W9-BRW-603

350
16-8

# "DON'T JUST SIT THERE, *BLEND!*"

He nodded to the others to begin the Blending, and then—

The entity containing the flesh form Korge was born, much strengthened from all but the last time it had been called forth. The other four entities hung back, giving it the honor of floating out first.

The villagers down among the dwellings were no longer going about their various mundane tasks. Instead now they ran screaming, as the first of the aliens came into view. The strongest entity floated toward the alien enemy, the other entities following, and attacked.

But to no avail. The aliens seemed entirely unaware of the strongest entity's presence. The other four surrounded the aliens and attempted to increase their strength by reflecting it back and forth between themselves. An urge came for the fifth entity to flee and preserve itself, but instead it attempted to add its own superior strength to the effort of the others. But still the aura surrounding the enemy remained untouched. Which brought the strongest entity distant fear.

And now the enemy began to slay those flesh forms it found among the dwellings . . .

Other Books by Sharon Green

**ATTENTION: ORGANIZATIONS AND CORPORATIONS**
Most Eos paperbacks are available at special quantity discounts
for bulk purchases for sales promotions, premiums, or fund-
raising. For information, please call or write:

**Special Markets Department, HarperCollins Publishers, Inc.,
10 East 53rd Street, New York, N.Y. 10022–5299.
Telephone: (212) 207-7528. Fax: (212) 207-7222.**

# DECEPTIONS

Book Two of THE BLENDING ENTHRONED

## SHARON GREEN

An Imprint of HarperCollinsPublishers

*For my sweetie, Dean Sweatman,*
*who's worth more than just a few words.*

This is a work of fiction. Names, characters, places, and incidents are the products of the author's imagination or are used fictitiously and are not to be construed as real. Any resemblance to actual events, locales, organizations, or persons, living or dead, is entirely coincidental.

EOS
*An Imprint of* HarperCollins*Publishers*
10 East 53rd Street
New York, New York 10022-5299

Copyright © 2001 by Sharon Green
ISBN: 0-380-81294-0
**www.eosbooks.com**

All rights reserved. No part of this book may be used or reproduced in any manner whatsoever without written permission, except in the case of brief quotations embodied in critical articles and reviews. For information address Eos, an imprint of HarperCollins Publishers.

First Eos paperback printing: April 2001

Eos Trademark Reg. U.S. Pat. Off. and in Other Countries, Marca Registrada, Hecho en U.S.A.
HarperCollins® is a trademark of HarperCollins Publishers Inc.

Printed in the U.S.A.

10  9  8  7  6  5  4  3  2  1

If you purchased this book without a cover, you should be aware that this book is stolen property. It was reported as "unsold and destroyed" to the publisher, and neither the author nor the publisher has received any payment for this "stripped book."

Sometimes I think that keeping this journal is a round-
about way of torturing myself. As I write about how Dis-
lin Marne, governor of Eastgate in the empire of Gracely,
told everyone about the invaders, I feel again the fear and
disbelief I felt when it happened. Strangers had come over
the ocean in ships, had landed near Eastgate, and then
had proceeded to attack the city and kill everyone they
could reach.

But it wasn't just the attack itself that turned everyone
in the room pale. Governor Marne had said that the invaders couldn't be touched by talent, that the High talents
in his city hadn't been able to stop them. That statement
was where the disbelief came in, and it was also the basis
for everyone's extreme fear. It wasn't possible that something or someone couldn't be touched by talent, and I
wasn't the only one who suffered through a strong flash of
helplessness. I know I wasn't the only one . . .

# ONE

"I think we need to go into a few more details about exactly what happened," Lorand said into the deeply shocked silence filling the large room. "If those invaders have a way to keep themselves from being touched by talent, it might very well be possible to negate whatever method they're using. Governor Marne, were your High talents able to learn anything?"

"Too many of them learned how easy it is to die," Marne answered after taking a long drink of the water someone had given him. The man was a short step away from exhaustion, not to mention in pain from his wounds, but he and his companions couldn't be allowed to rest yet.

"Are you trying to say they died uselessly?" Tamrissa put in, for once speaking soberly and quietly rather than sharply cutting. "If those invaders are to be stopped before they kill everyone in this empire, we have to know as much as we can about them. If you didn't notice anything, maybe one of your companions did."

"It wasn't possible to notice things," one of the men with the governor said with a headshake, his hand and the cup it held trembling ever so slightly. "The invaders are beasts—animals—and when you see women and children being cut down along with everyone else it's hard to notice much more."

"But that's on a conscious level," Jovvi pointed out very gently, speaking to the assembly members as well as to the men who had come to ask the assembly's help. "Deep in our minds we do notice other things, but after a time of great stress we need help to reach those observations. If these gentlemen will allow the assistance, surely one of your Spirit magic members can reach the information."

"Of course we can," a woman said, one of the two other women in the assembly besides Antrie Lorimon. "Or, perhaps I should say *I* can do the job. Step aside, please."

It wasn't hard for Lorand to see that the woman was larger than Antrie Lorimon and very brisk in her movements. She had brown hair and brown eyes, an ordinary face, and a thin body that she seemed to be holding back from moving nervously in some way. Jovvi stepped out of the woman's way with a faint smile, and somehow Lorand suddenly knew that the assembly woman wasn't as strongly sure of herself as she pretended to be.

"Allow me to present Banta Fullnor, a member of our assembly," the big man called Cleemor Gardan said dryly. He clearly spoke to Lorand and his Blendingmates, the dryness of his tone apparently an attempt to apologize for the abruptness of the Fullnor woman.

"We don't have time for the amenities now, Cleemor," Fullnor told her fellow assembly member without turning to look at him. "We have a crisis on our hands, and we have to settle it as quickly as possible. Now, Governor Marne, this won't hurt at all so please relax as much as you can."

The wounded and exhausted man looked more disturbed than relaxed, an odd expression in his eyes. He stared up at Fullnor for a long and silent moment, and Fullnor was the one who broke the silence.

"Why are you fighting me?" the assembly woman demanded with annoyance clear in her voice and expression. "I can force my way through to your mind, but I don't know why that should be necessary. What are you trying to hide?"

"He isn't trying to *hide* anything," Jovvi said at once, taking one step closer to the two people. "He doesn't want to relive what he went through, and that's what he thinks you'll make him do. If you'll just distance his conscious mind from the memories, he won't fight you any longer."

"Why don't you mind your own business!" Fullnor

snapped, turning her head to glare at Jovvi. "This is *our* country and our problem, so stop trying to mix in!"

"If the people here in *your* country don't solve the problem, then it becomes ours," Jovvi countered with a sharpness that surprised Lorand. The tone would have been more fitting coming from Tamrissa . . . "Instead of standing back and waiting for all of you to be killed before we do anything, we'd rather get involved now. And it's pointless for you to refuse to admit that you can't distance the man's mind from his memories. If you *were* able to do it, it would already be done."

"It isn't very intelligent to challenge someone on her home ground," the woman growled at Jovvi, fists closed tight at her sides. "If I decide to crush you I can do it, and the law can't protect you. You aren't one of us, so it doesn't apply to you."

"I don't think you want to crush me," Jovvi said calmly to Fullnor while Antrie Lorimon, Cleemor Gardan, and a few others began to protest what their fellow assembly member had said. "What you want to do is cooperate with everyone here to counter the crisis, not use the opportunity to advance your political plans. Only a mindless fool would jeopardize a country to gain personal aggrandizement for the short time it would last. Don't you agree?"

"Yes, of course I agree," Fullnor answered at once after taking a deep breath, her anger completely gone. "I was foolish to see this as an opportunity, and I won't make the mistake again. Go ahead and do what's necessary—I won't try to stand in your way."

"I appreciate your cooperation," Jovvi told the woman graciously while the other assembly members stared at both of them. Lorimon, Gardan, and the others obviously had no idea why Fullnor had done such a complete about-face, but Lorand was certain *he* understood. Jovvi had taken over the woman before she could attack, and now had the woman responding to reason rather than to selfish desires for bettering her place in life.

Lorand knew that Jovvi would have had a fight on her hands if she hadn't done what she had, but he wasn't quite sure he liked what she'd done instead. A second or two went by while his mind considered the matter, and then he came to a conclusion that was mildly surprising. Taking over the woman's mind had been an invasion, but if the woman had attacked Jovvi then Jovvi might well have had to destroy the woman. Jovvi had chosen the gentler means of self-protection, and Lorand found no willingness inside himself to argue the choice. The outlook was so unlike his usual one that it surprised Lorand, but he had no time to think about anything but what was going on with those who had brought news of the invasion.

"Governor Marne, my name is Jovvi Hafford," Jovvi said to the wounded man, taking Fullnor's place when Fullnor stepped aside. "I do have to make you relive what you went through, but you don't have to be aware of it. If you'll allow me to touch you, we can get the information we need without giving you added pain."

"I have no doubt that you can, Exalted One," Marne answered with a mirthless laugh. "I'm sure you can tell that I also have Spirit magic, and I'm strong enough to know that you're telling the truth. I also appreciate being asked rather than ordered to cooperate, so please go ahead. I don't know how much longer I can keep from passing out."

"I should be able to soothe and sustain you for a short while," Jovvi murmured as she looked down at the man. "After that you and these others will *have* to be allowed to rest, or we'll be in definite danger of losing some of you. Please describe as objectively as possible what the invaders look like."

"The invaders look like ordinary men, but I've never seen clothing like theirs," Marne replied, a small frown creasing his brow. "It looked as though they'd wrapped themselves tightly in leather that had small metal circles sewn all over it, and they wore close-fitting hats that were all of metal. They carried very long knives in leather sheaths that were just as long, knives whose blades measured three feet at the very least."

"Swords, what they carried is called swords," one of the other men put in, his tone thoughtful. "I remember reading about swords a long time ago, but I can't remember where."

"And they killed people with these swords?" Jovvi asked next as people muttered all over the room. "Did they hesitate at all, or did they just wade in joyfully and kill everyone they came across?"

"They weren't hesitant *or* joyful," Marne said, frowning again. "I hadn't realized it sooner, but they just went ahead and killed as though they were weeding a field. We tried to close the gates of the city against them, but they had already sent a number of their people inside the gates and they kept us from closing them. We should have closed the gates as soon as we sighted their ships, but it's been so long since we had to fight anyone at all . . ."

"What happened when your High talents attacked them?" Vallant asked after moving up to stop next to Jovvi. "How were the invaders able to fight off what was bein' done?"

"They *didn't* fight off the attack," Marne said with a shake of his head and a disturbed expression. "The invaders didn't even seem to know they were *being* attacked, and nothing anyone did affected them. Our Spirit and Earth magic people screamed that they couldn't reach the invaders' minds, and our Air magic people couldn't take away what they breathed. After that we all began to run in different directions, but it's fairly clear that the Fire and Water talents had had no luck either."

"That sounds like they were being protected by something," Tamrissa mused from where she stood. "What is there that can protect someone from the use of talent?"

"The only thing I can think of at the moment is a stronger talent," Vallant said with his own headshake. "But it doesn't sound as if that's what was bein' done. Did any of your Highs get the sense of a stronger talent bein' used?"

"If a stronger talent was involved, all of us would have felt it," Marne denied, all life having left his voice. "Our families and friends were cut down before our eyes, and all we could do was watch. If it hadn't been absolutely essential that we bring a warning to Liandia and the assembly . . ."

"No, please, you can't afford to be lost with the others," Jovvi said at once when the man's words trailed off into a sigh. "You were right to save yourselves and come here, and you'll understand that once you've had a chance to rest. Does anyone have any other questions?"

Lorand watched Jovvi glance around at the men and women of the assembly, but they all either shook their heads or simply looked frightened. They seemed to be completely out of their depth, which suggested to Lorand that they were too used to playing politics and not enough used to dealing directly with problems.

"We'll have to try to negotiate with those people," one of the assembly members said into the silence, his gaze on nothing and no one. "And that's rather lucky, since negotiation is much better than warfare."

"How do you negotiate with people whose sole aim is to kill you and everyone around you?" Tamrissa asked the man, and this time her tone was filled with impatience. "If you absolutely *have* to be a fool, please do it somewhere else."

"Young woman, you can stop that impertinence right now!" another of the assembly members snapped, his heavy face flushed. "Negotiation happens to be the best way to achieve anything, something you would know if you were a proper member of this assembly."

"Do you mean if I were a fool male like you two?" Tamrissa returned immediately, her tone sharp rather than defensive. "I happen to be fond of negotiation myself, but that's because I have experience with the alternative. I doubt if anyone here but my Blendingmates has the same experience, and you still haven't answered my question. How do you negotiate with someone who wants nothing but to kill you?"

The man's face went even more red, but despite his glare he seemed to be out of words. That made the silence unanimous again, which allowed Jovvi to take advantage of the lack of opposition. All five men put down the cups they were holding and leaned back in their seats, and a moment later they were all asleep—to Lorand's vast surprise.

"They should be taken to bed now," Jovvi told Gardan and Lorimon as she turned away from the wounded men. "And please remember that when they wake up they'll need strong support against the terrible depression they'll be feeling. If they don't get that support, they may not survive."

"I'll make sure they have everything they need," Lorimon promised quietly as she stared at Jovvi. "Am I mistaken, or do all of you intend to help us with this crisis? I think it's fairly clear we'll be needing all the help we can get, but why would you involve yourselves? Were you that impressed with the . . . warmly unique way we greet our visitors?"

"You think we ought to turn around and run for our lives?" Jovvi asked while Lorand and the rest of their Blend-ingmates smiled at Lorimon's question. "But if we do turn and run and your country is conquered, where do we run to next? The Astindans might take us in, but what happens when it gets to be *their* turn?"

"You're saying you're doing this for selfish motives, but I don't quite believe that," Gardan said, apparently taking the words from Lorimon's mouth. "Not unless you mean to do nothing but stand back and watch while we and our people go up against these invaders and take our turn with dying. Am I wrong in believing that you don't intend to just stand and watch?"

"We've discovered that we're bad at doing nothing," Tam-rissa put in at once with an amused smile. "If those people really can't be touched with talent we might not be of much help, but the least we can do is try. Assuming you don't mind if we do try, that is."

"Don't you people understand *anything*?" the first man who had spoken about negotiating suddenly demanded, his frightened gaze now on those he spoke to. "You're not sup-posed to offer us help without demanding a terrible price first, it just isn't done! You're supposed to play politics no matter *how* many lives are at stake . . ."

Lorand felt embarrassed when he noticed that the man was crying, but the expressions on too many other faces lessened the discomfort. The fearful hope on all those faces was nearly painful, and the smile Antrie Lorimon showed was almost as bad.

"What my fellow assembly member means to say is thank you," Lorimon told them as she looked around. The five wounded men were being carried out of the room, but that wasn't what took her attention. "All our thanks are truly sincere—unless you *do* intend to ask a terrible price for your help."

"Would a cup of tea be too much to ask?" Tamrissa put in dryly, breaking the mood by making almost everyone smile. "Preferably *without* an attack by unknown forces coming first?"

The last of that comment brought out embarrassed laughter, and the man Gardan shook his head.

"The tea I can promise, but I'm not certain about the attack," he told Tamrissa ruefully. "We'll get an investigation started into who was behind that first attack, but we probably won't have the time to stay around to learn the results. I think that those of us who are going to Eastgate need to leave as soon as possible."

"I expect that you're right," Vallant agreed with the man, sounding just as rueful. "But since not everyone will be goin' with us, it won't hurt to try findin' out who dislikes us so much. Just to be certain it isn't someone who *is* goin' with us, you understand."

Gardan stepped closer to Vallant and Tamrissa to continue the discussion, and Lorimon joined them while some of the other assembly members began to make their way to a long table standing at the back of the room. Lorand also felt the need for some tea, but even more pressing was the need to speak to Jovvi. He began to step toward her, but found that she was already on her way over to *him*.

"If you're going to ask me how I put those men to sleep, the answer is I have no idea," Jovvi murmured as soon as she was close enough. "Do *you* happen to know how I did it?"

"Certainly," Lorand answered as he looked down into her beautiful but anxious eyes. "What you did was borrow *my* talent, something I'm sure about because I felt you drawing on it. The part I'm not clear about is *how* you did it."

"I wish I knew," Jovvi said with a sigh that Lorand had the urge to join her in. "Something like this shouldn't be possible, but we've just proven that it is. Do you think we'll be lucky enough to discover that we're imagining things?"

"We haven't had much of that kind of luck lately," Lorand pointed out, letting himself take a deep breath instead of sighing. "It's fairly obvious that our list of new things has just grown, and we're going to have to tell the others about it as soon as possible. And we need to discuss again whether or not to tell these people how to grow stronger in their talents."

"And that won't be an easy decision to make," Jovvi said with a nod, understanding at once. "If those invaders really can't be touched with talent, making our new allies stronger won't accomplish anything. If the invaders *can* be defeated with talent, once the threat of their invasion is over we'll be back to dealing with the Gracelians."

"And the Gracelians are people who are obviously used to playing politics with everything," Lorand finished up. "If we give them a toe, they'll soon have the foot all the way up to the knee at least. The only possible advantage we have is that they don't like the idea of war. The need to avoid a fight with us should turn them reasonable—as long as they don't decide they can *win* a fight with us."

"Which brings us back to the question of how wise we would be to give them something that might make them believe they could win against us," Jovvi fretted, the point clearly bothering her. "We'll have to think about this for a while, and then maybe we can—"

Jovvi's words broke off as screams and shouts erupted from the back of the room, where the table with refreshments stood. Most of the assembly members were over there, and even as Lorand watched, two more people fell to the floor one at a time. There were others already down, but at least none of Lorand's Blendingmates was among them.

"Lorand, what's happening to them?" Jovvi asked in a shocked voice as another man screamed while falling bonelessly to the floor.

"They've been poisoned," Lorand answered savagely before heading for the fallen, his temper beginning to rise as it had never done before. "Dom Gardan, I'll need as many Earth magic healers as you can get, and that as quickly as possible. Two of those people are already dead, but we might be able to save the rest if we hurry."

Gardan and Lorimon had been staring at their fellow assembly members in shock, but Lorand's words seemed to galvanize them. Gardan ran from the room while two people came forward from the audience part of the room, and then Lorand had no attention to spare for anything but the fallen. A glance had told him which poison had been used, and he quickly explained to the two volunteer Earth magic users what had to be done before starting to use the procedure himself.

The next hour or so was a very long one for Lorand. The two volunteers were no more than Middle talents, and although the men seemed to have some skill in healing, what they didn't have was enough strength. Lorand reached out to his waiting link groups and tapped into *their* strength, then somehow spread the strength around. That act not only added to the volunteers' strength but let Lorand work on more than one victim at a time.

By the time other Earth magic users hurried into the room, one more person had died but the rest had been stabilized. Lorand stepped back, expecting to be exhausted, but he was no more than just normally weary. Antrie Lorimon waited next to Jovvi, and when Lorand joined them the Gracelian put her hand on his arm.

"Now we have even more to thank you for," she said, her voice almost fading to a whisper. "I can't imagine what you must think of us now, but I swear that this doesn't happen as a usual thing. Will—will they be all right?"

"Three of them are dead, and a fourth will probably never recover completely," Lorand answered with weariness coloring his tone. "The rest should be all right, but there's something I'd really like to know: Were they the targets of this attack, or was it supposed to be us who died?"

"It can't possibly be your group alone that was the target of the attack," Antrie Lorimon said at once, her hand closing more tightly on Lorand's arm. "Those refreshments were meant for everyone, and there was no guarantee that you and your Blendingmates would eat or drink first. It looks like whoever is behind all this doesn't care if innocent bystanders die. That's more than simple dislike or ordinary resentment."

"And you still have no idea who it could be?" Jovvi asked, a frown of disturbance creasing her brow. "Someone like that would have to be completely insane, and that sort of insanity ought to be completely noticeable to those who aren't forbidden the use of their talent."

"We did have someone among us who was that badly unbalanced," Lorimon admitted slowly with her own frown. "The man did horrible things to a number of people as well as to his own Blending, but when we found out what was going on we stripped him of his position and his talent. He can't possibly be the one behind all this, not when he doesn't have gold any longer either."

"If he didn't find a way around all those drawbacks, you've got another of the same sort on your hands," Jovvi said with a headshake. "Since your own people are just as much at risk as we are, I would suggest that that investigation be started as quickly as possible. But now what's going to happen with Eastgate? Three of your people capable of Blending are dead, and more than half of the rest are probably in no shape to travel."

"If we have to we'll replace the dead at once, and then take the resulting Blendings with Cleemor's and mine," Lorimon answered with a sigh. "The three new major talents will have to practice with their Blendingmates on the trip, which will hopefully let them be of real help once we find the invaders. If we can't find experienced volunteers and the new major talents aren't of real help . . ."

The woman's words trailed off as she performed a small shrug, and Lorand didn't need to have her finish the sentence. When they met the invaders they'd need all the help they could get, and not having what they needed could well mean their defeat . . .

# Two

Zirdon Tal let himself be helped into his house by his servants, those who had come running out to help as soon as his carriage pulled up. It seemed that everyone had heard about the attack in the assembly building, and high feelings were flying all over the city. Some people were outraged that their leaders could be hurt and killed with such ease, and others were terrified that the same thing could be done to *them* much more easily.

"Yes, this is fine, thank you," Zirdon told his very concerned servants as they helped him into a chair in his study. "And a cup of tea, if you please."

"Certainly, Exalted One, certainly," one of his servants answered, trying to hide his continuing surprise. Ever since that fool Ebro Syant had been punished for what he'd done to people, Zirdon had been treating his servants as though they were actually worth something. Just as a precaution, of course . . . "Are you sure you don't want to be put to bed, Exalted One?"

"I'm mostly unharmed, so bed is unnecessary," Zirdon replied, forcing himself not to scream at the man. "Just bring me the tea, and then leave me alone to rest for a time."

The servant bowed and passed along the cup of tea that another servant had already filled, and then the whole gaggle of them left. Zirdon no longer kept a servant in the room with him at all times, and the new practice came in very handy now.

"That miserable slime," Zirdon muttered once the door had closed behind his staff, his hand closing very tightly around the teacup. "That colossal fool Syant! When I see him I'm also going to see how close I can come to killing him without actually doing it!"

Zirdon's insides hurt, and it was all that fool Syant's fault. Luckily Zirdon wasn't one of the first to take some of the refreshments, and so he'd only had a single sip of wine when people began to fall as if they'd been poleaxed. Panic had made Zirdon begin to throw up, and once begun the process had continued on its own. Zirdon now felt as though he'd been beaten with fists in his stomach, and it was all because that imbecile Syant hadn't warned him.

"The idiot may have been counting on the fact that I usually don't eat or drink anywhere but at home or in certain select dining parlors," Zirdon muttered after taking a sip of tea. "He'll probably claim that that's what he was counting on, and it's merely an odd quirk of fate that I was so upset at the news of the invasion that I took wine and because of that nearly died with the others. He may even beg me not to hurt him, but that won't do him any good. Of all the mindless, insane things to do . . ."

Zirdon found himself gulping the tea, and it was almost beyond him to stop. Syant had said that the next part of his plan would disrupt the assembly, and it certainly had. But "almost destroy" would be more descriptive than "disrupt."

The little slug obviously cared nothing about what turmoil his actions caused, which meant that Zirdon would have to monitor the madman much more closely in future. And make sure that he, Zirdon, knew exactly what was going on, so that next time *he* didn't fall victim along with the others. A precaution like that was necessary at any time when dealing with a madman, but especially now—

"Oh, by the Highest Aspect," Zirdon said with a groan, closing his eyes for a moment. "That invasion . . . We can't continue on with the plan when our empire is in danger of being destroyed around us. I've become a victim of the worst possible timing, but having control of a dead empire isn't what I had in mind."

Which meant that Zirdon would have to meet with Syant today after all. The Fire magic user had meant to let the little slug wait at the meeting place until the fool turned blue, but now the fool had to be reined in and the madman inside him put under control. Not to mention the fact that Zirdon needed to know *everything* that was part of the plan. It might be possible to let some of it continue without interruption, but the rest of it would definitely have to be delayed.

Zirdon rang for a servant to have his teacup refilled, and then he worked to pull himself together while he sipped the tea. He *was* going to be late to the meeting, but since the way Zirdon felt was Syant's fault, the small madman wouldn't have been able to complain even if he'd been allowed the freedom.

After the second cup of tea, Zirdon sent for his carriage. The servants fussed over the request like a bunch of disapproving old nannies, but refusal on their part was out of the question. Once the carriage was outside the front door Zirdon left, but not briskly or even quickly. His insides hurt too much for that, so his pace was even less than a stroll.

Zirdon's driver was instructed to keep the horses at a pace that would allow the least amount of jostling, so it took Zirdon longer than usual to reach the meeting place. He had taken some time to decide on the safest place for him to meet Syant, but once Zirdon remembered that his favorite dining parlor wasn't far from a public bath house, the decision was made. Zirdon would usually enter the dining parlor and have something to eat, then he would go out the back of the parlor and make his way to the bath house. No one he knew—or who knew him—would *ever* be found in a public bath house, so the meeting place couldn't be bettered.

Today Zirdon was in no condition to eat even the smallest snack, so he entered the dining parlor and then immediately left it again by the back door. Those who ran the parlor were discreet to a fault, which meant that no one ever questioned Zirdon's comings and goings.

It took longer than usual to reach the bath house, of course, but Zirdon wasn't far from the bath house's back door when his steps faltered. A small crowd had gathered not far from the door, every person in it staring intently at whatever was going on inside. The door itself was open, and figures could be seen moving about beyond the opening.

"What's happening, Chirn?" a voice said, and Zirdon looked around to see another newcomer approach one of the men in the crowd. "Why are you out here instead of being inside bathing?"

"We were all made to leave," the man addressed as Chirn replied with a sigh and a headshake. "The guard took our names and where we can be reached, and then we were told to go outside. I don't know if they mean to let the bath house be opened again today."

"But today's our usual day," the second man protested, much of his attention on what was going on inside the building. "Why would they decide to close a perfectly good bath house?"

"A man was just killed, Tavva," Chirn replied with a shiver. "I was just starting to get undressed when two or three men who looked like beggars came in and went up to this other fellow. The one they approached was small and very quiet, and I'd had the impression that he was waiting for someone."

"Why would he be waiting for beggars?" the man called Tavva replied, his expression now puzzled. "And would beggars spend the copper they'd collected on a bath unless they absolutely had to?"

"The small man wasn't waiting for the beggars," Chirn returned with a sigh. "When he saw them he acted as if he didn't recognize them, but they certainly knew him. They said that they'd followed him, and now they wanted whatever copper or silver the small man meant to use to pay for the bath. The small man said he didn't *have* any copper or silver and that he was waiting for someone else, but the biggest of the beggars laughed and called him a liar. They'd waited a short while to see if there *was* someone who came to meet the small man, they said, but no one had appeared."

"Maybe the one he meant to meet was unavoidably detained," Tavva suggested, obviously not the swiftest fish in the stream. "Why didn't he tell the beggars that?"

"The beggars weren't interested in anything the small man had to say," Chirn told his friend with a headshake. "They demanded his copper or silver again, and when he repeated that he *had* no copper or silver the big one who had done all the talking pulled out a knife and stabbed the small man. The small man collapsed, and the big man tried to search his clothes for the copper or silver. He checked as many places as he could, then he cursed something terrible and led the others out again at a run. Someone had gone for the guard, you see, and the big man knew it."

"So the big man got all the small man's copper and silver," Tavva said, nodding his head in understanding. "Is the small man talking to the guard now, telling them who the big man was?"

"There *was* no copper or silver," Chirn said with something of a sigh. "That's why the big man cursed before he ran off. And the small man isn't talking to the guard or anyone because he was killed. You do remember I told you that, don't you? The small man didn't die right away, of course, but no one had the cost of calling a healer. How could we have called a healer if we didn't have the cost?"

The man called Chirn seemed to be somewhat upset over not having had the cost of a healer, but Zirdon felt too numb with shock to be upset. He'd been in the midst of telling himself that it must have been some other little man who had been killed, that it couldn't possibly have been Syant. But then the body was carried out to be put in a waiting wagon, and it certainly *was* Syant.

Zirdon moved slowly away from the fringe of the crowd, and once he felt sure that no one could see him he turned and ran. His insides protested the exertion of the run, but the Fire magic user couldn't have walked even if his life had been at stake. He ran until he reached the dining parlor, and then only just managed to make himself slow down.

Moving through the dining parlor was like moving through a nightmare. Zirdon had no idea why he didn't stumble and fall, but somehow he found himself back at his carriage. His driver took him home again, and the numbness in his mind continued until he was alone with a glass of wine in his hand. He sipped once . . . twice . . . and then he began to tremble in earnest.

"Now what do I do?" Zirdon whispered, feeling chill terror wrap him completely around. "Syant was the only one who knew exactly what was going to happen, and now he's dead. I don't even know who his secondary intermediary was, so I can't find out anything even through *that* man."

Zirdon put his wineglass down and closed his eyes, fighting to keep from throwing up again. Without someone to cancel the orders, Syant's plans would continue on no matter how desperate the situation was. Just when the assembly needed to be an effective, cohesive whole, they would be attacked and disrupted and made to look like a bunch of bumbling fools. At least the ones who survived would look like that . . .

"And I can't even take advantage of the confusion," Zirdon moaned with more than a little pain. "If I forced myself into leadership of the assembly, they would all expect me to come up with a way to stop the local attacks as well as the invasion. With Syant alive I *could* have stopped the attacks, but now . . ."

Zirdon moaned again, this time wordlessly. The invasion was a serious matter and needed to be responded to with strength, assembly Blending strength. It was almost guaranteed that that fool Marne of Eastgate was wrong about talent being useless against the invaders, and Zirdon could have led his peers in wiping out the intruders. It was a priceless opportunity, and now it had to go to waste . . .

Zirdon felt a frown creasing his brow as an idea suddenly came to him. The man who led the effort to stop the invasion would be the greatest hero Gracely had ever had, and that hero would have no trouble making himself the empire's sole ruler afterward. If Zirdon ever wanted his plans to work *he* had to be that hero, and there just might be a way to accomplish that *without* having to get involved with whatever attacks Syant's plans still called for.

A smile bent Zirdon's lips as he realized that he could assign the attacks problem to someone else if *he* were in charge. Lorimon and Gardan ought to be completely out of favor with the surviving members of the assembly now after what they'd allowed to happen. If Zirdon took over he could challenge the two to handle any further attacks while *he* saw to removing the invasion menace.

"Yes, that has definite possibilities," Zirdon murmured as he straightened in his chair. "I think an emergency meeting of the assembly this afternoon is called for, one to make sure that the proper people are in charge of the proper things."

Zirdon rose to call a servant, his former terror long gone. The little slug Syant's plans would still be for *his* benefit, and now it wasn't even possible for anyone to link him with Syant. Lorimon and Gardan would be left to face whatever came—and hopefully fail to survive it—while *he* was safely out of the city seeing to the invaders. Yes, things were going to work out right after all . . .

"Thank you, Antrie, that was a wonderful lunch," I heard Jovvi say as I finished the last of the tea in my cup. "We very much appreciate your hospitality."

"It was the least I could do," Antrie Lorimon answered ruefully. "I may not be certain about how safe the rest of the city is right now, but I *am* sure about my own home. And you really ought to consider staying here rather than going with us to the meeting this afternoon."

"Too many of your assembly members have been hurt or killed already," Lorand said, answering the suggestion that had been put to all of us. "We'd really rather not go up against those invaders alone without at least *some* of you along to separate friend from foe, so we'll play bodyguard for you and the others as best we can. That is, if you don't mind."

"Truthfully, I'm relieved and delighted to have you," Antrie answered with a weak smile. "Cleemor and I have used our talent to protect ourselves to a certain extent, but hardened air can't stop poison or any number of other things that can kill us. I just wish we knew who was behind these attacks—and who it is who's being attacked."

"I think it's fairly obvious that we're all the targets," Cleemor Gardan said from where he sat at the other end of the table, his expression an extremely unhappy one. "That first physical attack could have been just for our guests' benefit, but not the poisoning. It would have been nothing more than good manners for us to sample the food and drink before offering it to our guests, to prove it wasn't tampered with. If the poison had taken longer to work then the attempt would have been a serious one against our guests, but as it was . . ."

Gardan's shrug was rather eloquent, but Lorand still sighed to show his own unhappiness.

"I just wish I could have gotten to that table sooner," Lorand said with a headshake. "The poison was subtle but still visible, and I would certainly have seen it. If I'd been there, your people would still be alive."

"But chances are *we* would not be sitting here and talking like this," Antrie pointed out, suddenly looking more alert than disturbed. "If you'd found that poison before it killed our people, Lorand, what would you and your Blending-mates have thought?"

"That you were trying to kill *us*," Jovvi said at once while Lorand frowned. "I'm almost sorry you noticed that, Antrie, because it means that we're up against someone who really knows how to think. No matter what happened, that situation was designed to cause chaos. Do you really have no idea who could be behind this?"

"If I did, I think I would hesitate not at all in using my Blending to question them," Antrie answered with her hand to her brow, the disturbance back in her gaze. "You probably consider me terrible for saying that, but it's precisely the way I feel. Whoever is doing this cares nothing for human life, and I think it most fitting that we return the compliment."

"*Your* questioning would probably be a lot less terrible than mine," I pointed out, giving the woman a smile when she looked at me. "I really detest people who attack from hiding, and I tend to want to show them how I feel. Why should *you* be any different?"

Antrie was about to answer me when a servant appeared, showing in the man Frode Mismin. Since Mismin was in charge of looking into what had happened we all gave him our immediate attention, but he just shook his head.

"So far I've been able to find nothing at all," he said, sounding as depressed as his announcement made the rest of us feel. "Those people who were involved in the attack outside the assembly building this morning have no idea who might be behind it all. They were hired by a man in a mask and told what to do, and were supposed to pick up the rest of their pay once the attack was successfully concluded. Since the attack *wasn't* successfully concluded, it came as no surprise that no one appeared at the scheduled rendezvous."

"Wonderful," I muttered while everyone else made different sounds of disappointment. "That means we're back to where we were."

"Actually, we're worse off than that," Mismin told me with a smile that had no amusement in it at all. "We had an ousted assembly member that I considered a good suspect, and the last time I checked he'd disappeared. Unfortunately my people found him again this morning, or at least they found his body. He'd been killed in a public bath house by 'beggars,' according to the reports of the witnesses. The beggars demanded his copper or silver, he told them he had none, and one of the beggars then knifed him before searching his clothes. After finding nothing in the way of coin, the beggar and his companions then ran away."

"But if he had no money, what was he doing in a public bath house?" I asked, confused over the point. "Aren't people charged for using the facilities in this city?"

"Of course they are!" Cleemor Gardan exclaimed, staring at me before moving his gaze to Mismin. "Frode, you have to follow up on this. If the man had no funds, he must have been there to meet someone and we *have* to know who that was. Take gold with you as well as silver, and don't let anyone refuse to answer your questions. If the person with the information won't take a bribe, tell him that the next ones to question him will be a full Blending, and we won't offer silver or gold."

"That should open him or them up," Mismin answered with a real laugh, depression completely gone. Then he turned to send me a smile. "And thank *you,* Exalted One, for the priceless insight. It never occurred to me to wonder about the point."

"You might say I'm something of an expert when it comes to bath houses," I returned, making my Blendingmates laugh. "We spent a lot of time traveling before we went back to Gan Garee to . . . finish up our business there, and at one point we had something of a problem. There was a public bath house in the town we stopped in, but there were also a very large number of us. Paying for the baths would have cost almost all the gold we had left, so we had to give up the idea of bathing that day. Let's just say I wasn't very gracious about having to make the sacrifice."

" 'Not very gracious' is puttin' it mildly," Vallant said with a grin. "She was ready to start a war, but no one was foolish enough to try standin' against her. If she ever accepts a bribe, it won't be gold. It will be a bath that she really wants."

"Well, now I get to see if someone with information we need *will* accept a bribe in gold," Mismin said after joining everyone's laughter. "If that and the threat of a Blending visiting doesn't work, I now have something else to offer. If you'll all excuse me?"

Mismin bowed while most of us nodded, and then he strode out of the room again. He'd exchanged a brief smile with Antrie before leaving, and suddenly I knew that those two were involved in a relationship. How I *knew* wasn't clear, but there was no time to poke at the question.

"You know, Antrie, I'm beginning to wonder how we got along before our guests arrived," Cleemor Gardan said while grinning in my direction. "And I'm also beginning to be very glad that they came."

"It's an unfortunate fact of life, but people grow close quickly during emergencies," Jovvi said with a smile while I fought the urge to blush. "If there had been no trouble during our visit, we never would have gotten to really know one another."

"And that would have been a shame," Antrie said with her own smile that looked a bit sad. "It grieves me that people had to die, but it helps to know that their lives weren't wasted. Shall we stroll in the garden for the short time before we have to leave for the meeting?"

"Antrie, you may not have noticed, but it's rainin'," Vallant pointed out as we all began to stand. "How are we goin' to stroll in the garden in the rain without gettin' soaked?"

"Vallant, Cleemor and I have Air magic," Antrie countered with a better smile. "The least we can do is protect our guests while we show them the garden."

"My brothers and sisters aren't used to that kind of service," Rion put in with a faint, odd smile. "We all got into the habit of choosing to be wet over choosing to waste strength that might be needed to defend ourselves."

"You must have had a really terrible time before you defeated those nobles," Antrie said, her expression filled with compassion as she looked around at us. "I don't think it will strain relations between us if I say I totally disliked the few nobles I met."

"They all seemed to think they were more than special because of the families they were born into," I said, swallowing the disturbance I always felt at the memory of the "Seated High" in Fire magic. "They lied so often to the whole world that it's no wonder they never noticed they were also lying to themselves. One of our biggest problems at home will be figuring out a way to keep another nobility from forming."

"I thought *our* way worked well until I took a good look around," Antrie said with a grimace, leading us out of the dining room and toward the back of the house. "Being constantly challenged *should* keep our major talents from falling into the 'noble' mind-set, but it doesn't help with those major talents who were raised in wealthy families. They start out expecting the world to cater to them, and becoming a member of the assembly only makes the problem worse."

"A prime example of that is Zirdon Tal," Cleemor Gardan said with his own grimace as we all approached double doors which obviously led to the outside. "The man was clearly raised to believe that he was meant for great things, but he isn't bright enough to accomplish more than the ordinary. I've been told that he considers everyone his inferior, and the way he acts confirms that."

"Children *should* be raised with a positive point of view where the future is concerned," Naran said, the first words she'd contributed all morning. "But the wise parent will quietly add moderation to that outlook, so that becoming 'great' isn't the child's only ambition. Some people just aren't meant for greatness, but that doesn't mean they can't still be happy."

"There are all sorts of ambitions people can have, and some of them don't even ruin the people as decent human beings," Jovvi put in, her expression suddenly serious. "We haven't discussed what was done to our army, but I think the time has come to ask a question. If you were able to put those nobles under your control, why didn't you make them forget they *had* an army and free those poor people they had enslaved? Do you have any idea how badly they were treated?"

Antrie and Cleemor Gardan both stopped near the door without trying to open it, and the glance they exchanged seemed to be filled with deep disturbance and possibly even agony. Antrie also looked undecided, but a moment later her expression turned determined.

"We . . . figured something out a short while ago that I think you ought to know," Antrie said, then held up one hand toward her countryman. "No, Cleemor, we *have* to tell them. We'll soon be in a position where we have to trust one another completely, and if we hold back information then we don't deserve their trust."

"You know I agree with that, Antrie, but *I* know you'll take too much blame for what was done," Gardan told her quietly. "We were guilty of no more than being outvoted, and we didn't even *know* about the rest of what Tal had done until those people were freed. If anyone is going to pay for the horror, let it be the one who caused it."

"What horror are we talking about?" Lorand asked, his close attention divided between the two Gracelians. "You sound as though there's more involved than simply not freeing the members of the army."

"There *is* more involved," Antrie answered with a sigh. "We didn't free those poor people because we were afraid that your nobles would learn of it and send a much larger force that we would find impossible to control. But that isn't the worst of it. Cleemor and I believe that . . . the nobles leading the army were . . . made to treat the army members so badly that . . . they would all . . . die. If the people died of mistreatment, it couldn't be considered the fault of anyone but the men in charge."

Antrie finished the last of her confession on a single breath, obviously hurrying to get the words said before she lost the nerve to speak them. I stood there with my mouth open, so shocked that I barely noticed the deep silence surrounding us, and then the silence was broken.

"Are you sayin' that that Tal slime couldn't be bothered with makin' the nobles *think* the army members had died?" Vallant demanded in a growl. "Why in the name of sanity would anyone choose to kill that many innocent people when it wasn't necessary?"

"When ordinary people mean nothing to you, why would you bother about what happens to them?" Cleemor countered, his voice filled with bitterness. "And don't forget that it takes intelligence to realize that the people don't have to die if they can be thought of as dead. Tal doesn't have that intelligence, and he probably can't even spell the word 'compassion.' If we had any proof that Tal actually did what we suspect . . ."

"Proof isn't difficult to get," I found myself saying in a voice much harder than my usual one, not quite looking at anyone. "If he confesses, for instance, what will be done to him?"

"If the only proof we have is a confession, nothing will be done to him," Antrie said with a sigh that brought my gaze up to her face. "Do we need to tell *you* how easy it is to make someone confess to something they didn't actually do? If there isn't separate and independent verification of what was said in the confession, it can't be used against him."

I wanted to argue with that, but as angry as I felt I still couldn't refuse to see reason. If Jovvi made the man tell the truth I knew it would *be* the truth, but not everyone could be expected to believe that. And taking someone's word for their good intentions isn't something *I'd* be overly anxious to do either . . .

"Don't worry, Tamrissa, we'll figure out *something*," Lorand said in almost the same growl Vallant had used. "That would-be noble won't get away with what he did."

I wanted to believe Lorand, I really did, but as we dropped the discussion and followed our hosts outside I wasn't sure I did believe. And I also didn't know if I could make myself wait until we managed to figure out something else . . .

# THREE

Vallant entered the assembly building with everyone else, but most of his attention was on Tamrissa. The woman he loved was more disturbed than she'd been in quite a while, and she'd also become much too quiet. Vallant didn't know how he knew so certainly about Tamrissa's disturbance, but there wasn't a doubt in his mind about it.

So Vallant had to quiet his own anger in order to keep an eye on Tamrissa's. The emotion inside her was an almost tangible thing, so much like his own when he'd been younger that Vallant wanted to ask how that could be. But there wasn't time to ask questions that might not have answers. All Vallant could do was try to stay alert . . .

"This is supposed to be a meeting of what's left of the assembly," a voice stated almost as soon as they all entered the meeting room. "Do we really want the intrusion of outsiders?"

"These outsiders last intruded to save the lives of some of this assembly," the big man Gardan said at once, nothing of friendliness to be heard in his tone. "At the very least, they have the right to observe."

"In an effort to learn how to do things properly?" the man who had spoken, a tall, supercilious fool, said with a smirk. "If that's the case, then by all means let them come in and listen."

"Yes, we mean to watch what *you* do and then do just the opposite," Tamrissa said as she chose a chair just outside the

inner circle of assembly seats. "That, I think, is the best way
to learn what not to do to make fools of ourselves."

"Your opinions are of no interest to us, *woman*," the tall
man snarled, his skin darkening when he heard the chuckling coming from other members of the assembly. "But
we're all here now, so let's get the meeting started. I demand
to know what's been done to find the person responsible for
the attempted murder of this entire assembly. You and Lorimon *were* responsible for keeping everyone safe, weren't
you, Gardan?"

The big man Gardan seemed to be searching for what to
say while the other members of the assembly muttered in
abrupt anger. Everything that had happened had suddenly become Gardan's and Lorimon's fault, but that was nonsense.

"As I understand it, Gardan and Lorimon were supposed
to keep *us* safe," Vallant put in at once from the chair he still
stood in front of. "Since there's nothin' wrong with us, that
job's been done. Now what you need to ask is why none of
your people with Earth magic knew there was somethin'
wrong with the food and drink."

"And if you're all that concerned with being protected,
why didn't you have someone on guard to make sure the
food and drink wasn't tampered with?" This next question
came from Lorand, who hadn't given the tall speaker
enough time to answer the first question. "If you don't make
any efforts of your own, you can't blame others for doing as
you did."

"This is none of your concern, and if you don't keep quiet
I'll have you put out!" the tall man snarled to both Vallant
and Lorand, his anger having increased. "You can't distract
me—us—from the fact that nothing has been done to find
the person responsible for this atrocity, and that person *has*
to be found. I move that the search now be *made* the concern
of Gardan and Lorimon, and if the search isn't successful
that *they* be held responsible."

"Just hold on there, Tal," another assembly member said,
a heavy man with a gravelly voice. "I think we all know how
much you'd enjoy seeing Gardan and Lorimon given trouble, but the fact that you lost your coalition to them doesn't

make them guilty of anything but being better leaders. Someone *is* behind what was done, and that's the someone we'll save our anger for."

"You stay out this too, Dinno," the man called Tal snapped as his skin darkened again. "Just because you've become Gardan and Lorimon's lapdog doesn't mean those two are innocent. People are *dead* and others suffering, all because two members of this assembly were concerned only with the protection of that group of intruders. That's why someone was able to tamper with our provisions, so Gardan and Lorimon *are* responsible."

Tal's little speech ended on a note of triumph as he managed to find a line of logic that supported his stance. His expression also showed his triumph as others began to mutter darkly, and he quickly followed up the advantage.

"Now that we know who really is responsible, they do have to be also made responsible for catching the murderer," Tal continued. "Someone has to be punished for what was done, and if those two can't make amends for letting it happen in the first place, then I say we can punish *them*."

There was far too much agreement in the newest muttering from the assembly members to suit Vallant, not to mention how pale Gardan and Lorimon had grown. Vallant, now seated with his Blendingmates, exchanged glances with them, but before either he or Lorand could speak again Tamrissa rose to her feet.

"I think it ought to be perfectly clear who was behind the poisoning," Tamrissa announced calmly, but with an odd tension that seemed to crackle from her. "Someone here has a grudge against two people, and now those two people are being held responsible for something they had nothing to do with. Is it a coincidence that the one holding the grudge now insists that the people he hates be punished? Is the one holding the grudge all that concerned about people that he would hesitate to kill some of them in order to accuse those he hates? I really don't think so."

The last of Tamrissa's words were drowned out behind screams and shouts as assembly members almost flew erect from their seats. Tal was the one screaming incoherently, more than aware that the other assembly members were shouting and shaking fists at *him*. But Tal was so furious with Tamrissa for ruining his malicious work that he was nearly beside himself. When Tamrissa sat down again with a small, private smile on her face, Tal finally lost all control.

The loss of control was immediately clear when flames suddenly erupted very near Tamrissa. Vallant had water in his mental grip instantly, ready to apply it where needed, but nothing began to burn—and Tamrissa never lost her smile.

"If that's the best you can do, you might as well give it up," Tamrissa drawled to Tal in the shocked and abrupt silence. "And is this the way you always answer charges? By attacking the person making the charge? How very . . . convenient for you."

The flames near Tamrissa seemed to intensify, but they still weren't able to touch her or anyone else. Clothes, floor, chairs, everything was being kept from burning, and Vallant knew when Tal finally realized how ineffective his efforts really were. Tal paled visibly, and the flames near Tamrissa disappeared as abruptly as they'd formed.

"The woman was lying, and all of you ought to know that," Tal said shakily to the assembly members, who still stood staring at him. "Not only is the charge absurd, but I was also a victim. If that poison had taken any longer to work, I'd be dead along with the rest right now."

"How convenient," Tamrissa repeated at once, before the frowns of doubt on the faces of the assembly members could be vocalized by any of them. "You're also a victim, so you can't be considered guilty. Of course, for that excuse to mean anything, people would have to forget that you *didn't* die. In fact, you didn't even have to be worked on by a healer, did you? How very, very, lucky . . ."

One glance showed Tal that the frowns of doubt shown by the assembly members had been replaced with glaring, and that seemed to be too much for the man. The look on his face said he wanted to scream again with pure rage and madness, but instead of that Tal simply strode from the room. No one said a word until the furious man had disappeared, and then Gardan stirred in his seat before standing.

"We do need to have the truth behind the poisoning, but that isn't all we're concerned with today," Gardan said to the assembly, his tone somber. "We don't dare forget about that invasion, and those of us going to see what we can do will leave tomorrow morning at first light. I suggest you all consider who else will be going with Antrie and me, and let us know as soon as possible. We'll be at our homes, getting ready for the trip."

This time the disturbance was of a different sort as Gardan offered his arm to Antrie and the two of them began to leave the meeting room. Again Vallant joined his Blendingmates as they followed the two Gracelians, and their procession didn't stop until they were outside and alone.

"That was absolutely incredible," Antrie blurted, finally losing the pleasantly aloof expression she'd been wearing as she turned to Tamrissa. "I don't know when you realized that Zirdon Tal was responsible for the poisoning, but I'm delighted you told us about it when you did. What gave you the first hint?"

"You actually believed that accusation, didn't you?" Tamrissa answered with a delighted laugh, studying Antrie's face. "It sounded so good that *I* almost believed it, but I wasn't sure everyone else would see it the same. You didn't realize that I was just making things up as I went along?"

"Making things up?" Antrie echoed, shock clearly taking control of her. "You didn't figure things out—you just made them up?"

"That's marvelous!" Gardan exclaimed with a deep, hearty laugh, beaming at Tamrissa. "If it hadn't been Tal I might be feeling guilty right now for considering *him* guilty, but I enjoyed that too much for guilt to have a chance. Just imagine . . . For once Tal is innocent, but no one believes it."

"But Tal *isn't* innocent," Jovvi put in quietly while everyone else laughed and congratulated Tamrissa. "His reactions were so clear that it's a wonder no one else noticed. He *was* involved in the poisoning in some way, even though I don't believe he tampered with the provisions himself."

"This is getting almost too complicated for me, and that's

saying a lot," Antrie put in with a groan. "So Zirdon *is* guilty, but we still can't prove it. That means he'll be getting away with murder again, and I simply can't stand it. I'm afraid I'll—"

"Excuse me, but we're about to have another emergency," Lorand suddenly interrupted. "I remembered that while we were in the meeting room the floor struck me as odd, so I just reexamined it from another angle. I can see now that the wood's been weakened, and it's sure to collapse at any minute. We've got to get those people out of there before they go with the floor."

Antrie Lorimon and Cleemor Gardan both exclaimed aloud before turning and hurrying back into the building. Rion followed them without hesitation, but Lorand stopped Vallant with a hand on his arm as he was about to go with the others.

"This is a job for Air magic users, I think," Lorand said softly when Vallant raised questioning brows. "Besides, there's something the rest of you need to know. I'm not the one who spotted the coming emergency."

"*I* saw it, and with unexpected clarity," Naran said softly, her tone as disturbed as her expression. "The probability of the floor collapsing is close to a certainty, but the possibility of more deaths isn't the same. Those people can be saved if they're gotten out of there quickly enough."

"And, happily, Lorand's quick thinking let you give the warning without admitting who it really came from," Jovvi said with a warm smile for the two, but then she sobered. "Does that mean the . . . flux or whatever it is has finally cleared up, I hope?"

"No, the nasty stuff closed in again immediately," Naran said, sounding uncharacteristically annoyed. "I've decided that being so close to the coming collapse let me see it in spite of the flux, or that someone is deliberately blocking me. I don't know who could be doing the blocking this thoroughly, I just know it isn't anyone in my link groups. But who does that leave?"

"Only the whole rest of the world," Tamrissa said, mirroring Naran's annoyance. "And this is just what we needed at the moment: another mystery to solve."

"I think I'm gettin' more angry than tired of it," Vallant put in, meaning every word. He did feel the way Tamrissa and Naran obviously did, but the rest of his comment was interrupted when people began to hurry out of the building.

Quite a few people had appeared when there was a very loud crash accompanied by a storm of dust erupting from the doors and windows. The people closest to the building cried out in fear as they cringed away, but Vallant was most concerned about those who hadn't yet come out. He quickly used water to blot up the dust in the air nearest the door before taking a step toward that door, but going inside wasn't necessary. The three Air magic users walked out, completely unbothered by the swirling dust and debris.

"Being able to keep yourself untouched is obviously a handy aspect of talent," Lorand commented with a relieved grin. "I'd have to pull all that dust out of my clothing and hair, but they won't have that problem."

"And I'd have to rinse it out," Vallant agreed, matching Lorand's relief. "I'm glad there was a reason to let them go inside alone."

Vallant glanced at Naran with that comment, and only because of the glance did he catch the tail end of drawn worry on Naran's face. The next moment her face looked completely unconcerned, a look that was surely for Rion's benefit. They'd have to do something about the breach between Naran and Rion soon, or be faced with a problem like his and Tamrissa's all over again . . .

And then a shouting babble erupted, aimed mostly toward Rion and the others. Some of the assembly members were trying to thank the people who'd saved them, but a few of the others were demanding to know who was responsible. No one mentioned aloud that Zirdon Tal was no longer present, but more than one person must have been thinking it.

"Please try to calm yourselves," Cleemor Gardan shouted over the tumult, both of his hands raised high. "Once we Air magic users got inside you were no longer in any danger, not when we were able to put a platform of hardened air under your feet. I suggest you go home now while I get in touch with Frode Mismin. Once he puts his people on the alert, nothing like this should happen again."

Very few of the assembly members looked convinced about the reassurances, and a couple of them seemed more than a little determined. What they were determined about wasn't Vallant's business, but curiosity touched him for a moment. Then the heroes left the people they'd rescued and rejoined *their* group, which meant they were able to leave as well. Vallant needed to speak to their people back at the inn outside the city, and he also needed to get in touch with the group following some hours back.

Their Blending would be leaving tomorrow along with the Gracelian Blendings, and Vallant meant to take along volunteer link groups. But that meant real volunteers, since they weren't going to be riding to a party. Hopefully there would be enough volunteers to fill out tandem link groups for all of them, but he and the others would be going even without link groups.

Vallant just prayed that they would not find that necessary. If the invaders really were untouchable by talent it might make very little difference, but then again the difference might be between living and dying . . .

Zirdon Tal stormed into his house, his mood blacker than it had ever been in his life. He'd been one step away from putting his plan into practice, the plan that would have put *him* in charge and his enemies in trouble, and then that— that—*female!*—had opened her mouth and ruined everything . . . !

Thought of what that ruining entailed made Zirdon feel pale, so as soon as he was in his study with a glass of wine in his hand he chased out his hovering servants. Once alone he took a swallow of the wine rather than just a sip, and only then let himself remember what had been said—and done. The accusation had been bad enough, coming as close as it had to the truth, but the aftermath . . .

"How can that cursed woman be so *strong*?" Zirdon demanded in an intense whisper, a shudder running through him. "She kept me from touching anyone and anything with my fires, and I don't understand *how*! How was it possible?"

It was perfectly obvious that those Gandistran commoners were able to do things their betters in Gracely couldn't, and Zirdon cursed the fact that he'd been too disturbed to say that aloud. Making those intruders look like dangerous animals would have gotten the other assembly members to stop staring at *him* in silent accusation. But he'd been too upset to think of the ploy, and now it was too late to use it.

Or was it? Zirdon straightened in his chair, examining the marvelous new idea he'd just gotten. Lorimon and Gardan had been spending a lot of time in the company of the Gandistrans, so it shouldn't be too difficult to suggest that the pair had sold themselves to the intruders. Yes, that would be the note he had to take, that they'd accused *him* to conceal the fact that *they* were planning something against Gracely's best interests.

The decision to counterattack made Zirdon feel a good deal better, but not all of his upset was soothed. It still wasn't possible to understand how that woman had linked *him* to the attacks, not when the trail now ended at Syant's dead body. And it was frightening how quickly everyone had believed the accusation. Could it be possible that those intruders *were* using some aspect of talent to control everyone?

"Even if they aren't, it's worth making the claim," Zirdon muttered after another sip of wine. "If I can discredit the Gandistrans, Lorimon and Gardan will be marked with the same brush. And I *have* to do something about them, I simply have to."

Another sip of wine was needed to calm Zirdon's agitation, but the calming effect didn't last long. As soon as Zirdon had a definite plan of action, his mind insisted on returning to the question of Syant's unknown plans. How it would be possible to avoid what was meant to affect the other assembly members Zirdon didn't know, and that uncertainty threatened to unman him. It was almost as if Syant hadn't cared *who* was hurt, the man in control of him included . . .

Zirdon brooded over that impression for a while, but all

too soon he discovered his glass to be empty. The one glass of wine was obviously not going to be enough to calm him completely, so he rang for a servant to refill the glass. The man seemed agitated over something when he entered, and once Zirdon's glass was refilled he discovered what the something was.

"Your pardon, Exalted One, but something terrible has happened," the servant blurted after handing him the glass. "May I tell you about it?"

"Since you've already begun to tell me, you might as well continue," Zirdon replied with a dryness that the fool couldn't possibly appreciate. "Has our daily delivery of milk gone bad?"

"I wish it were only that," the man replied, actually looking deeply troubled. "Word has come that the assembly was attacked again, and if not for a timely intervention all the surviving members would have been killed. The Highest Aspect be thanked that you yourself weren't there."

Zirdon stared at the servant, his hand tightening around the glass as all traces of amusement fled. There had been *another* attack so *soon*? And if he hadn't left when he did, he would have been in the middle of it again?

"Exalted One, you've turned pale," the servant observed with concern as he bent over Zirdon. "Please, take a sip of the wine."

Zirdon took more of a gulp than a sip, and once the wine had warmed away some of the ice inside him he felt able to speak again.

"Tell me what happened," Zirdon commanded in a choked voice before a thought occurred to him. "Or don't you know any of the details?"

"Apparently Earth magic users weakened the floor of the meeting room the assembly uses," the servant replied at once. "That floor would have collapsed, taking everyone with it, but two Exalted Ones and one of the visitors, all with Air magic, saved everyone. The three are considered heroes now, of course, and feeling is very high against whoever is behind all these terrible doings—"

"All right, that's enough!" Zirdon interrupted with a snarl, control of his temper completely beyond him. "Get out and leave me alone!"

The fool of a servant bowed immediately and quickly left, and the solitude allowed Zirdon to curse long and feelingly. Not only was he shaken by how close he had come to being put in danger again, the rest of it made him feel even worse.

The Air magic users mentioned had to be Lorimon and Gardan, and now they were considered *heroes*! And he, the man who had been accused of being behind the attacks, had left the room rather abruptly! Right now the law said he couldn't be put on trial without actual proof of his guilt, but how long would it be before irate assembly members changed that law? If they used a Spirit magic Blending to question him . . .

The glass of wine went down Zirdon's throat almost before he knew it, but this time he rose to fetch a refill himself. In spite of all his efforts, Lorimon and Gardan were now considered heroes and *he* was being regarded as a villain. It wasn't fair, it just wasn't fair, but Zirdon didn't know what to do to change matters!

Zirdon returned to his chair to drink and brood, and he didn't know he'd fallen asleep until one of his servants awoke him with a shake.

"Please excuse the intrusion, Exalted One, but there are other Exalted Ones here to see you," the servant blurted with wide eyes and a pale face. "We tried to tell them that you didn't want to be disturbed, but they demanded to be brought to you. If you haven't agreed to see them in five minutes, they mean to come in here anyway!"

Zirdon put his hands to his face, fighting to pull himself together. His head ached abominably and he felt absolutely hollow, the darkness outside the windows confirming the probability that he'd missed dinner. He wanted nothing more right now than a good meal, a hot bath, and then his bed, but he had "visitors . . ."

"All right, show them in, but tell them that I'm still not feeling well from having been poisoned this morning," Zirdon directed. "And have someone bring fresh tea."

"Immediately, Exalted One," the servant agreed with a

bow, and then the man was gone. Zirdon took the opportunity to straighten his clothing and smooth down his hair, and then he had to force himself to his feet. Olskin Dinno led three other assembly members into the room, and none of them seemed in the least friendly.

"It's about time," Dinno said, his voice its usual rumble as he looked Zirdon over with no approval whatsoever. "Do you do this sort of thing often?"

"Are you asking if I get poisoned on a regular basis?" Zirdon countered as he stiffened in insult, in no mood to be charming. "No, my dear Dinno, that isn't one of my usual habits, and what's more—"

"Please make the effort to be less of a fool, Tal," Dinno interrupted before Zirdon was able to introduce the topic of how dangerous the Gandistrans were. "I'm a High practitioner of Earth magic, and as such I can tell that it isn't poison throwing you out of focus like this, but too much wine."

"And what makes that *your* business, you lowborn lout?" Zirdon snapped, humiliation and the headache forcing him to speak his mind for once. "I've never had to account for my actions to *anyone,* and I don't mean to start now."

"We're not terribly interested in your personal problems, Tal," one of the others, Satlan Reesh, put in before Dinno could comment. Reesh was a heavy man with the proper low opinion of women that Zirdon had made use of in the past to counter Lorimon. Now Reesh looked at Zirdon with that same condescending attitude, and Zirdon wasn't in the least pleased.

"We're here to tell you something important, Tal, so try to pay attention," Reesh continued. "Do you by any chance know what happened in the meeting room after you left this afternoon?"

"Yes, my servants brought me the news," Zirdon replied, still bristling with insult. "What has that got to do with this . . . this . . . invasion of my privacy?"

"It has quite a lot to do with our visit," Dinno took up the explanation, his wide face covered with very obvious distaste. "Most of us believe that you *are* responsible for these attacks against the assembly, and it's your good fortune that we have no proof to add to the suspicion. If we did have proof . . ."

"Then it would be our pleasure to show you how we feel about you," Reesh finished the sentence when Dinno didn't, giving Zirdon a sudden chill. Those men really seemed to hate him . . . "But lovely daydreams won't help us, so we've decided to do something that will. Dinno and I have decided to take our Blendings to join Gardan and the Lorimon woman tomorrow when they leave to look into this invasion matter. With that in view, you and your Blendingmates will join us as well."

"In other words, we'd rather have you where we can keep an eye on you," Dinno added flatly while Zirdon stared at Reesh with astonishment. "And a word to the wise, Tal: If anyone in the expedition so much as catches a cold, we will hold *you* responsible. At that point we won't wait any longer for proof, but will simply have you questioned. And if you admit to being guilty as I think you will . . ."

This time no one added to the ominous words, and even Zirdon was too shaken to comment. They were going to drag him along on the expedition against those savage invaders, and weren't prepared to accept his refusal. If he tried to refuse anyway, chaos knew what they would do to him . . .

"We'll be leaving at first light, and will meet before then at the assembly building," Dinno said, his tone still completely flat. "Don't be late, or we'll come after you."

All four men stared at Zirdon for a few seconds longer, and then they turned and simply left. A servant had brought in a fresh tea service, but Zirdon's visitors hadn't even sat down much less accepted refreshment. The whole episode made Zirdon's head spin, and rather than go to the tea service he returned to the wine decanter and took a clean glass. His previous glass was still on the floor, where he'd dropped it after falling asleep.

A good swallow of the wine let Zirdon get control of himself again, and the first thing he did was take a deep, settling breath. He needed a clear head if he was to think his way out of the trouble he found himself in, but he also needed the steadying effect of the wine. He'd just been told that he would be going after the invaders, and he had to decide what to do about that—

"Oh, for pity's sake," Zirdon muttered, suddenly remembering that he'd *wanted* to go after the invaders. It would let him get out of the city and away from Syant's insane plans, and also allow him to become the empire's greatest hero. And now Dinno and the others had made it possible to do just that. Not to mention giving him the opportunity to repay those Gandistran intruders for the way they'd made him look like a fool. He might not be able to match that miserable woman's strength on his own, but with the help of his Blending . . .

Zirdon spent some time laughing in delight before he went to tell his Blendingmates about their upcoming trip . . .

# FOUR

High Lord Embisson Ruhl felt vastly confused. He'd awakened in this bed beneath him not long ago, the room about him completely unfamiliar. For some reason he also felt very weak, and not until he tried to move did he understand the weakness. Pain flared throughout his body strongly enough to make him gasp, most of it coming from his back. And that, oddly enough, was when he suddenly remembered what had happened.

"Those chaos-forsaken traitors," Embisson growled, abruptly so furious that his head began to spin and his vision blur. Sembrin Noll and his bitch-wife, Bensia . . . They had to be the ones who had sent some of the men meant for their new "guard" to kill him. How those two had gotten control of the men was completely beyond him, but there was no longer any doubt that they had. Obviously, he should have listened to Edmin's words of warning—

"Edmin!" Embisson gasped, now also remembering how insanely he'd argued with his son. Some part of him had known he was wrong and Edmin was right, but thick clouds of unreason had kept him from acting rationally. And that night the men had come . . . The house had been completely empty of both Edmin and the servants, and the murderers had tried to ask *him* where they were. Happily he hadn't known, otherwise he would certainly have betrayed his own flesh and blood in madness-induced anger—

Suddenly the door to the room opened, admitting three

41

strangers. The two men and one woman appeared perfectly ordinary, and in fact were certain to be commoners. Since Embisson still had no idea where he was or with whom, he made no effort to speak first.

"Ah, our guest is not only awake, he also seems to be aware," the man in the lead said as he came nearer, studying Embisson's face. "How is he doing, Eslinna?"

"He's weak and in some pain, but that's to be expected," the small, faintly pretty woman answered with a smile. "Other than that he's coming along quite nicely. Are you going to tell him who he owes his life to?"

"Of course, once he's a bit stronger," the man replied with his own smile. "It might or might not do him some good to know, but telling it will do *me* good. Are you ready to talk to us, Ruhl?"

"If you know my name, you also know I have titles that you're ignoring," Embisson pointed out in little more than a whisper, now knowing he lost nothing by making the statement. "I am a legally appointed leader of this empire, and trying to deny my orders will make you a lawbreaker. You will immediately tell me who you are and where I am, and then you will put all the forces at your command under *my* command."

"If it's the law you'd like to discuss, I'll be glad to oblige you," the man returned with a laugh that looked like true amusement. The commoner was tall and solidly built, less than handsome but apparently unconcerned by his physical lacks. His dark hair was too long for Embisson's tastes, and the insolence in his gaze begged for the proper disciplining.

"You'll oblige me by using my titles and acknowledging my position," Embisson returned with all the annoyance he now felt. "I don't *discuss* things with underlings, I simply give them orders to obey. You've been given yours, and now I'm waiting for the obedience."

"Now, see, *there's* where you're making your mistake," the man said, showing nothing of defensiveness or angered embarrassment—much less obedience. "You think our positions are such that I'm required to obey you, but that's completely wrong. To begin with, the so-called nobility of this empire forfeited their positions because they thought they could get away with cheating on their responsibilities. They were wrong."

"How dare you," Embisson began, vastly insulted, but the man waved an intrusive finger at him.

"Please don't waste all our time trying to deny the charge," the man said, the briskness of his tone showing something of the annoyance he'd kept hidden until now. "I happen to know that you were right there in the middle of the fraudulent game, the one that helped Middles be Seated as the strongest Blending in the empire. Even *my* Blending could have defeated your usual puppets, and that fraud alone was enough to disenfranchise you and your sort."

"Charges like that are all well and good if you can prove them in court, which you certainly can't," Embisson pointed out stiffly. "With that in view, all the theories and guesswork in the world won't make your position legal."

"The worry about legality didn't stop *your* lot from knocking out the real winners of the competition for Seated Blending," the man countered immediately. "That alone would prove the charge for us, even if we were interested in being fair with you people—which we're not. There isn't one of you who understands the meaning of fairness, so we're treating you the way *we've* been treated all these years. Now: I'm Wilant Gorl, duly appointed substitute for the legally Seated Blending in this empire. Tell me who you came to this city with, and what you all intended to do."

" 'Duly appointed substitute,' " Embisson repeated with a sneer, letting the man see how much contempt he felt. "In other words, you haven't the ability or the intelligence to make the position yours rather than someone else's. Or is that the real reason you've come to me? If you want my help to make you and yours the ones with the power, you'll have to pay for that help. You may begin the payment by kneeling to me the way you should have when you first came in, and then we'll see about what else I want."

Embisson was delighted with the way things had worked out, the certainty about the commoner's desires coming to him in a flash. He realized that it might take a moment or two before the common trash was able to force himself to his knees, but it was certain to happen. If Embisson didn't understand the need for power then no one did. But the reaction he'd anticipated came sooner than expected—and turned out to be vastly different from what he'd pictured.

"You expect me to kneel and beg so that my Blending can take over being the actual Seated Blending?" the man asked after laughing with what looked to be incredulity. "If we were stupid enough to want the position permanently, we could compete for it in a year's time without having to lick *anyone's* boots, you fool. And with the number of Blendings already formed out there, no one will ever again be able to twist the competitions to their own ends. You're obviously out of touch with the world as it is today, so I'll say this just once more: Are you going to answer the questions I've asked, or do you need a bit of help?"

"You expect me to believe that you don't want the power?" Embisson demanded, trying not to show how shaken he felt. "Everyone wants power, so that's absolute nonsense and I won't—"

"Vindren, help me out here, please," the man Gorl interrupted, turning to the second man of the group. "I don't want this taking all day."

"Certainly, Wil," the man addressed as Vindren replied, his expression mild and pleasant. This was a slender man with brown hair and eyes, and Embisson's outrage over being interrupted again disappeared immediately—along with the other disturbing emotions he'd been feeling.

"What were the questions you had?" Embisson found himself asking, the words causing only a small disturbance deep down inside himself. "I'm afraid I don't quite remember."

"I wanted to know who you came into the city with, and what your plans are," Gorl repeated, a gleam of satisfaction in his eyes. "And you might also tell me who stabbed you, assuming you know who it was."

"I came into the city with my son Edmin, Sembrin and Bensia Noll with the woman's cousin Rimen Howser, and a large number of men who were to form a new Guard force,"

Embisson answered at once, now finding no reason to withhold any of the information. "Our plan was to reestablish our power here, with me in charge. Unfortunately, though, something made me begin to act oddly, and I had a falling out with Edmin. Before I could overcome the oddness, Noll sent some of the men to my new house to murder me."

"It wasn't 'something' that made you act oddly, it was *someone*," Gorl told him with a small frown. "When you were first brought here, Vindren noticed that you'd been put under layers of commands by someone with strong Spirit magic. Do you know who could have done that to you?"

"My son has Spirit magic, but it couldn't have been him," Embisson answered, seriously considering the question. "Even if he were of a mind to do something like that to me, he would hardly have arranged things so that he and I would argue. No, it has to have been one of the Nolls, probably the woman. If Sembrin had been the one, he would have been intelligent enough to work on Edmin as well as myself."

"Meaning that your son is probably too strong in Spirit magic not to notice someone trying to tamper with him," the man Gorl murmured, exchanging a glance with the other two people who had come in with him. "Where are the Nolls and your son now?"

"The Nolls claimed they were returning to their old house here in the city, but I no longer believe that," Embisson said with a bitter smile. "They knew I would probably try to find them when I discovered that the men *I* paid for were no longer available to me, so I'm certain they went elsewhere. Edmin left with our servants before those men came to murder me, and I now remember that the men also asked me where Edmin was. Obviously he was scheduled to be killed as well, and when I couldn't answer their questions the men availed themselves of the one victim in their grasp."

"So we now have two groups to worry about," Gorl growled, his unhappiness very clear. "Your son Edmin isn't likely to join forces with the Nolls again, which means they'll both be trying to take over but in different ways. It's a good thing you didn't ask me to beg to get *rid* of this marvelous power, Ruhl. I might have obliged you."

"How much damage can they possibly do?" the woman called Eslinna asked with her own frown. "It isn't as if there are hundreds or even dozens of other former nobles in the city, just waiting for someone to lead them in rebellion. If we can locate and arrest the men they brought with them, the nobles shouldn't be a problem all by themselves."

"How are we supposed to locate those men?" the Spirit magic user called Vindren asked in a reasonable tone. "And even if we should find a way, how can we justify arresting them if they haven't done anything? People are supposed to be free to come into this city, after all, and if we start to arrest some because we think they *might* do something wrong, I for one won't want to live with the precedent that sets."

"I think we can find a way to be fair and still keep our people safe," Gorl interrupted when the woman started to argue what Vindren had said. "It isn't as if we have no way to find out if strangers have nasty intentions, and if they do we can throw them out of the city instead of arresting them. Unless they're the sort who take lives casually, of course. You're not seriously worried about *their* rights, are you, Vin?"

"As long as we're sure what type of person we're dealing with, no," the Spirit magic user allowed after a very short hesitation. "I just don't want us to make a habit of pushing everyone around because we think they might be guilty of something."

"Everyone is guilty of *something*," Embisson put in, faintly amused by the innocence these people showed. "If you remember the point when you deal with them, you never make the mistake of being too generous."

"It's nice of you to share your expertise with us," Gorl said, and Embisson had the odd impression that the man had spoken dryly. "We'll certainly remember your advice, and right now I'd like some more of it. What do you think your son and the Nolls will do to gain the power they're looking for? How will they start?"

"The obvious thing for them to do is to gather a local power base," Embisson said, surprised that even a commoner would fail to know that. "They'll search out the dissidents in the city, those poor fools who believe they should be important simply because they want to be. Those people will be able to move about freely and gather information on your weakest points, at the same time spreading rumors that will make you monsters in the eyes of the credulous masses. And the Nolls will also contact the people who worked for them before they left the city, of course."

"Of course," Gorl echoed in a mutter, his mind obviously working behind a distracted gaze. "If I'd stopped to think about it, I would have seen how obvious those moves are. Is there any chance that they'll use the men you all brought into the city in an open attack against the palace or some other point?"

"Only as an absolute last resort," Embisson answered, remembering ruefully his own mad plans along those lines. "Or in a situation where your own people are inadequate to protect a location, and a quick, unexpected strike will shift the location into their hands. And the location needs to be significant, like the palace."

"I think we'd be wise to set some of the new Blendings on guard in pairs," the woman Eslinna commented almost in a murmur. "That way we'll be warned if any of them make a try for the palace, and at the same time our Guard force will have help. They aren't High Blendings, of course, but that still makes them more capable than anything those nobles have."

"You really do have to stop that nonsense of making more Blendings and training the peasants," Embisson said, letting the youngsters see his disapproval. "You keep power by not letting others have even a taste of it, unless you need to toss them a crumb or two. Then you keep the crumb very small, and only lead the fools to *believe* that they can earn a larger crumb. You use the lure to keep the fools moving, and never have to use the larger crumb at all."

"I think I've had enough instruction for one day in how to be a mindless noble," Gorl surprised Embisson by saying with unexpected derision. "If you people had had any intelligence at all, you would have understood long ago that keeping people from doing anything effective also robs *you* of what their efforts might have produced. We're learning new things every day to make life easier and more pleasant, things we never would have known about with *you* fools in charge. Eslinna, Vindren, let's go. We have things to do."

The other two people followed Gorl out, leaving a puzzled Embisson behind. By rights he should have felt outraged, and on some distant level he did. But he also couldn't help wondering what new things Gorl had spoken about. It was true that nothing new had been done with talent in more than a century, but the lack had been a necessary one. You can't turn people loose with all kinds of knowledge and still expect to rule them. But if you could . . .

Embisson hadn't felt serious pain since the trio had entered his room, and now he moved just a little in the bed to get more comfortable. He remembered clearly how bad the pain had been when that Mardimil woman had had him beaten up, and how long the pain had lasted. If this current lack of pain was any indication of the new things the peasants could do, their progress was something he had definite interest in. There really should be a way to have the new and useful without losing control, so Embisson decided to think about the problem. After all, he didn't have much else to do right now, and as soon as Edmin freed him from capture the ideas could be put to use . . .

Rimen Howser drifted through the shadows of early evening, moving along the street in a way that kept him from the attention of the animals. And animals there were aplenty, including a surprising number of unaccompanied bitches. With people of true quality no longer about to show what actual humanity was, the animals paraded around pretending that *they* were human. But they weren't, and Rimen knew that better than most.

A narrow alleyway appeared on Rimen's left, so he eased into it and found a place behind trash bins to sit down for a time. It had taken him most of the day to reach this part of the city on foot, but the effort had been worth it. His right leg throbbed with pain, a reminder of the way the leg had been broken that would be with Rimen for the rest of his life. He now walked with a limp, his posture bent a bit to the left because of the way his ribs had been cracked. He no longer looked the part of true humanity the way he had before the beating, and for that the animals would pay . . .

Tears filled Rimen's eyes as they did so often lately, another legacy of the beating. He'd thought he'd be so safe with guardsmen to protect him, but a great mass of animals had gathered around them all. When Rimen demanded the gold that was due one of the Seated Blending, expecting the animals to obey the way they always had, those animals had turned on him and his escort instead. The guardsmen had gone down first, most of them killed, and then the animals had dared to turn their attention to *him* . . .

Ripples of shuddering took Rimen over at the memory of that beating. It had been the worst thing ever to happen to him, and to this day he had no clear memory of how he'd managed to get home. At times he thought there had been animals who had helped rather than hurt him, but that couldn't be. Animals did nothing but bring a man pain and disgust, and the time had come to repay the pain and ease the disgust.

Rimen smiled as he considered his plans, plans that would let him get more than just his own back. Once he would have let everyone know what was being done and who was doing it, but now secrecy was essential. Real people were no longer in charge of the city, but if the animals didn't know who was culling their herds they couldn't stop him. And he would *not* be stopped, not until he'd avenged himself a hundred times over.

Labored breathing forced Rimen to control his rage, a restraint he'd lately had to learn. Losing his temper now meant to also lose the ability to control his broken body, and Rimen simply couldn't afford that second loss. His Water magic wasn't very strong, but when his mind was calm he could use his fragile talent to locate the positions of people—and animals. It had become time to use that talent, and as soon as the forced calm flowed over him he did exactly that.

The small alley should have been perfect to find the first of his victims, but Rimen searched uselessly over and over

again until impatient anger flashed through him. For some
reason there weren't any ragged, hungry animals seeking a
nesting place in the alley, and it occurred to Rimen that he
hadn't sensed the presence of animals in the other alleys
he'd passed either. At one time the streets in this part of the
city had been clogged with scruffy, disgusting animals begging handouts or shuffling along looking for cast-off food or
clothing. Now . . .

"Now they're all pretending to be human," Rimen muttered, disturbance and a trace of fear coloring the thought.
"I'm not strong enough to face a healthy animal directly and
win, so what am I to do?"

Rimen knew well enough that he had only two choices—
either to give up and go back to where he'd come from, or to
think of a plan that would allow him to continue on. Giving
up was unthinkable, so there was nothing for it but to come
up with a plan.

The alley he sat in smelled terrible, a nausea-making reek
that threatened to turn his stomach. He decided it might be a
good idea to find another place to do his planning, so he
struggled to his feet. Standing up meant needing to lean
against the wall for a moment until he caught his breath, but
Rimen was almost used to the restriction. He recovered
fairly quickly and was about to leave the alley, when a door
abruptly opened to spill light out into the darkness.

Rimen was too far to the left of the door to be caught in
the light, and then the animal that had opened the door
closed it almost as quickly. But the animal had stepped out
into the alley, and now staggered to the section of wall opposite the door as he groped at his clothing. A moment later Rimen heard the sound of water spilling, an increased stench
in the air telling Rimen that the obviously drunken animal
was relieving himself.

Outrage gripped Rimen so suddenly that he almost did his
own staggering. The nerve of that animal, to come out filled
with drink so that he might relieve himself in public! The action was so disgusting that Rimen's stomach heaved, but he
suddenly realized he had no time for catering to his delicate

digestion. His plan was formed immediately, and just that quickly he put it into action.

Moving as quietly and swiftly as possible, Rimen drew the knife he'd taken from the house and moved up to a place behind the animal. His left hand flew to cover the animal's mouth as his right hand thrust the knife deep into the animal's back, and a screaming grunt was stifled against Rimen's palm as the animal spasmed and then collapsed.

Rimen made no attempt to hold the animal erect, but instead followed it down to the ground as the knife continued to rise and fall as though Rimen's arm had a life and will of its own. No other sounds came from the animal, which was very fortunate as Rimen's palm was no longer over the animal's mouth. Over and over again Rimen drove the knife deep into the animal's body, the motion bringing Rimen such pleasure that he found it impossible to stop.

Exhaustion alone brought an end to the pleasure, and Rimen had to crawl back to the shadows in order to rest. He felt completely drained, but the sensation was one of extreme gratification and intense pleasure that was better than anything he'd ever experienced. The knife was covered in blood and probably so was he, but that mattered not at all to Rimen. The important part was that he'd begun to mete out the vengeance those animals had earned, and now had the perfect means to continue with that vengeance.

It took a number of long minutes before Rimen was able to get to his feet again and leave that alley, but his movement was no longer aimless. He would now search out taverns and inns, and await the disgusting animals in the alleys behind those loathsome establishments. When others came out to make filthy water, they would become his as easily as that first one had.

Rimen wasn't visible in the shadows he clung to as he moved along the street, but if he *had* been visible an observer would have noticed the delighted smile that now covered him like a blanket . . .

# FIVE

Driffin Codsent was so deeply into his own thoughts that the coach he rode in reached its destination without his being more than vaguely aware of the trip. The ride itself was faintly disturbing in that he still wasn't used to going places by coach, but that had become the least of his worries. Today was the day he and a Spirit magic user would try to heal someone who suffered from mind sickness.

Driffin took a deep breath and blew it out slowly, wondering if he'd been kidding himself. He knew he was as good a healer as someone with only a Middle talent in Earth magic could be, but everyone around him seemed to think he was capable of miracles. In reality he knew himself to be no more than a small man who had survived on the streets for quite a long time, eventually rescuing others and helping them to survive as well. As far as doing miracles went, that should rightfully be left to High talents.

But it was some High talents who had gotten him interested in this project, and they seemed to think he could handle the job. He'd thought the same for a while, the idea of doing something new exciting him, but now that he was actually about to try that something new he had begun to develop doubts . . .

"Well, do you intend to sit there all day, or do you mean to come inside?" a female voice demanded, gentle humor rather than acid sarcasm behind the words. "I don't come out to greet *everyone* who visits here, so you ought to be flattered."

Driffin looked up to see that the coach had come to a stop in front of the large house that had been pressed into service by the new government. Gensie Landros stood at the bottom of the walk where his coach had stopped, and he hadn't even noticed her approach—or the coach stopping. Gensie was the High in Spirit magic he would be working with, and although her plain brown hair and eyes added nothing to her rather plain features, the size of her talent made up for any other lacks.

"Sorry, Gensie," Driffin said at once, trying to hide his embarrassment as he began to get out of the coach. "I shouldn't have let my mind wander, especially not to the point of having no idea where I was or who was with me."

By then he stood on the walk beside Gensie, but she didn't respond immediately. She waited until the coachman started to drive the coach toward the stables at the back of the house, and then she gave her entire attention to Driffin.

"Why are you suddenly feeling so unsure of yourself, Driff?" Gensie asked, concern clearly marked on her face. "Don't you understand *yet* how good you are?"

"Sure I'm good, Gensie," Driffin answered, giving her a smile with absolutely no humor in it. It isn't possible to hide your true feelings from a High in Spirit magic, so Driffin didn't even try. "I'm probably the best Middle talent healer around, but what I can't understand is how I let myself get involved with High talents. I'm not in that class and never will be."

"No, that's true," Gensie granted with another version of her gentle smile. "You never *will* be a High talent, but there's a fact you seem to have missed somehow. Except for Lorand Coll, you manage to be a better healer than anyone even *with* High talent. Don't you know that, or is it just that you don't believe it?"

"Where did you get *that* idea?" Driffin demanded, staring at the small woman. "I know that I'm usually called in to help with the more difficult cases, but that's because I'm handy and also willing to drop what I'm doing when I'm called. How does that make me a better healer than a High talent with Earth magic?"

"I haven't the faintest idea how it works," Gensie returned with a dismissive shrug. "All I know is that it does work like that, and you *are* a more effective healer than any of the High talents. Why else do you think I dragged you into this? Because you're handy and willing? Really, Driff, I thought you had a better opinion of me."

Once again Driffin stared at the woman, this time wordlessly. Gensie might be a High talent in Spirit magic, but even she couldn't lie to him. If she hadn't been telling the truth he would have known instantly, but the truth of her words shone brightly to his talent. It took a long string of moments before he was capable of speech again, and then he shook his head helplessly.

"I think I need to sit down somewhere for a while," he finally managed to get out, still shaking his head. "I know *you* believe what you just said, but I'm not up to sharing that belief yet. And the way I feel now I may *never* be able to believe it."

Driffin muttered the last of his comments, but Gensie still heard it and actually laughed.

"You're really funny, Driff," she said, her chuckle somehow sounding deliberate. "Have you ever heard of a Middle talent who could do anything at all against a High talent? I know *I* haven't, but there you stand, telling me you know I'm speaking the truth. Being able to do that doesn't give you the hint that you can do other things as well?"

Driffin lost the ability to speak again, but the pained look on his face must have told Gensie that he hadn't been joking about needing to sit down. Instead of continuing the discussion she put an arm around his shoulders and led him up the walk to the broad steps of the house, and then took him inside.

The house was really rather large, almost as large as the one where Driffin had healed the former noble of the stab wound that was about to kill him. There were a couple of people dressed like servants in the wide front hall, but when they smiled and nodded to Driffin he realized that they were both High talents in Earth magic.

"We need various High talents here to help with the residents, but it would hardly be wise to advertise what they are," Gensie murmured as she led him to the left of the hall, toward a discreetly closed door. "The people residing here may be disturbed in one way or another, but they aren't stupid."

No, the people in that house weren't stupid, Driffin knew, just terribly confused. They seemed to have an instability inside them that being allowed to use their talent had . . . freed, it might be easiest to say. The instability took different forms, some milder than others, but being taught how to use talent made all of them dangerous.

"I still don't really understand why we have this problem," Driffin said as Gensie led the way into a small room that was comfortably furnished with chairs and hand tables and not much else. "Why would two people, with the same abilities and the same opportunity, react so differently?"

"Why does the same thing happen even when talent *isn't* involved?" Gensie countered, speaking over her shoulder as she headed for a large tea service. "You've told me how you lived on the street, spending a lot of effort helping others. Did everyone who lived on the street do the same?"

"Some of them had been too badly hurt to be interested in helping others," Driffin answered soberly, remembering those times with a small inner shudder. "It was all they could do to keep *themselves* safe, and what they'd gone through made that the most important effort of their lives. They couldn't bring themselves to the point of understanding that other people had been hurt just as badly."

"Sometimes I think it's lack of imagination that hurts certain people the most," Gensie said, paying only partial attention to the cup of tea she filled. "They know their own hurts and troubles well enough, but can't see that others suffer from the same. I wonder if that's what being self-centered is all about."

"Some people are self-centered because they were raised to be like that," Driffin said, walking over to take the cup of tea Gensie had poured. "At one time I thought only the nobles were like that, but I quickly learned better. You'd see a small child blasting through people and things at the market, and the child's parent would be right there, making excuses about why the child was doing as it pleased. You don't have to beat a young one to teach it how to behave, but too many people don't seem to understand that."

"That's very likely what's wrong with our first patient," Gensie said, a sigh accompanying the bleak look in her eyes. "He's actually a Low in Earth magic, but once he finished the training class he somehow made better use of his talent than some Middles. He started a 'health protection' business, first bringing people almost to the point of a heart attack. Once he released them and they recovered, he told them they would stay 'healthy' if they paid him a certain amount of silver on a regular basis. He didn't think anyone would have the nerve to report him—or that anything would be done if they did—but he was wrong."

"Only because the new government actually cares about what happens to people," Driffin replied with a frown as he sipped the hot tea, studying the idea that had just come to him. "It's a really big change in attitude from what the nobles showed, and makes all the difference. If there was some way we could change that patient's attitude . . ."

Driff let the words trail off as he stared at Gensie, asking the question without actually speaking it. She *was* a High in Spirit magic, after all, and ought to know what was and wasn't possible.

"I think you're onto something, but I'm not quite sure what that is," Gensie answered slowly, staring at him in the same way. "How would we change the man's attitudes?"

"Well, it seems to me that how we act depends on what we remember about what we learned as children," Driff replied slowly, putting the odd idea straight in his mind as he also put it into words. "If we remember being smacked the couple of times we tried to run wild, we may *feel* the urge to run wild but we don't act on it. But if we remember nothing unpleasant happening . . ."

"Yes, yes, that's it, I think," Gensie said at once, a new enthusiasm burning in her eyes. "If we can change those memories we can change their attitudes, but it won't be an easy process for the patient. Do you think you can keep them stable while I rearrange their past lives?"

"The only way to know is to try it," Driff said, eagerness also growing in *him*. "If anything goes wrong we can stop at once, and then undo what was done, can't we? If we can't undo it, we really shouldn't start at all."

"Oh, yes, I can undo anything I do," Gensie assured him, and once again Driff could tell she wasn't lying. "Let's go see how it works."

Driff finished his tea in a single gulp before putting the cup down and following Gensie out of the room. It came to him fleetingly that he'd wanted to sit down, but for some reason the urge wasn't there any longer. He still felt vaguely nervous about being part of such an important project, but the eagerness that had risen pushed the nervousness aside.

Gensie went back out into the front hall, then led the way up the wide stairs to the second floor. There were people dressed as servants up here as well, but only some of them were actually working. The others seemed distantly alert, so they must be High talents keeping tabs on some of the house's residents. Most of the doors to either side of the long hall were closed, and Gensie ignored them as she led the way to what was apparently a sitting area in the midst of the rooms.

"Is this kind of thing usual in the houses the nobles lived in?" Driff asked as he looked around. "Aren't there sitting rooms enough on the ground floor?"

"I suppose that whoever owned this house didn't want to be bothered with going downstairs all the time," Gensie answered with a shrug. "Personally, I find this area very handy. I've held more than one general meeting here, and if someone has to leave abruptly to take care of some trouble, they don't have far to go."

"So you use it for the staff rather than the residents," Driff said with a nod. "Are we going to be using it for our own project?"

"I thought at first that we would, but I've just changed my mind," Gensie said as she also looked around. "It's too open here, and any of the residents could come along at any time. I'll feel better if we keep our first attempt private, for our sake as well as that of our patient."

Driff definitely agreed with that, so he simply nodded and followed Gensie again. Two doors down from the sitting area she stopped to knock, an effort she had to repeat twice more before there was an answer. Driff had known there was someone in the room, but the resident had apparently taken his time with answering. Driff sighed as he followed Gensie into the room. It looked like they really had their work cut out for them . . .

Idresia Harmis, Driffin Codsent's partner in life, was much more busy than she looked. She'd taken a job waiting tables at the Tiger Tavern, and usually rushed around when the place was crowded. Middle of the day brought only a few patrons, but they were the ones she was actually there for. The Tiger Tavern had become a meeting place for the unhappy and disaffected, those people who had developed a strong hatred for the new way of doing things. They had different reasons for their hatred, but the emotion itself was enough to bind them in a definite way.

Lounging around not far from the only customers of the tavern was part of Idresia's job, and the look on her face was only to be expected. An observer would consider her bored almost to tears and completely distracted, but that observer would be wrong. Idresia had taken over Driff's spy network, and usually directed the others she'd recruited to the effort.

But one of her people had alerted her to the meetings held in the Tiger Tavern, and she'd decided to oversee *this* place herself. Almost everyone in the city was deliriously happy with the new government, but there were those who would have found fault with the home of the Highest Aspect itself. People were entitled to be as miserable as they liked, but those who were miserable by nature had a tendency to want everyone else to be just as miserable.

Driff had been warned that there were people in the city who would try to make trouble for the new government, so Idresia had joined the effort to see that that didn't happen. Life had become too good for her to simply stand by and watch the terminally foolish ruin things for everyone. Waiting tables in a tavern wasn't the easiest thing to do, but it did let Idresia listen carefully to what was being said.

"I tell you we just can't let this go on without doing something," one of the men at the table urged heatedly. "Those users don't want ordinary people for anything but servants, just like the nobility before them. Name just one position of importance that someone not a High talent has been given since they took over."

"They've put a lot of Middle talents in as class instructors, Meerk," someone pointed out without the diffidence that most of the others showed. "And they've also opened a lot of clinics with Middle and High healers. My sister wouldn't have been able to afford a healer for her broken leg, but the clinic she went to didn't charge her. You're still complaining because the new Seated Blending didn't let you put yourself in charge of everything."

"I would have done things right, not the way *they're* doing them!" the man called Meerk snarled, his face red with fury. "I deserve to be in charge because I can handle the job, but those fools never even gave me the chance. And teaching classes or working in clinics isn't the same as being part of the government, something you'd understand if you weren't a fool!"

"Oh, right, *I'm* the fool," the other man returned with a snort of disdain. "That great job you claim you can do would let you start a new nobility, with you at its top. If you don't know how lucky we are to be rid of the old nobility, you're a bigger fool than I could ever be."

"If you're so unhappy with the way I look at things, what are you doing here?" Meerk demanded, now cold in his anger. "Why don't you go and be a good dog, and let your new masters find some property for you to stand guard over?"

"As a matter of fact, I just came by to tell you what I thought of your endless complaints," the other man countered, showing a nasty grin. "I enrolled in one of those useless classes you think so little of, and now that I've completed the course I've also found a group to Blend with.

We'll be starting instruction in Blending tonight, and in a day or two we'll be helping to guard the palace and keep an eye on the city. And doing other incredible things you'd never understand. If the rest of you are smart, you'll leave Meerk to complain to empty chairs and get on with your life the way I did. Doing beats complaining any day of the year."

And with that the man rose to his feet and headed out of the tavern, the four silent men at the table staring after him. The man called Meerk was the only one showing a scowl; the other four looked disturbed, and it wasn't immediately clear exactly what had disturbed them.

"Now, that's the kind of wrongheadedness we have to guard against," Meerk growled after a moment, and Idresia had the impression the man was very much aware of the reactions of the others. "That idiot obviously thinks he's getting somewhere, but all he's doing is becoming a tool of the High Blendings. If they won't give important positions to people who deserve them, they certainly won't give anything worth having to *him*."

"Don't thet depend on whut you figure's worth havin'?" one of the remaining men asked quietly, his gaze as sober as his words. "Useta be there warn't nothin' I culd do as wus worth havin', but now I been lookin' around. The way I talk don't matter none t' 'em, so I'm gonna do whut *he* done. An' mebbe you ain't got whut *you* want 'cause you ain't done nothin' t' earn 'er."

Meerk's jaw tightened in anger at what had been said to him, but he let the other man leave without commenting. Once the second member of his group was gone, he turned to the others.

"Is there anyone else here thick enough in the head to agree with those two?" he demanded, glaring at the three remaining men. "If so you can leave right now, and *without* the ignorant comments."

The man's remaining cronies avoided his gaze as they shook their heads, which eased some of Meerk's anger. Idresia yawned behind her hand, delighted that she'd been able to witness those two scenes, but it was fairly clear that her presence wasn't necessary. The man Meerk would never be a real threat to the new government, not when he preferred to demand things rather than work for them. One of Idresia's agents would be enough to keep an eye on the group.

It wasn't possible for Idresia to simply walk out of the tavern and away from the job, not when she was supposed to be filling in for the woman who was her agent. Waiting until it was time to go home would be necessary, but in a couple of hours the tavern would begin to fill. Then Idresia would be too busy to have to worry about boredom, and the hours would fly by. Until then . . .

Meerk signaled to have his flagon refilled, and Idresia was in the midst of doing that chore when the door opened to admit a newcomer to the tavern. The man was rather hard looking and Idresia expected him to take a table alone, but surprisingly enough he walked to Meerk's table and sat without waiting for an invitation. He also gestured toward Idresia, showing that he wanted a flagon.

"In case you hadn't noticed, this table is taken," Meerk told the newcomer, a faint nervousness behind his tone. "I think you would be best off finding a table of your own."

"I won't be here long enough to need a table of my own," the man responded in a voice that didn't carry very far. "I'm just here to deliver a message and have a drink, and then I have other stops to make."

Idresia had quickly gotten an empty flagon from the bar, and then had filled it for the man. She also pretended that her mind was elsewhere during the pouring, but didn't miss the way the newcomer glanced at her. He seemed to be checking to see if she were paying attention to what was being said, and when he decided she wasn't he went back to the conversation.

"You have a message for *me*?" Meerk asked with a frown, having waited until Idresia moved away from the table. "Why would anyone send a message instead of coming to see me personally?"

"Some people have better things to do with their time," the man answered after taking a long pull at the flagon, giving Meerk a flat, humorless smile. "Also, some people would rather not be seen by everyone in the city. I'm told you're unhappy with the way things are going these days, and would like to see matters returned to the way they used to be. Would you be willing to join a group dedicated to making that happen?"

" 'Eager' would be a better word than 'willing,' " Meerk said, showing that eagerness as he leaned forward. "I know you're not from those fools running the government now; they already know how I feel, so there would be no reason for them to send someone to make sure. Who do you represent, and what are they willing to offer for my cooperation?"

"Those are questions you have to take up with them," the man returned, his narrow, sharp-angled face still showing that same smile. "You'll meet them at the time and place written on this slip of paper, and you'll come alone. If you don't, or if you tell anyone about this, you won't ever have to worry about who's running this empire again."

Meerk took the slip of paper the other man held out, staring at it rather than unfolding and reading it. It seemed as though Meerk might have a second thought or two about joining people who were willing to kill him, but the hard-faced man didn't give him the chance to change his mind. The man emptied his flagon in one long swallow, wiped his mouth with the back of his hand, then got up and left.

Idresia made no effort to watch the man leave, or even to see what Meerk did with the slip of paper. She quickly looked at a drunk sitting at a corner table, and nodded once. The "drunk," who was one of her agents and not drunk at all, immediately got shakily to his feet and staggered out of the tavern. It would be pure coincidence that he went in the same direction as the hard-faced man, who shouldn't notice that he was being followed. The hard-faced man's first glance around the tavern had completely dismissed the "drunk," which was just the way Idresia wanted it.

Excitement made Idresia's heart thunder, also making it harder for her to continue her act of being uncaring and un-aware of what went on around her. But the act was necessary, so she barely glanced at Meerk to see what he meant to do with the paper. It would have been nice if the man had read the contents of the message aloud to his cronies, but he must have been thinking about the warning he'd been given. He opened the note and glanced at it, then refolded it and put it away in a pocket before lifting his flagon again.

*Looks like I'll have to take off after all,* Idresia thought, adding a yawn to her performance. *Someone has to follow that man Meerk, someone with Spirit or Earth magic. If there's a serious plan afoot to make trouble, I will know about it.*

As she drifted toward the back door of the tavern, Idresia smiled to herself. She would certainly tell Driff what she'd learned, but would be careful not to mention that she'd learned it personally. The man was always so worried about her that he would throw a fit if he found out how personally involved she was. He had no idea how silly his worry was . . .

Idresia stepped out the back door—then cried out as two hands suddenly grabbed her from behind. She also began to struggle, but the hands belonged to a man and they refused to let her go!

# SIX

Lord Sembrin Noll was fairly well pleased when he entered the dining room. Bensia walked in just ahead of him, and when he held her chair she sat, then turned her head to smile at him.

"If lunch is as good as breakfast was, I'll have no complaints," Bensia said in a murmur as he took his place at the table beside her. It was a small private dining room and very small table they used, since there were only the two of them taking the meal.

"*I'll* have no complaints if the men are as successful at finding malcontents for me to work with as they were in finding servants," Sembrin said as he settled himself. "So far they've located only two supposed 'leaders,' and that's not nearly enough."

"Use the two to help you find others," Bensia said as she helped herself to a roll from the folds of the towel keeping the contents of the basket warm. "But you'll probably be best off keeping the number of peasants you use to a minimum. They'll certainly expect to be ennobled, and we don't want the lesser nobility to outnumber the higher by *that* much."

"The more peasants I use, the better off *we'll* be," Sembrin pointed out, taking a warm roll of his own. "If there are only a few of them, they could well make a pact against us. If there are six or more in the group, they'll be too busy trying to show each other up and gain an advantage to make any pacts. Peasants always act that way and probably always will."

"Well, you do know them better than I do," Bensia conceded with a smile as she added butter to her roll. "You must do as you think best, but please keep me informed. It won't hurt to question the peasants every now and again to find out what their true intentions are."

Sembrin felt the urge to tell her to stay out of what was supposed to be *his* concern, but the urge faded immediately behind the awareness that he did want her to know what he was doing. It would be best for everyone concerned, he realized, and could do no harm.

"The children will be eating later, but I wonder why Rimen isn't joining us," Bensia remarked, taking Sembrin's thoughts away from the previous topic. "The servants tell me he's still asleep, which is most unusual."

"It's not terribly unusual if you know what time he got back to the house," Sembrin said, immediately annoyed. "The men tell me he limped home just before daylight, and spent a long time in the bath house before going to bed. I have no idea where he went or what he did, but I certainly mean to find out as soon as he's awake again."

"Frankly, I felt relieved not to have him hanging about the house brooding," Bensia said after swallowing a bite of roll. "His whole inner being has turned so dark that I wonder how wise we were to bring him with us. If he was out in the city . . . If you need the children's help to find out if he told anyone about us, they should be back from the errand I sent them on in just a little while."

"If your broken cousin told anyone about us, the peasants would already be here to arrest us," Sembrin pointed out as he reached for the bottle of wine the servants had put on the table. It was a passable vintage, so he began to uncork it. "I'm not worried about what he *said,* only about what he might have done. He's really unbalanced, Bensia, and it might become necessary to sacrifice him in order to protect ourselves."

Sembrin was trying to lay unobtrusive groundwork for what he fully intended to do with the madman, but Bensia still felt it necessary to resist.

"He's my flesh and blood, Sembrin, so I won't allow him to be killed," she stated firmly, turning her head to look at him. "If it becomes necessary to restrain him, I'll use the children to do it."

"As you wish, my love," Sembrin agreed immediately, privately retaining his original intentions. "As long as the children *can* restrain him . . . Wasn't he given instructions not to leave the house? You'd better have them look into the matter, just to be on the safe side. And aren't you ready yet to ring for the meal to be served?"

"There's still one matter we haven't discussed," Bensia answered, taking up her wineglass as soon as Sembrin had filled it. "I can't believe that the men have found not a single trace of Edmin Ruhl. The man has to be *somewhere,* and we need to know where that is if our backs are to be protected."

"I know that even better than you," Sembrin grumbled, back to being extremely unhappy. "Edmin is ruthless and capable and a definite danger to us, but he seems to have disappeared like morning mist. I have no idea whether or not he knows yet that his father is dead, but I sincerely hope he doesn't. He put together much too effective an organization in this city, and he'll certainly find it possible to rebuild at least a part of it. If we don't stop him, he could well become our most serious rival."

"And if the peasants we use have a choice of masters to serve, we'll never be able to make full use of them," Bensia added, sharing Sembrin's sourness. "I will *not* have that man ruining all our hard work, and we can't afford to forget how much gold he has at his disposal. We should never have let the Ruhls keep most of the gold in *their* coach."

"At the time, we had very little choice," Sembrin reminded her, refraining from mentioning that leaving the gold with Embisson Ruhl had been *her* idea. "We didn't want them to know what we meant to do, and if Edmin hadn't left his father we would have had the two of them to kill and the gold ours to take. Now . . ."

"Now we *have* to find the man," Bensia repeated, her hand tightening around the glass she held. "When are you supposed to meet with the peasants? You might be able to use *them* to find Edmin."

"I'll be meeting with them tonight, suitably masked, of course," Sembrin answered with a small headshake. "I'll try to make use of the peasants, but I won't count on getting much help from them. I have most of the men out searching the city, and *their* chances of finding Edmin are much better—or at least I hope their chances are better. If the peasants find Edmin first, they might talk to him rather than killing him immediately."

"Our own people should also want to talk to him first," Bensia said sharply. "Killing him before finding out where he put the gold would be a foolish waste."

"If the men find him in some deserted area, they'll torture the information out of him," Sembrin told her wearily. "If they have to choose between finding out about the gold and losing him again, I've told them to kill him at once. I'd rather do without the extra gold than take a chance with having him still out there plotting against us."

"I really dislike using our own gold to fund this enterprise," Bensia complained, her attitude beginning to give Sembrin a headache. "It would be so much more fitting to use Ruhl's gold and what he collected from the others around the Bastions area. If you try to do it my way, my dear, I'll really appreciate it."

She gave him one of her seductive smiles before ringing the bell to tell the servants to begin serving the meal, which saved Sembrin the trouble of having to answer her. Her smile had made him feel the usual strong urge to please her and do as she asked, but this time the gesture had less strength behind it than usual. Possibly that was because of the pretty little serving girl who had come with the others, the girl who had proven to be so agreeably willing . . .

Sembrin watched the platters with their food being put on the table, his smile only on the inside. He had a few things to do this afternoon to prepare for the night's meeting, but there certainly weren't so many things to do that he would have no time to visit with a girl who asked nothing more of him than a bit of attention . . .

\* \* \*

It had turned full dark hours earlier, but Edmin Ruhl still moved through the streets with utmost care. The fact that so many people walked unconcernedly through the night-dark-ened streets still disturbed him, and he reached his destination with so deep a frown that he could feel it twisting his features.

"What's wrong?" Issini asked as soon as she'd closed the door behind him, her lovely blue eyes filled with concern. "Did you have trouble?"

"No, not really," Edmin replied, waiting to let her lead the way through the fairly large house. Issini Randos was a courtesan Edmin had known for years, a woman who had started out as nothing more than a female he used to give him pleasure in bed. Somehow, without his noticing quite how, Issini had become a friend and confidante, someone who would listen and comment but never pass on what was said by him. Although she was no longer a girl, she re-mained a beautiful woman with a marvelous body that al-ways had the ability to tempt him. And her soft blue eyes and golden hair made him forget that she was in no way part of the nobility that had meant so much to him.

"The changes in the city are still bothering you," Issini said as she opened the door to the small sitting room she used for special visitors. "But I have the feeling that those changes are bothering you in a different way now."

"You could say that," Edmin granted wearily, going to his favorite chair and collapsing into it. "I saw a pickpocket be-ing arrested, and if I hadn't been watching carefully I would never have known what was happening."

"It bothers you that the city guard no longer beats people to the ground as part of arresting them?" Issini asked, faint amusement in her voice as she walked over to the sideboard to pour him a glass of wine. "That pickpocket you saw ar-rested would probably have *preferred* to be beaten, but he— or she—won't be given the choice. They were all told to find jobs or leave the city, and those who are caught now are *made* to leave. In a way that won't ever let them come back."

"And the same has to go for other sorts of criminals," Edmin mused aloud, the frown still firmly with him. "That's why all those people walk down the streets so confidently. They know their safety is all but guaranteed by their new leaders. I'd still like to know, though, what their new safety is costing them. There has to be a cost they're not seeing or simply not admitting."

"The cost of their new safety is supporting the new government," Issini answered, turning from the sideboard with his glass of wine. "Everyone has to do his or her part while the new arrangements are being put in place, helping others in whatever way they can. Most people would rather pay silver than give up their convenience, so the cost isn't as low as you obviously consider it."

"But none of this makes any sense," Edmin grumbled as he took the glass of wine that he needed rather badly. "A government's main purpose is to keep itself in power, and the best way to do that is to amass mountains of gold and keep the people under them firmly in control. These fools who have taken over the reins of government aren't doing the thing properly, and before they know it they and their new ideas will be out in the street."

"Which is where they obviously want to be," Issini said with a laugh as she sat near a cup of tea she'd clearly been drinking before his return. "Our new Seated Blending doesn't *want* to be in power, which is why they're doing so much to train others for the competitions next year. At first very few people believed the Blending would give up their place—or do what they promised to—but now there are very few who don't believe they'll continue as they started. And there are even fewer willing to let them go."

"But that makes no sense at all," Edmin protested after having taken a fortifying sip of wine. "Why would anyone dislike the idea of power, and why would the peasants want to keep people like that as their leaders? If one *must* have leaders, one chooses the strong rather than the weak."

"Edmin, my dear, you really must stop trying to fit everything into an old niche," Issini scolded gently with a fond smile. "Those who have a strong sense of duty can't use their power for themselves alone, their natures won't allow them to do that. They have to work as hard as they can for others, even while those others are constantly trying to force them into behaving as *they* think people should. And the . . . peasants you mentioned aren't so thick in the head that they don't understand how much better off they are with reluctant leaders who also have a sense of duty. Duty makes those leaders perform the functions that are necessary while their reluctance keeps them from trying to get a death grip on those under them. The . . . peasants win all the way around."

"It's fairly obvious you dislike my use of the word 'peasant,' " Edmin observed, studying Issini's lovely face. "But they *are* peasants, you know, whether or not you approve of the term."

"Using the word means you're still living in the past, my dear," Issini said with a sigh, no longer amused. "I know you hope to bring the old nobility back into power, but it's time to tell you that that won't be happening. No one wants to go back to being a slave, especially not after tasting what freedom brings—in addition to having enough silver to keep a family alive and healthy. If you treat people as something better than peasants, most of them respond by rising above the state."

"That's a noble thought, but it won't keep the masses of them safe from what the Nolls plan," Edmin pointed out, feeling annoyed by Issini's "patience" with him. "The Nolls will turn this entire city upside down, and they have the manpower to keep it that way. When their private 'guard' starts to beat people back into line, you'll see how quickly those 'free' people become peasants again."

"And *I* think you'll be surprised to see how quickly those free people fight to *stay* free," Issini countered, the response quiet and assured. "You said you saw a pickpocket being arrested. Can you describe exactly what you saw?"

"I found the whole thing a bit confusing," Edmin admitted after a moment and another sip of wine. "I happened to be touching the power, you understand, to be certain that no one recognized what I was without my being aware of it. Passing through that area of taverns with crowds all about is always a bit risky, so I try to stay alert."

Issini nodded her understanding, so Edmin continued.

"People were moving along the street in all directions amid more indications of talent being used than I ever before experienced. It's possible that only those, like myself, with Spirit magic, were using their talent, but that isn't very likely. I slowed for a moment, trying to see if people were using their talent rather than just touching the power, and that was when I felt the surge. It was as if more than one person with Spirit magic . . . *shouted* with their talent."

"Yes, that's the way it's done, I'm told," Issini said with a nod and a smile. "I have Air magic myself so I can't confirm that from personal experience, but please do go on."

"Well, no more than moments after the surge, newcomers appeared in the street," Edmin related, a frown he could feel finding a place on his features again. "The newcomers all seemed to see a sign I, myself, did not. They converged on a haughty-looking woman who had been making a slow way through the crowds. When the woman saw them she screamed in fury and tried to run, but she was already surrounded. When the newcomers had their hands on her, they began to pull pouches out of her loose robes. The pouches had been cut from the belts of their owners, and there was quite a variety."

"Yes, she would have found easy pickings in a crowd these days," Issini said, still showing a smile after she sipped at her tea. "And once the pouches had been returned to their owners, she must have been taken away. Did she continue to scream and struggle?"

"No, as a matter of fact she didn't," Edmin confirmed, now studying Issini. "I could feel Spirit magic being used, and afterward she just stood calmly while the pouches were returned. Once that was done she left with the newcomers without a single trace of resistance."

"You haven't yet remarked on the strength of the Spirit magic used by the newcomers," Issini said, also studying *him*. "Since you *could* feel that strength, how did it compare to your own?"

"I've never felt strength like that," Edmin muttered, knowing that that was one of the things disturbing him so badly. "I don't know who those peasants were, but they shouldn't have been using strength like that for nonsense. They could be establishing themselves in power, not wasting their time playing with unimportant pickpockets."

"They're High talents, my dear, and the base force of the new Guard," Issini informed him gently, her expression so close to pity that Edmin was truly disturbed. "They're helping people be safe instead of establishing themselves in power because, as strong as they are, they aren't nearly as strong as the new Blendings. Two Highs did try to carve out their own domains in the city right at the beginning, but their efforts lasted no more than a day and a half. One of the experienced Blendings went after them, and that was the end of their effort."

"I simply don't understand why that would be," Edmin said, his tone perilously close to being plaintive. "If those peasants have so much strength, what could possibly be keeping them from using it to their own benefit? Are they that afraid of what their Seated Blending might do to them? Or—Wait! Maybe they were put under the control of that Seated Blending. Yes, that's probably the answer. They aren't working for their own benefit because they've been put under control."

The sudden idea made Edmin feel a good deal better, but not for long. Issini's slow headshake was like the throwing of cold water, and the following words were even worse.

"No, my dear, they haven't been put under control," she said, just as though she knew the matter for a fact. "Some of the newly trained Middle talents in Spirit magic thought the same thing, so they made the effort to find out. We've been assured that none of the High talents is under anyone's control, which proves that they *are* getting a benefit in doing what they do. Haven't you ever felt the very great pleasure there is in helping those who are weaker and less able than you?"

"What pleasure can there be in helping the weak?" Edmin asked, completely at a loss. "It's possible to gain standing of your own by helping the strong, but what can the weak do for you? Nothing but drain your own strength, and then abandon you once you no longer have what they can use. Surely you know that yourself, Issini."

"What I know is that there's a difference between helping the strong and helping the weak who *aren't* the sort of self-ish slugs *you're* talking about." Issini's tone was very firm, a perfect match to her serious expression. "When you help the strong, they always look at what you do with the knowledge that you're only helping because you expect to gain some-thing from the act—even if you expect no such thing. They can't see your efforts in any other way."

Edmin made a gesture that showed the woman merely mentioned the obvious. Those with strength were intelligent enough to see the truth.

"But when you can't get anything from helping someone, that someone looks at the effort differently," Issini contin-ued, a wry amusement behind her gaze. "When they show their gratitude for your help, that gratitude is real and brings you a marvelous payment for your effort. And when the gratitude is real, it can become help in turn if *you* happen to need it. First you get the pleasure of helping someone who can't help himself, and then, if you happen to need it, you have help in return. Are you trying to say that that return help is worthless?"

Edmin would have said just that, but his own situation suddenly brought itself to his attention. His friendship with Issini had caused him to do various things for her while he still had power and position, the doings basically unimpor-tant but still necessary for *her*.

When he left his father that night in Zolind Maylock's house, he'd been more upset than ever before in his life. He'd chosen an empty house not far from where his father was, and had left the servants and the gold there. After that he'd crept back to Zolind's house, intending to see if he could bring his father back to his senses before it was too late, but he'd reached the house to find that it was already too late.

The men who stood talking to his father were clearly members of the new guard force that the Nolls had taken over. As Edmin watched through a window from outside, the men spoke briefly with his father—and then stabbed the old man with a knife. Edmin had nearly cried out as he watched his father's body crumple to the floor, the old man not quite dead but soon to become that way. And having no idea where to find a healer these days, Edmin hadn't even been able to *try* to help.

He'd run blindly into the dark, and by the time lack of breath had forced him to stop he'd had to face the fact that his father was dead and beyond help. The Nolls had undoubtedly meant for Edmin to die as well, and his leaving had been the only thing to save his life. But the Nolls weren't likely to leave things as they were. They would send the men out searching for him, and whatever house he chose to hide in would eventually be found.

It had taken Edmin almost an hour of plodding through the dark before he thought of Issini. He would certainly be able to hide himself and the gold with *her,* but the servants his father had been so concerned about would have to be abandoned. They were only peasants so they didn't concern him overmuch, but losing their service would be a hardship. That, however, was better than losing his life . . .

So he'd returned to the house where he'd left his belongings, and the servants were all asleep. That made things easier, since they'd left the horses still attached to the coach, just as he'd told them to do. The gold was still hidden among his belongings, and it took some effort to get his clothing and the gold into the coach. But once it was done he'd left, making his way to Issini's house in the slowly brightening daylight.

Issini had welcomed him without the least hesitation, and had even helped him to unload the coach. Afterward she'd insisted that he drive the coach a good distance away from her house, a precaution that unfortunately made sense. The men with the Nolls knew what the coach looked like, and there was no sense in finding the perfect place to hide if that place was given away by the presence of something as large as the coach.

So for the moment Edmin was safe from the Nolls, and the point Issini had made was painfully clear. Her previous gratitude had turned into desperately needed help, a benefit he'd never anticipated when he'd found it amusing to give *her* help . . .

"No, help in return for gratitude is anything but worthless," Edmin admitted with a sigh after the moment of reflection. "If anyone knows the truth of that, I have to be the one. But as far as the rest of it goes . . ."

His gesture was one of helplessness, indicating his inability to understand the rest of what she'd been trying to explain. The circumstances of his life had certainly changed, but he'd found nothing to show that his lifetime beliefs ought to do the same.

"At least you're able to see *one* thing differently," Issini said with the marvelous smile that always warmed him. "The rest will take time, Edmin, but I have confidence that you'll eventually understand everything. In the meantime, what progress have you made in our campaign?"

"I've actually made more progress than I expected to," Edmin said, smiling at her use of the phrase "*our* campaign." He'd expected her to stay out of his war with the Nolls, but she'd insisted on being a part of it . . . "I found more of my former agents than I expected to, and as you suggested I told them that there were those about who were going to make trouble for everyone in the city. All but two of the men I spoke with were sincerely interested in helping to stop the trouble, and the last two won't be able to ruin my plan. I gave them false information about future meetings, and won't approach them ever again."

"So even if they try to betray you to the Nolls, they won't be able to," Issini said with an approving nod. "Have you considered my other suggestion?"

"You mean about sending anonymous information to the . . . *authorities*?" Edmin asked, then nodded when he saw Issini's nod. "Yes, I did consider it, but for the moment I've decided against sending the warning. I want the heads of Noll and his family as my own trophies, and won't share the chance of getting those trophies unless I absolutely have to. Can you understand that?"

"Yes, it so happens I can," Issini said with something of a

sigh. "I'm not very fond of the Noll woman myself, not after she had a friend of mine hurt because Sembrin Noll was visiting my friend. Can you imagine, hurting a courtesan because your husband is one of her clients?"

"With that particular woman, I can more than imagine it," Edmin said, an automatic growl entering his tone. "She pretends to be nothing more than a powerful noble's bauble, but even a Low talent in Spirit magic would be able to feel the wild thirst for power bubbling beneath her surface. You can have as much of her as you like—after *I* get through with her."

"Since she's probably the one responsible for your father's death, I won't challenge your right to first licks," Issini said with a gentle, compassionate smile. "But now that you've made contact with your people, what are we going to do first?"

"First we're going to locate the Nolls, and then we're going to spend some time ruining whatever plans they've put in motion," Edmin answered, not caring that his answering smile must look soulless. "I want them to suffer before they die, Issini, and the best way to make them suffer is to let them think that they're getting somewhere and then crush their hopes without warning. And I'm going to be there to see those hopes crushed . . ."

"We'll both be there, but not without some very necessary changes," Issini answered, studying him in an odd way. "The last thing we want is for those people to recognize you, so we have to work at making some changes. Will you agree to letting me do that?"

Edmin raised his brows in puzzlement, but still gave her the agreement she wanted. That made her laugh softly, and it took a short while before Edmin understood the laughter . . .

# SEVEN

Kail Engreath sat leaning against the wagon's tailgate, glancing over his exhausted work group. He was more than a little tired himself, but the people who worked at his direction were close to collapse. Under other circumstances he might have pitied them, but Kail had learned not to waste pity on people who brought disaster on themselves.

In the short time they'd been working to reclaim the ruined Astindan land, they'd accomplished more than Kail had expected them to. The people in Kail's work group—and in most of the others—worked only because they had no other choice, at first making no more than reluctant effort. But two days of having to continue working into the dark of night to finish their assigned area had changed that somewhat, and now they finished in time to be taken back to their barracks by nightfall.

A small sigh of exasperation escaped Kail, one that was mostly composed of the wish that he didn't have to spend most of his time with these people. He'd been born to the Gandistran nobility in Gan Garee, but he'd never really been one of them. Their selfish, ruthless attitudes had always grated on his sense of reality, telling him that these people weren't nearly as important as they thought they were.

And the most exasperating part of it all was that most of the bound former nobility *still* thought they were due some sort of deference and obedience. He'd been put in charge of this work group, but the people in it obeyed him only be-

cause they were forced to. And some of the twenty didn't
even obey completely . . .

"Just you wait, you traitor," a woman's voice suddenly
came, pain and exhaustion clear behind the words. "When
we're finally freed from this unjust slavery and returned to
our proper positions, I will personally see to it that you suffer the most horrible tortures before you die. You have the
word of a High Lady on that."

Kail looked at the woman who had spoken so venomously
to him, and was surprised to discover that there wasn't the
least amount of disturbance inside him at the accusation. He
still didn't know the woman's name, and truthfully had no
interest in learning it.

"You have the nerve to blame *me* for what the overseer
did to you?" Kail replied with a snort of derision for what
she'd said. "Unless you're deaf, you heard me tell you more
than once that you weren't doing your share of the work.
You ignored me just the way you're ignoring the fact that
you'll never be considered 'noble' again, and you paid for
that stupidity. If you ever learn to take responsibility for
your actions, I'll probably please you no end by dying of the
shock."

"You, young man, will kindly watch your tone when you
speak to a lady of station!" one of the men snapped, his own
tone stuffy and highly outraged. "And having that low peasant of an overseer force her to work so much harder *was* your
doing, a truth all the lies in the world won't cover. You betray
your own to the enemy, and that does make you a traitor."

"Are you people taking some sort of drug the rest of us
don't know about?" another man demanded, looking back
and forth between the man and woman who had spoken.
"That female isn't a 'lady of station,' she's a slave worker
just like the rest of us, and I'm more than tired of the way
she tries to put on airs. If the boy hadn't reported her to the
overseer *I* would have, most especially since she's the one
doing the betraying. In a situation like this, standing around
idle while everyone else does all the work is the worst kind
of betrayal."

"He's right and you know it, you pompous oaf," another

woman put in immediately when the first man opened his mouth with the obvious intent to argue. "The two of you keep dragging your feet while the rest of us break our backs, and it did us all good to see that 'high lady' being made to do some real work for once. I hate all this even more than you do, because the two of you knew what was being done to this country and I didn't. I let fools make the decisions that would affect *my* life without trying to find out what those fools were doing, and now I'm paying for the stupidity. If we ever get out of this nightmare and back to a normal life, I'll never make the same mistake again."

The man and woman who had started the complaint against Kail looked around, the sudden alarm in their expressions telling Kail that the two had noticed the entire group now agreed with what they'd been told. Everyone was dressed in what they would all have once considered rags—plain, dark gray skirts and trousers with lighter gray tunics—but the rest of the work group suddenly looked like people in power. Even the small, sullen members had apparently found targets for their dark and bubbling rage, and those targets weren't the Astindans.

Kail found himself surprised by the reactions of his work group. Everyone had started out blaming the Astindans—and Kail—for what they were being put through, and Kail would have bet gold that these people would never change their narrow-minded stance. But it looked like some of them *were* changing, coming around to his own way of thinking. The woman and man who had spoken first now sat with petulant put-upon expressions, suggesting rather strongly that *they* would never change, but the rest . . .

The unexpected reaction from the balance of his work group held Kail's thoughts for the rest of the ride. When they reached the barracks area torches were already lit against the fall of night, and it was possible to smell the stew that would clearly be their evening meal. The members of the work group stirred as the aroma reached them, all of them at least as hungry as Kail himself, and as soon as the wagon stopped they began to get to their feet. Kail quickly opened the tailgate and jumped down, and the others followed.

The work groups were given the chance to wash up before they had to form a line for the evening meal, but some members of the various groups never bothered. They went directly to the food line instead, to make certain that they would be among the first who were given food. It was no surprise that the whining man and woman were that sort, but Kail would never be able to understand that particular reaction. Eating without first washing up would have turned his stomach no matter *how* hungry he was.

People were moving all around the area, some heading for their barracks to wash, others to the food lines after having already cleaned themselves up. Kail went toward the supervisors' barracks, wondering if Renton Frosh was back yet. His friend Ren also supervised a work group, but Ren was far too gentle with his people. At first they repaid the man by working so slowly that Ren's group was the last one back, but too many nights of eating cold leftovers had reached them the way Ren's gentle admonishments never could.

"Ah, Kail, you've finally made it, I see," Ren's voice came from his sleeping mat as soon as Kail entered the barracks. "I expected to find you here as soon as *I* got in, but you must be falling down on the job."

"We were delayed because one of my group had to be disciplined by an overseer," Kail explained, making no effort to take his dirty, sweaty presence anywhere near the sleeping mats. "The woman will never learn to really pull her own weight, but at least now she's been taught what that consists of."

"I'll bet the rest of your work group was happy to see her being instructed," Ren said with a laugh as he got to his feet. "Some of mine came around more quickly than I'd expected them to, and they really enjoyed it when one of the others needed to be instructed. I'll walk with you to the washstands out back, and then we can get something to eat."

Kail accepted the offer with a smile, and it didn't take him long to wash away the remnants of the workday. He washed his tunic before washing himself, pulled the water out of it once the tunic was clean, then had a freshly laundered tunic to wear once he'd dried himself. Ren had hung his own washed tunic on a drying line, and Kail pulled the water out of it for his friend once he was done with his own things. Ren took the dried tunic inside and put it away, then the two of them headed for the food lines.

The Astindans worked their new slaves hard, but they also made sure their slaves didn't go hungry. A healthy chunk of buttered bread was added to the bowl of stew Kail was given, and large metal cups of tea stood lined up on the serving table waiting to be claimed. Kail took one of the cups that had had sugar added to it while Ren took one without sugar, and then the two found an unoccupied patch of ground where they could sit and eat.

"I never imagined that plain food could ever taste so good," Ren said with a sigh after at least half of the food had gone down his and Kail's throats. "I used to console myself with food when I felt as if I didn't belong, which was most of the time. Every dining parlor in our part of Gan Garee knew me on sight and I knew every one of their best dishes, but even the best of the best from back then wasn't as good as this stew."

"That's because you weren't working hard back then, at least not physically," Kail pointed out after swallowing. "Now you're getting all sorts of exercise, so of course the food tastes better. Your body needs it more than it did back in Gan Garee."

"I hope the new job doesn't let me get fat again," Ren said, his face creased into an uncharacteristic frown. "I like being able to bend without effort, seeing my toes without a paunch in the way. I—What's the matter?"

"What you just said is the matter," Kail answered, still staring intensely at his friend. "What new job are you talking about? Are you just wishful thinking out loud, or were you told something by the Astindans?"

"Why, I was told something, and I thought you were told the same," Ren answered, surprise widening his eyes. "The overseer told me to pick out someone to take my place as supervisor, because all the current supervisors were being given new jobs. Didn't the overseer give you the word?"

"No," Kail muttered, suddenly not as hungry as he'd been.

"Maybe the man was distracted by having to discipline one of my workers, but he didn't say a thing. Are you sure you were told that *all* supervisors would be doing something else?"

"Yes, I'm very sure," Ren answered, his expression having grown concerned. "What's wrong, Kail? I thought you would be as happy as I am to get away from our 'highly important' workers."

"As a matter of fact, I was wishing not long ago that I *could* get away from them," Kail replied with a headshake. "It's just that . . . If I'm not out with the work group, I won't get to see . . . someone I've grown to like."

The someone was Asri Tempeth, the woman who brought water around for the workers. Asri was a former member of the nobility just as Kail was, but more importantly she was just as glad to be free of her former life. In point of fact Asri was even more pleased to be out of Gan Garee for her baby's sake, and the thought of never seeing her again was more than Kail could bear. He'd looked for her in the barracks area more than once, but she was apparently being quartered elsewhere.

"You must be talking about Asri," Ren said, surprising Kail. "She's always so sweet and pleasant that I'll miss her myself—unless you're talking about something more than a casual, pleasant exchange. *Was* something more developing between you?"

"I'd like to think so, but I'm not sure," Kail admitted after a brief hesitation, deciding he might as well speak of the matter aloud. "Her visits quickly became the high points of my days, but I never found the right time to do more than exchange pleasantries with her. After all, we're not exactly free to make careers for ourselves here, and when you like a woman you want to be able to offer her something more than your corner of the barracks."

"I hadn't thought of that," Ren said with a sigh, sympathy clear in the gaze he sent to Kail. "That's a definite drawback to our . . . 'idyllic' life here, but there isn't much we can do about changing things. So what are you going to do?"

Kail was about to say that he didn't know, but the words

and intention were interrupted by the appearance of his overseer. The man came over to where Kail and Ren sat, and then crouched down.

"It came to me a short time ago that I neglected to speak to you, Engreath," the man said to Kail with the seriousness all Astindans seemed to show. "As you're to be reassigned tomorrow, I'll need the name of someone in your group to take your place as supervisor. Can you give me a name now?"

"I would recommend the man named Dalsin Fort," Kail answered, faintly surprised that his inner mind had already considered the matter. "His attitudes have been changing, and something he said today leads me to believe that he won't allow the others to slack off."

The Astindan nodded as he reached for the paper, pen, and ink that he had in his pouch. The man Kail had recommended was the one who had taken Kail's part in the short argument during the group's ride back to the barracks area, and Kail really did think the man would do well as supervisor. He watched the Astindan writing down Fort's name, hesitant to push for information the Astindans seldom gave without reason, but the matter was too important to Kail for him to let it slide.

"I'd—like to ask about what will become of the woman named Asri Tempeth," Kail said in something of a rush before the Astindan finished writing and left. "She's the one who brings water around to the workers, and she's more than willing to do everything she can for the people of this country. She thinks of herself as having been rescued by your people, which means she's being wasted as someone who does no more than cart around water."

The Astindan overseer glanced up, faint annoyance starting to show in his expression, but the annoyance disappeared almost immediately. Kail wondered if the man had seen something in his face or eyes that gave away how he truly felt, and then that thought was swept away by the shock of seeing the hint of a smile turning the corners of the Astindan's lips.

"The Tempeth woman is also being reassigned," the overseer said as he refolded the paper he'd written on and put everything back in his pouch. "We have too few resources left in this part of the country to waste any of them."

And then the Astindan straightened out of his crouch and walked away, leaving Kail to stare after him. It took Kail a moment or two to notice that Ren also stared at the man's departing back, and then Ren shook his head.

"I would have bet gold against your being told anything at all," Ren said after having taken a very deep breath. "Some of them seem to be really decent, but I'm sorry *I* missed the opportunity. If the man was in the mood to talk, I could have asked him what we'll be doing instead of supervising work groups."

"I doubt if he would have told us *that*," Kail said, returning his attention to what was left of his meal now that his appetite had returned. "I may not get to see Asri as often as I used to, but at least I know now that I'm not leaving anything of value behind and can enjoy the thought of moving on. Do you have any idea at all about what we'll be doing?"

"Not the smallest shadow of a hint," Ren denied with a headshake as he also returned his attention to the food. "I just hope it's more interesting than what we've *been* doing. Making one's body fit and healthy is fine, but some of us also have a mind that needs to be exercised."

Kail nodded his agreement with that, as he'd also been growing extremely bored. Well, after they ate they'd walk around a bit, and then they'd go to bed. When they woke up tomorrow morning, all their questions would be answered.

After breakfast the next morning, Kail's curiosity was still with him. The group of former supervisors stood around while the work groups were sent off to the day's labors, and when the wagons returned, Kail and the others were loaded into two of them. Rather than heading toward the work area, the wagons went in an entirely different direction. Kail exchanged an interested glance with Ren, but their interest faded when the trip began to drag out.

Kail found that he'd actually fallen asleep when he jerked awake at the change in the wagon's steady pace. The position of the sun in the sky showed that hours had gone by, and a single glance around showed that they were no longer out in the countryside. The buildings of a city or town rose on both sides of the wagon, and there were even people walking in the streets.

"This looks much more promising, but I'm almost afraid to hope," Ren said in a murmur as he, too, looked around. "Do you think it's possible that we've been brought here because the wealthy people in this city need well-mannered servants? We're the ones who gave the overseers the least amount of trouble, after all."

"Unfortunately that's more than possible," Kail allowed with an inner groan, his rising eagerness for something new beginning to fade. "If they do want us as servants, I'm going to insist on being taken back to the work area. Breaking my back to repair the destruction my own people caused is acceptable. Picking up after Astindans with too much gold isn't."

"I feel the same way, of course, but I don't know if I'll be *able* to insist on being taken back," Ren fretted, disturbance in the glance he sent to Kail. "If I'm offered an actual bed to sleep in and the chance to look about the city during my free time . . . I'm a creature of cities, Kail, and I really do miss having one to wander about in."

Kail nodded without speaking, more than aware of how much Ren had suffered despite his bantering about how good for his physical well-being the work had been. Renton Frosh was a man of emotions rather than of cities. He had always seemed to need serenity and happiness and outright enjoyment around him, even if he had rarely felt or shown those emotions himself. It could well have something to do with Ren's Spirit magic, and the hatred and misery of the workers must have been a constant nightmare for him.

"We all do what we have to in order to survive, Ren," Kail said after a moment, sending his friend a true smile. "We'll both do what we have to, but let's not rush into anything. Demanding to be taken back—or asking to stay—can be done after we find out the actual reason we've been brought here."

"Yes, jumping to conclusions is an exercise I tried to

avoid even when all others were beyond me," Ren said with a small laugh. "Thank you for being a true friend, Kail."

Kail shook his head with a dismissive gesture, but Ren continued to look much more at ease. He'd apparently been worried about Kail's opinion of him and about what he meant to do, but now knew he had nothing to worry *about*. They would remain friends no matter what point the future brought them to.

But the future took its time appearing. The wagons continued along the street at the slower pace, nearly half an hour disappearing before they turned into the drive of a building that seemed to be their destination. The building was a large and gloomy construction of stone, a perfect match to the humorlessness of the Astindans. Both wagons pulled up near the wide and heavy wooden doors of the structure, and the Astindans who had ridden with the wagon drivers jumped down and came around to the back of the wagons.

"Follow me, please," the Astindan who opened the tailgate of Kail's wagon said, his manner still as unexcited as ever.

Kail joined everyone else in climbing out of the wagon, and then followed along with the groups from both wagons into the large building. Most of the people they passed only glanced at them, as though two wagonloads of strangers arriving was an everyday occurrence. But that was so only until they reached the building.

Inside there was a wide entrance area, and half a dozen more Astindans looked around at their appearance. These others seemed to be waiting for them, and they approached the doubled group in a small group of their own.

"You've been brought here today for a specific reason," one of the half dozen greeters said, stepping out from the others and looking around as he spoke. "We've been told that you people have shown concern and a cooperative attitude right from the beginning, so we've decided to offer you the chance first. Those of you who can contribute something to our society will, after a time of trial, be given the opportunity to become full citizens of Astinda. If any of you feel that accepting our offer isn't something you can, in all good conscience, do, just let us know and you'll be returned where you came from. Take a moment to think about the matter."

Ren looked as shocked as Kail felt, and a glance around showed Kail that he and his friend weren't the only ones who had been taken by surprise. They weren't just being offered productive jobs, they were being given the chance to become a true part of this new land. Kail found it impossible to picture his former peers ever doing the same, which suggested rather strongly that these people were definitely better human beings. These Astindans were willing to pay an honest price for whatever skilled help they might need . . .

"All right, you've all had a moment to consider your decision," the same man said after a brief time. "Is there anyone here who would prefer to be taken back to the work area?"

Kail fully expected there to be no answer to that question, and was surprised a second time when two men, standing together, raised their hands.

"It's rather painful to admit, but neither my friend nor I can accept your offer," one of the two said with a sigh. "We may not have done what we should have with our Gandistran citizenship, but that doesn't change the fact that we're Gandistrans. We hope that someday, after all the hurts have had a chance to heal a bit, we'll be permitted to return to our home. That's the place we hope to make amends."

After listening to what the man had to say, three others in the group also raised their arms slowly. Kail could now understand their reasoning, but the five were all older men who had spent most of their lives being Gandistrans. Kail's life in Gan Garee had been mostly composed of misery, and if he never saw the place again it would not upset him in the least.

"I find myself surprised as well as impressed with your honesty," the spokesman for the Astindans said with raised brows. "We thank you for that honesty, and will do what we may to see that you never regret it. You'll be fed and allowed to rest before you're returned to the work area."

The five men nodded, and when a female Astindan stepped forward and gestured to them, they followed her toward the left side of the building. They seemed to be heading toward one of the doors there, but before they reached it the spokesman reclaimed the attention of those who were left.

"You'll be separated into six different groups, and then taken to be interviewed," the man said, looking around again. "If at any time you change your mind about wanting to be one of us, just speak to your guide and you'll be allowed to join the people who are being seen to elsewhere. This is an opportunity, not a requirement, and none of you will be forced to comply."

The Astindan glanced around one last time to see if anyone had already changed his or her mind, and when no hands were raised he got on with separating the groups. Kail managed to stay with Ren, and they exchanged a glance before following their new guide. They still had no real idea of what lay before them, but Kail hoped with all his being that he'd be able to find *something* to offer in return for his rescue . . .

# EIGHT

Rion rode along in his place in the column, faintly amused and not quite certain why he felt that way. The enlarged group's progress had been slower than what he and his Blendingmates had been used to, but the Gracelians weren't up to moving quickly and without effort. They were also unconsciously reluctant to find and face the enemy, so the going had become even slower.

The amusement Rion felt seemed to stem from the circumstance of their presence among these strangers. The trip had begun with the various Gracelian leaders quietly vying for the position of overall leadership. Playing their political games seemed to be an ingrained part of their whole existence, even during a time when game playing was entirely inappropriate. And they'd also been very firm on the point that the visiting Blending from Gandistra was only there to help if it became absolutely necessary.

Jovvi and Vallant had conferred, and then they'd told the rest of them—and the members of the link groups—that their role had become one of hanging back. If the Gracelians were that determined to fend for themselves, the only thing to be done was to let them try. This was the fourth day of the attempt, and the Gracelians hadn't even put out advance scouts. It ought to be amusing when they ran into the first of the trouble without the least prior warning . . .

"Good morning, Rion," a voice came, and he turned his

head to see Tamrissa moving up to a place beside him. "Nice day, isn't it?"

"It certainly is," Rion agreed in a matching tone of unconcern, his glance going to their surroundings. They rode along a wide, beautifully paved road, with fields and woods appearing in turn to either side. There were also occasional farms to do no more than dent the monotony, since breaking monotony isn't an easy thing to accomplish.

"I've been asked to pass on the word that we'll be seeing action of some sort soon," Tamrissa continued in a much softer voice, her expression a match in blandness. "Our advance probings have shown some sort of group not far ahead of us, and they seem to be hiding to either side of the road. Also, our most solitary host seems to have let his brooding egg him into showing how much he thinks of us. All indications are that that Tal fool will attack us when the column stops for lunch."

*All indications,* Rion thought wryly. *That has to mean Naran's ability is coming into play, but we don't mention Naran and her abilities aloud. Not in front of the Gracelians, and certainly not in front of me . . .*

"Tamrissa, I need to ask you something," Rion said after nodding at what he'd been told. "You, as a woman, may well understand a certain happening, whereas our brothers are unable to explain the matter to me because of their own lack of understanding. You see—"

"You approached Naran in an attempt to heal the rift between you, and she refused to listen," Tamrissa interrupted to sum up in admirably few words. "Is that what you wanted to ask about?"

"Yes, that's the matter exactly," Rion admitted with raised brows. "I wasn't aware that you were present at the time."

"That's because I wasn't," Tamrissa answered with an annoyingly bright smile. "Naran told Jovvi and me about it afterward. You spoke to Naran yesterday afternoon, and she told us about it last night. You must have the world's worst way of expressing things."

"How kind of you to say so," Rion responded stiffly, finding his own amusement disappearing as Tamrissa's grew.

"And do let me apologize for intruding with a question you obviously find so unimportant—"

"Oh, Rion, please stop being so stuffy and formal," Tamrissa interrupted again, this time with a sigh. "That's one of the things you did wrong with Naran, and I'll be glad to explain the matter if you're willing to listen."

Rion opened his mouth to insist that he wasn't being stuffy in the least, then swallowed the words instead of speaking them. He did need Tamrissa's help, and driving her off wasn't the way to get it.

"Allow me to apologize a bit more sincerely this time," Rion said instead, chagrin coloring the words with actual sincerity. "I'd truly like to know what I—'did wrong' with Naran."

"Actually, it was a combination of things rather than just one," Tamrissa said, faint annoyance and a small frown apparently aimed at her memories. "She felt that you were trying to patch things up between you for the sake of the Blending rather than because you really wanted to be back with her. Can that be true?"

Again Rion held his tongue, but this time with mortification. How could Naran possibly have guessed . . . ?

"I . . . don't quite know how to explain," Rion groped, using one hand to gesture vaguely. "All of you have spoken to me at various times, concerned about *my* concerns, so I thought I could . . . ease everyone's mind. And I do miss Naran terribly . . ."

"But you still aren't past expecting yourself to 'betray' Naran again," Tamrissa said with another sigh. "You haven't settled that problem in your own mind, and that's why you were so stiffly formal with her. She said you sounded as though you were proposing a business arrangement."

"I was simply trying not to raise her hopes too high again," Rion whispered after closing his eyes. "I'm not a man she can rely on, not when my head was turned so easily the first time. I'd like to think that the same won't happen a second time, but there's no way to be certain of that."

"Nonsense," Tamrissa stated, and Rion opened his eyes to see that his sister now looked impatient. "Tell me, Rion, do you really think you're the only person to ever feel tempted by someone other than the one you love? That feeling is called lust, and is differentiated by another name because it's just physical attraction. It's only human to find someone other than your love attractive, and there's nothing wrong with experiencing the feeling. Unless you mean to let the lust rule you from now on. Some people do, you know, and you could well be that sort."

"What sort is that?" Rion asked, confusion covering him again the way it had in the beginning. "And do you see some . . . sign that I *am* the kind to fall to lust again?"

"People who let lust rule them are either desperately in need of being loved or are completely self-centered," Tamrissa explained, her tone more gentle as her lovely eyes examined him. "The self-centered ones are just out for the pleasure, having no interest in sharing another person's life. Sharing often calls for sacrifice, and they have no intentions of sacrificing for anyone. Do you think you're *that* sort?"

"No," Rion answered, relieved to be able to give a positive reply to at least one question. "I found my greatest pleasure *in* sharing with Naran, not in simply taking solitary pleasure. But what of the other sort?"

"The ones who desperately need to be loved?" Tamrissa asked, studying him with her head to one side. "Considering the way you were raised you do need to be loved, a circumstance I understand only too well. But the people in that group need constant reassurance that they're wanted, which is why they go from lover to lover. Staying with one would be too dangerous, because that one might grow bored and then distracted. Are you afraid that Naran might grow bored with you and go looking for someone else?"

"I constantly marvel that Naran has found any interest in me whatsoever," Rion answered with complete truthfulness. "If she were to grow bored with me and look about for someone more interesting, I would be devastated but not unduly surprised. Is that the same thing?"

"No, it isn't, so stop looking so woebegone," Tamrissa said at once, putting a hand to his arm. "Your whole problem is that you're not used to having anyone find you attractive. No matter what the rest of us tell you, you still believe the lies that woman fed you while you were growing up. You see yourself as an unwanted outcast, but nothing could be farther from the truth. Why, if I hadn't met Vallant and you hadn't met Naran, I would probably be chasing after you myself right now."

"You would?" Rion asked, his brows having risen of their own accord. "But, Tamrissa . . . You're an extremely beautiful woman, turning the heads of most of the men who see you. Why would you possibly look to *me*?"

"I would look to you not only because I know how decent a person you are," Tamrissa answered firmly, doing nothing to avoid his gaze. "I would also look to you because you're an extremely handsome man, broad-shouldered and tall and overall trim. You're also a marvelous lover, and it must be very difficult for you now that you're not sharing Naran's bed. But there's a very easy way to solve that problem . . ."

Tamrissa's words ended with a suggestive smile, and at first Rion was disconcerted. He really did find Tamrissa attractive, just as he did Jovvi, but Naran was more than simply attractive. And yet, he suddenly believed that Tamrissa did find him just as attractive. If he were able to resist *her* after easing himself, then he could be a good deal more certain about resisting strange women. Yes, her suggestion was a really good one . . .

"Yes, let's do solve the problem," Rion said, turning happily to Tamrissa. "We can lie together tonight once we've made camp, thanks to the obsession with privacy that the Gracelians indulge so thoroughly. I'll await you in my tent, and Tamrissa . . . thank you."

He touched her hand to show his thanks more completely, then urged his mount to a faster pace. He was now very eager to reach the place they would camp tonight, hoping fervently that his experiment would work. If he *was* able to resist Tamrissa after lying with her again, then he would be able to approach Naran with an easy mind and full heart. If not . . . No, he would *not* consider defeat, not unless—and until—he had no other option . . .

I watched Rion ride away, still too stunned to speak a single word. I'd been trying to tell the man that he could get back together with Naran if he made himself forget the nonsense that was keeping them apart, but instead he'd interpreted my suggestion in an entirely unexpected way . . .

A deep and feeling groan escaped me, a vocalization of everything churning around inside me. After the groan I turned my mount and went looking for Jovvi, not about to struggle with *this* problem alone. She'd been the one who had suggested I speak to Rion, after all, so now she could figure out what to do about *this* turn of events. Or at least I *hoped* she'd be able to figure something out . . .

"Why are you so agitated?" Jovvi said at once when I reached her, a small frown creasing her forehead. "Obviously things didn't go *well* with Rion, but they couldn't have gone *that* badly."

"Would you care to put gold on that opinion?" I countered after turning my horse to pace beside hers, no longer at a loss for words. "I tried to make Rion believe how attractive he is, just as we agreed I would. I also tried to hint that he could ease his bodily demands if he only approached Naran in the right way, but the last part of that suggestion got lost somehow. Rion thanked me for my suggestion with a tear in his eye, and tonight will be waiting for me in his tent."

"Oh, dear," Jovvi said as she flinched, obviously picking up my newest emotions without anything to buffer them.

"Don't you dare 'oh dear' me!" I hissed, so furious it was a wonder that the whole world hadn't gone up in flames around me. "My flirting with Rion was *your* idea, and now he expects me to lie with him tonight. How am I supposed to stomp on all that gratitude he showed? How am I supposed to explain to Naran what I'm doing? And above all, how am I supposed to tell Vallant why I won't be in our tent tonight?"

"Please, Tamma, you really must calm down at least a little," Jovvi said in a choked voice, her hand coming to my arm in a pleading way. "For some reason I can't block you out completely the way I used to be able to do, and my head is threatening to split. If I can't think, I won't be able to help . . ."

"The only help I can use right now is you volunteering to

take my place," I told her bluntly, but still forced myself to let go of some of the fury inside me. "And why *aren't* you able to block me out? Are you losing strength for some reason?"

"Thank you," Jovvi said sincerely after taking a deep breath, and then she shook her head. "As far as I can see I'm just as strong as ever, so I don't understand this newest development either. Not to mention the fact that I certainly don't like it. And at the risk of starting you up again, I'd be glad to volunteer to take your place, but that just isn't possible."

"Why not?" I asked, very aware of the growl in my voice. "Since this was all *your* idea, the least you can do is exercise your old profession."

"As a courtesan?" Jovvi said, moving her shoulders in a way that suggested they needed loosening. "That's one of the reasons why I can't take your place. Rion knows I was a courtesan, so my lying with him would mean nothing. And even if I thought I *could* take your place, don't you think my suddenly being there instead of you would give him the certain belief that he isn't attractive after all? The rift between him and Naran would grow wider than ever, and might even grow beyond the point of ever being correctable."

"And my lying with Rion will *please* Naran?" I countered with a sound of ridicule. "Somehow I doubt that, but she isn't my greatest concern. Vallant is, especially after the way he was with Alsin Meerk. Do you really want Vallant challenging Rion to a physical fight?"

"Oh, I seriously doubt he would do that," Jovvi all but scoffed, the assurance ruined by the continuing expression of worry on her face. "Vallant knows that Rion is one of us, so he would never react the way he did with Alsin Meerk. He might, however, be upset with *you,* so we'll have to explain the circumstances to him—and to Naran as well, of course."

"Oh, of course," I agreed dryly with a short nod. "But where does this 'we' come in? If I'm the one who will be visiting Rion tonight and it's just too impossible for you to take my place, then you can be the one doing all the explaining. After all, if one of the two decide to get violent, you're the one who can calm them."

"We *hope* I'm the one who can calm them," Jovvi said with what was obviously a deeply heartfelt sigh. "I couldn't do any calming a moment ago with *you*, but maybe the new development hasn't affected them yet. And yes, fair is fair, so I'll speak to them alone when we stop for lunch. If everything goes right, you won't know how they feel about all this until I come over and tell you."

Meaning that if one or both of them exploded, I'd know about how they felt without being told by Jovvi. I nodded to show I agreed with the hope, and we continued our ride in silence.

It wasn't quite noon when we reached a stand of woods to the right of the road. The woods were thin enough to show that nothing and no one was hidden there, and thick enough to give us some cool shade to take our meal in. Most of the column had already entered the woods by the time *we* got there, the rest of our Blending having mostly ridden with their link groups. That was the only thing that had kept our previous conversation private, but the members of Jovvi's link groups were eyeing Jovvi and me in a wary way. They obviously knew *something* was up, but were being discreet by not asking about it.

The wagons that were part of our entourage were left on the road, but the horses pulling them were put around the edge of the woods with our mounts, where they could all graze while we ate. The Gracelians were scattered through the woods, either walking out their stiffness or sitting on the ground. They all seemed to be suffering from the unaccustomed exercise of being in a saddle for so many hours, and some of them went so far as to glare at those of us who showed nothing of discomfort. It was apparently beyond them to understand how long my Blendingmates and I and our link groups must have been on the road for us to be that unbothered.

As soon as Jovvi and I tied our horses where they could graze, she squared her shoulders and went off to take care of her chore. I didn't know if she meant to speak to Naran or Vallant first, but it didn't really matter. If either one or both of them had violent objections to my being with Rion, we'd have a very nasty mess on our hands. Even though both of them should understand that what helped Rion also helped the rest of us. After what Rion had gone through growing up with that miserable noblewoman pretending to be his mother, it was a wonder the poor man had any self-esteem at all.

Thought of the Mardimil woman got me just as angry as it always did, so I wandered through the woods thinking pleasantly dark thoughts while the Gracelian cooks prepared our meal. Halina Mardimil had been sent with the other deposed nobles to work in Astinda, which was a really fitting punishment for her years of doing exactly as she pleased to anyone who crossed her path. But if I could have managed a few private minutes with her first, I would have taken a great deal of pleasure in showing her how unhappy I was with the way she'd tortured Rion . . .

It suddenly occurred to me that my angry thoughts might be disturbing Jovvi during her rather important mission. I knew I had to rein in the anger, but I did so enjoy being furious with a woman like Halina Mardimil, who deserved every rotten thing that could be done to her. I let the anger flare just one more time in a sort of fond farewell, distantly wondering why I wasn't trying to suppress the surging emotion at once, and then—

And then I was under attack! Although I couldn't see it, I somehow knew there was an entity near me, a Blending entity that loathed me. That entity was strongly Fire talented, and clearly meant to burn me to cinders.

But my raging anger had been enough to hold off the entity's first attack, and then I was firmly meshed in with my link groups. If someone had told me that one person's talent, even augmented by tandem link groups, would be stronger than a Blending entity bent on mayhem, I would have laughed in that person's face. But I could feel that I *was* stronger, and my immediate response was completely automatic.

A new pattern suddenly appeared for me to work through, and I used it without a second thought. My fires turned so hot that anything exposed to them would be all but vaporized, and then those fires were sent into the Blending entity through the new pattern. I heard—and felt—a soundless scream, and then there were vocal screams added to the silent one. Not far away five people were suddenly writhing on the ground, and only when I saw them did I remember Naran's warning about an attack that would probably be launched by Zirdon Tal's group.

"Tamrissa, are you all right?" Lorand demanded as he ran up, uncharacteristic fury blazing in his eyes. "Am I wrong in believing that that Tal slime attacked you alone rather than all of us?"

"Yes, I'd say that Tal did make that mistake," I answered, pushing away for later consideration the slight shakiness that my new achievement had caused. "And the attack wasn't just him. He used his Blending entity against me."

"What sort of utter nonsense are you spouting, woman?" one of the Gracelians demanded from the agitated group that had also hurried over. "You couldn't possibly have survived against a Blending entity all by yourself!"

"If you weren't a complete fool, Dom Reesh, the fact that I'm still standing here would give you a clue about how wrong you are—as usual." Satlan Reesh was a member of the assembly who seemed to have a uniformly low opinion of all women, and I had no intention of telling him that I *hadn't* been alone. I was in no mood to be at all diplomatic, the way I'd been on the trip until now.

"Those people thought they were attacking me from behind by using their Blending entity, but they were just as wrong," I added. "In case you still doubt my word, you might want to try the same thing yourself and see what happens."

"Stop sputtering, Reesh, the girl is right and you *are* wrong," the man named Olskin Dinno growled to his fellow assembly member, distaste for the fool's speech clear in the words. "We all have our private likes and dislikes, but letting them control us to the point of idiocy is . . . idiotic. Now, I think, we ought to see why those five are still screaming. As far as I can tell, they aren't physically harmed."

"The reaction looks more like terror than pain," Lorand put in to Dinno as he frowned at the five people whose writhing around was beginning to quiet. "Let's see if we can find out what happened and what was done to them from their own point of view. Jovvi?"

My attackers were quieting because Jovvi had joined the group, and the easing had to be *her* talent at work. It still bothered me that the Gracelians never seemed to reach for the power and their talent unless they absolutely had to, not when using talent wasn't against their laws. It seemed that people got sloppy about exercising a right that could be exercised at any time, but it would probably be quite a while before the people in Gandistra became that blasé.

"Yes, we do need to find out what happened," Jovvi agreed, and then she gave her full attention to one of those on the ground. "Dom Tal, please tell us what brought you and those others to this state."

"It was all *her* doing," Tal answered sullenly, a flicking gesture of his hand and finger indicating me. "She sided with my enemies against me as though she were of true importance instead of being just a backward intruder, so I decided to teach her a lesson. My people and I Blended and then our entity tried to singe her, but there was a . . . a . . . shield of some sort in the way. The shield protected her, and then her strength increased so greatly that our entity was stunned. After that she did something to our entity that was so painful even *we* felt it for a moment. Then our entity was gone and we were left with the memory of agony."

"So your cowardly attack against her was *her* fault, was it?" Cleemor Gardan growled while most of the others in the group muttered darkly. "I think that that action justifies our asking you other questions as well. Did you have anything to do with the attacks against the assembly?"

"It wasn't me, it was that slug Syant," Tal protested, actually looking annoyed. "When I decided to use Syant against you and Lorimon, I apparently neglected to give the mad fool detailed enough instructions. He arranged all sorts of things he didn't tell me about, and then he got himself killed before I could question him closely. I have no idea what he arranged or with whom, but it really doesn't matter. I'm no longer in the city where the real danger lies, and when I return from this foolish little outing a hero I'll be the sole leader of our empire."

"And he called Syant mad," Dinno commented in his own growl with an accompanying headshake. "Does anyone here doubt the truth of what we just heard?"

"Not only don't I doubt it, I can also see that this imbecile had the cooperation of his Blendingmates," Reesh said, surprising more people than just me. "I say we remove the whole lot of 'em, and put them on trial for murder and attempted murder. I had a good friend who died from that poison . . ."

"I agree that something definite has to be done, but we must go carefully here," Gardan cautioned with one hand held up as he looked around at the others. "We have nothing but Tal's—ah—assisted word concerning the details, and that's not enough for the law to condemn him. He is, after all, still a member of the assembly—"

"Excuse me, but that last isn't true," Lorand said, interrupting whatever else Gardan had been about to add. "If those of you with Earth magic will look closely, you'll see that Tal no longer has the talent to be a member of the assembly. The same is true for his former Blendingmates, none of whom will ever Blend again. Any fool who attacks a third-level High in Fire magic deserves whatever he or she gets."

Wails of misery came from Tal's Blendingmates while Tal himself frowned with what looked like lack of understanding. Nervous mutters came from many of the other Gracelians, and the way they glanced at me made me feel the least bit uncomfortable. I hadn't known I'd burned out the talent from those who had attacked me, especially since I'd gone through their entity to do it. Under other circumstances the revelation might have made me feel guilty, but with Tal involved there wasn't even the smallest trace of guilt.

"What foolish talk is that?" Tal demanded, his frown still firmly in place. "The only way my talent can be taken is for the entire assembly to find me guilty of something. Since there isn't any proof for me to be found guilty of anything, I *will* retain my seat in the assembly and I *will* have my talent returned. The lot of you lowborn fools have no choice."

The man's smirk worked what can only be called a miracle. The moment he finished speaking everyone standing around just stared at him, all nervousness and tangential accusation toward me gone at once. Everyone was too busy glaring at Tal for his colossal nerve to do or think anything else, and that was when Antrie Lorimon stepped forward.

"I think we all know now what our former associate's opinion of us is," Antrie said with a faint, humorless smile. "It's apparently beyond the silly little brat to understand what his true position is, so I propose that we teach him the truth in the most direct way possible. We've brought no servants with us, and more than one of us has noticed the lack when something needs to be fetched or carried. Instead of sending these five turncoats back to the city to sit quietly while awaiting our return, let's keep them here and make full use of their presence."

"And I second that," Reesh said at once, surprising everyone again. "Don't anyone ever say I don't know a good idea when I hear it."

After that everyone added their own agreement, and Tal's four co-conspirators were either in shock or crying. Tal himself blustered and tried to throw his weight around, but people came forward to pull him to his feet while ignoring everything he had to say.

"While they're not doing their job as servants, we'll keep them tied," Cleemor Gardan said as he looked around at his fellow assembly members. "No sense in leaving them free to make mischief while we sleep."

Again everyone agreed with the idea, and all five of the new servants were pulled to their feet and hurried away. I'd expected Jovvi to say that it wasn't necessary to tie the five to keep them from doing something nasty, but she never said a word. Instead she pulled Lorand off to the side and began to speak to him, and after a few minutes the two of them walked away.

I thought about following Jovvi and Lorand, then gave up on the idea and found a cool place to sit down instead. We still had a problem of our own to take care of, and once Jovvi solved it—assuming she did—I'd then be able to hear all about it . . .

# NINE

With all the excitement over for the moment, Jovvi put a hand on Lorand's arm.

"Lorand, I need to speak to you," she said in a very soft voice. "I need your help and your support, and most of all your understanding."

"I like to think you have all that without asking," Lorand replied with raised brows. "Is something wrong?"

"Yes," Jovvi answered without beating around the bush. "And it's all my fault, for talking Tamma into doing what I thought was best—and safe. Let's step over there and I'll explain as quickly as I can."

Lorand still looked bewildered, but that didn't stop him from following her away from the crowd. As soon as they stood alone, Jovvi turned to him again.

"I thought it was a good idea to ask Tamma to flatter Rion a bit, to build his self-confidence," Jovvi said in a rush, wishing there was time to hem and haw. "If things had worked out he would have been more sincere when he spoke to Naran again, but somehow he misinterpreted what Tamma was saying. She told me he was incredibly grateful that she wanted to lie with him again, and thanked her with a tear in his eye before riding away. He now expects her to come to his tent tonight, and if she fails to show up he'll be crushed."

"To borrow a phrase from you, 'oh, dear,' " Lorand said, his face now showing the flinching distress she herself felt. "What is Tamrissa going to do about it? If Vallant finds

103

out . . . I'm not sure how he'll react, but it won't be pleasant. And what about Naran? How will *she* feel?"

"Those are the things *I* have to take care of," Jovvi told him with a sigh. "Since Tamma's speaking to Rion was *my* idea, she insisted that I see to the problems before they *become* problems. Will you come with me and support whatever I say? I'm still not sure what will be involved, but I have this strange feeling that you're part of the solution."

"If I can be of help in some way, of course I'll do it," Lorand, the love, volunteered at once. "Do you have any idea what makes you think you'll need me?"

"Not really," Jovvi answered with a small headshake. "And it's so annoying, as if I've seen a clue somewhere but can't remember it completely or understand it. Well, maybe I'll understand later, so let's go find Naran first."

"Why are you taking Naran first?" Lorand asked as he followed her back toward the area of woods where their own people were resting and waiting for lunch. "Isn't it Vallant who's likely to make more of a fuss if he isn't calmed down quickly?"

"Vallant won't make a fuss until he finds out about the proposed change in sleeping arrangements," Jovvi pointed out over her shoulder. "Since he shouldn't find out until tonight, we have some time with him. Naran, on the other hand, might learn about the situation at any time if that flux clears up enough for her to See something. I know she's been acting detached and uncaring, but that isn't what she's really feeling."

"What gets me the most about this mess between Rion and Naran is that it isn't their fault," Lorand said, sounding unusually savage. "If Rion's self confidence hadn't been deliberately destroyed by that woman who raised him, he would not be filled with so many doubts now. I only wish we'd done something more to her than simply send her to Astinda with the others."

"Why, Lorand, you sound more like Tamma than she does," Jovvi said, sincerely surprised. "Since when have you become so . . . aggressive?"

"Certain things seem to set me off lately," Lorand said in a way more normal to him, shaking his head ruefully. "I think Tamrissa may be a bad influence on me."

"Then it's a lucky thing she'll be lying with Rion rather than with you," Jovvi said, making sure she showed a smile to let Lorand know she was joking. Then the smile suddenly disappeared. "There's Naran, sitting by that tree, and she's more upset than her expression shows. That could mean she already knows . . ."

Jovvi let her words trail off as she led Lorand over to where Naran sat, her talent flowing out in front of her. It was still possible to touch Naran a bit with easing, and if there was ever a time that easing was necessary . . .

"I've been expecting you, Jovvi," Naran said as she looked up with a small, unamused smile. "I don't know what I'm about to tell me, but I do know I won't like it."

"It isn't a tragedy, so don't start to think that it is," Jovvi said at once, sitting down beside Naran and putting a hand on her arm. "There's been a . . . very complicated mix-up, and you need to know about it before even more complications arise."

"The situation may be more of a tragedy than you know," Naran disagreed with a small headshake. "Rion is about to do something, and the results of that something will have a strong impact on his relationship with *me*. I couldn't See how it will turn out, but the probabilities of a simple, happy outcome are on the low side."

"Naran, you've got to be very careful," Lorand said suddenly, startling Jovvi. "I know you can't keep from looking at the probabilities whenever you can See them, but you have to learn to be more objective even when your own life and happiness are involved. You know even better than I do that low probabilities have become reality before this, but you still let yourself become upset. If you keep doing that, you'll drive yourself crazy."

"Lorand's right," Jovvi said, tightening her grip on Naran's arm while Naran stared at Lorand with large, vulnerably innocent eyes. "We're all working on a plan to get you and Rion back together, in a way you can both accept and live with. The only problem is, we've had a small . . . snag in our plans."

"I could almost see you flinching when you said the word 'snag,' " Naran commented in surprise, now studying Jovvi. "If I weren't feeling so depressed, I'd be really eager to hear your explanation. It must be incredibly entertaining—under other circumstances."

" 'Entertaining' is not the word *I* would use," Jovvi muttered, very aware of the way both Naran and Lorand looked at her. "I . . . asked Tamma to see if she could do something to increase Rion's self-confidence, since it was lack of belief in himself that started the trouble between you two. She came back to say that Rion had . . . misinterpreted her intention, and had thanked her sincerely for volunteering to lie with him. Then he rode away before she was able to think of some way to . . . clarify her true position."

"Oh, dear," Naran said, and then suddenly she and Lorand were laughing uproariously. Jovvi couldn't quite see what was so funny, especially since it was another minute or two before Naran was able to speak normally.

"We really must stop rubbing off on each other," Naran said after taking a deep breath, her eyes still sparkling with the tears of laughter. " 'Oh, dear' wasn't what I meant to say, but the words just seemed to pop out on their own. From Lorand's reaction, he must have said the same."

"I certainly did," Lorand confirmed with a chuckle. "And when *you* said it as well, I just couldn't hold back. Come on, Jovvi. Admit that you said exactly the same when Tamrissa first spoke to you."

"All right, so maybe I *am* rubbing off on all of you," Jovvi grumbled, still not terribly amused. "Those words may not be the most satisfying when you're angry or upset, but they do have the benefit of not making a bad situation worse. If you're both finished with being amused, I'd like to get back to what really is a serious situation. Tamma is more than a little upset about how you'll feel, Naran. She really had no intention of doing anything that would hurt you."

"I know that, Jovvi, and I don't blame either of you for this—snag," Naran said at once, smiling gently when she spoke the last word. "It's just possible that Tamrissa *can* help Rion by lying with him, and helping him will help me as well. It's just that I Saw something . . . complicated ahead, but it was just a glimpse so I didn't get any details and certainly didn't understand it. What bothers me most about this whole thing is that I could use some . . . comforting myself, but I'm not likely to get it."

"Why not?" Jovvi asked without thinking. "Aren't we all closer than a family? Why can't Vallant or Lorand—"

Jovvi's words broke off at the look on Lorand's face, an expression that was completely different from the one she would have expected.

"Now I think I understand why you needed to have me with you," Lorand said to Jovvi, his brows high with surprise. "If I take the honor of comforting Naran, you'll be free to console Vallant in the same way. If we ask Vallant to lie with Naran, Tamrissa—and possibly even Rion—will think Vallant is simply trying to get even with Tamrissa for lying with someone else."

"You know, that makes a good deal of sense," Jovvi said, startled to find that the observation was perfectly true. "But Lorand . . . You don't *mind* both of us changing partners? That isn't at all like you."

"I know, and I'm even more surprised than you look," Lorand answered with a rueful smile. "I can remember being really upset by the idea of either one of us lying with someone else, but it isn't the same now. These are our brothers and sisters we're talking about, after all, and it isn't as if we haven't done it before . . . Are *you* the one bothered by the idea now?"

"It may be hard to believe, but for a moment I was," Jovvi admitted with a small laugh. "I don't know why I felt that way, but the feeling is gone now so we don't have to worry about it. All we have to worry about is how Vallant will take the news."

"This time your flinch had mine to keep it company,"

Naran said, obviously addressing Lorand as well as Jovvi. "I should be really upset by what's happening, but now that I've been told about it I feel easier than I did before. Do you think there's a chance Vallant will be just as reasonable?"

"You of all people should know that nothing is certain, not even Vallant's temper," Jovvi pointed out with another sigh. "It's just that I have this feeling . . ."

Surprisingly, both Naran and Lorand nodded their agreement without waiting for the details that Jovvi couldn't provide. They seemed to share her feeling, which wasn't, in her opinion, a good sign. Well, the job still had to be done, so there was no sense in just sitting there. Vallant couldn't be very far away, and maybe he *would* be just as reasonable as Naran had been . . .

Vallant finished up with his people and walked briskly away after getting the report he'd wanted. Every time the column stopped because one of the Gracelians thought it was time for a meal or a rest, Vallant had one of the more experienced Blendings scout the road ahead of them. That was how he knew about the ambush that would take place not long after they were moving again, but he still hadn't decided whether or not to speak to Gardan and Lorimon about it. He and his Blendingmates *had* been told to stay out of what was supposed to be a Gracelian matter . . .

"Gracelian matters," Vallant growled under his breath, still more than a little furious about what had almost happened to Tamrissa. That man Tal was supposed to be one of their matters, but instead of putting the fool where he could do no more damage, they'd invited him along. Well, Tamrissa had settled *his* hash well enough, and without the help of their scouting Blending.

At first Vallant had thought that the scouting Blending entity had returned soon enough to give Tamrissa protection and support, but once the Blending had dissolved, the members of it assured him that their entity had been too far away to help. So Tamrissa had apparently stumbled on another trick, but that didn't mean Vallant hadn't aged until he'd been assured that she was all right.

Vallant had almost run straight to Tamrissa, but all the action was over by the time he learned about what was happening. All his people had assured him she was fine, so he'd made himself stay and get the report. Now that the business of everyone's safety was taken care of, he meant to find Tamrissa and see for himself that she wasn't harmed in any way.

It wasn't possible to see exactly where Tamrissa was, not with all the people in the woods, but Vallant's search lasted no more than moments. Almost as soon as he started Vallant ran into three of his Blendingmates, who acted as though they were looking for *him*.

"Ah, there you are, Vallant," Jovvi said in a way that was much too jovial, immediately making Vallant worry. "We were looking for you, and here you are."

"What's wrong with Tamrissa?" Vallant asked at once, barely noticing that he'd been right about who the three were looking for. "Was she hurt after all? I knew it was wrong stayin' and listenin' to some report when my woman was almost killed, but they swore she hadn't been hurt. What did they lie about, and how bad is it?"

"Vallant, calm down, Tamma is perfectly fine," Jovvi quickly assured him, Lorand and Naran adding their own assurances. "We'll have to remember to ask her later how she managed to stand alone against a Blending, but there's no doubt that she did. Or should I say, a former Blending? She burned the talent out of Tal and his Blendingmates, and the Gracelians have taken Antrie Lorimon's advice to make the five of them general servants for the rest of us."

"And when they're not serving, they'll be tied up to keep them from making trouble," Lorand added with what looked like grim pleasure. "At first I wondered why Jovvi didn't mention that the five don't *have* to be tied, not with a Spirit magic user like her around, but now I think I know. Being tied like an animal for the night should be a humbling experience for Tal, and the others may need it as badly as he does. And even if the experience *doesn't* make the man humble, he more than deserves the humiliation."

"So there's really nothin' wrong with Tamrissa?" Vallant

just had to ask again, to be absolutely certain. "Where is she, by the way? I'd enjoy seein' and holdin' her for a bit."

"She went to sit down, and you can certainly join her in a moment or two," Jovvi said, stepping closer and looking up at Vallant soberly. "Before you do go, though, we'd like to have a word with you about something important. You know that Naran and Rion still haven't gotten back together."

Jovvi hadn't asked a question, but Vallant still nodded after glancing at Naran. Mention of the trouble in her presence made Vallant uncomfortable, but oddly enough she didn't seem as upset as usual.

"Well, I decided that something needed to be done about the situation, so I asked Tamma to talk to Rion," Jovvi continued, now looking more hesitant than assured. "I asked her to encourage Rion and help build up his self-esteem, but the effort . . . went awry."

"She made Rion feel worse instead of better?" Vallant asked, more surprised than annoyed. "I find that hard to understand, seein' as how Tamrissa has always been really fond of Rion."

"No, as a matter of fact, the awry part went in the other direction, so to speak," Jovvi answered with a sigh as Lorand and Naran seemed to find other things to look at. "Rion took her flattery wrong, and told her how grateful he was that she'd offered to lie with him tonight. Then he rode away before she could set the matter straight."

"How embarrassin'," Vallant said with a chuckle as he shook his head. "She must be spendin' her time tryin' to find the kindest words to explain Rion's mistake. Are you here lookin' for me because she wants me to go with her when she tells him he's wrong?"

"Vallant, Tamma *can't* tell Rion he's wrong," Jovvi got out with a look that seemed to say she felt some kind of pain. "He thinks he can't trust himself because he lacks self confidence and life experience, and her refusal to lie with him now will only make those conditions worse. And it isn't as though she hasn't done it before, so—"

"So why should she have to do it again?" Vallant interrupted to ask, all amusement suddenly gone. "In case you're forgettin', our 'inexperienced' Rion managed to lie with both Tamrissa and you almost before Lorand and I made our first moves. And she and I haven't had such an easy time of it that I don't mind givin' her up. Or are you forgettin' how long it took Tamrissa and me to get together?"

"Vallant, it's only for a single night, and she's doing it to help *me,*" Naran put in when Jovvi simply closed her eyes and sighed more deeply. "You of all people should understand when I say that I feel only half alive without Rion, and that I want him back more than I want to continue breathing. But he has to come back in the right way, or the deep love we had will never be reborn. Isn't it worth a night away from Tamrissa to help try to make that happen?"

Vallant closed his own eyes and rubbed at them, wanting with every part of his being to say that *nothing* was worth being parted from Tamrissa for even a single night. Even when it wasn't possible for them to make love, just lying beside her made the world complete for him. But he *did* understand Naran's loss as few others would, so he couldn't speak the words that would show how he really felt. What he *could* do he had no idea, but then Jovvi's hand touched him.

"If you're picturing lying alone tonight, missing Tamma's presence, it won't be like that," she said softly with clear commiseration. "Since I can't take Tamma's place with Rion for reasons she understands, the least I can do is take her place with *you.* Unless you'd rather not have me. Lorand will be lying with Naran so none of us has to be alone, but if you'd *rather* be alone . . ."

Vallant opened his eyes to glance down at Jovvi, but Lorand was the one he looked at directly. Lorand had always been less willing to share Jovvi than Vallant was willing to share Tamrissa, but now he'd suddenly changed his mind?

"Yes, what Jovvi said is absolutely true," Lorand assured him with a wry chuckle, obviously reading Vallant's thoughts in his expression. "If it were anyone other than you or Rion I would *not* be this understanding, but the six of us share something even closer than lovemaking. How can I be upset over sharing Jovvi with what can almost be considered another part of myself?"

That question made Vallant stop and think for a moment. Rion had always called Lorand and him brothers, but the relationship was a good deal closer. At times they *were* a single individual, even more so now than at first. Now when they Blended Vallant saw clearly and individually through the entity's eyes, and Water magic was only the Vallant entity's strongest talent. The other talents were also there, as were his Blendingmates in a . . . blended sort of way. It shouldn't bother Vallant in the least that Tamrissa meant to lie with Rion, but for some reason it did bother him . . .

"You don't really have to feel good about this as long as you can bring yourself to not make a fuss," Jovvi said, still speaking gently. "And you can even reject me if you like, I promise I won't be insulted—all that much . . ."

Her teasing smile made it impossible for Vallant to retain the heaviness of his thoughts. He still wasn't in the least happy, but that certainly wasn't Jovvi's fault.

"Tamrissa is good at drivin' me out of my mind, but I'm not *that* far gone," Vallant finally said with as good a smile as he was able to manage. "If the day ever comes that you find me rejectin' *you,* Jovvi, you can be sure it isn't me you're talkin' to. As long as you're certain about this, Lorand . . . ?"

"Naran and I mean to comfort each other," Lorand answered with a smile that looked perfectly true and natural. "But if I had to leave Jovvi alone for the night, neither Naran or I would find that comfort. Your agreement to this arrangement helps more of us than just Rion."

"That's me, always willin' to be of help," Vallant muttered with a sigh. "Is it all right if I go lookin' for Tamrissa now? She's probably thinkin' I'm too busy organizin' things to worry about somethin' as unimportant as her."

"I'm sure she knows better, but just in case we'll go with you to reassure her," Jovvi said with one of her ordinary beautiful smiles, no longer teasing. "And I did want to ask her about how she withstood the strength of an entire Blending."

"I can tell you that she did tap into the strength of her link groups," Vallant said softly as they all began to walk in the direction he'd taken originally. "Two of the members of her link groups made sure to mention she'd done that, but only after Tal did the attackin'."

"So that's what she used to burn the talent out of the five, but we still don't know how she held off a Blending," Lorand put in just as softly. "I'm just afraid she'll say she doesn't *know* how she did it. If I have to hear that again, I may end up getting violent."

"You'd better save bein' violent for that attack that's comin'," Vallant said, still keeping his voice down. "I've been tryin' to decide whether or not to tell Gardan and Lorimon about it, but they joined the others in sayin' we were to keep back and not get ourselves involved in *their* business. If we'd done as they asked, we'd know nothin' *about* the attack."

"Cleemor and Antrie were just trying to keep us safe," Jovvi pointed out with a small frown. "That's why they didn't object when the others insisted we stay out of what they consider their affairs. Showing them that we aren't *letting* ourselves be left out could hurt the friendliness we've developed with them, but letting them be attacked without warning could hurt them worse in a different way."

"I wonder if it would be possible to defend against that attack without letting the Gracelians know we're doing it," Naran said in her usual thoughtful way. "That so-called flux eases up no more than every once in a while, so I can't tell you how successful something of that sort is likely to be. But if we get caught defending everyone, we can always play innocent and pretend we just have faster reflexes than the Gracelians."

"I have a better idea," Vallant said, pleased that the discussion had triggered the thought. "Lettin' the Gracelians get attacked is just the thing to make them understand how little they know about the right way of protectin' themselves. We'll do the protectin' and then we'll yell, rubbin' their noses in their lacks. If they don't reconsider lettin' us show them how it's done *then*, I'm for lettin' them get jumped on next time."

"That might be the most practical solution," Jovvi said slowly, obviously examining the suggestion as she spoke.

"We don't need to teach our good friends here *everything* we learned about conducting a war, but considering what we're riding toward we do have to teach them enough to survive. If we don't, then all too soon we'll have our own turn at showing the invaders how good we're supposed to be."

"Which none of us wants to have to do," Lorand put in, Naran's nod making the decision unanimous. "This means we have to encourage the Gracelians to start touching the power all the time. If they don't, they'll never be able to defend themselves from attack in time for the defense to do any good. But that also means they'll notice their strength increasing just the way we did."

"Keepin' them weak with those invaders around just doesn't make any sense," Vallant pointed out with a sigh. "But that doesn't mean their strength will be comin' very close to ours. Don't forget that they have only a single High talent in each of their Blendin's. Unless they change that—and they don't seem very willin' to do it—we and our people will still be stronger."

Everyone murmured agreement with that comment, but Vallant was no longer listening. He'd spotted Tamrissa sitting under a tree, and almost left the others behind in his eagerness to reach and hold her.

But then he remembered that he'd promised to go along with what Tamrissa would do with Rion. Making a fuss over her and then *not* making a fuss over her lying with Rion would be hard, so he'd better not make a fuss at all. If he pretended to take everything in stride, no one but Jovvi might notice his true feelings . . .

So Vallant continued to stroll along with the others, paying a high cost for keeping a casual smile on his face. If anyone but his Blendingmates had been involved . . . But it wasn't anyone else, and he couldn't let them all down . . .

# TEN

I watched Vallant and the others strolling over, wondering if Jovvi had spoken to him yet. He seemed awfully calm and easy for someone who had been given unacceptable news . . .

But maybe the news wasn't as unacceptable to him as we'd all thought it would be. The idea came as a rather unpleasant revelation, but I quickly decided not to jump to conclusions. There had been enough misunderstandings between Vallant and me to last a lifetime. Before I let myself get upset, I'd make very sure that I had what to get upset *about*.

"Tamma, we need to talk to you," Jovvi said as the group came up. "We'd like to know how you managed to withstand a Blending entity *before* you drew on the strength of your link groups."

"A little while ago I would have said I didn't know, but I've been thinking about it," I answered, paying attention to the question and my response rather than anything else. "Just before Tal's Blending attacked me, I was wrapped up in a good strong mad against the woman who ruined Rion. Getting mad seems to increase my strength more than slightly, and in this case I think it was the edge I needed. Tal's Blending was really strong only in Fire magic, so that's what it used. But I ought to mention that I knew the entity was there even though I couldn't see it. The entity's presence came across as a very strong conviction, one that turned out to be right."

"Now that's something I hadn't expected to hear," Lorand commented with raised brows, a reaction the others shared in different ways. "I didn't know it was *possible* to detect a Blending entity in any way, but I also have a different question. How did you burn the talent out of those five with their entity right there to protect them?"

"The new pattern I found let me pour incredibly hot fires into the entity itself," I responded with a small headshake. "I had no idea what good that would do, but along with the knowledge of the pattern came the conviction that that was what I *had* to do. Apparently it did more good than any of us would have realized."

"So an entity can be attacked by somethin' other than another entity," Vallant mused, seemingly concerned with nothing more than what I'd said. "Knowin' the entity is there makes it vulnerable, a point we need to keep in mind. But what does your new pattern look like?"

Everyone else supported his question about the pattern, so I shrugged to myself and drew a small example of it in fire in the air. Jovvi, Lorand, and Vallant all made sounds of satisfaction, as though they'd just been reminded of something they'd forgotten until now. Naran, though, showed a different reaction.

"Why does that pattern look so familiar?" she asked, frowning at what I'd drawn in the air with flaming curves. "I know nothing about Fire magic, so why . . ." Her words trailed off as her frown deepened, and then suddenly her eyes opened wide. "Of course! There's a way *I* can use that pattern, and fire has nothing to do with it. How odd!"

"Naran, hasn't any of us showed you the basic patterns we learned?" Jovvi asked, looking at Naran with her own frown. "I know we taught them to our people once we freed them from the army, so you must have seen some of them then."

"Actually, I never did," Naran denied with a faint smile. "If you'll remember back, I was trying to keep from having to show a 'normal' talent at the time, so I avoided the training classes on purpose. Since then I've heard you all discuss 'patterns,' but since I'd never seen any the word meant nothing to me."

"Then someone will certainly have to show you the rest of the patterns," Jovvi said after making a sound of self-annoyance. "I should have made sure you knew what the rest of us did, but you were supposed to have been trained by your own people . . . Well, if we can't find a time sooner, Lorand can show you the patterns when he comes to your tent tonight."

"Lorand is going to Naran's tent tonight?" I blurted as Naran nodded with her usual pleasant agreement. "Then what about *you*, Jovvi?"

"I'll be supplying Vallant with company," Jovvi told me with a smile that was just as pleasant as Naran's. "You'll be with Rion, after all, and there's no reason for any of us to be alone."

"No, I guess there isn't," I muttered, realizing that both Naran and Vallant knew what was happening and neither of them seemed to mind. Which was what we'd been hoping for, of course, but still . . .

"But I've been waitin' to see for myself that you're all right," Vallant said as he stepped closer to sit down beside me. "That fool Tal didn't hurt you in any way, did he?"

"No, not in any way at all," I said as Vallant's arm went around my shoulders and he hugged me to him. "I'm perfectly all right."

He made a sound of satisfaction as his other arm also went around me, holding me as though I really meant something to him. It was fairly clear that he *was* concerned about me, but I discovered that I no longer felt sure just how deep that concern went. Did it go all the way to love, the way mine went for *him*? Yesterday I would have sworn it did, but today . . . I've always hated possessive men like my late husband, but shouldn't a man who loves you show *something* in the way of regret when you'll be lying with another man . . . ?

Confused questions roared around in my head all through our lunch stop, and I couldn't even remember what I'd eaten when we were ready to get back on the road. The others had told me that the column would be attacked in a short while, and that we would be defending the Gracelians to make sure they weren't wiped out. After the attack we would insist on teaching our hosts the right way to conduct a journey like the one we were in the midst of. If they still refused to listen to us, the next time we would stand back and let them get hurt. I agreed with that plan, and it would have been nice if we'd been able to put it into effect *before* Tal and his group attacked me . . .

But that would have meant having Tal and his Blendingmates still free and in charge of themselves, which right now they weren't. The Gracelians had given each of the members of the former Blending a different dirty job to do, Tal himself being forced to check the horses. The former High in Fire magic had screamed and thrown temper tantrums almost without stop, but that hadn't kept him from having to do the chore assigned to him.

"Excuse me," a voice came as I was about to untie my horse. I turned to see Cleemor Gardan and Antrie Lorimon, and Lorimon smiled weakly at me. "We always seem to be apologizing for something to you and your Blendingmates, and that's a habit I wish we hadn't gotten into. You seem to be completely unharmed by what you went through, and we're very grateful for that. The others asked us to say how truly ashamed we all are that one of our own behaved in so honorless a way, and we'd like to know if you'd enjoy having your former attackers serve *you* tonight. You've earned at least that from them, so—"

"No, that's all right," I said at once, holding up one hand. "I'd rather see them serving you and the others. If I had to look at them around me during the meal, I'd probably lose my appetite. But I *would* like to know how close we are to where we're going. So far none of you has been willing to tell us that."

"We just didn't want you to worry, or to think that we meant to take advantage of your presence," Gardan answered with a faintly shamefaced expression. "We know that your Blending is stronger than any of ours, but this is a crisis we have to take care of ourselves. If we fail then it will be your turn, but until then . . ."

"We should be at our destination by tomorrow night," Lorimon put in quietly when Gardan's words trailed off in a way that said he wasn't going to answer my question with what I wanted to know. "Eastgate is about half a day beyond the town we'll spend the night in, so only our Blendings will be going on from there. Will you and the others be going with us?"

"Yes, we certainly will be going," I answered, seeing Gardan's glance of annoyance at Lorimon. But I also saw Lorimon's expression of intense relief, and knew immediately what her problem was. "But being afraid is nothing to be ashamed of, and you ought to know that. Going ahead with something that doesn't frighten you is nothing special, but going on in spite of your fear *is* special. We may look cool and unconcerned to you now, but we were nervous wrecks while we were fighting our way through the countryside of Gandistra—not to mention when we entered the palace. This is just more of the same."

"We *hope* this is just more of the same," Gardan muttered, his deep voice a rumbling grumble. "After all, your lot *won* the last fight you were in. But speaking of fights, just what *did* you do to Tal and the others? We've all been trying to figure it out, but now we have to admit that we're stumped."

"Answering that question would take too much time right now," I said, glancing over to where the column was beginning to form again. "Not to mention the fact that your people don't have enough grounding in the basics to understand the explanation. If we all live through the next few days, we may be able to help you fill in the gaps."

And with that I turned back toward my horse, not missing the flashes of frustration in Gardan's and Lorimon's eyes before I turned. It was fairly clear that they hadn't come over to apologize but to play their version of politics. I sighed as I climbed into my saddle, all but shaking my head over their antics. Playing politics is such a lame thing for adults to spend their time doing, and I'll never understand why people waste energy on it. Maybe it's because they're *afraid* to face things head-on . . .

Once we were back on the road, Rion came over to ride next to me. He gave me a smile before returning his attention to where we were going, and I was grateful for his silence. Not having to cope with conversation meant I could think about the coming attack, which helped me to *not* think about other things. Doubts about Vallant's feelings for me wasn't a subject I felt prepared to cope with right now.

Rion and I braced ourselves in our saddles, knowing that we could be pulled into the Blending at any moment without warning. We were waiting until we were almost on top of the hidden attackers, to keep from giving away what we meant to do. Jovvi was being guided by the Earth magic member of our scout Blending, who would tell her when the head of the column reached the proper place.

We'd been riding again for less than an hour when there was a sudden shout up ahead. It was one of the Gracelians who had shouted, and then I was the Tamrissa entity rather than myself alone. Floating above the column gave me an excellent point of view, from where I could see five Blending entities forming almost as quickly as I had.

The newcomer entities, which appeared smaller than myself in some way, spread out quickly to either side of the road. There were flesh forms in hiding a short distance ahead, flesh forms which had been poised to show themselves in attack. Instead, the flesh forms *were* attacked, swiftly and without hesitation. The flesh forms were in large numbers, fully half as many as those who rode in the column, but none was able to withstand what the various entities did to end them. They were ended in droves, uselessly thrown away, destroyed completely before this entity's very senses.

And then it was me back again, appalled at what I'd seen and beginning to get really angry. The Gracelians apparently *had* had someone looking ahead, and that's what the shouting had been about.

"Did you see that?" Lorand demanded as he and the others rode up to where Rion and I sat staring at one another almost in shock. "They just murdered all those people without the least hesitation!"

"They probably did it because they weren't given more than a minute's warnin'," Vallant put in, sounding really savage. "If they'd been scoutin' ahead the way we were, they could have captured those people instead of just endin' them."

"They acted in panic, and now they're really pleased with themselves," Jovvi added, a tinge of disgust in her tone. "They have no idea how foolishly they've acted, and I don't know if telling them will do any good."

"But we're goin' to tell them anyway," Vallant said, a statement he knew no one would argue with. "They're *all* fools, and if we don't find a way to straighten them out then we'll be facin' those invaders all on our own."

That conclusion was much too true, so we all urged our mounts ahead after Vallant. The Gracelian assembly members were gathered together at the head of the column, and only Gardan and Lorimon weren't laughing aloud and congratulating themselves. The rest were obviously filled with the thrill and pleasure of a job well done, especially the man named Thrybin Korge. Korge was young and handsome, blond hair and blue eyes, carrying less weight than Satlan Reesh but in his own way was just as offensive. His arrogance was the quiet sort, unannounced but definitely always there.

"Ah, and here come our esteemed guests, to add their own congratulation," Korge called out once we were close enough. "The fact that we had no need to call on their . . . sometimes overbearing assistance must please them no end."

"Wrong all the way around, Korge," Vallant answered as we all drew rein not far from the Gracelians. "We're here to talk about your shortsightedness and stupidity, not to mention your cold-blooded wastefulness. Is doin' things wrong a trait you require in assembly members?"

"How dare you?" Korge demanded as he drew himself up, all amusement gone from him and Reesh and Dinno. Gardan and Lorimon just looked upset, but Vallant gave no one else a chance to speak first.

"It's never a matter of 'dare' when instructin' the ignorant," Vallant growled, locking gazes with Korge. "You made no effort to look more than a short distance ahead of this column, so findin' those people waitin' in ambush frightened you. Instead of neutralizin' them and then askin' questions to find out why they were there, you just jumped out like fools and killed them all. You had no right makin' those people pay for your own shortsightedness."

"But of course we knew why they were there," Korge countered with haughty coldness as Reesh fumed beside him. Dinno frowned with what looked like thoughtfulness, but made no effort to interrupt Korge. "Those people were certainly outlaws, lying in wait to murder us and take what we have. We did nothing more than defend ourselves, and self-defense needs no excuse."

"Then why are you makin' one?" Vallant demanded in turn, no more impressed with Korge's speech than I would be. "You have no way of knowin' for certain that those people were outlaws, not when you killed them all before they could be questioned. For all you know they were refugees from the fightin' up ahead, and were lyin' in wait to attack any of the invaders who followed them."

"And if they *were* outlaws, you all ought to be ashamed," I couldn't keep from putting in as everyone but Korge paled to some extent. "The number of outlaws in an empire reflects on the job being done by that empire's ruling body, the greater number of outlaws, the worse the job. If you were doing what you should, the outlaw population would be firmly kept down."

"No, let's not get into an argument about that because they're right," Dinno said suddenly, looking at his fellow assembly members one by one. "I remember thinking that those 'outlaws' appeared rather too well fed for people living in the forests, but by then it was too late to stop the massacre. I joined in because I *was* frightened, most especially by the suddenness of it all. Now all I feel is ashamed."

"No, Korge, don't say it," Gardan put in quickly as the other man opened his mouth with a ridiculing expression on his face. "Our guests *are* right, and I agree with Dinno. We all acted out of fear, and may have made a terrible mistake. What we have to keep firmly in mind is the fact that we have no experience with this sort of thing, but the Gandistrans do. If we aren't *complete* fools, we'll start to take their advice."

"Why don't you simply hand over the assembly to them and have done with it?" Korge countered, the words heavy with disgust. "Our marvelous guests can do no wrong, but the rest of us are idiots. Well, you may feel that way but I don't. Those people we defended ourselves against *were* outlaws, and many of them were probably the criminal element in Eastgate who had to relocate when the city was taken. The rest of you may find it impossible to think for yourselves, but I don't have that trouble. And now I think it's time we got moving again."

Korge turned his horse and began to move up the road again, Reesh following right along after sending a look filled with daggers toward the rest of us. I had the impression that Reesh clung to Korge and his very convenient explanation as a way to keep from admitting that he'd made a terrible mistake. Some people can't handle that sort of knowledge, and Satlan Reesh seemed to be one of them.

"What do you people recommend that we do now?" Dinno asked Vallant, ignoring the departure of the two other men. "I'd dearly love to know the truth of what happened here, but unfortunately it's too late to find out."

"You could try askin' yourself if that large a number of criminals found it possible to get out of Eastgate when everyone else was bein' killed," Vallant pointed out sourly. "But that really is beside the point, when it's possible to keep this same thing from happenin' again. You have to take turns sendin' out your Blendin' entities to scout ahead of the column, and that should keep you from bein' surprised again. And if there *is* a next time, use your Spirit magic to take control of whoever might be waitin' instead of killin' them."

"And then we'll be able to question them," Dinno agreed with a nod and a sigh. "Now that the horses are gone, we make sure that the barn is firmly locked. But we really do need to get moving again."

That was one point no one could argue with, so the column formed again and began to move after the two men who were a short distance up the road. My Blendingmates and I hung back to take up our original positions near our own people, giving the Gracelians the privacy they probably needed. They'd begun to talk in low tones, hopefully arranging which of their Blendings would act as scouts when.

"They seem to be takin' my advice seriously, but we won't be givin' up our own scoutin'," Vallant said quietly after a moment or two. "And I think that our link groups ought to start takin' turns keepin' an eye out tonight."

"Against our allies, if our enemies don't happen to be close enough to worry about," Jovvi put in dryly, obviously agreeing with the idea. "That man Korge is furious, and I have the impression he has a private agenda much like the one Tal had. He also intends to go home a hero, at the expense of every one of us if necessary."

"I just love ambitious men," I grumbled, still not in the best of moods. "Maybe we'll get lucky, and he'll also decide to attack me."

"We can do without that kind of luck," Vallant said at once as he glared at me, clearly unamused. "Korge isn't the fumbler Tal was, and he also isn't a Fire magic user. His talent is Water magic, and if he comes at you without warnin' you could be a pile of dust before you know anythin' is happenin'. That means you'd better not try givin' him a *reason* to attack you."

"All right, I'll stay away from the man," I grudged, not terribly happy about being yelled at, but finding my mood just a little lighter. Vallant's worry was so thick I could almost taste it, and it was fairly obvious that that worry wasn't simply for the Blending's sake. Apparently I did mean more than a little to him, and it was possible he simply wasn't *showing* how he felt about my lying with Rion. If that were so, then I felt quite a *bit* better . . .

The rest of the day's ride was uneventful, and we made camp at sundown in a wide glade near a fast-running stream. Once the tents were all up and the horses taken care of, we indulged in a bit of creative bathing. Vallant took water from the stream and formed it into a large oval, and then I warmed the water before we began to take turns stepping into it. It's more than possible to wash while holding your breath as you stand completely submerged, but adding soap gets a bit tricky. We did manage it, though, and afterward felt much better.

Dinner didn't come long after we were all in clean clothing, and we discovered that our link groups and other Blending had done just as we had about bathing. The Gracelians, on the other hand, looked tired and hot and sweaty, and Antrie Lorimon actually came over to us to ask if we'd gone into the stream. She seemed about to tell us how dangerous swimming in a stream was, and hearing how we'd really bathed turned her wordless.

"It's not very difficult, you know," Vallant added while the woman still stood searching for what to say. "It only takes a small bit of strength to form the oval of water, so anyone with Water magic should be able to do it. Didn't it ever occur to you that somethin' like this could be done?"

"I never really stopped to think about it," Lorimon admitted ruefully with a shake of her head. "I suppose we're all just so used to going to a bath house to wash . . . It seems that hardship has a beneficial side we hadn't considered. When you have a need, you tend to find a way to satisfy it."

"Only if you stop complaining long enough," I put in, matching her rueful smile. "If I'd spent less time complaining and done more thinking before this, we could have had baths any time we wanted them. And don't forget to have a Fire magic user warm the water. Cold baths don't do the same job."

"I'll certainly remember, since my Blending and I will be trying out your method right after we finish eating," she said with a laugh. "Thank you for sharing that with me."

We watched her walk away to rejoin Cleemor Gardan and the others, and then we gave our attention to the food we were about to help ourselves to. Zirdon Tal and his former Blendingmates had apparently been put in charge of setting out the meal, so we made very sure that Lorand was first in line. Jovvi stepped up right behind him, and when they both turned to smile and shake their heads we knew that the new servants hadn't done anything to ruin the meal.

We took our time eating, all of us sitting more or less together in a loose circle. There wasn't much in the way of conversation, but it still came as a small surprise when Lorand and Naran rose and left together without saying anything. A couple of minutes later Jovvi and Vallant did the same, and that left just Rion and me.

"Are you ready to retire yet, Tamrissa?" Rion asked after another moment, what looked to be a single swallow of tea left in his cup. "I don't mean to rush you, of course. If you'd rather sit here a bit longer, I'll fetch fresh tea for the two of us."

"No, actually, I *don't* want to sit here any longer," I realized aloud, surprised to feel that way. "Let's go to your tent now, and save the tea for tomorrow."

"Are you certain that I'm not rushing you?" Rion asked as he stood up with me. "It would be boorish of me to be inconsiderate of someone who has granted me such a marvelous favor."

"Rion, please stop thinking of this as a favor," I asked as I took his arm, both of us leaving our plates and cups for the "servants" to clean up. "I happen to remember my first time with you, and you gave me great pleasure. You're a handsome, beautifully made man, and I've been thinking about being with you all day."

I may have been stretching a point with the last of my comments, but the statement was certainly no lie. Rion smiled in a way that made him even more handsome, also making me glad I'd said what I had.

"I've also had *you* in my thoughts all day, lovely sister," he responded, patting the hand I had on his arm. "I consider myself fortunate indeed to be part of a family such as ours, a family that Blends in mind as well as body. The thoughts have made me wonder if I would be able to perform at all with a woman I had not shared minds with."

"Now that you mention it, I think I'd hate to have to lie with a man who wasn't part of our Blending," I said, glad for

Naran's sake that Rion had thought of the point, but also telling the truth. "As far as *wanting* to lie with a man who wasn't one of us, I can't imagine ever doing it. I might find a strange man attractive physically, but only to look at. For anything more I'd want a man of my family."

"I'd been about to ask if you would be flattered by the attention of someone who wasn't one of us, but that would be a foolish question," Rion said, his smile now rueful. "I know you've had far too much attention of that sort to be flattered, and that's another point I hadn't considered. Perhaps, under certain circumstances, it's more of a benefit than a drawback to be ignored."

"During my marriage, I spent many nights crying and wishing I'd been born ugly," I said in a very low voice, still finding those memories painful. "I'm sure there are beautiful women around who are perfectly happy, but I'd be willing to bet that there are many more who aren't. It seems to be part of most men to want women who are beautiful, but the twisted men only want to possess that beauty and care nothing for the woman herself."

"Well, at least you don't have to worry about that with *our* family," Rion said, holding his tent flap aside and urging me in ahead of him. "We care about you first and your appearance second, a truth I hope you're aware of."

"If I weren't aware of it, I would have gone elsewhere a long time ago," I assured him while he laced the flap closed. "I'm still here because I belong here, just as all of us do . . . Do you think it's possible we were somehow *meant* to be together?"

"I have no way of knowing that," he answered with a shrug as he straightened up and turned toward me. "What I do know, however, is that I'm eternally grateful to be one of the family, and that's one of the reasons why I felt so upset over having found another woman's interest flattering when I had Naran. It was the basest kind of betrayal of what I consider most important in life."

"Well, it wasn't betrayal, it was just a normal reaction," I replied, putting my hand to his face as I looked up at him before stroking his cheek gently. "I know that because Jovvi felt flattered at a strange man's attention, and she's had more experience with being attractive and attracting than both of us put together. Shall we take our clothes off now?"

"By all means," Rion answered with the sweetest smile, and then his hands were on my arms. "It would also be my pleasure to assist you."

We ended up assisting each other, laughing over how silly we must look. Once our clothes were gone we slid onto the sleeping pad and under the quilt the tent came equipped with. Those Gracelians surely did enjoy their comfort, but at the moment I had no argument with that outlook. Rion took me in his arms as my hands stroked his body, and then we shared the sort of kiss that used to frighten me rather badly.

The first time Rion and I had lain together, it had taken quite a lot of effort on his part to make me ready for him. This time, however, it took very little effort before we were both more than ready. I welcomed Rion into my body and his sang with a pleasure that he shared beautifully in the way that seemed to be a part of him. We moved together for a very long time, the sensations exquisite, and not long after my body erupted in release Rion allowed his own to do the same.

After a moment or two Rion kissed me and moved to lie beside me, but I was already mostly asleep. I did, however, have the passing thought that the pleasure I'd had might have been more intense than what I'd lately been finding with Vallant. And Rion *was* attractive, more so now that he'd learned more about the way the world worked. If things never went back to the way they'd been between him and Naran, possibly another arrangement could be worked out . . .

# ELEVEN

It was a pretty new day when Jovvi joined Vallant in leaving their tent. The pretty day was a fitting match to the feelings of satisfaction inside Jovvi, feelings she seemed to have been missing lately. Vallant was *so* attractive and such a marvelous man, it was no wonder that Tamma had worried so about him . . .

"We'd better get a move on this mornin'," Vallant commented after taking a deep breath of the beautifully fresh air. "It will be rainin' by nightfall, and I'd like to be indoors by then."

"Yes, so would I," Jovvi agreed as they began to make their way toward the area where breakfast was being prepared. "I just hope that the town is large enough to have accommodations for all of us. This is much too large a group for me to be sure we'll have no trouble."

"We can worry about that when we get there," Vallant told her with an amused glance as they walked along. "The Gracelians might have trouble findin' places good enough for them, but our own people have spent too many nights in stables for it to be a problem. We'll make do, just as we always have."

"You're right, of course," Jovvi conceded with a laugh as she shook her head. "And this is much too nice a day for worrying in any event."

Vallant used a nod to agree with that sentiment, but before either of them could say anything else they were joined by

Lorand and Naran. The newcomers also seemed to be enjoying the pretty day, and their emotions were filled with happiness and satisfaction.

"I was just telling Naran that we ought to find some way to hurry the Gracelians," Lorand said as they all came together. "There will definitely be rain tonight, and I'd hate to have to put up with our hosts' wailing if they happen to get wet."

"Say, that ought to be the key," Jovvi exclaimed, pleased to have seen the point. "The idea of getting wet ought to make them hurry."

"Even if very little else would," Naran put in with amusement. "They seem to have the idea that hurrying is only for the unimportant, so they really don't want to be caught doing it."

"I'd be willin' to promise not to look," Vallant suggested in a drawl that made them all laugh. "If promisin' would make them move faster, I'd be willin' to promise almost anythin'."

"Are we talking about getting some speed out of our hosts?" Tamma asked as she and Rion joined the group. "Rion tells me that the air pressure suggests we'll be having rain later, so why don't we mention how awful they'll all look if they get wet and bedraggled?"

"Yes, that's exactly what we *were* talking about, and we can add your suggestion to mine," Jovvi said as everyone laughed again. "Unless, that is, they already know about the rain and have decided to hurry on their own."

Jovvi had made that comment because of the flurry they were approaching. The Gracelians seemed somewhat agitated as they took their meals rather more quickly than usual, and the servants in charge of cleaning up were already rushing around. It looked like the change in weather had already been announced, so Jovvi joined her Blendingmates in getting their meal. It didn't take long to finish eating, and once they were done they all moved out of the way of those doing the cleanup.

"It will still be a short while before we're on the road, so why don't we take a quick look around before going to our horses?" Jovvi suggested once she and the others were back among their own people. "Sitting down to Blend is easier than doing it while on horseback."

"I'm all for doing things the easy way this morning," Tamma said after yawning. "I think I'm getting really tired of always being on the move."

"There were supposed to be nomad groups in this area at one time long ago," Naran said as she and the others made themselves comfortable on the ground. "For the longest time I felt like a nomad myself, and I hated never being able to settle down anywhere. Now, though, I know that the traveling won't continue on forever, so I actually have something to look forward to."

"You also have *my* company in doing that looking forward," Jovvi assured her while everyone else made sounds of agreement. "I know we weren't happy living in the palace and were pleased to leave Gan Garee, but running away isn't the way to solve a problem. If we weren't happy with things as they were, we should have done something to change them. But that's for later, as we have other concerns right now. Is everyone ready?"

Since the others indicated their readiness with nods or short sounds, Jovvi initiated the Blending. She quickly became the Jovvi entity, but today something felt odd. The Jovvi entity wasn't quite certain what that oddness was, and it took a moment to understand. The bonds between her flesh forms were somewhat out of balance, but that matter could be easily seen to later. At the moment there was something else that needed to be done.

The road wasn't far from where the flesh forms had made their camp, but the Jovvi entity remembered that road well enough that it was unnecessary to float back to it. Flashing there was much more practical, and then the Jovvi entity floated quickly along the road to see what might be ahead.

For a short distance the entity discovered nothing but the usual small life to be found in woods and fields, but then there was an intrusion in her perceptions. There seemed to be something up ahead that didn't fit, and when the Jovvi entity reached that something she was perplexed.

Large numbers of flesh forms were spread throughout the woods and fields, some of them having apparently lain right beside the road. The clothing of these flesh forms was dirty and torn, most had no more than odd bundles with them, and more than a few very young flesh forms accompanied those who were fully grown.

Even as the Jovvi entity watched, many flesh forms hurriedly took to the road and moved as quickly as possible in the direction the Jovvi entity had come from. Exhaustion seemed to cover the flesh forms despite the rest they'd presumably had, and yet they continued to travel . . .

"There seems to be a bigger problem than rain coming," Jovvi said after dissolving the Blending. "If those people are coming from the town we're headed for . . ."

"Then the invaders are makin' better time than we are," Vallant finished for her as he got to his feet. "And findin' someplace to get out of the rain tonight might not be as easy as I was thinkin'. I'd better let our hosts know what's happenin', if for no other reason than to keep them from killin' those people headin' for us."

"And I'll go with you," Tamma announced as she also stood. "I have the feeling that some of those people will make trouble when they hear what you have to say, and there's no need for you to face that alone."

"Truthfully, I have the same feeling Tamma does," Jovvi said as she did her own rising. "I have the impression that there's going to be some kind of difficulty, and I think we should all be there."

"They're right," Naran agreed from where she already stood when the others glanced toward her. "They must have gotten the same glimpse I did when we were Blended, a faint suggestion that we could well have some trouble with our hosts. And the trouble will be less if we're all there."

"Then we must certainly all be there," Rion stated from where he stood beside an equally erect Lorand, whose firm nod showed he also agreed. "If you'd care to lead the way, Vallant?"

Vallant nodded and headed toward the other side of the camp, and Jovvi joined the others in following. She and her

Blendingmates were usually close, but this morning they seemed almost to be one person. No doubts, no rivalries or personal problems, just six people fully prepared to support one another. Jovvi found herself basking in the feeling of oneness, enjoying it to the full. The attitude wasn't likely to continue forever, so Jovvi was determined to enjoy it for as long as it did continue.

The Gracelians still weren't hurrying, but the briskness of their movements suggested that they also weren't wasting any time. The cooking area was cleared, the tents were almost all down, and the horses were already saddled. The new group of servants hurried around looking exhausted, but everyone was almost ready to go.

"You people are looking rather grim this morning," Cleemor Gardan remarked when he turned from his horse to see them. "Is something wrong?"

"One thing wrong is that you people still haven't taken our advice," Tamma answered bluntly before Vallant could say the same in a more diplomatic way. "I thought you agreed to do some scouting before blundering ahead into the unknown?"

"But we did do some scouting," Gardan answered with a small sound of protest. "Korge over there had the duty this morning, and he reported the road to be clear as far as he could reach."

"Well, either Dom Korge has a very limited reach, or he decided that scouting wasn't worth wasting his time on," Tamma returned with a withering glance for the miscreant in question. "In either event, there *is* something ahead on the road that everyone needs to know about. Hordes of people are heading this way, and unless outlaws in this country take their women and children along on raids, they aren't outlaws. There is, however, an excellent chance that they're refugees from that town we were supposed to be heading for."

"Which means that the invaders got there before we did and now there's no town worth headin' for," Vallant said, finally getting a word in edgewise around Tamma. "Instead of rushin' around to get out of here, we'd better sit down and make some plans."

"We don't need *your* help to make plans," the fool Korge said with a cold sneer as he came up with the others to join the conversation. "We're perfectly capable of running our lives without the assistance of gutter filth who have no morals."

"You're trying to avoid being blamed for not doing what you were supposed to by calling *us* names," Jovvi put in quickly before one of the others lost his or her temper and slammed into the idiot man. "This situation is too serious to play games with, or haven't you noticed that yet?"

"What I do or don't do isn't *your* concern, slut," Korge snapped, his face flushed with annoyance and partial embarrassment. "You're all sluts and knaves, and anyone who listens to you is a fool."

"What in the name of chaos are you talking about, Korge?" Gardan demanded as Satlan Reesh rumbled something from beside Korge that sounded like agreement. "You can't hope to keep from being condemned by making nebulous and ridiculous accusations against our guests—"

"Then why don't I make solid accusations rather than nebulous ones?" Korge returned as Jovvi fought to keep her Blendingmates from exploding in fury. "Do you know what they did last night after dinner? They paired off in *un*mated fashion, and then indulged in disgusting displays of rut. And these are the animals you want us to treat as honored guests."

The disgust in the man's voice got through to Jovvi's Blendingmates the way arguing would never have done. They all seemed to understand that Korge was seriously bothered by what he called unmated displays, and the other Gracelians were all looking at Jovvi's group oddly.

"Is this true?" Antrie Lorimon asked quietly to mask the agitation inside her. "We were given the impression that you were two matings and two individuals in composition. Did you really pair off outside your matings?"

"I don't understand why you're so disturbed," Jovvi said before Tamma could tell the woman that what they did was none of her business. "Aren't High talents in Gracely allowed to choose bedmates and lie with them any time they please? And isn't the act supposed to be an honor for those bedmates?"

"Of course it's an honor," Lorimon answered, riding over whatever Korge tried to say. "Ordinary people are delighted to share our glory, even for a short while. But the same rules do *not* apply to dallying among Blending members, unless those members are officially mated. The situation would be outrageous and simply isn't done."

"Outrageous, they call it," Tamma said with a laugh that had rather grim amusement in it. "Now we know why I was able to stand against one of their Blendings. These fools aren't bonded."

"If that comment is supposed to mean something, you'd better explain it," Olskin Dinno put in, his rumble covering exclamations of insult from the other Gracelians. "What sort of bonding are you talking about, and what has it got to do with Blending?"

"Bonding is what we call the strengthened tie between members of the Blending," Lorand said quickly, giving a more thorough—and reasonable—explanation than Tamma would have done. "Before lying together the bond is tenuous and . . . temporary, you might say. Our Blending entity helped us to learn about that necessity, so I wonder that yours didn't do the same."

"Possibly it's because our entities don't spring from *sluts,*" Korge stated without hesitation, looking around in a haughty, superior way. "How much longer do we have to stand here and listen to this filth?"

"Oh, don't pay any attention to *him,*" Naran spoke up in a light and casual way as Tamma began to bristle again. "He's just afraid that someone will find out how pitiful his performance usually is. The rest of you, though, don't have that to worry about, so why don't you try to think rationally instead of emotionally?"

Korge screamed in fury, and then somehow Jovvi felt the presence of an entity very near Naran. For that reason Jovvi was just about to initiate their own Blending when Korge screamed again, this time in pain.

"Yes, blockin' your effort with Water magic, even with

your Blendin' behind you, wasn't hard at all," Vallant told the man who had just fallen to his knees. "I don't know which of us is makin' you howl like that, but whoever it is I say more power to 'em. You deserve whatever you get."

"I was just warming some of his body parts a bit," Tamma said with a bland smile, watching Korge fold in on himself where he knelt. "If attacking someone with a Blending isn't against the law here in Gracely, you people might not be *worth* saving."

"The laws aren't meant to protect *demons*!" Satlan Reesh choked out as he bent to a weeping Thrybin Korge. "If we listen to anything more from you, we'll end up turning into the same kind of demon!"

"How many fools like that do you *have* in your ranks?" Tamma said to Gardan and Lorimon with a short jerk of her head in Korge and Reesh's direction. "And how did this weird system of yours ever get started? Having just one High talent in a Blending and four Middles doesn't bring the Middles up, it pulls the High down. If the Astindans had been moved by an interest in invasion rather than just looking for revenge, this country would now be called East Astinda."

"What makes *your* way right and ours wrong?" Dinno put in over Reesh's blustering outrage. "We've been doing things our way for more decades and centuries than you have years, but there you stand, telling us we're wrong. With the small amount of experience you people have, isn't it possible that *you're* wrong?"

"No," Vallant answered without the least hesitation, his tone firm but gentle. "As the old sayin' goes, the proof of the puddin' is in the eatin'. If your way was better than ours, two of ours wouldn't have been able to stand alone against two of your Blendin's. Talkin' a good show is for nothin' but those childish political games you play. This is the real world out here, and you're outclassed every time you turn around. Not admittin' to bein' outclassed isn't the same as actually bein' equal or better."

Dinno stared back at Vallant with desolation in his eyes, Gardan and Lorimon showing an equal disturbance. But none of the three could argue with what they'd been told, and Jovvi knew that the remaining two assembly members were too agitated to speak. Hatred and envy flowed so strongly from Korge that Jovvi's head began to throb, so she did the only thing the present circumstance allowed for.

"I think we're all forgetting about those invaders who aren't as far ahead as we thought," Jovvi said into the silence, drawing everyone's attention. "We need to make some definite plans *now,* and for that reason I've . . . calmed Dom Korge. He isn't interested in cooperation, only in causing as much dissention as possible which he can then take advantage of to put himself forward. If the rest of you don't yet know that about him, then you can't possibly have spent any time in his company."

"Oh, stop sputtering, Reesh," Dinno growled as everyone now examined the placidly kneeling Korge. "The man may have led you to believe that you and he are soul mates, but I happen to know that he doesn't even like you. I would never have mentioned that if we were back in the city, but out here we have to stop playing games and learn to tell the truth. Our lives literally depend on it."

Jovvi watched Reesh's emotions change as he looked at Thrybin Korge, a painful sense of betrayal in his gaze. The man Reesh clearly wasn't popular among his equals, and he seemed to have been leaning rather heavily on the friendship he thought Korge had offered. Reesh looked down on women because he needed *someone* to look down on, not because he really thought himself superior. His true feeling was the fear that he might not even be equal to others, and only the air of superiority kept him from falling apart. Jovvi felt a great deal of sympathy for the man, but there were other matters that needed their attention now.

"I think we need to decide first what to do about all those people on the road," Jovvi said after taking a deep breath. "Most of them have brought almost nothing with them, and there are quite a few children who looked hungry and exhausted."

"We don't have enough food with us to feed hordes of hungry people," Cleemor Gardan said, but with regret rather than selfishness. "We should be able to give each of them *something,* though, and then urge them along toward that last small town we passed. A town should be able to care for them better than we can."

"And moving this camp closer to what will probably prove to be a battleground doesn't make much sense," Antrie Lorimon said after nodding her agreement with Gardan. "We'll leave the tents and things here with the servants and cooks, and just take our Blendings with us."

"You would also be wise to arrange for a meal that can be taken easily and eaten on the move," Rion put in, his inner being steadier than it had been in days. "There isn't likely to be any forage, and there won't be time to stop and cook."

The others nodded distracted agreement, and then Lorimon gestured Reesh into joining them. The man hesitated a brief moment before doing so, his mind warming with what he took to be acceptance. It obviously hadn't occurred to him that the Gracelians were marshalling what was left of their resources and ignoring personal preferences. But that was just as well, Jovvi understood. The man would perform much better if he felt a part of the group . . .

Vallant led the way back to their own people to tell them what was going on, and by the time they all returned to the Gracelian part of camp with their horses, the Gracelians seemed almost ready to leave. Chunks of cooked meat and cuts of bread were given to everyone, and Jovvi sighed as she wrapped up her share and put it in her saddlebags. The meat wasn't likely to last very long in the heat of the day, and the bread would harden rather quickly. The Gracelians were definitely trying, but they still had a lot to learn.

A few minutes later they were all on the road, and everyone rode in a silence composed of their own thoughts. Jovvi wondered if the Gracelians would increase the strength of their Blendings by lying with their Blendingmates, but the chances of their doing that weren't good. Korge may have been left behind in the camp with his own Blending, but his point of view continued to color everyone's thinking. The Gracelians had centuries of the wrong attitude to overcome, and Jovvi didn't know if they would find that possible to do.

It took about two hours before the head of the trimmed-down column reached the first of the refugees. Some of the walkers just continued to plod on, but most of the ragged mob hurried over to stand in the way of the horses and beg for help. The din was incomprehensible as well as pitiful, and the Gracelians didn't seem to know what to do other than force a way through the throng. Before they actually did that, though, Jovvi led the rest of her Blending forward to help.

"Please try to calm yourselves," Vallant shouted to the people while Jovvi drew on the strength of her link groups to quiet everyone in reach. "We're here to help, but we can't do much without knowin' exactly who and what you're runnin' from."

"There are strangers killing everyone they can find," a man gasped out as Jovvi's efforts began to make a difference. "They came to our town from the east, and before we knew it people were dying everywhere. Some of those fleeing with us stopped at that village back there, but I wasn't about to do the same. It's too close to our town, and if the invaders are marching west . . ."

"All right, taking care of the invaders is what we're here to do," Reesh shouted as the babble of distress started to rise again. "We're members of the assembly with our Blendings, and we'll handle the matter."

"But you have to keep moving right now," Antrie Lorimon put in as people began a ragged cheer. "A short distance up the road you'll find our last camp, where you'll be given a small something to eat. We don't have much, so you'll have to continue on to the next village before you can stop to rest. Please pass the word back for us, as we have to continue on now."

Most of those around the horses were reluctant to step back, but they knew they had very little choice. Once there was enough room Vallant led the way to the grassy verge beside the road, and everyone followed. Trying to get through the massed escapees on the road would have taken too long and been too difficult, most especially since everyone seemed to want them to stop. The crying and begging was pitiful, but they just had to ignore it and continue on.

"The town of Velcia, gone," Antrie Lorimon muttered where she rode beside Jovvi. "My people were originally *from* Velcia, but now . . ."

When Lorimon's words trailed off, Jovvi put a hand to the woman's arm in sympathy. Destruction is never easy to accept, but destruction of something personal was another matter entirely.

After another hour of riding, they were able to return to the road. The last of the stragglers had already passed, and Jovvi couldn't help but notice that although the groups had been strung out, there weren't really a lot of people in them. The escapees seem to number about one percent or less of the people a large town ought to hold, and thinking about where the rest of the people might be simply made Jovvi shudder.

It was past noon when the column slowed and left the road again. Jovvi took that to mean they were close to something that required stealth, but it couldn't be the town of Velcia. That still lay hours ahead of them, but the village that man had mentioned wouldn't be the same. That village had to be what they were nearing, and when they entered a stand of woods and everyone began to dismount, Jovvi discovered she was right.

"We're goin' to sneak up on the village ahead on foot, and see what there is to see," Vallant said once everyone in their Blending and link groups was gathered around. "At the rate those invaders are movin', we need to be sure we don't ride right into the middle of them."

Everyone agreed that that was the wisest thing to do, and a moment later they were all trying to walk as quietly as possible. The woods thinned rather quickly, and when they reached the last of the trees they all stopped to stare. The village they were looking for wasn't that far ahead, and even from where they stood they could hear the sounds of what seemed like battle.

Once again, it appeared that the invaders had reached a place ahead of them . . .

# TWELVE

As soon as Lorand heard the sounds of what seemed to be fighting, he stretched out his senses as far as they would go. The fringes of the village were close enough to be seen from the woods they stood in, so he found what he'd feared he would rather quickly.

"People are hurt and dying over there," he said into what seemed like a shocked silence. "Instead of just standing around here, why aren't we over there seeing what we can do?"

"We're about to do just that, Lorand," Vallant answered at once, his tone soothing. "You assembly members can take your Blendin's in first, and we'll be right behind you. Let's get goin' before there's nothin' left for us to save."

The Gracelians were definitely nervous, but none of them refused to Blend. A moment later Jovvi initiated their own Blending, and the Lorand entity looked about himself. Those flesh forms called link groups stood ready to lend strength, but they also stood guard over the Lorand entity's own flesh forms. The lesser entity of those flesh forms accompanying the Lorand entity's flesh forms was also present, a shining presence of strength a good deal more supportive than the four entities ahead.

Those four entities which led the way toward the disturbance among the dwellings were puny indeed, not simply in strength but in arrangement as well. The bonds holding the entities *as* entities were frail and almost tenuous, weakening the entities to the point of their having no idea how badly they fared. These four were seriously crippled entities, making it no wonder that the Lorand entity and his lesser follower were needed.

The crippled entities reached the scene of disaster a bare moment before the Lorand entity, at which time they all hesitated. Odd-looking flesh forms were moving about among the terrified flesh forms of the dwellings, slowly and calmly ending each dwelling flesh form as it was reached. The odd-looking flesh forms carried long lengths of sharpened metal, and although there were less than two dozen of them, the dwelling flesh forms seemed unable to resist them.

Three of the crippled entities attempted to halt the odd-looking flesh forms, and then the fourth added its own efforts. All, however, were unsuccessful, as each of the odd-looking flesh forms was covered with an aura of protection. It took a moment for the Lorand entity to recall the details surrounding auras of protection, but then the memories were in reach.

A Blending entity with sufficient strength was able to generate an aura of protection about a large number of flesh forms. Once the auras were established, they were sustained by the power of the flesh forms themselves. The strength of the aura reflected the strength of the entity generating it, of course, and could be breached only by an entity of even greater strength.

With these facts in mind, the Lorand entity floated forward and gave the auras his close attention. An entity of great strength had generated these auras, and a brief attempt to negate them showed the Lorand entity that he, himself, had a lesser strength. For that reason he signaled to his associate entity, and the two of them formed echoing boards to increase their strength.

The Lorand entity sent his full power toward his associate entity, which being added its own strength and echoed back what it had received. Each re-echo increased the strength of the sendings, the power flaring back and forth so quickly that it was difficult even for the Lorand entity to follow.

The level of power rose and rose and rose again—and

then it was sufficient for the purpose at hand. The auras surrounding the odd-looking flesh forms were breached and banished, leaving those flesh forms susceptible to being taken over. The Lorand entity felt great curiosity about these odd-looking flesh forms, and many questions would be answered when—

The Lorand entity found itself startled when one of the crippled entities flashed over the odd-looking flesh forms and destroyed them completely as it went. Anger followed immediately that a crippled entity should presume so, and then it was Lorand alone back again, and anger had turned to rage.

"You chaos-taken fool, what have you done?" Lorand demanded, turning toward a Satlan Reesh who had also returned and now sat among his Blendingmates looking completely triumphant. "You idiot, you destroyed them all!"

"Of course I destroyed them," Reesh countered with usual bluster, his satisfaction looking only slightly dented. "In case you've forgotten, that's what we came here to do."

"How many times do you have to be told that you ask questions first?" Vallant shouted, obviously as furious as Lorand felt. "Endin' people can always be done later, *after* you find out whatever you can from them. And since it wasn't you makin' it possible to end them, you had no right jumpin' in like that!"

"And for your information, those people weren't acting on their own!" Jovvi added to a now-scowling Reesh. "They were under heavy control, and probably had no real idea what they were doing. They were, in effect, innocent, and you murdered them!"

"You lot have a nerve criticizing other people," Reesh huffed with red-faced anger and embarrassment. "Why didn't you tell us before that you had another Blending with you? You let us believe you were all alone, and—"

"What can that possibly have to do with your stupidity?" Tamrissa demanded, her anger so great that there was an almost-visible aura of flames about her. "If we *hadn't* had an associate Blending with us, we wouldn't have been able to breach those auras, you incredible fool. And why *wouldn't* we have another Blending with us? Do you take us for the same sort of mindless idiot that *you* are?"

"Please, recriminations now are useless," Antrie Lorimon said with her own disturbance, her hands held up in front of her. "What's done is done, so it's pointless to—"

"No, it is *not* pointless to weed out incompetents," Rion interrupted, the coldness in his voice a full match to Tamrissa's heat. "That fool first hesitated and hung back when you others went forward to attack, and then he jumped in without thought once the invaders were no longer protected. Thanks to him we now have to look for others of the invaders in order to learn anything at all about them."

"But one thing we know beyond doubt," Naran said, surprising Lorand to a certain extent. "Your Blendings are too weakly linked to be in the least effective against those people. If we hadn't been here, you would have been able to do nothing more than stand back and watch your people die. Isn't that enough to make you think twice about 'your' way of doing things?"

Lorand watched all four of the Gracelians—and their Blendingmates—stiffen where they sat, which was a clear enough answer.

"You're wasting your breath, Naran," Lorand said, making no effort to hide the disgust in his tone. "They'd rather be crippled than go against their marvelous traditions, so there's no sense in expecting anything else. I vote that we go home and gather our own people at the border, then take on the invaders once they're through with these fools. That should give us enough time to—"

"No, you don't understand, so please don't abandon us!" Lorimon blurted, her disturbance having increased to the point where it was more than clear. "We aren't refusing to strengthen our ties to our Blendingmates, we're trying to say that it simply won't work. Our Blendingmates have to defend their positions every month, and we ourselves have to defend our places every three months. What's the sense in strengthening the ties in a Blending that could well have a different composition every few months?"

"There's *no* sense in it, which means your arrangement is another thing that has to change," Jovvi said without hesitation. "Limiting the number of Blendings to fifteen is as foolish as having only one, and mixing talent strength makes it all even worse."

"If you want just fifteen assembly members, then limit that to the fifteen strongest Blendings," Tamrissa said while the Gracelians all looked upset again. "If you'd rather not go by strength, then figure out another way to choose the members but do *something*. The way you do things now is as bad as the way the nobility handled things in our own country, and the only choices you have are change or go under. If you can't bring yourselves to change, then you're wasting *our* time as well as your own."

"But you *don't* understand," Cleemor Gardan objected, fretfulness coloring his disturbance. " 'Strengthening ties' might be fine for the others, but I'm a happily married man. My wife doesn't happen to be part of my Blending, so how am I supposed to explain to her that what I'm doing is for the good of the country? I know how *I'd* feel hearing that from *her,* so how can I expect her to—"

"Oh, for goodness sake, grow up!" Tamrissa interrupted with her usual impatience. "If your wife refuses to understand that strengthening ties *is* for the good of the country, it's only because she doesn't *want* to understand or isn't capable of seeing the truth. And if you'd had proper Blendings to begin with, you wouldn't have gone outside them to look for mates. You're all doing nothing more than making excuses, and I for one am really tired of it."

"Which is another way of sayin' put up or shut up," Vallant concluded while Gardan scowled at Tamrissa. "And don't try talkin' about how sensitive your ladies are. Some of our own ladies had less than an easy time of it in the Blendin' to begin with, but they did what was necessary for the sake of our need. So what's your final decision?"

"This isn't something that can be decided after only a moment or two of discussion," Olskin Dinno put in when the others hesitated visibly. "We've done things our own way for centuries, and that can't be pushed aside by five minutes worth of talk. My associates and I will have to discuss the matter, and then we'll tell you our decision."

"You can do your discussin' when we get back to camp," Vallant said after exchanging glances with Lorand and the rest. "We'll give you until tonight, and then we'll make our own decisions. We still need to find out who these invaders are and what they mean to do—assumin' we stay here to help. If we don't, we'll need the time to assemble our own people against the crossin' of the border."

Lorand saw Reesh begin to tremble where he sat, the reaction certainly brought about by the thought of losing the help of those stronger than he. The man was really pitiful, and had no business being in the forefront of a situation like this one. Trust the Gracelians to consider politics before practicality.

They all got to their feet then, and went to see what could be done to help the surviving villagers. Most of the people were hysterical even if they weren't hurt, and when Vallant was finally able to tell them that they had to get their possessions together and leave, the hysterics started all over again. Even their hosts hadn't seemed to realize that the invaders would send a stronger contingent when the first never returned, which annoyed Lorand thoroughly. It's one thing to have no experience with warfare, quite another to be incapable of logical thought.

Once all the wounded were seen to, the "saviors" were able to retrieve their horses and head back to the camp. Some of the villagers were already on the road, and they made no effort to get out of the group's way. That actually annoyed some of their native "saviors," causing Lorand to shake his head. This alliance they'd made was getting more interesting by the minute. Maybe they'd get lucky and have the Gracelians tell them to get out and mind their own business . . .

Antrie Lorimon was exhausted even before they'd finished their evening meal, but lying down to sleep was out of the question. She and the others hadn't been able to meet and talk earlier because of the large numbers of refugees streaming past and into the camp. Now, thank the Highest Aspect, the refugees were asleep elsewhere and it was possible to think and talk again. Antrie had also wanted to have some private words with Cleemor, but hadn't been able to manage that either. Now, with the others all gathering around, it simply wasn't practical . . .

"You're all fools for letting the Gandistrans take over like that," Thrybin Korge sneered as he took his place near the fire. He'd been released to return to his usual self, and Antrie couldn't help wishing he'd been left under control. "I told you they weren't just innocent neighbors offering help to allies, and now—"

"Stop wasting our time, Thrybin," Antrie snapped, all patience gone with her strength. "If you haven't yet realized that this isn't the time for ambition, you really are too stupid to survive. And we wouldn't have survived either if the Gandistrans hadn't been with us. We might not have died right then, but it would have happened eventually."

"Those people had no right to speak to me as they did," Satlan Reesh complained from the place he'd taken near Korge. "All I did was what any of us would have, what all of us *should* have. It isn't wrong to destroy your enemies before they destroy you."

"It *is* wrong to destroy them before you find out what they know, so close your mouth, Reesh," Olskin Dinno growled from his own place to Korge's right. "Our friend Korge has obviously tickled your need for acceptance again, but since he wasn't there this afternoon his opinions don't count. And we have more important things to discuss than your stupidities and Korge's ambitions."

"I think the first question has to be, Can we believe what the Gandistrans are telling us?" Cleemor said, his manner still as reserved and disturbed as it had been all afternoon. "We all saw how much stronger their Blendings are, but can we believe what they claim the reason for that is?"

"What do you mean, their *Blendings*?" Korge interrupted to ask, glancing daggers at Reesh before looking around at everyone else. "No one told me they had more than one Blending."

"Well, they do," Cleemor answered, faint annoyance now tingeing his tone. "If you hadn't acted like an idiot and gotten yourself excluded from the foray, you would have found out everything along with the rest of us. There are two of them, both incredibly strong, and it took both of them to breach the protection those invaders had. My Blending felt like a ghost next to theirs, but I'd like an answer to my question."

"How *can* we answer your question, except with opinion?" Dinno responded, clearly exasperated. "And my own opinion is that I'm not sure. Our own Blending entities are a good deal older than theirs, but theirs are so much more complete and able. And yet it's possible that the state comes from something other than what they claim it does."

"What good would it do them to lie to us?" Antrie asked, catching Dinno's troubled gaze. "They really do need us to be as strong as possible to save them from having to face the invaders next, but I—just can't—get around the requirement."

"Of course you can't, and you shouldn't have to," Cleemor said with heavy concern, reaching over to pat her hand. "When a male High honors a girl from the general population, he's doing his part to spread his talent as far as possible. Since the same doesn't hold true for a female High, it makes no sense for her to put herself out. And don't think that my Blendingmates aren't as disturbed as I am. A Blending is supposed to require their minds, not their bodies."

"I told you they were all sluts, and their purpose is obvious," Korge said with intense distaste. "They want to drag *us* down to their level, but I for one refuse to be sullied. My Blending is one of the strongest among us, thank you, and that's quite strong enough for me."

"But none of this solves our problem," Antrie pointed out wearily as she accepted a cup of tea from one of the servants. "If we refuse to rearrange our lives the way the Gandistrans are insisting we do, they'll leave us to face those monsters alone. And we *can't* face them alone without being destroyed."

"We also can't rearrange things to please the sluts," Korge stated, obviously having been briefed on *this* point, at least, by Reesh. "Having an unlimited number of Blendings will destroy our method of governing, not to mention set people to rioting. Who would want to be just one High talent among five? Being the major talent in a Blending is what every High dreams of becoming, and if we try to take that dream away from them . . ."

"Then they'll riot, yes, yes, we get the point," Dinno grumbled with a headshake. "What you can't seem to get through *your* head, Korge, is the fact that the people rioting is the least of our concerns. No one can riot if they're dead, and that's what they'll be if we don't stop those invaders. And we can't stop them without the help of the Gandistrans."

"Which we won't have if we don't agree to do things their way," Cleemor said, sounding as though he were ready to explode. "By the Highest Aspect, how did we get cornered in so terrible a place?"

Antrie watched her friend's torment, knowing exactly what it stemmed from. Tenia Gardan, Cleemor's wife, was a very beautiful woman who had Cleemor firmly wrapped around her finger. Tenia played the delicate flower for her husband, delighting in every gift he brought her, but Antrie had noticed that those gifts had quickly stopped being the valueless love tokens they'd been at the start. Tenia was now given nothing but expensive gifts, and her delight had grown accordingly.

But Tenia's delight would disappear completely if Cleemor even thought about lying with the female members of his Blending. The woman would torment Cleemor until his actions became the reason for the end of the world, and it *would* be the end of *his* world. Cleemor wasn't capable of looking at the matter objectively, but he was one of those who had to make a very necessary decision.

Not that the rest of them were any better, Antrie admitted to herself. Thrybin Korge was a narrow-minded bigot with sky-high ambitions, someone who didn't care who he walked over to get where he wanted to be. He'd never give up the prestige of being a major talent, not under any circumstance. Death held no fear for him in this matter, since death would be preferable to being less than important.

Satlan Reesh was a man composed of fears—fear of not being accepted, fear of not being adequate, fear of looking like a fool or a coward. He would be lost among other High talents, no longer of the least importance even for his ability. And as far as lying with him went, what woman of High talent would want to? His Blendingmates associated with him, but only because they had to. If that requirement disappeared . . .

Olskin Dinno was a far more complicated man than she'd realized, but Antrie also knew that the man was currently plagued with doubts. He believed in the way Gracely had been doing things for so long, and simply tossing those methods aside could well be beyond him.

And then there was her, Antrie Lorimon. Antrie grimaced inwardly, finding it only just possible to admit to herself that she *couldn't* lie with her male Blendingmates. She felt a great deal of closeness to them, of course, but she'd been raised to believe that a woman shared the bed of no man but her husband. How was she supposed to ignore those beliefs? How was she supposed to turn her back on the life she'd lived for so long . . . ?

"How did we get cornered in so terrible a place?" Dinno suddenly repeated Cleemor's question, his voice full of bitterness. "We made the mistake of being invaded, that's how. And now that we *have* been invaded, we still have to figure out what to do about it."

"Changing our ways is completely out of the question," Korge stated, surprising no one by his stance. "If we have to face those invaders ourselves, then so be it. Those sluts managed to vanquish the invaders, so I see no reason why we can't do the same. Moral integrity does stand for *something,* after all."

"You're not worried about moral integrity, you're worried about not fulfilling your ambitions," Dinno said to Korge flatly, an unexpectedly calm outburst. "Reesh is worried about having the world know how useless he is, Antrie is worried that she may enjoy lying with men and won't want to stop, and Gardan is worried that his sweet and manipulating wife will cut him off entirely. That leaves me, and what worries *me* most is what our realm will be like if we do go ahead with the changes. It certainly won't be the same realm we've known for so long."

And with that he rose to his feet and walked away, leaving everyone else to stare after him in silence. Antrie felt her cheeks burning from what Dinno had said, but the others were too busy being irate over what they'd heard about themselves. And Dinno's accusation had been so wrong! Antrie had been raised to be a lady, and ladies didn't—

"The fool is just jealous," Cleemor suddenly muttered, apparently speaking more to himself than to the others. "He would love to have a woman like Tenia, and resents the fact that I have her while he doesn't. I'd like to see how fast *he* would risk losing—"

"Am I supposed to believe that no one else in the world is ambitious?" Korge muttered, vindictiveness still clear in his voice. "*His* problem is that he knows he can't do what I can, so he's trying to talk me out of even trying. But he *can't* talk me out of it, not in *this* lifetime. I *will* have what I was meant to have . . ."

When Cleemor got up and walked away with as little notice as Dinno had given, Antrie immediately decided to do the same. She needed the solitary privacy of her tent very badly, and was already in her nightdress before she realized something: They hadn't made the decision the Gandistrans had demanded of them.

"But that probably won't matter," Antrie said to herself softly, the idea immediately making her feel better. "Those people won't abandon us, not when they refused to be left behind in the first place. They were only bluffing, and if we call their bluff in a delicate enough way, they'll accept our decision."

That understanding eased Antrie's mind, and let her go to bed filled with relief instead of fear.

\* \* \*

Zirdon Tal struggled against the ropes tying him, but the struggle did no more good than it had for the last endless days. It was humiliation that forced Zirdon to struggle, that and a continuing sense of disbelief. This couldn't possibly be happening to *him,* not to *HIM*!

But, like a persistent nightmare, it *was* happening to him. First that outrageous female who had somehow stood up to the might of his Blending, and not only stood up to it but also destroyed it. They were all of them talentless now, and his former Blendingmates were still in shock.

Zirdon had also been in shock for a time, refusing to believe that all his marvelous planning had come to naught. He'd left the city with thoughts of being ruler of the empire pleasantly filling his mind, and now he'd been reduced to less than nothing. Forced to serve those who weren't good enough to polish his boots, forced to refrain from doing them harm by tampering with their food . . .

"But tampering with food isn't the only way to do someone harm," Zirdon whispered fiercely to himself. "And not being able to use talent isn't the end of a search for revenge. That madman Syant got *me* to do what he couldn't, and I can use the same method—but a bit more wisely."

Yes, he'd definitely have to be more cautious than Syant had been, but he also had a much better pawn to use. Satlan Reesh wasn't bright enough to know when he was being put to the service of others, a fact easily shown by how quickly the man jumped when that disgusting Korge whistled. Korge was an interloper with no family worth mentioning, but Zirdon, now talentless, still had *his* family.

And his family would be properly furious at what had been done to him. There would be just as much gold as there had ever been to use, and Zirdon meant to spend it to destroy everyone who had dared to try making *him* a servant. And to destroy those outlanders, most especially that horrible female. She and they would die first in a great deal of pain, as slowly and horribly as Zirdon could manage.

The ropes bit into Zirdon's flesh again, making him feel

like a captured animal. In the morning he would be stiff and movement would be painful, but that would not stop those creatures from making him do their disgusting chores. And he felt so exhausted all the time now, not to mention outraged when he was required to serve *peasants*! There was so much he had to get even for, but he would do it, oh, yes, he certainly would . . .

Thrybin Korge pulled closed the flaps of his tent, and only then allowed himself to smile faintly. In spite of a few niggling difficulties, things were proceeding marvelously well. His decision to come along on this . . . venture was the best one he'd ever made.

Thrybin was about to take himself to his sleeping mat when he heard a faint scraping at the tent flaps. He turned back immediately and murmured an invitation to enter, and Restia Hasmit slipped in.

"It's hard to believe, but no one is moving around or watching out there," Restia said with a soft laugh, gliding close to Thrybin. "I thought at least one of the others would be doing the same thing we are."

"Reesh doesn't have the brains or the nerve, and the others can't bear the thought of it," Thrybin answered with a laugh that was just as soft, his hands going to Restia's waist. "I hope you know that I've always wanted to do this, but couldn't bring myself to ask you to go against tradition. But now we have a *reason* to go against tradition that will soon be shared by everyone, and doing it now will simply make us first."

"And first will hopefully also make us best," Restia responded, leaning even closer. "If none of those other Blendings can stand against us, they also can't keep us from taking over and running things right. And my Spirit magic tells me that the outlanders won't interfere once the deed is done."

"They won't interfere because they consider themselves 'honorable' people," Thrybin agreed with a great deal of amusement. "What we do in this realm is our business and none of theirs, they believe, and they're the only ones who might stop us. The others can be forgotten about, each and every one of them."

"Not *all* of them," Restia corrected, her amusement increasing. "You were right to ask me to watch that Tal fool, even though he no longer has any talent to worry about. If I'm not mistaken, the way Tal gazed at Reesh says he means to try using the ugly lump. But how does he expect to get away with it?"

"Tal is an idiot who thinks that having a rich family can cure any ill," Thrybin answered, then began to lead Restia to his sleeping mat. "He'll probably pretend to want Reesh as a friend, intending to offer gold afterward, and doesn't realize that Reesh will never associate with anyone who isn't *important*. Reesh needs that association to feel important himself, and standing is much more important in his mind than gold. Tal no longer *has* that standing, but we'll find it amusing to watch him try to use Reesh."

"I'm continually amazed that you read people so well without Spirit magic," Restia murmured, stroking Thrybin's face with one hand as she returned the brief kiss he gave. "And I think I'm going to really enjoy . . . strengthening our ties. What luck that no one in our Blending is ugly."

"Luck had nothing to do with it," Thrybin answered with a chuckle as he took her down to the sleeping mat with him. "The wise man plans everything in his life, and the clever man makes those plans work properly. We're all the same on the inside, Restia, we just happen to be wearing different bodies. And soon those bodies will be ruling this empire."

"And then we'll make it an empire in fact rather than just in name," Restia agreed, reaching for his tunic as he began to remove hers. "Yes, we *are* all alike on the inside, but I'm glad the same isn't true for our outsides. I'd enjoy this a good deal less if you looked like *me*."

Thrybin laughed his complete agreement, and then he got down to serious enjoyment. His Blendingmates *were* just like him, and together they would make every one of his plans come true. Luckily for him the others were all Middle talents, otherwise they would all try to run things in his place. No, adding other High talents would ruin everything, and Thrybin was *not* going to ruin things.

He was just going to make them much, much better . . .

# THIRTEEN

Honrita Grohl paced back and forth in the sitting room of her small apartment. Until today she'd been oddly content to live in this house she'd been brought to, but after breakfast this morning she'd found the contentment gone. She also realized that she hadn't been doing anything with her newly strengthened talent in Spirit magic, and that realization had shocked her.

"I don't understand why you *haven't* done anything," she said to herself, speaking as sternly as she'd been spoken to as a child. "Did you work that hard in class just to let yourself go back to being a nonentity that everyone walks over? Haven't you earned the right to exercise a talent that belongs to *you* rather than to someone else? Just what is *wrong* with you?"

That demand was very familiar, so familiar that Honrita fell silent the way she had as a child. Back then it was some chore that she hadn't done properly, but the final point was still the same. She hadn't been behaving the way she was supposed to, hadn't acted the way her new position in life demanded—

A knock at the door stopped the self-recrimination, but only for a time. Honrita was really annoyed with herself, and now the annoyance spread to cover whoever was at the door. There *was* such a thing as disturbing someone's privacy, and no reason to let people get away with the intrusion. So she walked over and pulled open the door to see who it was who was bothering her.

"Dama Grohl?" the woman standing outside asked, her expression calm and serene. "I'm Gensie Landros, and my companion is Driffin Codsent. We're here to speak with you for a short while, so may we come in?"

The woman was no taller or larger than Honrita herself, and the man was even a bit smaller. Neither one of them looked terribly important and certainly not imposing, so Honrita sniffed the way so many of her employers had done.

"My time is really too valuable to be wasted on nonsense," Honrita said, looking only at the woman. "If it isn't something important—"

"The matter is very important," the woman interrupted, her smile soothing Honrita's annoyance instantly. "We'll be glad to discuss the situation with you in detail, but not from out here in the hall."

"Come in, then," Honrita found herself inviting, stepping aside with the words. For an instant she considered that very odd, but then all disturbance was swept away behind a feeling of complete happiness and contentment . . .

"I'm hoping that will do it," Driff said to Gensie after the hours of effort they'd put in, wiping sweat from his brow with the back of his hand. "Why don't *you* ever sweat the way I do?"

"My part in this is more passive than yours," Gensie said as she studied the expressionless face of the woman they'd just been working on. "All I have to do is encourage the patient to remember the episodes in his or her life that caused the problem. You're the one who has to heal the damage done by those episodes."

"I don't think I'll ever get over being astounded that it's possible to heal someone's *mind*," Driff told Gensie with a small shake of his head. "Physical healing is a lark compared to this, but mind healing is so . . . so . . ."

"So much more difficult and yet even more satisfying," Gensie finished when his groping produced nothing in the way of words. "We couldn't be there the first time these people were harmed by those around them, but now that we *are* here we can undo the harm. Or at least I hope we undid it. Let's find out. Dama Grohl, how do you feel?"

"Why, I feel fine, thank you," the Grohl woman answered as she suddenly came alive again. "And please call me Honrita. Do we know each other? I can see that you're a High in Spirit magic, but I don't remember having met you."

"I'm Gensie Landros, and my associate is Driffin Codsent," Gensie said with a smile as she gestured to Driff. "We introduced ourselves when we first got here, but you weren't feeling very well at the time so that could be why you don't remember. Driff helped to heal you, so I'm glad to hear that you're feeling better."

"I'm also feeling confused," Honrita admitted openly with something like vulnerability in her tone. "What was wrong with me that I needed to be healed?"

"That might be difficult to explain," Driff answered, since he was the one she'd addressed her question to. "You could say you were hurting from old injuries, but now they shouldn't bother you any longer. You seemed angry when we first got here, and you told us that you didn't want to waste your time with us. Do you remember saying that?"

"Why, yes, I do remember that now," Honrita replied, her brows rising with surprise. "Why in the world would I say something like that?—Oh, yes, I understand now. I felt I was too important to be bothered with trivial distractions."

"*Are* you too important?" Gensie asked, her smile still calm and soothing. "And what makes a visitor at your door trivial?"

"I'm more important than I was, but I'm not really *important,*" Honrita answered with an amused laugh. "I've always seen those people around me who considered themselves important acting like everyone else's business was trivial, so that was the way *I* acted. I hadn't realized that if you really are important, you don't have to act that way to let people know. Others find out about it all on their own."

"Yes, they do," Gensie agreed happily. "What are your plans for once you leave here?"

"Well, I was hoping to get a position teaching one of the starting classes," Honrita said, her brows now drawn together in consideration. "For some reason I seemed to think I could handle an advanced class, but I'm not good enough for that yet. Or strong enough. But I'd really like to help those poor unfortunates like me who have very little self confidence. They need something to make them feel like worthwhile human beings, and I have a need to help them develop that something."

"And we have a need for more teachers with your attitude," Gensie said as she rose from her chair. "We could also use your help here in this house, so would you mind not moving elsewhere for a time? We'd really appreciate that."

"You've changed me in some way," Honrita said as she got to her feet once her visitors were both standing. "I don't really understand what you did, but I'd like to. Is there any chance I can be told some details?"

"As soon as we have a few minutes to spare, we'll try to tell you everything you want to know," Gensie promised the woman. "Do you mind waiting?"

"Yes, but I don't see that I have any choice," Honrita replied with a laugh that surprised Driff. "But I'll find something to occupy my time while I wait, and I'll be glad to help out here in this house. What would you like me to do?"

"You'll need to speak to the resident High in Spirit magic about that," Gensie said with a shrug. "I wasn't given any details, just asked to pass on the request. I'll ask him to stop by and speak to you a bit later."

"Yes, please do," Honrita said as she accompanied them to the door. "And both of you: Thank you for whatever you did. I feel so much . . . cleaner and freer now."

"It was our pleasure," Gensie assured the woman, and then led the way out of the apartment. Driff followed after saying his own good-byes, and once the door closed behind them and they'd moved a short way down the hall, Gensie turned to him. "So, what do you think? Did we do a complete job, or will we have to come back to try again?"

"From where I sat, the woman told the truth every time she spoke," Driff answered with a sigh. "The only question I have is, when did you release her from your control?"

"I released her no more than five minutes after I woke

her," Gensie replied with a wide grin. "We'll have to come back in a few days to make sure, but I think we did it again, Driff. I think the woman is cured."

"I certainly hope so," Driff said, trying to share Gensie's enthusiasm. "Another cure would add nicely to our numbers, but there's *something* . . ."

"Oh, you're just in a dark mood for some reason," Gensie scoffed, dismissing his comment with a brisk gesture. "We both felt that she was telling the truth, so what could be wrong?"

"If I knew, I wouldn't be in such a dark mood," Driff answered dryly. "The woman responded just the way we wanted her to, but there was something different about this one. She *is* our first Spirit magic patient, after all, so maybe we rushed things a bit."

"Just to soothe your vague discomfort, we'll come back in a couple of days to look at her again," Gensie promised with a supporting pat to his arm. "I don't expect that we'll find anything wrong, but if that's what you need to ease your mind, that's what we'll do."

"That *will* make me feel better," Driff admitted as he and Gensie continued along the hall. "I know I'm probably imagining things, and I'll be happier when I find out I'm wrong. But right now I'm going home to change and rest a little. I'll see you tomorrow?"

"Tomorrow right here, same time," Gensie agreed with a smile. "I have to let the resident Highs know we're done for the day, and then I'll be heading home as well. When they erect statues to honor our marvelous work, I'll want to look well rested for the sitting."

Driff shook his head with a laugh as he parted company with Gensie, heading for the front door while she went searching for the people she needed to speak with. Driff really enjoyed working with Gensie, but despite her very strong Spirit magic talent, Driff felt that she wasn't quite in touch with every aspect of the real world. She hadn't grown up as roughly as he had, and that had a lot to do with the matter.

"But maybe we'll find that I'm too suspicious and she was

right all along," Driff murmured to himself as he headed toward the carriage that had brought him to the house. "I won't mind in the least, but I can't get rid of the feeling that *something* isn't quite right . . ."

Driff really was tired, so as soon as the carriage started to move he got as comfortable as possible and let himself drift off into a doze. In a couple of days they'd find out which of them was right . . . And hopefully *he* would turn out to be wrong . . .

Honrita waited until her former visitors left the hall for the stairs, and then she turned and hurried into her bedchamber. It had really tickled her to fool them the way she had, and she laughed softly as she began to pack the things she needed to take with her. As a child she'd watched others pretend to be what they weren't, but she'd never had the nerve to try it herself. For some reason she now had the nerve, and the aftermath of the pretense felt marvelous. She really should have tried this sooner . . .

"But I wasn't *able* to try it sooner, not until they did whatever it was they did to me," she murmured to herself as she packed. "Now that I'm not afraid of my own shadow any longer, I can do anything I please. And I also won't ruin things again by trying to play important. I'll keep what I'm doing very quiet, and then one day I'll really *be* important."

That thought made Honrita smile with anticipation. Her parents had battered at her constantly when she was a child, forcing her into doing nothing but obey them, but she'd only been overwhelmed, not blind. It wasn't possible to miss the fact that those who took what they wanted got to enjoy what they took. Those who sat around like good little tykes waiting to be given things never quite got anything worthwhile.

So Honrita's first move would be to get out of that house, and then she'd be able to start taking. It was fairly clear now that they'd had her under some sort of control, so she had to get out before they tried to reestablish that control. The act she'd put on for her visitors had bought her a small window of opportunity, and if she missed out on using it then shame on her.

It came to Honrita to wonder how she'd managed to fool a High talent in Spirit magic, and her packing was done by the time she came up with something of an answer. The reason Honrita had been so good at pretending was that she'd noticed as a child that the best liars always believed completely whatever they happened to be saying. So while she'd been speaking, *she'd* considered what she said to be perfectly true. It was that belief that had fooled the High talent and, if she should run across another, it would do the same again.

"And now for the start of my *real* new life . . ." Honrita murmured with a happy smile as she picked up her battered old bag and took the first steps toward slipping out of that house.

Tolten Meerk felt foolish knocking at the door of a shack, but simply barging in wouldn't have been very wise. He'd agreed to meet that stranger here, the hard-looking man who had approached him in the Tiger Tavern. Tolten's Middle talent in Earth magic had told him that the man was speaking the truth about wanting a serious talk, so there was nothing to be lost in finding out what the man had to say. If Tolten didn't like what he heard, he could always walk out again . . .

His knock brought an immediate response. The door opened without the squeal of old hinges that he'd expected, and the man who had approached him in the tavern looked out of the narrow opening. When the man saw who had knocked he quickly stepped aside, and Tolten took that as an invitation to enter.

"Thank you for joining us," the man said without inflection as Tolten looked around. The shack was slightly less shabby on the inside, since its walls didn't seem to be peeling as badly as on the outside. In addition to a small cot heaped with dirty linen, there was a table and more than half a dozen chairs scattered around, and someone seemed to have wiped away most of the dust.

"If you'll take a chair with the others, my employer will be here shortly," the man said after Tolten had had a chance to look around. "When he arrives, he'll tell you why you were asked to come."

Tolten had been about to demand explanations *now,* but a glance at the hard-faced man made him change his mind. The man was nothing but a flunky, after all, and probably didn't *have* any answers. It was annoying, but he'd just have to wait. No sense in walking away before he found out what was going on.

So Tolten walked toward one of the chairs, finally letting himself glance at the two other men who were already there and seated. The hard-faced man hadn't used Tolten's name and hadn't tried to make introductions, so these great conspirators probably didn't want their three . . . guests to know each other's names. And that was a shame, because Tolten already *knew* who the other two men were.

Relton Henris sat scowling and looking uncomfortable, probably feeling frustrated that he wasn't able to tell people how many shop owners he represented. Tolten had seen Henris when the man had tried to control the new Seated Blending, but Henris hadn't had any more luck at it than Tolten had had. They'd both been flung off the path leading to true importance, and Henris had even come down a bit in life. Less than a handful of the new shop owners still considered him their representative, but Henris insisted on carrying on as though nothing had changed.

The second man sat quietly with a faint smile curving his lips, looking as though he might be among close friends in their well-appointed home. He was tall and on the thin side, thinner than the last time Tolten had seen him. The man was Holdis Ayl, former second in command of the Guild, and was currently being hunted by every guardsman and official in the city. Tolten had heard it said that Ayl had used up all his followers and was now on his own, but as the newcomer also took a chair he wondered if that rumor was true. Ayl and his people were fanatics, but that didn't also mean they had to be stupid . . .

Nothing in the way of refreshment was offered to Tolten and his fellow conspirators, but at least the wait turned out to be fairly short. Tolten had the time to shift only once in his chair before the door opened, and a man wearing a privacy mask entered. Four more hard-faced men entered behind the masked one, which made Tolten feel very uneasy.

"Good evening, gentlemen, good evening," the man in the privacy mask sang out as he approached the chairs, sounding as though he hadn't a care in the world. "I very much appreciate your accepting my invitation."

"We didn't come for pleasant conversation, or at least *I* didn't," Henris growled, his tone surly. "I was told I would be given a chance to help turn things back the way they were before *those* people were Seated. If you really have a way to do that, I want to hear about it. If you don't, I have better things to do than waste my time."

"If you're that eager to return to things as they were, you may begin by showing me the deference due my station," the newcomer snapped, no longer sounding languid and easygoing. "You will, after all, be due the same deference when *you* become a member of the nobility, or perhaps I should say the *new* nobility. Most of those who claimed the title before these . . . difficulties have forfeited their right to retain those titles."

"You're a member of the former nobility, then?" Ayl asked the man in an offhand way, the faint smile never leaving his face. Tolten sat as silent and thunderstruck as Henris, replaying in his mind what they'd just been told. *They* were to become the new nobility, and those ungrateful upstarts on the throne would be out in the street!

"There's nothing former about *my* position in the nobility," the man in the privacy mask responded to Ayl's question, the words solid with assurance. "I remain as I have always been, and very soon that will be proven to everyone in the empire. In the interim, you all may address me as 'lord.' "

"I may very well give you my approval to use that title," Ayl said with a nod, his faint smile beginning to disturb Tolten. "First I must hear what you have in mind to restore this city to its former condition. Your primary plans, I hope, revolve around destroying those liars on the throne. And I must have some assurances that my people and I will actually receive what we're being promised."

"The word of a born noble is all the assurance anyone could ever need," the man replied smoothly, and again that certainty was in his tone. "What *I* need to know is how many people each of you is able to bring into this effort. You'll be responsible for passing on my orders to them and seeing that those orders are carried out, and all efforts must be coordinated. Are you all willing to cooperate fully?"

"I can bring in at least thirty men," Henris said at once, his eagerness pathetic in Tolten's opinion. "I may even be able to get more, but they won't also become nobles, will they? They'll be working for *me,* so I should be the only one—"

"I can bring in fifty men," Tolten interrupted the disgusting display, forced to stretch the truth a bit. "And, yes, I'm prepared to cooperate fully . . . lord."

"We still haven't heard anything about what your plans entail," Ayl put in, still as quietly unimpressed as he'd been all along. "And in my experience with 'born nobles,' more than their 'word' is required to bind them. I'm waiting to hear what you mean to do and what assurances you can give that my people and I *will* get what we're being promised."

"My plans entail disrupting the pitiful efforts of those now running this city," the noble answered, a faint trace of annoyance to be heard behind the words. "When all of you have decided to commit yourselves fully to this enterprise and have convinced me of your dedication, you'll then be given details. And you haven't yet said how many men *you* expect to supply for our use. If that means you don't have *anyone* . . ."

"I have two hundred and seven men and women dedicated to obeying my every wish," Ayl said when the noble's words trailed off in doubt, his easygoing manner finally turning the least bit stiff. "Now I *will* hear what assurances you're prepared to offer, or I'll leave rather than ask again."

"Contracts of agreement that are legally perfect are now being prepared," the noble responded with a growl, the words clearly being forced out of him. "Does that arrangement meet with your approval, my dear High Lord?"

"For the moment," Ayl replied, his spare body relaxed back into a languid pose and his faint smile restored. "Now I need to know when and where we'll meet again."

"You'll be told when and where we'll meet next when I decide on the matter," the noble answered, his tone having turned cool and distant. "It will definitely be in the next few days, though, so I expect you all to have your people ready to move. You're all to remain here for the next quarter hour, and then you may leave. If you try to leave here before that, my people will know."

The masked noble looked at each of them one last time, and then he turned and strode out of the shack. All of his men, including the one who had greeted the three seated guests, left at the same time, and there was a long moment of silence. Tolten was in the midst of picturing his suddenly beautiful future when Henris made a sound of scorn.

"And where do *you* expect to get fifty men?" Tolten heard, which made him turn his head to find that Henris spoke to *him*. "You know you'll be lucky to find five men, so you only said that to make *me* look bad."

"Don't you worry about how many men I'll get or where I'll find them," Tolten retorted at once, ignoring the heat he could feel in his face. "I still have plenty of people willing to listen to me, even if *you* don't. And don't try to count in those four shopkeepers who still think of you as their representative. The last thing *they* want is a return to the way things were."

"They won't mind going back to the old ways if *they're* the nobles this time," Henris returned with heat, his face darkening with anger. "And they'll all take my orders for the chance, don't you think they won't. I just won't tell them about that contract, is all . . ."

"What fools you two are," Ayl said suddenly, his amusement no longer faint as he looked back and forth between Tolten and Henris. "What good do you expect *contracts* to do you, when that useless lump will control all the courts? If you try to hold the man to what he's promised, that very important *'lord'* will simply have his bullies take you somewhere and no one will ever hear from you again. You won't be made into nobles, you'll just be used, so don't think for a moment that you'll have exactly what you want."

"You think *you* know it all?" Tolten demanded, hating the way Ayl was trying to ruin his dreams. "Even after he's back in power that lord will *need* people to back him up, and I'm going to be one of those people. Are you trying to talk us out of cooperating because you want what's to be had all for yourself? If so, then you're wasting your time. You don't have two hundred people following you any longer, not after so many have been arrested, so how do you expect to make a better showing than me?"

"All my people are still with me, and I don't expect to make any sort of showing," Ayl replied with that same faint smile as he rose to his feet. "I came tonight simply to find out what that leech is up to, and now that I know I'll have to include him in my plans. No one will ever become a noble in this city again without *my* express permission, and neither you nor he have that permission. Waste your time with the fool as you like, but don't expect to get anything out of it but an end to all misery."

And with that Ayl headed for the door. Tolten felt too . . . disturbed to say anything, but Henris yelped.

"Hey, you can't leave yet!" he called after Ayl, his nervousness plain. "We were told to wait fifteen minutes, and the time isn't up yet!"

"Don't be more of a fool than you have to be," Ayl replied, only pausing to glance at Henris. "I can tell easily that all those people are gone, so what would be the purpose in waiting any longer?"

And then Ayl was gone as well, leaving Tolten to sit staring at Henris—who returned the stare. There was another moment of silence between them, and then Tolten shook his head.

"That freak really is completely out of his mind," Tolten said, hating the way his voice wanted to shake. "He truly believes he'll be able to name the next nobility, and he believes he still has all those followers. He's dangerous, and I wish someone would lock him up and then forget where they put him."

"We'll have to tell the lord about him at the next meeting," Henris said with a distracted nod. "I can't see Ayl doing any real damage, not when he has nothing in the way of talent, but it won't hurt to keep our eyes open."

Tolten nodded his agreement, reflecting that he'd rather associate with Henris than with Ayl any day. Henris obviously meant to wait the fifteen minutes just as he did, and if the lord had anyone waiting in hiding to see if they obeyed, then only Ayl would be in trouble.

But Ayl didn't count, especially since the madman didn't intend to come back. Tolten knew he would have no trouble proving himself the better man with only Henris to compete against, and then he, Tolten Meerk, would have the rewards he should have had long before this. Life would finally be worth the living, and Tolten couldn't wait . . .

# FOURTEEN

Idresia Harmis stood in the shadows with Tildis Lammin, one of the boys Driff had rescued from the streets. Tildis had insisted on helping Idresia with her investigations, and the boy—who was rapidly becoming a man—still had too many street connections for Idresia to refuse his help. Although some of those connections now made Idresia nervous about standing there in the dark . . .

"Don't worry, I don't think that night prowler is anywhere around here," Tildis whispered to her, obviously knowing how she felt. "And if the one killing people in alleys *does* show up, just do to him what you did to me and we'll both be fine."

Idresia shook her head just a little, remembering how Tildis had frightened her when he'd grabbed her in the alley outside the Tiger Tavern. She hadn't been able to break his grip on her, so she'd used her Fire magic to put flames under his hands. She'd expected to burn herself as well as him, but for some reason Tildis's hands were the only things that were singed a bit.

"My heart almost stopped when you grabbed me," Idresia murmured back, not joking in the least. "The next time you'd better warn me in words about something like that. If you ever do the same again, I'll send my flames somewhere other than under your hands."

"You have my word," Tildis promised, holding up both of the hands in question. "If that ever happens to you again, it *won't* be me doing it. Ssh! Someone is coming!"

They both moved back even more deeply into the shadows, watching the five men approach the shack they'd followed Tolten Meerk to. One of the five newcomers wore a privacy mask, and the other four reminded Idresia of what guardsmen used to look like before the change in government. One of the guardsmen opened the door to the shack, and all five walked in.

"Now we'll get to see if our idea works," Tildis whispered as the door was closed behind the five men. "They didn't notice any of us as they approached, so there's a good chance they're not touching the power."

Idresia was about to say that if any of the five *was* touching the power, that one couldn't possibly be a Fire magic user. But before she was able to voice the words, other words began to reach them. Tildis and another of Idresia's people with Air magic had done something to some of the air inside the shack, and now those in the shadows outside could hear every word spoken. And Idresia had ten people with her, scattered and hidden all around the shack.

Tildis was properly silent while they listened, and Idresia was grateful for the boy's common sense. Discussing what they heard could be done later, once all the talk was finished. Unfortunately there wasn't a *lot* to hear, only enough to prove that what Driff had been told was true. There *was* a member of the old nobility here in the city, trying to put things back to the way they'd been. If the other two men who had met with the noble were as soured as Tolten Meerk, together they might be able to make some real trouble . . .

When the noble left he had five men with him rather than four, and once they were all out of sight Idresia began to stir. Her people would now be following the noble and his bullies, and hopefully she would soon know exactly where all of them were hiding. Tildis parted his lips to say something, but additional conversation interrupted him. That man who had gotten the noble angry by pressing him . . . He had words with the other two and then left, with one of Idresia's people following carefully. When Idresia finally learned who the man was when one of the others mentioned his name, she felt shocked.

"That was Holdis Ayl," Idresia whispered to Tildis once the last two men fell silent. "He's that renegade Guild man everyone has been searching for. How in the world did they *find* him?"

"They probably left word at one of the drop points he has around the city," Tildis replied with a shrug. "People take messages for him without messing around because they're afraid of him. Now I understand *why* they're afraid."

"But I don't," Idresia said with an annoyed shake of her head. "The man is clearly insane, but he doesn't even have talent to call on. He can be stopped even more easily than a normal person, so why would everyone be so afraid?"

"Mostly because they don't have your personality," Tildis answered with a wry smile. "I know that because *I* don't have it either, that assurance you show and probably also feel. Insanity frightens anyone who can't blithely protect himself against an attack, and that man Ayl will certainly attack even if he isn't cornered. If he *is* cornered . . ."

Tildis let his words trail off, giving Idresia a better idea of why the boy found Ayl so frightening. The madman *would* attack without hesitation, using whatever he possibly could to do damage. Idresia considered that only to be expected, but it was now clear that others didn't look at it the same. Well, that was something to keep in mind . . .

The last two men waited the full fifteen minutes the noble had told them to, and then they also left the shack. Just before they walked out Meerk used the other man's name, so Idresia now knew that the third conspirator was called Henris. Meerk and Henris separated to go different ways, and some of the rest of Idresia's people silently followed.

"Well, I think *we've* had a good night," Tildis said as he stretched widely once the last two men were gone. "If our people don't lose any of that group, we'll know exactly where the Guard can find them."

"I seriously doubt if we'll know where *all* of them are," Idresia disagreed as she did her own stretching. "Our people are bound to lose at least one of that group, if not more. They have strict orders not to let themselves be caught, and to let the person they're following get away if the choice is between continuing or being found out. I just wish I knew *which* of the group will escape."

"That noble will probably be one of them," Tildis said sourly, his good mood having evaporated. "And Ayl will be the second, leaving us with no one but those two useless fools. Do you think Ayl was right when he said the noble would cheat them?"

"I think that that former lord probably cheats everyone he comes in contact with," Idresia said, turning to look at Tildis even though the boy was hard to see. "But don't keep calling him a noble, or you'll be giving him an extra edge over you. We don't *have* nobles in this country any longer, so that man is nothing but a renegade trying to bring back a way of life that should have died years ago. Do you understand what I mean?"

"You mean it's like someone telling me I have to listen to him because he's smarter or more important than me," Tildis said with a slow nod. "If I just take his word for it rather than make him prove what he's saying, then shame on me for letting him get away with telling what could very well be a lie. I'd be throwing away my own chance to be important or show how smart *I* am."

"You've got it," Idresia told him with a pat on the arm, then looked around. "I think it's time we gathered up the others and went back to the warehouse. Everyone will go *there* once they're successful or they fail."

"I think you've missed noticing that we don't *have* a lot of others to gather up," Tildis said, faint amusement in his tone. "Jobry is the only one of our people left besides us, probably because Driff told him to stick with *you*. Jobry's Earth magic talent is almost as strong as Driff's, and Jobry himself is about three times Driff's size."

Idresia made a sound of ridicule over Tildis's last remark, then led the boy toward where Jobry still stood in the shadows. Jobry wasn't three times *anyone's* size, but twice would be only a small exaggeration. The man *was* big and Idresia felt better having him close by, even though Jobry was as sweet as he was big. But most people had no interest in finding out if Jobry really would tear them apart if they did the wrong thing, so just having the big man around stopped most trouble before it could start.

It didn't take long for Idresia and her two male companions to get back to the warehouse. The location was no longer a closely guarded secret, but the warehouse itself *was* still guarded. She and Driff would be moving into a house soon—or so Driff said—but the warehouse was still home to a number of the children they'd rescued. And it was the perfect place for the headquarters of Idresia's spy network.

"Someone's here to see you," Rimdal told Idresia as soon as she and the others had been admitted. "Issini Randos brought someone she says can help, but we don't know him. And besides, the guy is *old*."

"Please, Rim, you think *I'm* old," Idresia returned with a laugh, letting the large boy know she only teased him. "Besides, let's find out what he's offering to do before we decide he can't do it. Hopefully the others will be back here soon, so please keep an eye open for them."

Rimdal nodded his agreement with the engaging grin that made most people overlook his size, so Idresia led the way back to the sitting room she and Driff used when friends came to call. Issini Randos was a long-time friend, but her name was too much like Idresia's for most people's comfort. For that reason they'd taken to calling each other different names when they were together, to cut down on the confusion.

"Har, you're back!" Issini said with a welcoming smile as soon as Idresia entered the room. Tildis had gone off to his own room, but Jobry was still right behind her. "My dear, it's been much too long."

"That isn't *my* fault, Ran," Idresia countered even as her friend rose to exchange hugs. "I'm not the courtesan who's so popular that she has no time for her friends. If you aren't wealthy by now, shame on you."

"There's wealth and there's wealth," Ran said with a fond smile as she examined Idresia. "Gold is a part of it, but so is friendship. And speaking about friends, I'd like you to meet one of mine. He knows there's a noble in the city who's trying to bring back what used to be, and he wants to help stop the man."

"Does he really," Idresia murmured, turning to look at Ran's companion. The man had white hair and a white beard and mustache, so their door guard hadn't been all that wrong to call him old. He also sat bent over a bit, using a staff to hold him up that he obviously also used to help him walk.

But somehow the man looked *too* old, as though he were trying to project the image of frailty. He'd been sitting straight in the chair when Idresia had first walked into the room, but now . . .

"That's a good disguise, Ran," Idresia commented after only a short pause. "Was it your idea or his?"

"I told you she'd be hard to fool, Edmin," Ran said with a laugh as she turned to the man. "For someone with Fire magic, this girl makes a good Spirit magic user."

"And I can confirm the fact that she isn't guessing," the man called Edmin said with amusement as he straightened in the chair again. "It's rather fortunate that your friend is on our side instead of against us."

"It's interesting that you use the word 'us,' " Idresia said at once, before Ran could comment. "If I'm not mistaken, you're speaking with the cultured accents that were used by members of the nobility. Who are you, and what did you expect to gain by coming here?"

"I expected to gain allies," Edmin responded at once before a now-disturbed Ran could intervene. "I'll freely admit that I came back to this city with the intention of doing everything in my power to take over, but now my intentions have changed. The man and his wife who are your real enemies had my father killed, and now my only purpose is to watch those people go down to failure and death. If you'd rather not be part of my effort just say so, and I'll continue alone."

"*Your* effort?" Idresia echoed with a small, mirthless laugh. "If you came here expecting to take over, you can guess again. Even assuming we agree to let you become part of what we're involved with, that's all you'll be: a part of *my* effort. So that seems to be the first thing we have to straighten out. Can you live with *taking* orders rather than giving them?"

"You seem to think that no one in the nobility ever found it necessary to take orders," Edmin replied, the words somewhat stiff. "Yes, I'm able to take orders, but first I must know what obeying will bring me. How soon do you expect to find it possible to locate *our* enemies?"

"My people are currently working on that," Idresia said, still studying the man. "If I decide I can trust and believe you, you'll find out when I do. In the meantime, tell me what I can expect from *your* end of the bargain."

"You can expect to have details about your enemies you would not ordinarily have," Edmin offered, a grim satisfaction behind his words. "The man's name is Sembrin Noll, and his wife's name is Bensia. Her Spirit magic is rather strong, and she uses it to manipulate people into doing as she wants them to. They also have the large number of men we brought into the city, men who are meant to become the new Guard force."

"Men who look just like the *old* Guard force," Idresia commented, realizing that she'd already guessed that part of it. "I saw some of them just a little while ago, and it isn't possible to miss what their purpose is. But if there are a large number of them, they can't all be staying in one place. Do you have any idea where they *are* staying?"

"I've managed to locate three of their hidey-holes," Edmin told her, smiling faintly when he saw her surprise. "Yes, I do still have contacts here in the city, and, yes, I've been using them to look around. If you don't mind the suggestion, having their 'guardsmen' disappear a few at a time ought to do quite a lot to disturb the Nolls."

"It certainly would, but managing that will take some doing," Idresia said, now more bothered than surprised. "If those men aren't breaking any laws, we'll have no concrete reason for telling them to leave. If you start to force possible enemies to leave, you next find yourself doing the same to people you don't quite approve of. As someone who isn't often approved of by others, I'm not very comfortable with starting that kind of effort."

"She's right, Edmin," Ran said when he looked about to argue the point. "Would you like it if *you* were asked to leave the city simply because of what you looked like? You don't have a position and lots of gold to protect you any longer, so think about the matter from a personal point of view."

"You're quite right that I'd dislike an outcome of that sort intensely, but that isn't the main point involved here," Edmin returned, his tone having turned weary. "If we wait for those men to start their depredations, the Nolls will have their position strengthened much too far. If the people are afraid of what Noll's men will do, they'll be much less likely to oppose his demands."

"I'm more concerned about the innocent people who will be hurt, but that just adds to the validity of your argument," Idresia was forced to say with a headshake of annoyance. "We have to stop those men *before* they start to do whatever this Noll wants done, but we can't break the law to accomplish it. Or maybe we *can* break the law, which could well be better than changing the law to suit someone's whim . . ."

"What have you got in mind, Har?" Ran asked, her gaze bright as she looked at Idresia's face. "Your expression says you have *something* in mind, and knowing you it must be really good."

"Those men can't be approached *officially,* but what about unofficially?" Idresia asked slowly, still trying to sort out the idea in her own mind. "If we can convince one of the new Blendings to question those groups, the answers to those questions ought to be enough to convince the Blending to send the men out of the city with orders not to come back again. And if the Blending is acting on its own, they're not likely to make a habit of it. If they try, they'll probably be in trouble with the new government."

"One of the *new* Blendings," Edmin echoed as he shook his head. "You have no idea how odd that sounds to me, and I really do have to ask: how many Blendings *are* there these days?"

"I'm sure *someone* is keeping track, but personally I have no idea," Idresia responded honestly. "The Blendings in charge of running things are Highs, of course, but now there are also Middle Blendings and even one Low Blending, I heard. The Low Blending isn't very strong, but it's able to do things together that its members can't do individually. What we want is one of the new Middle Blendings, I think, one whose members will be open to persuasion. I'm sure Driff will know who that might be."

"Driff has certainly been making a name for himself these days," Ran commented, a faint worry in the expression in her eyes. "He's not only doing all that healing in the clinics, he's also working closely with High members of the government, I'm told. Are you sure he won't decide it's necessary to . . . mention what we want to do to the wrong person?"

"Driff hasn't stopped being loyal and practical, if that's what you're asking," Idresia returned, trying not to sound stiff and insulted. "He might not agree with my idea, but even if he doesn't he would never 'report' me. But I also can't imagine him *not* agreeing, since stopping those people is so necessary. And I'm just about convinced that we'd even have official help if we needed it. Those new government people are different from any I've ever seen."

"Probably because they aren't interested in gathering personal power," Ran said in a very offhand way that likely meant more than Idresia could fathom at the moment. "If you're just there to do a job, you look for the best and most efficient way to do it. If you want to make yourself powerful, you come up with all sorts of rules that you force everyone to obey. The need for personal power ruins things, especially if those things are governments."

"If half of what Driff tells me is true, then we don't have to worry about those people making useless and annoying rules," Idresia assured her guests. "And if they *were* that sort, then neither Driff nor I would be working with them. So . . . when will you be prepared to share those locations, Edmin?"

"As soon as you've decided whether or not to allow me to join you," Edmin replied, the faint smile curving his lips having appeared after Ran had had her say. "Do you have any idea when that will be?"

"Yes, it so happens I do," Idresia replied with a smile of

her own. "I'll tell Driff what's happening, and then I want
him to meet you. Once he does, you'll have our decision.
Can you come back tomorrow at about this time? If Driff
can't make the meeting, I'll send you word."

"I'm definitely not used to dealing with people who don't
consider torment a natural part of the dealing process," Edmin said with a fractionally wider smile as he stood. "Yes,
tomorrow will be fine, and I'll trust to your discretion about
who and where I am. I've been discovering that at certain
levels of life, which I've never before been a part of, trust is
taken for granted because it's rarely if ever violated. That
sort of thing takes quite a lot of getting used to."

"Just be sure you don't get used to it with the wrong people," Idresia found it necessary to say. "The nobility aren't
the only ones who had people among them who couldn't be
trusted, so make sure you consult with Ran—Issini—before
including anyone else in on your secret. And I really do hope
you're sincere about not wanting to bring back what was. I'm
not the only one who would rather die than see that happen."

"So I'm learning," Edmin agreed, his tone more perplexed
than sarcastic. "It was a pleasure to meet you, dear lady, and
I look forward to seeing you again tomorrow. Issini, my
dear, if you would?"

Edmin had gestured toward the door, and by the time
Issini had it opened the man was bent and old again. As he
shuffled out of the room Issini smiled her thanks, and then
they were both gone with the door closed behind them.

"Jobry, did you follow all of that?" Idresia asked, finally
turning to her bodyguard. "And if you did, what do you
think? Was the man telling the truth?"

"He definitely told the truth about how he feels over his
father's death," Jobry answered slowly, obviously considering his words. "I could almost feel how much he hates that
noble we're all after, but as to whether or not he's given up
his own ambitions . . . I think you'd better let Driff answer
that one."

"I was afraid you were going to say that," Idresia responded with a sigh. "Nothing seems to want to work out
the easy way these days . . . All right, my friend, you might

as well go and relax now. And please keep what you heard to yourself."

"Of course," Jobry agreed with a smile, and then he left as well. Men Jobry's size were supposed to be stupid, and Jobry usually did nothing to disabuse people of that notion. But the man was far from stupid, and could be relied on to be circumspect as well.

Which still left Idresia with a problem she couldn't wait to discuss with Driff. That man Edmin thought his father was dead, but unless Idresia had mistaken something Driff had told her, the older man was still alive. Driff had been called to heal a noble who had been stabbed, and the man was now recovering in the palace.

"So how eager will Edmin be to offer his help once he finds out that his father isn't dead?" Idresia murmured, really disturbed as she made her way to the tea service. She'd been so deeply involved in questions without answers that she hadn't even offered tea to her guests, but those guests didn't seem to have noticed. She and Ran were good enough friends that Ran would have *asked* for the tea if she hadn't had other things on her mind. It was clear to Idresia that she wasn't the only one involved who felt disturbed.

"So why isn't Driff back yet?" Idresia murmured again as she filled her cup. "And what about my people who are supposed to be following that noble and the others? Chaos, but I *hate* waiting!"

Which thought didn't do a thing to bring her wait—for anything—to an end . . .

Edmin let the coach driver help the "old man" climb in and seat himself, and then it was Issini's turn. Only a pair of moments after they were both seated and settled the coach began to move, and that was when Issini turned to him.

"What did you really think of my friend?" she asked, clearly trying to keep from sounding intrusive. "Did you really mean that about trusting her?"

"Yes, I really, really meant it," Edmin answered with a smile, surprising himself by actually teasing Issini. "I couldn't help but notice that your friend doesn't care for nobles at all, but in spite of that she treated me as though I were simply a stranger who had yet to prove himself. That she clearly means to allow me the *chance* to prove myself is rather impressive."

"Why do you consider that impressive?" Issini asked, her brows raised in surprise. "I had the feeling you expected her to . . . act differently."

"Do you mean I expected her to be overwhelmed with who and what I was and to begin bowing and scraping?" Edmin put with even more inner amusement. "Yes, it so happens I did expect something like that, along with wheedling for gold and hidden resentments that weren't all that well hidden. Your friend didn't even begin to feel those things, and she spoke the truth when she said she would not betray me. She *was* disturbed, but I would have been surprised if she hadn't been. Other than that, she handled the situation admirably."

*Which came as a great surprise to me,* Edmin refrained from adding aloud as Issini said something about how glad she was that everything had worked out right. Edmin had been expecting dull, unintelligent, furtive little people who were hiding in that warehouse. Instead he'd found an efficient organization merely using the warehouse as a handy headquarters, an organization run by an impressive woman.

Edmin had expected to be able to take over the group easily, but the woman called Idresia had put a stop to *that* idea with very little effort. She hadn't tried to defend her supposed right to run things, she'd simply stated how matters would proceed and let it go at that. She exuded an air of competence that only a very few of the more powerful members of Edmin's former class had been able to match, and Edmin found himself fascinated. He'd never dreamed that the lower classes would produce such a leader who was also a woman, and couldn't help but wonder what other surprises his new associations would bring him.

And, most of all, he wondered if there might be *some* way for him to meet Idresia again tomorrow *without* looking like a frail old man . . .

# FIFTEEN

Driffin Codsent had the carriage drop him off a few blocks from the warehouse and then he walked the rest of the way. In a matter of days he and Idresia would be moving to that house he'd found, but Idresia still meant to use the warehouse as a base of operations. That meant it would do no harm to continue being circumspect about the place, to protect Idresia if for no other reason.

Rimdal was the door guard on duty, and Driff nodded to the large boy before continuing on to his and Idresia's private quarters. If she hadn't been in, Rimdal would have said so. That meant Driff expected to be greeted by Idresia, but not in the way it actually happened.

"Driff, where have you been?" Idresia said as soon as she saw him, sounding more upset than angry. "I've been waiting and waiting and waiting . . ."

"Idresia, what's wrong?" Driff asked at once as he put his arms around her. "You're more agitated than I've ever seen you to be, so tell me what's happened."

"It isn't anything really bad, at least not yet," Idresia quickly assured him with a brief smile and a pat on the arm. "I'm still waiting for my people to report back, and that on top of this—"

Her words cut off as she shook her head hard, and then she took a deep breath.

"You also don't know why I'm waiting for my people to report back, so let's see if I can relearn how to speak and act coherently," she said with obvious self-annoyance. "You sit down and I'll get you a cup of tea, and then I'll start from the beginning."

The sudden display of brisk efficiency was more like the Idresia he knew, so Driff took a seat as she'd requested, and then he listened to a recital of the matter she'd been involved with. His brows went up rather quickly, and when she reached the part about sending her people after those who had attended the meeting he had to comment.

"No wonder the waiting has been making you jump around like a crazy person," Driff exclaimed, seriously impressed. "You actually found the renegade noble, a number of his men, two pawns he means to use, and Holdis Ayl! If your people are able to follow the noble and Ayl, you can hand them both over to the temporary ruling Blending tied up in ribbons. If they don't name you woman of the century, I don't know them nearly as well as I think I do."

"That's only part of the story," Idresia returned, surprisingly looking disturbed rather than delighted. "When I got back here I had a visitor waiting, and that visitor was another noble who had come into the city with the ones we're hunting. He told me he wants to help hunt down those others, because they had his father killed."

Driff opened his mouth to say he didn't understand, but then various pieces of information returned to his memory.

"That noble I healed, the one who had been knifed," Driff said slowly as he stared at Idresia. "Can *that* be who the man's father is?"

"I had no way of checking, but I'm sure of it," Idresia returned, giving him a quick, warm smile for understanding so quickly. "The man wants revenge against the people who killed his father, but his father isn't dead. He has the locations of three of the places their hired bullies are staying, men who will be used to hurt people and disrupt everything in the city. If we tell Edmin that his father is still alive, will he still be so eager to betray someone who's really one of his own? But if we don't tell him the truth, what will he do when he eventually finds out? I don't know what to *do*, Driff, and it's driving me crazy!"

"I can see your problem now," Driff admitted ruefully as he patted her hand. "But what's this about the location of hired bullies? It won't do us any good to know where the men are, not when we can't arrest them or throw them out of the city before they actually make trouble."

"We can't wait for those men to make trouble, not when innocent people will be hurt," Idresia denied with a shake of her head. "That's something else I needed to talk to you about, so let's do it now. Do you think you can talk one of the newer Middle Blendings into helping us to get rid of those men? We don't have to arrest them or charge them with anything, all we need to do is make sure they leave and don't come back as long as they still want to hurt people. And if any of them want to change sides and work *with* us, we can let *those* men stay."

"I'm glad you're not a High talent interested in taking over the city," Driff commented as he blinked at Idresia. "If you were, I think even the Seated Blending would be in trouble . . . Idresia, I don't know what to tell you. I can let *myself* be talked into going along with your schemes, but luring in an innocent Blending . . . I'll have to think about that for a while."

"Don't think about it *too* long," Idresia cautioned with a sigh. "If those men start to make trouble before we chase them away, we'll be directly responsible for every bit of harm done. If you can stop troublemakers and don't—"

"I know, I know," Driff interrupted wearily, holding up one hand. "If you can stop troublemakers and don't, you're responsible for whatever happens afterward. You may recall that *I'm* the one who first told you that saying."

"Then you ought to know I'm not just making it up to hurry you," Idresia returned mildly, then her expression changed. "But what are we going to do about that noble Edmin? I gave him my word that we would not betray him to the authorities, but I refused to commit myself beyond that until *you* were available to meet him. He'll be coming back tomorrow at the same time he came tonight."

"Then I'll have to be here to meet him," Driff said with a thoughtful nod. "If he's serious about having given up his plans to reinstate the nobility and actively helps us catch his former friends, then we'll owe him our discretion about his presence here in the city. If he's lying to us, we won't owe him anything."

"Now, that's something else," Idresia said, as if just remembering the point. "He doesn't want the people he calls the Nolls arrested right away. He wants to make them suffer by ruining their plans first, and only then will he be willing to see them arrested. Since he believes they had his father killed, I can understand why he wants to do it that way."

"If we can find out where the Nolls are and can keep a watch on them, that man's idea might be the best way to handle the matter," Driff said, the idea coming to him as something of a surprise. "If we just walk in and arrest the Nolls, other renegade nobles might get the idea that our finding the Nolls was just bad luck and that *they* could well be successful. If we 'play' with the Nolls for a bit before reeling them in, the lesson will be much sharper for anyone who happens to be watching."

"So now we just have the question of whether or not Edmin is sincere," Idresia said after sipping at her tea. "That question can't be answered until tomorrow night, so now I'm back to waiting for some word from my people. I know they won't *all* be successful, but I'm afraid to wonder which of them will fail."

"Looks like you won't have to wonder long," Driff commented when a knock came at the door. "That could be the first of them now."

Idresia was out of her seat and on the way to the door so fast that Driff would have blinked in startlement if he hadn't been expecting the speed. When she reached the door she yanked it open and stepped outside, then spent a few moments talking to whoever was out there. When she came back in again, her expression wavered between elation and annoyance.

"Planning ahead really does pay," she remarked as she returned to her chair and tea. "I had my people arranged in pairs, with the first of the pair doing the immediate following of the person or people they were assigned to. The second came a short distance behind the first, leading two horses. If the assigned quarry stayed on foot, so did the followers; if the quarry took to a coach or horseback, the followers mounted up."

"Are you getting ready to say that *all* of your people were successful?" Driff asked to cut short the tangential explanation. "If so, please just get it said."

"My people were *almost* completely successful," Idresia allowed, vexation shadowing her pleasure. "Those five bullies stayed with the noble, and even followed his coach when it turned into the drive of a house. It looks like they're 'bullies on tap' so to speak, and not lodged elsewhere. Meerk and that other man who met with the noble simply went to their respective homes, which aren't hidden in any way. The only one my people lost sight of before he reached a destination was Ayl."

"Wouldn't you know it," Driff grumbled, keeping himself from using stronger language only by sheer willpower. "Ayl is probably the most dangerous one of all, and not just because he's insane. He's also clever and creative, two things you never want your enemy to be. So how did your people lose him?"

"Ayl is apparently the sort to take precautions automatically," Idresia answered in her own grumble. "He didn't seem to know he was being followed, my man said, but first he walked through busy neighborhoods, and then through a deserted one. My man had to hang back to keep from being seen, and during one of those times Ayl disappeared. My man tried to find him again, but it was just no use. The only thing that strikes me as significant is the fact that my man lost him not far from the palace."

"And that makes a disturbing kind of sense," Driff agreed with raised brows. "Those who are looking for Ayl are probably assuming he would stay as far away from the palace as possible. Since most of his attempts against the Seated Blending were made at the palace, an ordinary leader *would* put a lot of distance between himself and where his people struck. They should have remembered that Ayl isn't ordinary."

"You know, I think I was almost hoping that my people would lose the noble," Idresia commented with a vague shake of her head. "Edmin wanted to know if I'd located Noll as yet, and I was able to tell him honestly that I hadn't. Even if we decide to trust Edmin and work with him, I'm not sure I'll be comfortable telling him where Noll is."

"Well, we know the man won't try to kill Noll, at least not at first," Driff reminded her. "If he wants his revenge done right, he has to wait while the Nolls' plans are ruined. And Edmin may decide against killing the Nolls at all when he finds out that his father is still alive."

"There are too many twists and turns in this whole situation to make me even a small bit happy," Idresia said, this time with a headshake that was definitely more firm. "If only Issini hadn't brought that man here . . . But since she knows about everything that goes on in this city and she and I are friends, where else would she bring him? He has to mean a lot to her . . ."

Driff watched Idresia float off into deeper thought, and couldn't keep from smiling to himself. She was obviously doing a marvelous job as head of his "secret" spy network, and would certainly continue to do the same. Driff's only problem with her efforts was that she'd put him very much on the spot with one of her requests.

The smile faded as Driff sighed, only just keeping himself from shaking his head. Idresia wanted him to recruit one of the new Middle Blendings to their cause, but doing that would be unfair to the people in the Blending he chose. If something went wrong *they* would be in the most trouble, a good deal more than him or Idresia. Individuals who broke the law might find themselves forgiven, but there would be no forgiveness for any Blending that erred.

So dragging in a new Blending was out, but those men did have to be seen to before they hurt innocent people. It surprised Driff to realize that he already knew what he'd have to do, and that was talk to one or more members of the Blending now running the city. It was downright shocking that *he* would do such a thing, the man who had been an out-law for so long. Going running to the authorities was for the law-abiding, not for someone like him . . .

But Driff was no longer *like* "him," no longer like what he used to be. He'd found himself fitting in incredibly well with those he'd never dreamed he'd ever associate with even tan-gentially. "Authority" was a concept he had never been will-ing to accept, but now he worked hand in glove with the current authorities and, what's more, he enjoyed it!

*That has to be because they've changed the meaning of the word "authority,"* Driff thought as he sipped his tea. *It used to mean those people who were in charge of cheating the most they could out of ordinary citizens, but that isn't what "authority" means now. Now the concept means tak-ing responsibility for what you do, and making an effort to help rather than harm. And taking risks that it isn't fair to ask others to take . . .*

But that part of it Driff carefully kept to himself. Tomor-row he'd have to ask some very direct questions without supplying any more information than he could get away with. If anyone tried to force him to tell more, he'd know that the people he thought of as friends were no such thing. But he didn't expect that to happen . . . Or he *hoped* it wouldn't happen . . .

Wilant Gorl looked up from his desk when Oplis Hen-den, Wilant's Air magic Blendingmate, stepped into the room after a brief knock on the door. Wilant felt annoyed that Oplis hadn't waited for permission to enter, but one look at Oplis's delighted expression banished Wilant's an-noyance.

"Don't tell me that something has gone right for a change," Wilant commented as he sat back to study Oplis. "I may not be strong enough to take news like that."

"*You* may not be strong enough, but *I* certainly am," Oplis returned at once with a grin, joining in the mutual teasing. "Now that we've reached the point where we can kid our-selves into believing we almost know what we're doing, we have to learn how to accept *good* news. Like the fact that my unofficial spy network has accomplished more than the entire Guard force."

"You're joking," Wilant said with brows high, finding the same delight that Oplis showed. "You can't mean they've tracked down our intruder nobles."

"I *can* mean it and I do," Oplis said with a laugh. "But I promised Driff that he could discuss the matter with more than one of us, because he seems to have something in mind. He's just outside . . ."

"Then bring him in," Wilant said at once, no longer bothered about intrusion. News like this wasn't intrusive, it was sent by the Highest Aspect . . . "Good morning, Driff. I understand you have some good news for us."

"I think you'd better wait a short while before deciding that," Driff answered, the small man having stopped next to Oplis. "My people *have* located the renegade noble, but there's more involved here than you may realize. Do you know that they've brought in more than three hundred men that they expect to turn into a new Guard force like the one we *used* to have?"

"*How* many?" Wilant demanded, all delight suddenly gone. "I suppose I knew they would have *some* men with them, but more than three hundred! Where are they hiding so many?"

"They're scattered around in various-sized groups, and we don't have all the locations yet," Driff said, going to the chair Wilant waved him into without seeming to notice what he was doing. "We'll hopefully have the locations of three of the groups later today, but unless your Blending or one of the other High Blendings running things is willing to break the law, knowing where the men are won't do us any good."

Wilant opened his mouth to ask what Driff was talking about, but sudden understanding came before the words.

"You mean we can't throw them out of the city legally if they haven't made trouble yet," Wilant said instead, hating the frustration he suddenly felt. "We have to sit back and wait for innocent people to be crippled or killed before we can do anything. I understand the need for that law and agree with it fully, and also find it terrible that not everyone sees it the same. We can discuss later exactly *who* doesn't see it the same, and I'll be giving you the information so you'll know who to stay away from. But in the meanwhile, was there anything else you wanted to talk about?"

"Yes, there *are* a couple of other things you need to know," Driff answered, his previous stiffness melting away like magic. "Your renegade noble has been trying to recruit local malcontents to help with his plans, and so far he's talked two men into joining his effort. One of them is Tolten Meerk, and the other is Relton Henris."

"What a surprise hearing *those* two names," Wilant observed as he sat back in his chair. "What did the renegade offer them to cooperate with him?"

"They expect to be made nobles once the renegade has taken over," Driff answered, adding a rueful headshake. "I love people who are completely against a ruling class—unless they happen to be members of that ruling class. But those two weren't the only ones who showed up at the meeting the renegade arranged. The third person was Holdis Ayl."

"What?" Wilant yelped, almost storming to his feet. "We have every High talent in this city looking for Ayl, and the *renegade* finds him? How in the name of chaos did he manage *that*, and what have they agreed to do together?"

"I understand that there are various message drops around the city that Ayl uses," Driff supplied, the tone of the man's voice more soothing than it had been. "People are afraid of Ayl, so they take messages for him and don't mention the fact to anyone. But don't worry about Ayl and the renegade getting together. Ayl went to the meeting because he was curious, not because he means to team up with anyone. He still has his crazy ideas, and doesn't seem ready to give them up."

"I'd love to ask how you know all that, but I think I'm better off not having the answer," Wilant said after staring at Driff for a moment. "It's too bad you weren't able to find out *Ayl's* location as well as the renegade's. Or did our luck suddenly turn more than sweet . . . ?"

Wilant found himself seriously hoping as the idea came to him, but Driff's headshake killed the hope quickly.

"Some of our people *tried* to follow Ayl, but the man apparently covers his tracks even when he has no idea he's being followed." Driff's expression now showed annoyance and frustration that mirrored Wilant's own. "One thing we do believe we've learned though . . . My people lost Ayl in a neighborhood that's very close to this palace. The madman must be getting a lot of pleasure out of living almost under your noses."

"That has to be why we haven't been able to find him!" Oplis suddenly spoke up, the first words he'd said since Driff had come in. "All the searchers assumed he'd be as far away from here as he could get."

"So living under our noses was the safest thing Ayl could decide to do," Wilant agreed with a slow nod. "Now that we know better than to look for him on the other side of the city, we might actually track him down . . . Driff, do you have any idea how much help you've been to us? Without you we'd probably still be floundering around trying to get started. I know you'll hate hearing this, but you've just earned another bonus in gold."

"That bonus will go to the people who did the actual work here, so I don't hate the idea at all," Driff said with a faintly embarrassed laugh. "I didn't do *any* of the work; I'm just the one telling you about it. But the story isn't quite finished yet."

Wilant's brows rose when he saw that the amusement had left Driff, but he refused to voice the sigh he felt on the inside.

"All right, I'll admit we're due some bad news after all the good." Wilant didn't quite grudge the concession, but it was a near thing. "What is it that you haven't mentioned yet?"

"It's . . . not exactly bad news," Driff got out, obviously choosing his words carefully. "I need to ask a question without going into details about *why* I'm asking. Do you think you can give me an answer without first hearing anything else?"

"I'd have to know what the question was first," Wilant said at once, refusing to lie to this man who had given them so much capable and varied help. "But if it's a question I can answer without knowing the background details, a straight answer is the least I owe you."

"All right, here goes," Driff said after taking a deep breath and letting it out slowly. "The confidence involved isn't mine, so it isn't for me to break it . . . If someone who used to be a noble works *with* us to bring down the renegade and his family and 'guardsmen,' can we promise the former noble that he'll be safe from being arrested and sent to the Astindans? Assuming he makes no trouble for the new government, that is."

"With that last provision firmly in place, I'd say the answer is yes," Wilant said after exchanging a glance with Oplis. "My Blendingmate here obviously agrees with me, and I'm certain the rest of our Blending will also agree. If someone makes a voluntary effort to repair some of the damage he's done, that calls for encouragement so more will follow the example. But how sure are you that this former noble means what he says?"

"I'm not sure at all because I haven't met the man yet," Driff answered, the look in his eyes faintly troubled. "I do know that the reason he's offered his help is a legitimate one, but—He's under a false impression, and once he learns the truth he could well change his mind about helping."

"If he does, then none of us will owe him anything," Wilant pointed out. "Can you tell me now who he is and what false impression he's under?"

"He's a man who thinks the renegade—*renegades*—had his father killed," Driff supplied after a very brief hesitation. "He wants to ruin their plans and destroy all their hopes before going after them personally, and I agree about ruining their plans—after we first deprive them of hired men who can do damage. Other members of the former nobility could well be watching, and we want them to see these renegades humiliated before they're crushed."

"To take away all interest in *their* trying the same thing," Wilant mused, liking the idea. "Yes, it ought to save us some future trouble . . . But there's something I don't understand. You said your man *thinks* the renegades had his father killed. How can you possibly know that they didn't?"

"I know because I'm the one who saved his father's life," Driff answered ruefully. "You do remember that noble who was knifed, the one you had moved here to the palace after I healed him? We're certain that that noble is the father the man is talking about."

"Embisson Ruhl's son Edmin?" Wilant couldn't keep from blurting, suddenly feeling very pained. "That man was almost as powerful as his father, I'm told, and also almost as influential. The only difference was that he hadn't been at it as long as his father. And *that's* the man you want us to pardon?"

"Assuming he's telling the truth about now wanting to help and no longer being interested in returning to power," Driff confirmed with a definite nod. "Why would pardoning be all right for someone else, but not acceptable for him? Do you know about some horrible incident involving innocent people that he's responsible for causing?"

Wilant was about to say he knew of no such incident but that that didn't matter, when it suddenly struck him that it *did* matter.

"You've made a very good point," Wilant conceded instead with a sigh. "There were people in the town I grew up in who insisted I couldn't be trusted because I'd become the leader of the rest of the kids my age. I had 'power' they didn't, so I simply couldn't be trusted. It made no difference to them that I'd become a leader because I didn't mind making decisions and the other kids did. In their minds I couldn't be trusted . . . All right. If Ruhl keeps to his word, so will we. You have *my* word on that."

"Which is more than good enough for me," Driff answered with a smile as he stood. "Now all I need to know is which Blending I'm to stay away from, and then you can go back to what you were doing before I interrupted."

"Oh, yes, I nearly forgot about that," Wilant said, swallowing a laugh. "I really do hate to name names, so I'll ask Oplis to *show* you the Blending you're to stay away from. If Oplis goes so far as to actually introduce you to the Blending members, that should make it even easier for you to remember who you have to stay away from. And don't forget to tell them when you would have needed them if you hadn't been warned to stay away from them."

"I certainly will," Driff agreed solemnly while Oplis shook his head at Wilant ridiculingly. Oplis was completely open and honest about everything he did, and refused to see that there were times to be circumspect about certain actions. As people standing in for the Seated Blending, they had no right to change or disobey any of the laws. If Jovvi and Lorand and the rest decided to change things, then that was *their* business. All Wilant and his people could do was *appear* innocently law-abiding.

And as Wilant watched Oplis and Driff leave, he hoped that he hadn't made a bad mistake. Edmin Ruhl would make a much more formidable opponent than the Nolls, even without all those heavies meant to start trouble and push people around. But one thing was for certain: he'd have to put a special guard on Embisson Ruhl now . . .

# Sixteen

"Well, that didn't take very long," Bensia observed with surprise as Sembrin entered the sitting room. She'd been reading, Sembrin noticed, but now her attention had been diverted. "Didn't your meeting with the peasants go as well as it should have?"

"For the most part it went exactly as expected," Sembrin answered, letting his annoyance take him over to the sideboard so that he might fill a glass with wine. "Two of those stupid peasants are already competing for my approval, but that third . . . A pity he's the one with more followers than the other two put together."

"Why is it a pity?" Bensia asked, amusement in her tone. "If the peasant lacks the proper attitude, the children can change the lack easily enough. You'll just take them with you to the next meeting."

"And use what as a reason for my children being with me?" Sembrin demanded as he turned to look directly at Bensia. "Even the first two peasants would be suspicious over *that,* and the third would certainly know I was up to something. The man is suspicious and demanding enough now; if he ever gets the idea that I mean to manipulate him, he'll be gone so fast that everyone will think he disappeared."

"The children don't have to show themselves until after they have the peasant under control," Bensia countered, her tone suddenly stiff. "And I would appreciate your not speaking to me like that again. I'm not a peasant you may be as

194

rude to as you please, and if something is disturbing you then you might do me the favor of discussing whatever it is."

Sembrin had had no intention of mentioning what really disturbed him, but suddenly he felt an overwhelming urge to put his feelings into words.

"After meeting those peasants, I'm . . . suddenly filled with doubt about how successful we'll be," Sembrin put forward gropingly after sipping at his wine. "After combing this city, our people were able to locate only three men who were unhappy with the new government and had any sort of following. Two of those three are the sort to talk rather than do, I think, and the third won't commit his followers without solid guarantees proving they'll get what I've promised. The first two had to be reminded to show me proper respect, and the third never did show respect. This isn't the same city we left, Bensia, and the differences make all the . . . difference."

"Nonsense, Sembrin, nonsense," Bensia disagreed with a smile and then an encouraging laugh. "You're simply tired, and that's why you feel discouraged. You've forgotten that as soon as the other peasants see how well your chosen three do, they'll begin to flock to our cause in order to do equally as well. When do you plan on seeing those three again?"

"I told them I'd send word, but I expect to contact them in the next day or two," Sembrin answered, for some reason feeling less encouraged than usual when Bensia spoke to him. "We really can't afford to waste any more time getting started with our campaign."

"Of course we can't, and that must be another thing bothering you," Bensia said with very clear sympathy. "We've really been doing very little to advance ourselves, and that has to be more than trying for you. But we're getting started now, and when you see those men again you'll take enough gold with you to widen their eyes and make them catch their breath. Having gold to spend will put the fire of enthusiasm into them, and their spending will recruit more followers for us than anything they could possibly say."

"Of course it will," Sembrin agreed in a murmur, not quite believing the assurance he spoke. He'd only gotten a glimpse of parts of the city he used to know rather well, but all of those parts looked different now. Peasants walked the streets happily and with confidence, run-down areas were either deserted or being renovated, beggars were gone from the places they'd squatted in for ages, and there seemed to be an overall air of satisfaction pervading the city. Even if his lackeys started to spend gold, how many of the city's people would leave their satisfaction to bring back what used to be?

"I think we'll do well changing the subject now," Bensia announced, her tone still bright and full of happy enthusiasm. "I asked the children to speak to cousin Rimen, a conversation that will have a double purpose. To begin with they'll find out for certain what he's been doing with his time, and if it's something that could put us in danger they'll make sure he *stops* doing it. That should satisfy the both of us, and will make one less worry for you to shoulder."

Sembrin parted his lips to ask when the children were scheduled to speak to Rimen, but the words were interrupted by the arrival of the children themselves. Travin, their eldest son, walked in beside Wesdin, his brother. The two boys were almost seventeen and almost sixteen, respectively, and both had Sembrin's height and their mother's good looks in male form.

The girls, however, were easily as beautiful as their mother. Solthia at fourteen and Liseria at thirteen both moved and behaved as though they were grown women, and both had many of their mother's mannerisms. It was more difficult for Sembrin to see any part of himself in the girls, just as though he hadn't been involved in their formation. But that was perfectly ridiculous, of course . . .

"Ah, children, your father and I were just talking about you," Bensia said with the enjoyment she always showed when looking at her offspring. "We'd like to know what you learned and did when you got together with cousin Rimen."

"Cousin Rimen had already left his apartment by the time we got there," Solthia answered for all of them, her gesture of dismissal the mirror image of Bensia's. "He sent for a meal when he awoke, but we didn't expect him to swallow it whole and then disappear. Tomorrow we'll have to visit him *before* the meal arrives."

"That's assuming he doesn't do something to get himself arrested *tonight*," Sembrin interjected with annoyance as Bensia was about to agree with what was actually the children's failure. "Do you really *want* him to lead those peasants to our door?"

"Cousin Rimen may be strange, Father, but he's still a noble born, don't forget," Travin put in soothingly with a smile. "Those peasants won't find it possible to put their hands on him, and tomorrow we'll see to the matter to your complete satisfaction. Won't that be acceptable?"

"Of course it will, Travin," Sembrin found himself saying with a matching smile. "Your seeing him tomorrow will be perfectly fine."

Everyone including Bensia smiled at that, and then Bensia began to discuss some planning with the children. Sembrin went back to refill his wineglass, and after the first sip the satisfaction and approval filling him began to fade. Tomorrow was *not* soon enough to take care of the problem Rimen Howser embodied, and even the children's talent wasn't enough to make Sembrin think it was.

Anger over being manipulated by his own children sent Sembrin out of the sitting room, annoyance growing almost as great when he realized that no one noticed his leaving. Bensia and the children were too involved with whatever plans they discussed, plans that had never been mentioned to the man who was supposed to be running that effort. Lately Bensia had gotten sloppy about making sure Sembrin believed *he* was the only one in charge, and it was time to take advantage of that sloppiness.

"While I can still remember that I *want* to take advantage of it," Sembrin muttered as he strode toward the door which led most conveniently to the servants' quarters that had been turned into a barracks. "It isn't hard to figure out now that Bensia makes me change my mind whenever she notices that I'm around. If our men were the sort to take orders from a woman or a bunch of children, she probably would have already disposed of me. I've got to counter her plans, but I also have to be careful doing it . . ."

Stepping outside silenced Sembrin's muttering. The men

he'd had on duty inside the house had been moved outside, a change whose only purpose was to cater to Bensia's preferences. Bensia preferred to think of the world as it used to be, a daydream that was disturbed by the near presence of guardsmen, so the guardsmen had to be moved out of her sight. But that, happily, also moved them out of her hearing . . .

"Were my orders obeyed?" Sembrin asked without preamble when he saw the pair of men on guard. "The man Howser has already left the house, I'm told. Was he missed by those of you who are supposed to be on duty?"

"No, sir, Howser wasn't missed," one of the guards answered, his tone more casually lazy than Sembrin cared for. "Two of our men are following Howser, and if he does anything he shouldn't he won't be coming back again. This time the man took a horse, and the ones following him will bring it back if Howser ends up not being able to do it himself."

"Excellent," Sembrin said with a nod of approval, his mood finally lightening a bit. "Pass the word that I want to know what happened as soon as those men get back—but I want to be informed privately. Where is your commanding officer right now?"

"He *was* out checking with the other groups, but he may be back by now," the same guard responded. "Do you want me to find him for you?"

"No, I'll go myself," Sembrin answered before leaving the guards at their post. The separate building meant to house the servants that this house boasted had proved to be perfect as a barracks for the guardsmen. The leader of this group had turned one of the barracks rooms into an office, and that was where Sembrin found the man.

"How are the rest of the men doing?" Sembrin asked when the man politely rose to his feet at Sembrin's appearance. "Are they ready to move?"

"More than ready, sir," the officer, named Jost Feriun, answered at once. "In fact, they're eager to be out and doing. If we don't make use of them soon, some of them may end up acting on their own."

"And we can't allow that, so we'd best begin to move,"

Sembrin said with a nod as he took a chair in front of Feriun's desk. "I'll want your man to contact those people again and have them meet me tomorrow night in the same place we met tonight. We'll be moving the very next day."

"That's good news, sir," Feriun said as he reclaimed his own chair and made a note on some paper. His dark face now showed a faint smile of satisfaction, and then his dark eyes returned his gaze to Sembrin. "Will we be using all of the men, and if so, how will they be deployed?"

"At first we'll only be using some of the men, but they should enjoy the effort," Sembrin answered after sipping at the wine he'd brought with him. "For the most part they'll be working in pairs, primarily in taverns and inns and eating parlors. The men you'll use will be ones who don't know where we, ourselves, are located. I'm sure you can guess why that is."

"So that if they're captured, they can't betray our location," Feriun answered at once with a shrug. "It's the reason we kept our location secret from the others in the first place. What will the men be doing in pairs?"

"One of each pair will enter one of the places I mentioned, and then the other will join him as though by chance," Sembrin answered. "After they've greeted each other, they'll begin a conversation that will be loud enough for the people near them to hear. One will complain about being badly treated by the new government, and the second will add his own tale of mistreatment. Then they'll discuss 'horror' stories they've heard about others having trouble, and they'll end with the theory that the new government soon plans to stop doing things for ordinary people. After that the government will start to use people the way they meant to do all along, and no one will be able to stop them."

"Yes, that ought to provide some action," Feriun agreed as he made further notes. "But what if the men are challenged to prove what they say?"

"Each pair will have at least one local along with them who will then come forward to support their claims," Sembrin explained. "If no one does challenge them, the local will simply come up to them and say he's noticed the same things. One way or another the complaints will be supported, and shortly after that the three will leave separately to go on to another location."

"And how long will we be doing that?" Feriun asked, raising his eyes again. "It shouldn't be too long before the government people hear about it."

"That's why we'll only be doing it for two days," Sembrin said, pleased that he didn't have to explain *everything* to the man. "By the third day the rumors will have spread all over, and then the men can begin haranguing groups to act before they're no longer *able* to act. We want those people to march on the palace, and the more out of control they are the better it will be. When they break into the palace our men will be right with them, and anyone official that they encounter is to be dealt with immediately.

"Once the palace is cleared, some of our men are to take over standing guard while the rest direct the mobs toward attacking anyone official who happened to be out of the palace during the first attack. We'll strike so fast and decisively that the peasants in charge will be dead before they realize that anything is happening."

"And then we get to quiet the mobs," Feriun said in a way that made Sembrin believe the man really looked forward to that part of the job. "Once all the dust has settled we'll be in charge, and the rabble will be too frightened to try rising again."

"Exactly," Sembrin agreed with a smile. "It's been done before, so we should have no trouble doing it again. Let me know when the messages to the peasants I mean to use are delivered, and we'll add more detail to the plan. At the moment I'll need one of your men to contact some of the people supplying me with information. My informants need to be situated around the city to tell me how well our rumors are working."

"I'll have the man go out at once, sir," Feriun said, and there was new respect in the officer's manner. "Shall I have all of your informants report to you?"

"Yes, but not all at once," Sembrin said, getting to his feet. "Most of them don't know about the others, and I'd like to keep it like that even after we take over. It never hurts to guard your back."

"No, sir, it certainly doesn't," Feriun agreed, again getting to his feet. "I'll have the men report to you as soon as your orders have been carried out."

"Good," Sembrin said with another smile, and then he left the man's office. Some of the informants were very strong supporters of Sembrin's plans, the promise of ennobling making them that supportive. When Sembrin asked two or three of them to secure Puredan for him, they'd get the drug without asking questions. After that, Bensia and her precious children would no longer be a problem, but until then Sembrin would have to stay away from them. If he wrapped himself in making their plans go forward, none of the five would get suspicious. *Hopefully* they would remain unsuspicious . . .

Rimen Howser stopped in the darkness for a moment to give his aching body a rest. Using a horse had gotten him to the part of the city he wanted much faster than walking, but riding had caused his body to hurt in a way that walking didn't. He would have enjoyed being able to lie down somewhere, but there were tasks to perform before that ease could be taken.

Thinking about those tasks brought a smile of pleasure to Rimen's face. Slaughtering animals was pure delight to him, and tonight he would put down as many as he possibly could. His knife would sink deep into helpless flesh, and a small bit of the outrage perpetrated against him would be washed away in the blood.

The ache in Rimen's body hadn't eased much, but his impatience set him to walking again. He would find another tavern and the alleyway behind it, and those drunkards who stumbled into his hands would never stumble away again. And if it took too long for a drunkard to appear, he might even pull an animal in off the street. All those animals were his to do with as he pleased, just as they were supposed to be. Changed conditions indeed!

Annoyance touched him as he remembered the lecture his

cousin's husband had tried to give him when they arrived in the city. Conditions are not what they used to be, Rimen, we can no longer do as we please, Rimen. Caution and circumspection are necessary, Rimen, at least until we regain our former power. After that, Rimen, you can certainly do as you please with the peasants . . .

Rimen had thought about telling the fool that *he* was already able to do as he pleased, but that would have wasted hunting time. Instead he'd left the house as quickly as possible after he'd eaten, and now he saw the tavern he would use tonight. If he'd wasted time in talk, his pleasure would have been much longer in coming.

The alleyway behind the tavern was as disgusting as Rimen expected it to be, but he ignored the stench and filth and positioned himself not far from the back door of the tavern. The knife he'd brought with him again was removed from its hiding place in his clothing, and it made a lovely weight in his hand. Now all he had to do was wait for the first of his animals to arrive . . .

Rimen had never needed to learn patience, and the need for it now quickly became galling. Time limped past slowly and painfully, as though it, too, had been savaged by uncaring hands. Rimen shifted in place a number of times, trying to *will* an animal to come through the door, but none of them did. And they must be refraining from coming out on purpose, he suddenly realized, simply to cause him even more agony. That couldn't be allowed to happen . . .

Decision firmed in Rimen, causing him to turn away from the outline of the door and back toward the night-sheathed street. If the animals refused to come to *him,* then he would go to them. They thought they were so safe, those mindless animals, but no animal had the right to be safer than a true noble like him. He would teach them, he would show them how wrong they were . . .

It took only a moment or two before an animal walking alone passed close enough to the deeply shadowed alleyway where Rimen stood poised. This was a male animal, not very tall and thin, a perfect sacrifice to Rimen's cause. Rimen reached an arm out as the animal passed, hooking the animal around the neck and pulling him back into the alleyway. His hold on the animal was also tight enough to keep the fool from crying out, and in a moment the animal would no longer be *able* to cry out.

Rimen raised the knife high, ready to plunge it into deserving animal flesh, but suddenly *he* was the one who cried out! Without warning it abruptly felt as though someone had lit a small fire beneath the arm Rimen had around the animal's throat. The flames weren't large or extremely hot, but they were enough to cause Rimen to release the animal with an exclamation of pain.

And then the air itself was lit by flame, enough so that Rimen and his knife were perfectly clear to the fearfully staring animal. The animal backed away slowly, one hand rubbing at his throat, and Rimen snarled in frustrated rage. That a miserable animal would *dare* try to deny him his due, that it would *dare* try to disobey him! Rimen was *not* going to allow that to happen, not now and not ever!

A scream of rage left Rimen's throat as he raised the knife again and pursued the animal as quickly as he could make his body move. It made no difference to Rimen's fury that he would be putting *this* animal down in the middle of the street. Doing as he pleased was Rimen's right as a true human being and noble, and no one would dare try to stop him. No one!

But then there were two other animals getting in the way, trying to keep him from his chosen sacrifice, trying to take his knife away. Rimen screamed again and slashed at one of the two even as the other tried to hold him still. The struggle grew more and more fierce, and then the animal behind him put an arm around Rimen's throat. Terror joined itself to rage in Rimen's mind as he began to fight even more violently, and then—

Deslen Voyt felt surprised at the strength of the madman he tried to hold still. He and Brange had followed Howser from the house according to orders, and when they saw the madman trying to kill someone they'd had no choice but to intervene. If the fool had kept his killing in the shadows where no one was able to witness what happened, they could have let the madman have his fun.

But making it so public meant Deslen *had* to interfere, intending to get Howser away from the area before anyone official stuck a nose into the row. But now it was him and Brange that Howser fought against, and that knife could do a lot of damage. Deslen tightened his hold just as Howser began to struggle even harder, and an abrupt snap stopped all the action at once. Howser went limp, and when Deslen let him go, the madman fell bonelessly to the ground.

"You broke his neck," Brange pointed out unnecessarily with an edge of accusation in his tone. "Now we're both in for it if the lady finds out instead of the lord."

Deslen knew that as well as Brange did, but before he could say anything or even suggest that they leave as fast as possible, they were suddenly in the midst of an excited crowd.

"Okay, what's going on here?" one of the newcomers asked, stopping to look down at Howser's body. "Who did this, and why?"

"They did it to save *me!*" the man Howser had been pursuing spoke up at once, the words rushing out together. "That one on the ground grabbed me and tried to pull me into an alleyway, but I've been through the training course. I may only have a Low talent in Fire magic, but now I can use it better than I used to be able to. I made that crazy man let me go, but then he started to come after me right into the street. I was so scared I couldn't think of anything to do, but then those two men came out of nowhere and tried to stop the crazy man. He went even crazier then and tried to kill *them,* but instead *he* ended up dead. That man was trying to hold the crazy still rather than hurt him, but the crazy twisted so hard that he broke his own neck."

"Well, it looks like we have a couple of heroes to thank," the newcomer who had asked the question said at once with a wide smile. "You men are to be commended, and there may even be some silver in it for you. When citizens do more than ordinary duty calls for, they deserve to be properly rewarded."

Deslen just stood and stared as the newcomer clapped him

on the shoulder before turning away to other newcomers. An accusation of murder was what Deslen had been expecting, but instead he was being called a hero and promised silver. A glance at Brange showed the other man to be as confused as Deslen felt himself, but then the confusion in Deslen began to turn to pleasure. No one had ever called him a hero before, and strangely enough it felt pretty damn good.

"You know, this city can use all the heroes it can get," the newcomer said as he turned back to Deslen. "I'm Redris Holm, by the way, officer of the watch at the moment. Have you men taken the new training yet?"

"No, no, we haven't," Deslen said quickly for both of them, trying to think of a reason why they hadn't. "It's just that . . . Well, we're Low talents, and—"

"That's okay, I understand," Holm interrupted in a kindly way. "A lot of Low talents think the classes can't do anything for them, but that isn't true. No matter how little strength of talent you have, once you've trained it you can become part of the city's guard force. And we'd love to have you, we really would. Brave men can always find a place with us, so if you decide to change your mind about taking the class, look me up once you've finished. I promise I won't forget who you are."

Holm clapped Deslen on the shoulder again before walking away, and now some of the other newcomers were seeing to Howser's body. Deslen caught Brange's eye and gestured with his head, and then the two of them were leaving the scene of action behind.

"I don't believe they didn't get all crazy about what we did," Brange murmured as soon as they were far enough away. "And that Holm called me a hero. No one ever said that to me before."

"It felt good, didn't it?" Deslen said, smiling as the pleasure returned in memory. "I never thought I'd like having people think of me as a hero, but I really do . . . What do you think about that class Holm mentioned?"

"He couldn't have been lying about them training Lows," Brange said, giving Deslen a longer glance. "I don't have much in the way of Earth magic, but that man we saved said *he* didn't have much in the way of Fire magic and they still trained *him*. And what they both said made me want to take that class myself . . ."

"Yeah," Deslen agreed, then fell silent. He also wanted to take the class, but that was part of the new world that had been built after the nobles were taken down. He and Brange were supposed to be part of the group trying to put things back the way they'd been, back to where no one was allowed to use talent . . . or be a hero . . .

"All right, let's talk about this before we go back," Deslen said once they reached the horses. They'd left their own mounts near Howser's, so they could take it with them without any extra fuss. "I want to be part of what those people have now, not just walking muscle in a uniform who doesn't count for anything at all. How about you?"

"I want the same thing, but how are we supposed to get it?" Brange countered, stopping next to his horse to look straight at Deslen. "We know too much for them to let us wander off, especially if we do end up joining the guard force. If we try to walk away we'll be dead before we take more than a couple of steps."

"That's true only if it's the two of us trying to walk away," Deslen pointed out, the idea coming to him rather quickly. "If we can get most of the men to leave *with* us, the noble won't be able to do anything to stop us. There are some we'd be fools to approach, but the rest . . ."

"The rest are like the way *we* were, disgusted with how little they'd gotten out of life," Brange said with eagerness when Deslen let his words trail off. "If we give them something better to do than run around helping some fool noble . . . I think we can do it."

"At the very least, we have to try," Deslen said before turning to his own mount. "Let's make up a list of names on the way back to the house. We'll talk to the ones we're sure of first, and get them onto our side. Then, if one of the later ones decides not to go along with us, we won't be only two anymore."

"Good idea," Brange said as he settled himself in his saddle. "We'll get all three of these horses taken care of, and then we'll get started. I want to start that class as soon as I possibly can."

Deslen wanted the same, and as they headed back to the house where the noble hid, he decided that it would *not* be long before he and Brange had what they wanted . . .

"I think that went very well," the man said comfortably to Redris Holm as they watched the two men ride away leading a third horse. "I've always believed that most sane people would rather be heroes than villains, and those two have just proven the matter for me."

"I wish I knew what was going on," Holm said in a low voice to the man whose name he hadn't been told. "I heard what those two were talking about, but I didn't understand a word. If they want to join one of the classes, why do they feel they can't?"

"They happen to be involved in something that we're aware of but can't discuss," the man said with easy amusement. "We've had people watching the place where they're staying, and when their small procession left the house there was just enough time to alert *my* small group. We saw you call the men heroes, and that's what gave us the idea. They would have liked the idea—and the thought of joining a class—well enough on their own, but we helped them along with really liking it. Now they're going to help *us* out by saving us a good deal of effort. And the end result of their efforts ought to be a lot of fun to watch."

"Now I'm more confused than ever," Holm said, staring at the man. "What small group are you a part of, and how did you let us hear what those men were saying from all the way over *here*?"

"It really isn't anything for you to worry about," the man assured Holm, giving him a warm and friendly smile. "I think you've guessed by now that I'm associated with the substitute Seated Blending, and that's all you really have to know at the moment. As long as you greet those men happily when they come to you for positions—and don't discuss any of this—everything will be fine."

"All right, all right, I won't ask any more questions," Holm gave up wearily with a shake of his head. "You people seem to like making things more complicated than they ought to be, but that's your business and none of mine. You can tell me or not in your own good time, the choice is yours."

"Thank you for your trust, my friend," the man said with a warm smile and a touch to Holm's shoulder before he turned and walked away. Holm sighed and shook his head again, then went back to his duties as officer of the watch. At least the madman who had been killing people was no longer a problem . . .

# Seventeen

Kail and Ren and the woman who was added to their small group were taken to another part of the large building and told to sit down. None of them spoke, not even Ren, and Kail wondered if that was because the other two were as nervous as he. He now knew he could earn Astindan citizenship, but still didn't know what would have to be done to earn that privilege. Kail could almost see and hear his father sneering at the idea that Kail would find it possible to do anything worthwhile at all . . .

"I think we should spend this waiting time talking to each other," Ren said suddenly, startling Kail and the woman as well. "If I have to sit here with nothing but my own thoughts to occupy me, I'll probably faint when they finally call my name. I've been wondering what will happen if I can't find anything useful to do to earn my citizenship."

"That's exactly what *I* was thinking," Kail admitted, feeling more anxious than embarrassed. "What can they possibly need that I could do?"

"Even if it turns out to be something I've never done before, I'll find a way to make it work," the woman said almost fiercely, speaking to Kail and Ren both. "I hate being anywhere near those parasites we were born among, and if I never go back to Gan Garee I won't miss the place for a moment."

"And my father used to tell me that I was the only one to find fault with the superior beings called the nobility," Ren said with raised brows as he examined the woman. "I've since learned that I wasn't alone in feeling as I did, but now it's become clear that I wasn't even first in feeling so by any number of years."

"I'm at least ten years older than you two, but I learned I wasn't first either," the woman said with a smile. She was a rather pretty woman of above average height, but definitely on the slender side. "My father didn't like the way I criticized what I saw among his peers, so he married me off to one of his friends. *That* man tried to beat me into keeping quiet, but I refused to accept being treated like that. I put Robris root into his lunch the next day, and when he was finally over wishing he would die I told him he *would* die if he ever touched me again. He also knew that if he threw me out I would tell everyone it had been done because he was terrible in bed, so we ended up living separate lives in the same house. But I still hated my life because it was so useless."

"Yes, being useless was the hardest part, I often think," Ren said to the woman with his own smile. "I'm Renton Frosh and my friend here is Kail Engreath. May I ask *your* name?"

"I'm Tansomia Elgrin," the woman supplied in a softer voice. "My father always tried to tell me that I was *supposed* to be useless because I'm a woman, useless for everything but childbearing. Since I refused to accept the first part of that dictum, I also refused the second. I never brought any children into the world to be ruined by their father, but I also never had any to be loved by *me*. That's been my greatest regret in life."

"But if you gain Astindan citizenship, you'll be able to marry someone of your own choice and have those children," Ren pointed out to her. "You're certainly not too old to have children, and I think you'll make a wonderful mother."

"Thank you," Tansomia answered with an incredibly shy smile, and that was when Kail realized that he hadn't been part of the conversation for the last few minutes. Ren and Tansomia were mostly talking to each other, but Kail found it impossible to feel insulted or shut out. The woman was a bit older than Ren, but if Ren felt attracted to her it was no one else's business. Tansomia did look at things the way Kail and Ren did, after all . . .

The chairs they'd been taken to were in a hall opposite a closed door, and suddenly that door opened. A man stepped out holding a sheet of paper, and he looked at the three people waiting before he said, "Kail Engreath."

"That's me," Kail said at once, finding himself on his feet without remembering the process of rising. The man gestured to Kail before going back into the room, and Kail wiped his palms on his trousers before following.

"Please close the door," the man said from where he stood behind a desk. Kail complied even as he looked around to see an unexpected mess. There were two chairs in front of the cluttered desk the man now sat himself behind, and books and papers seemed to be stacked everywhere. The two windows the room boasted had nothing at all covering them, and the only place that looked as though it had recently been cleaned was the fireplace.

"Please sit down and excuse the mess," the man said with a faint smile, gesturing toward one of the chairs in front of his desk. "I've only just moved into this office, and although I thought everyone knew what books and papers I would be bringing with me, no one provided places to *put* those books and papers. I've been assured that the problem will be solved very shortly, but until it is I've got to live with chaos. Why are you so nervous?"

"I'm afraid that I'll be found to be useless, and the offer of citizenship will be withdrawn," Kail answered at once, faintly surprised that he spoke so freely as he sat. "The chance to *earn* a respected place in the world has been a dream of mine for years, but if I can't find something worthwhile to do the dream will become a nightmare."

"You sound as if you've been taught to *expect* failure," the man mused, studying Kail as he leaned back in his chair. "Is that what people teach their children in Gandistra?"

"I don't know about the common people, but that's what the so-called nobility liked to do," Kail replied. "My father wasn't the only one who taught my brothers and me that we would be absolutely nothing without him and his contacts and power. My brothers were grateful for the chance to prove that our father hadn't wasted his time and efforts on their behalf, but I could never quite see it the same."

"I can't say that I blame you," the man remarked, the look in his eyes one of disapproval. "My own father taught me that I was a perfectly capable human being, and that whatever I chose to do in life would make him proud because I would certainly be a success. Not in the way of silver and gold, you understand, but in finding happiness. That's the real success in life."

"My father was happy when he got his own way, which was almost always," Kail said, remembering back to all those years at "home." "He was also happy when he made those around him miserable, which was also almost always. I suppose by your definition, my father *was* a success."

"Not really," the man disagreed, surprising Kail. "If your father actually *was* happy, he would have wanted to share that happiness with those around him. If he shared misery instead, that can only be because he was just as miserable. It sounds to me as though *he* was also made to feel like a failure while growing up, and he spent the rest of his life trying to disprove something he shouldn't have believed—but did. If a person truly is self-assured, he doesn't have to spend most of his time proving how good he is compared to everyone else."

"That never occurred to me, but, you know, I think you're right," Kail said, feeling as though he'd experienced true revelation. "I was always made to feel like less than a human being, but I know for a fact that that isn't so. I should be able to do anything I put my mind to, so . . . What is there for me to put my mind to?"

"Well, there seems to be more than one thing you're better than average at," the man observed as he glanced through the papers in front of him again. "You obviously dislike your former countrymen, but your supervising of them was fair and equitable at all times. That should mean you can be counted on to be the same with people you don't have hard feelings for. Would you *like* to supervise other people?"

"I will if that's all you have available, but I would really prefer to work *with* others," Kail said, again surprising himself. "I'd rather be *part* of something than be in charge of that same something, at least until everyone involved knows I *ought* to be in charge. Then taking over won't be distasteful at all."

"I think I can understand why you feel that way, so let's take a look at your other choices," the man said with a faint smile. "I'm told that you're a fairly strong Middle talent in Water magic, and it seems that you once tried to do something with that talent. Can you tell me what that something was and how far you got with it?"

"Well, it wasn't much of anything, really," Kail said, his embarrassment fading even as he became aware of it. "I only mentioned it when I was first interviewed because I was told to mention everything I'd done. Some friends and I got together whenever we could, intending to look into possible new uses for the various talents, but we didn't get very far. Everyone insisted that we were wasting our time, and even we weren't allowed to do anything we cared to with our talent. Gandistra has laws against the use of talent unless that talent is being used to earn more gold for the nobility."

"Gandistra no longer has such laws, I hear, and it's about time," the man said, now showing satisfaction. "We ourselves had no such laws before the invasion, but we were nothing but a large number of small independent areas that were most often at each other's throats. It took the invasion to unite us, and instead of each small ruler having a Blending or two to use against his neighbor, we began to share our knowledge about talents. And we learned to deal with former enemies without losing control of our tempers."

Kail was shown that faint smile again, and suddenly he had a theory about why the Astindans seemed so emotionless. Since they'd *had* to get along with each other, showing nothing at all in the way of emotion must have made the process easier for them. Now they seemed to do it out of habit, and had even extended the practice to the former nobles they'd taken as work slaves. It occurred to Kail that his former peers had no idea how lucky they were . . .

"Once we had the time, we began to wonder what else it was possible to do with talent other than destroy one's enemies," the man went on. "The wondering hasn't gone much farther than the intent to form groups to look into the matter, but it seems to be time to improve on that tiny beginning. Would you like to be a part of the effort?"

"I would love to be a part of it," Kail answered simply and honestly, excitement beginning to build in him. "I also have a theory that it might take greater strength to *establish* the new applications, but once established any number of those new applications should be useable by everyone including Low talents. How many people are already part of the group?"

"So far there's just you, but we'll see about changing that fairly quickly," the man said, looking up from having made a note on his papers. "I'll see if I can interest some of the others who came with you, and then we'll supply an equal number of our own people. While we're looking for and drafting suitable Astindans, you and the other former Gandistrans will have to be trained to use your talent properly. You can't hope to do your best work while you're still handicapped."

To say that Kail felt overwhelmed would be putting it mildly. He was being given the chance to earn what he most wanted by doing what he most wanted to do. Kail reached down and pinched himself to make certain he wasn't dreaming, and when he looked up again his interviewer was clearly rather amused.

"No, you aren't dreaming, so don't start to believe that you are," the man said in gentle admonishment. "There's a house not far from here where you'll be quartered with the others, and you'll also need to be fitted for some new clothing. Astinda will pay your expenses for six months, and then you'll be expected to take over supporting yourself. My name is Deslin Fodro, and if you need to reach me you'll find me here most of the time. Do you have any questions?"

"How will I get to that house you mentioned?" Kail asked, his head spinning with delight. "I'll be more than happy to walk if I'm given directions . . ."

"Once everyone has been interviewed, you and the others

will be guided to the house," Fodro told him, then rose to his feet. "If you'll wait outside I'll finish up as quickly as possible, and then we can get all of you settled."

Fodro led the way to the door and opened it, and Kail seemed to float through and back to his chair. Ren had obviously been waiting to ask how things had gone, but Ren was the next one called and so had no time to put the question. As soon as the door closed, however, the question came from another source.

"What happened in there?" Tansomia Elgrin asked in a soft but anxious voice, leaning a bit over Ren's empty chair. "You looked as nervous as I feel when you went in, but now . . ."

"Now there's nothing to be nervous about any longer," Kail answered, just short of laughing. "They really do want to give us a chance, and they're going to let *me* work at what I always wished I could. It isn't some sort of make-work and they aren't doing me any kind of favor. My ability got me the position, and that same ability will help me to keep it."

"Then I'm going to believe that they'll do the same for me," Tansomia said, sounding more hopeful than believing. "At first I was startled to see women working alongside the men on the way here, and then I couldn't help but feel envious. Those women held the same positions that the men did, and the Astindan men weren't condescending or trying to control the women. Remembering that will bolster my belief, and then things really will turn out as well for me as they did for you."

She lapsed back into silence then, and Kail joined her in that. The Astindans did seem a good deal more tolerant of women in their midst than the Gandistran nobility had been, and Kail hoped that Tansomia *would* benefit in the same way he had. This was a new beginning, after all, so why not have all sorts of new attitudes as well?

Kail sat floating in happiness until Ren reappeared, at which time Tansomia was called in. Kail saw Ren touch the woman's hand encouragingly as she passed him, and she, in turn, flashed him a grateful smile. Ren reclaimed his chair just before the door closed again, so Kail was able to turn immediately to his friend.

"So?" Kail demanded, suddenly worried that things hadn't gone as well for Ren as they had for him. "Are you going to be doing something worthwhile or boring?"

"The position will certainly be what I make of it," Ren answered, the bemused expression still on his face. "Do you remember that time in Gan Garee, when you invited me to join your supposed research group? Do you remember what I said?"

"You said we'd never be allowed to get anywhere, and you hated to waste your time and effort," Kail replied promptly if a bit impatiently. "What has that got to do with—Ren! Did they say you can join my group?"

"Rather than allowing me to join, Dom Fodro suggested I might want to consider the position," Ren answered, and then his smile widened until it was a gleeful grin. "I wasn't told I *had* to do as they wanted me to, the decision was left up to me. Do you have any idea how marvelous that felt, Kail? To these people I'm an actual human being."

"I know exactly how marvelous that feels, because I was treated in the same way," Kail assured his friend, quickly joining his delight. "I was also told that my father wasn't as sure of himself as he always seemed, otherwise he wouldn't have taken such delight in belittling others. That means my father's opinions of me have absolutely nothing to do with what I'm actually like, so I'm now free to be as much of a success as I can manage through my skills."

"I knew that about your father, just as I knew the same about my own," Ren said, sadness now coloring his smile. "What kept me in a constant state of depression was the fact that knowing the truth did me no good at all. Half the nobility felt they had something to prove no matter how much they'd already done, and the other half were spoiled brats who refused to even consider proving anything to anyone. I knew people like that were destined to trip and fall at *some* time, and that I would be taken down with them without having a say in the matter. I just had no idea I would be able to pick myself up again . . ."

"We needed some help to do that, but now that we've had the help we can continue on our own," Kail pointed out firmly to restore his friend's good mood. "I wonder what the house we'll be living in is like—and what the training of our abilities will consist of."

Ren threw off the sadness that had held him for a time, and joined Kail in speculating about what lay ahead. The two were only a short way into the discussion when the door opened again, and Tansomia Elgrin reappeared with Deslin Fodro coming out behind her. The woman was positively glowing, and Fodro wore his faint smile again.

"Well, it seems you now have a total of three members in your group," Fodro said to Kail in a warm voice. "I'll take you three to the place where you'll meet the rest of your housemates, and then you'll be escorted to the house itself. Lunch should be ready by the time you all get there, so you'll be able to settle in at once. Please follow me."

Kail and Ren stood at once and followed as they'd been told to do, but Ren took a moment to squeeze Tansomia's hand in silent congratulations. Kail felt a brief stab of envy at seeing that, but flatly refused to begrudge Ren the pleasure. Neither one of them had ever expected to find a woman they cared about, but now . . . Kail just wished that Asri could somehow appear and join them . . .

That was a wish Kail felt certain would never come about, and he sighed with resignation as he and the others followed Fodro through the large building. There were others moving through the building as well, some of them dressed in the same gray Kail and his companions wore. The vast majority, however, wore anything *but* gray, and one or two glances were anything but friendly. That was only to be expected, Kail knew, and the marvel was that there seemed to be so *little* animosity toward obvious former enemies. And soon, as Fodro had said, those who were no longer enemies would no longer be marked with that gray . . .

The man Fodro led the way into what seemed to be a very large meeting room, one where a number of other people already stood waiting. Kail glanced at the others in gray, then felt his heart leap with disbelief. One of those others was a woman holding an infant, and when she saw Kail her smile turned warm and welcoming. Obviously this *was* a day for making dreams come true, Kail thought as he and the others walked toward Asri Tempeth. Rather than be together as slaves, it looked like he and Asri would be together as future free citizens. He would soon have a life he could offer to share with a woman, and as soon as he did . . .

Deslin Fodro left his charges in the care of those who would take them to their new home, and took himself to a previously scheduled meeting elsewhere. When he entered the room everyone looked up, and Kestri Somore smiled at him.

"You're the last one to arrive, Deslin, so if you'll give me your report I'll have them all," Kestri said, her smile as warm as it usually was. "After that I have a report of my own to make."

"That sounds fair," Deslin allowed as he took the chair that had been left vacant for him near Kestri. "The Gandistrans I interviewed were as damaged as we expected them to be, but they're definitely salvageable. After interviewing some of the older Gandistrans I was afraid that they'd all been ruined, but happily I was wrong. None of the three fit at all well into their previous society, but they should do beautifully well in ours."

"And as far as you could tell they were all normal human beings?" Kestri asked after finishing a note on the papers she held. "No hidden reservations or resistances?"

"The one named Renton Frosh is a fairly strong Middle talent in Spirit magic," Deslin answered, suddenly curious. "He seemed to be holding off some of the conditioning given him in Gandistra, which means that everything he did was done freely rather than under duress. Is that the sort of resistance you meant?"

"No, and I'm glad to see that you found nothing else," Kestri answered, and then she began to address the entire group. "Most of the rest of you found the same lack of anything unusual, but there were two instances where the results didn't match. Luckily we had a High Blending standing by to help if they were needed, and their entity found the two

instances of discord. One of them was a man with strong
Spirit magic, and he didn't simply hold off some of the conditioning. He used his talent to judge the best moves to
make, and that's how he ended up among the other people
here."

"I take it that means he was less than truthful about wanting to become one of us," Gelden Rosh called out from the
other side of the room. "What did he want instead?"

"His intention was to infiltrate our ranks and get free of
observation and conditioning," Kestri replied with a sigh and
a headshake. "After that he planned to find the best place or
places to create havoc, using dupes that he would put under
his control. Once the confusion was at its height he planned
to free his peers, but what he would do after that wasn't certain. He couldn't decide between taking over here or returning to Gan Garee to take over there."

"The fool would probably have decided eventually to do
both," Gelden said with a matching sigh. "None of these
people seem to know anything at all about how talent works,
so they dismiss the matter completely from their calcula-
tions. As far as they're concerned, nothing in the world has
changed from the way it was when they were in power."

"Which hopefully means that even if we hadn't discovered the man's intentions now, he still wouldn't have been
successful," Kestri said with a nod of agreement. "The man
was sent back to work the land with his friends, and his conditioning has been strengthened to the point of severity. If he
tries to use his talent for his own benefit even one more time,
he'll lose the use of it permanently. The choice of what he
does, though, was left up to him."

"Since I'm sure he was also warned, what happens to him
next will be entirely up to him," Deslin said with a shrug that
many of the others in the group echoed. "If he hasn't the
sense to refrain from doing harm, his eventual loss will be
no one's fault but his own. Was the second odd instance similar to this first one?"

"Not really," Kestri answered, her expression having
turned disturbed. "The second instance is one no one under-

stands yet, not even the Blending entity that found it. One of the women interviewed . . . Everything about her says she's entirely sincere, but there's also something . . . odd about her. The only thing we can't discover is what that oddness consists of."

"How is that possible?" Deslin asked, feeling the frown he wore. "If there's something odd about the woman, the oddness itself ought to be perfectly plain. If it isn't, how was the oddness noticed to begin with?"

"It was the Blending entity that noticed the oddness to begin with," Kestri pointed out with continuing disturbance. "The Blendingmates involved *know* there's something odd about the woman, but even they can't say what the oddness is. The entity simply noticed the oddness, then seemed to dismiss the entire matter. Since the Blendingmates can't question their own entity, they can't think of a way to get more details."

"Then what are we going to do about the woman?" someone else called out, sounding as confused as Deslin felt. "We can't very well exclude her from this program without a more compelling reason, but to turn her loose would be foolish."

"We've decided to keep her in the program, but also to keep a close eye on her," Kestri said with a gesture of apology. "There's nothing else we *can* do, at least until we find out what's going on. But we do want all of you to be aware of the situation, so if you begin to get odd reports of some kind you won't simply dismiss them. If *anything* at all odd starts to happen, you're to report the matter immediately. And that, I think, is all we need to discuss at this time."

A babble broke out as soon as Kestri ended the meeting, but Deslin didn't contribute to it. The matter of that oddness really bothered him, but he didn't understand why it should. It was certainly a mystery, but mysteries were supposed to entice a man, not repel him. But there was something about the matter that touched him deep down, even though he had no idea why it should . . .

Deslin took a deep breath to banish foolish thoughts, then turned to Kestri again to get some of the data that had been reported. He wanted to put others into Kail Engreath's group, and his associates would have found out which of the others qualified. And doing the routine should let him forget about mysteries for a time . . .

# EIGHTEEN

When Jovvi awoke, it was a small surprise to find Rion sleeping next to her rather than Lorand. All six of them had gotten together the night before, and none of them had missed the fact that their Blending entity had felt out of balance. They also all knew *why* the entity was out of balance, and Tamma had put the matter most simply.

"It seems we've been spending too much time paired off with permanent partners," she'd said with a sigh. "I hadn't realized that the bond needed to be restrengthened on a regular basis, but I don't think we can argue the fact. I expected to be back with Vallant tonight, but it looks like going back to old habits will have to wait until tomorrow night."

"Yes, I'm afraid it does mean that," Jovvi had put in with her own sigh. "If we don't want a lopsided entity, Rion will have to lie with me, Lorand with Tamma, and Vallant with Naran. That ought to make the Gracelians even more thrilled with us than they already are."

"To chaos with the Gracelians," Vallant had said very flatly, his tone completely uncompromising. "They're a bunch of fools who would rather die along with all the rest of their people than change their way of thinkin'. If they don't tell us in the mornin' that they've come to their senses, we'll have to turn and walk away from them. If we don't, they'll just continue doin' things in the old way because *we'll* be there to save their necks."

"I hate the idea of abandoning the helpless, but I agree

that we'll have to leave," Lorand said, his tone filled with pain but just as unwavering as Vallant's had been. "Helping those who refuse to help themselves is something I'm not prepared to do."

"And staying after saying we would go will make things incredibly worse," Naran said, her gaze unfocussed again. "I can't see very much or very far, but one of those patterns Lorand showed me is helping to break through some of the flux. If we stay with the Gracelians even after they refuse to change their ways, the chances are excellent that it will destroy all of them."

"Which means that we'll have to think of something else to do," Rion had said with his own disturbance. "Just because the people in this country have fools for leaders, that doesn't mean they ought to be abandoned. Not long ago *we* had fools for leaders, and abandoning these innocents will feel like abandoning ourselves and our followers."

No one had been able to argue that statement, but the rain had started then so they'd all gone to the tents they meant to spend the night in. Jovvi had enjoyed the time with Rion fully as much as she'd enjoyed the night with Vallant, and now it was almost time to get up and face what the new day would bring . . .

"Good morning, lovely sister," Rion's voice came from the other side of the mat. "Allow me to say how devastated I am that our time together is now over."

"Oh, Rion, you do know how to make a woman feel marvelous," Jovvi answered with a laugh as she turned her head toward him. "You *are* looking awfully satisfied for a man who feels devastated, but I'm willing to overlook that fact. And please explain to your devastation that from now on we'll have to do this . . . exchanging more often. We have to keep our Blending entity well balanced, so the six of us will just have to force ourselves into doing the necessary."

"I can see that you consider that as terrible a fate as I do," Rion said with true amusement, raising one hand to touch her face. "I have faith that we'll find *some* way to cope with the horror being forced on us, but right now I have truly good news. My night's sleep seems to have brought me an

answer about what we might do once we leave these
Gracelians."

"You seem very certain that we *will* have to leave them,"
Jovvi pointed out as she sat up. "But as far as that goes, I feel
just as certain. So what have you thought of that we can do?"

"We can start the same kind of revolution that we started
in our own country," Rion answered easily as he also sat up.
"At home we taught all the High talents we found how to do
things the proper way, so we'll just have to do the same here.
By the time the assembly fools look about themselves, there
will hopefully be a large number of High Blendings to push
the fools out of the way while the new Blendings handle
matters properly. Or am I taking too much for granted? It
could well be true that the people are as wedded to their old
way of doing things as the assembly members."

"I think we'll just have to try your idea and see for ourselves," Jovvi told him, brows high after briefly considering
what Rion had said. "They may well refuse to go along with
us, but we do owe it to them to make the offer. If we're
turned down, we can return home with clear consciences."

Rion was quick to show his agreement, so they both rose
and dressed. The rain of the night before had ended to produce a fairly pretty day, so Jovvi and Rion strolled toward
where breakfast was being prepared. Not long after they began their stroll, Lorand and Tamma joined them from
Tamma's tent. They were just exchanging good morning
wishes when Vallant and Naran appeared to be included in
the exchange.

"Now that we've all spoken about what a good mornin' it
is, I have two bits of news," Vallant said in a soft voice. "The
first is that our night guards tell me we aren't the only ones
strengthenin' ties any longer."

"I don't believe it!" Tamma exclaimed with amusement,
showing she certainly did believe. "The Gracelians have actually decided to do things the right way?"

"Not *all* the Gracelians," Vallant corrected, answering
everyone else's questions and comments at the same time.
"It was just that Korge and his Blendin'mates, sneakin'"

around in the dark after the others were asleep. I really do wonder *what* he can be up to."

"I doubt if any of us has the least idea," Jovvi said just as dryly as Vallant had spoken. "First he makes the others ashamed to even consider something as 'disgusting' as bonding, and then he runs to do it himself. The fool is still playing politics without the first idea of how much serious trouble he's making."

"He wants to rule the country with his Blending of Middle talents," Naran commented with an impatient shake of her head. "He really believes that no one can stop him, but if Vallant's plan works he'll be stopped rather easily."

"Lorand's plan will do the same kind of stopping," Tamma said just as Jovvi said, "Rion's idea should take care of Korge and his ambitions." They all paused to look at each other with brows high while the men exchanged puzzled glances.

"All right, it looks like mine isn't the only plan," Vallant said after a moment. "Let's start with all of us mentionin' what we have in mind, and then we'll go with the best idea. Lorand, would you like to be first?"

"Certainly," Lorand agreed in his usual easygoing way. "I've become convinced that the Gracelian assembly members will refuse to change their stance, so our only option will be to find what Gracelian Highs we can and train them in the proper methods of becoming a real Blending. That way these people won't be left with no useful protection of . . . any sort . . . Why are all of you looking at me like that?"

"Personally, I was wondering how you and Rion can have come up with precisely the same idea," Jovvi told Lorand, and then she became aware of what Naran's and Vallant's re-actions had to mean. "Or should I say, how you and Rion and Vallant *all* came up with the same idea?"

"Yes, that's what you ought to be sayin'," Vallant con-firmed with a nod, his expression just as peculiar as every-one else's. "And I, for one, would love to know how it happened."

"Don't look to *me* for an explanation," Tamma said at once with a shake of her head. "I'm still trying to figure out what the weird dreams I've been having can mean—if I can even once remember what they were."

"You've also been having strange dreams?" Naran said to Tamma, obviously surprised again. "I thought I was the only one, and I'd dearly love to remember what the dreams were about. They feel important in an odd, tangential way."

The next moment everyone else was speaking at the same time again, but Jovvi had no trouble sorting out the comments.

"I'm going to make a wild guess and say that we've *all* had odd dreams that we can't remember," Jovvi stated as soon as the hubbub died down. "You're all agreeing with me, so we're going to have to remember to discuss this at another time. Right now breakfast seems to be ready, and even if I weren't so hungry we don't have much privacy for conversation here."

The others glanced around to see that their hosts were up and moving around the camp, so there was nothing to do but end their discussion and collect the breakfast that was now ready. Lorand was put on line first again, of course, but none of their "hosts" had decided to tamper with the food. Which was a good thing, since Jovvi really was very hungry.

The six of them shared a quiet but companionable meal, but the quiet didn't last much past the end of the food. Their hosts appeared in a body, showing a bland and political lack of expression, obviously having forgotten that Jovvi didn't need facial expressions to know what they were really feeling.

"Good morning, friends," Antrie Lorimon said with a warm smile, clearly speaking for the others. "We hope you slept well last night?"

"We slept very well, thank you," Vallant answered for *their* group, the words even and calm. "I'm assumin' you're here to give us your decision about whether or not you're willin' to change your ways, and we'd appreciate your gettin' right to it."

"Of course," Antrie answered with another of those sweet

smiles. "We've discussed the matter both last night and this morning, and we've come to the only decision we could. We've made no effort to force *you* into doing things the way we do, so we'd like to be extended the same courtesy. A difference of opinion doesn't mean we can't continue to work together, after all, so—"

"But it means exactly that," Vallant interrupted as he got to his feet, Jovvi and the others quickly following his example. "Courtesy has nothin' to do with what's goin' on here, and it isn't us but common sense doin' the forcin' you mentioned. If you don't change your ways you won't survive, and we have no intention of goin' down right along with you."

"I told you we were wasting our time trying to treat these sluts as though they were decent human beings," Korge stated with a smirk clear in his gaze. "They want to drag *all* of us down to their level, and if we listen to them we'll *deserve* to have people turn away from us in disgust."

"Listenin' to *that* one is the mark of a true fool," Vallant commented as he eyed Korge with the mentioned disgust. "He and his Blendin'mates went through the 'unnecessary' bondin' procedure last night, leavin' the rest of you in the dust. He still wants to be the one runnin' things in this country, and you're all playin' into his hands with your 'reasonable' refusal. But since that's obviously the way you want it . . ."

Exclamations of shock and demands for confirmation or denial finally interrupted Vallant, some of the comments aimed at Vallant, most of them aimed at Korge. That one had turned dark with rage, but he still stood there denying the charge until Olskin Dinno held up a hand.

"I can tell that you're lying, Korge, so don't waste any more of our time trying to deny what the man said," Dinno stated flatly with a growl. "All that talk about doing disgusting things was just to keep the rest of *us* from doing them. What do you expect to gain from such underhanded methods?"

"How can you stand there shouting at *me* when it's perfectly obvious that those interfering monsters have been *spy-*

*ing* on us?" Korge took his turn at putting a demand, obviously trying again to deflect outrage from himself. "If none of the rest of you have the stomach to denounce them for it, then I'll have to do it myself! They're supposed to be guests, but it's a sickening guest who sneaks around watching what his host is doing—"

"Give it up, Korge," Tamma said flatly, cutting off the flow of words from the man. "Your associates should know that with the invaders so close we set out sentries, something all of *you* should have done but didn't bother to think of. If you people don't get with it, you'll be dead before you learn how much of a waste of time and effort this playing politics is. Now: We'd like a final answer. Since one of your number has already started to do the right thing with his Blending, what about the rest of you?"

Tamma had glanced at the others with her question, but her gaze ended up resting on Antrie Lorimon. The small woman had been doing the talking for the rest of them until then, but now she seemed hesitant about continuing in the same vein.

"I . . . think we'll need some time to discuss this new turn of events," Antrie said after a short but definite hesitation, and then her smile came out again. "You've been so patient with us so far that I'm sure you won't mind waiting just one day more for—"

"No, we won't be waitin'," Vallant interrupted, his tone softer than it had been but no less firm. "We're goin' to get our people and possessions together, which will take a few minutes. If you don't have an answer for us by the time we're ready to leave, then we'll leave without the answer. We've wasted enough time with you people."

And with that he turned and walked away, leaving behind a group of people who looked shaken to the core. Or at least most of them were shaken, Jovvi told herself as she joined the others in following Vallant. Thrybin Korge was hiding his elation, but the other Gracelians were badly frightened.

"So, what do you think they'll do?" Tamma murmured as she came up to walk beside Jovvi. "Will they just let us leave, or will they agree to change their ways?"

"I'm afraid they *can't* change their ways," Jovvi answered with a sigh. "They're all more afraid of changing their practices than they are of the invaders, and nothing we say or do will alter matters. Even if they tell us they agree to make the changes, they won't be speaking the truth."

"Then we'll definitely be leaving," Tamma said with a nod. "I can't say I'm surprised, and I'm not even terribly disappointed. Having a tent to sleep in doesn't balance out what we've had to go through with that group of fools, so leaving them behind will be a definite relief."

Jovvi felt the least bit guilty about considering the matter in the same way, but there was no doubt that she did. Leaving the Gracelians behind *would* be a relief, but if the plan all three of the men had thought of worked they would certainly run into the assembly members again . . .

Cleemor Gardan wasn't a happy man as he joined the others in walking to a place where they might sit down to talk. Nothing was going the way it should have, but he couldn't think of a thing to turn the situation around again . . .

"Well, *you* certainly did a wonderful job keeping the Gandistrans here where they're needed," Cleemor heard Satlan Reesh say harshly. "I knew we were fools for giving a woman a chance to ruin things."

"Close your mouth, Reesh," Olskin Dinno said at once before Cleemor had the chance to say the same. "Antrie was the only one of us who had any chance at all of making the Gandistrans stay, and it wasn't her fault that she failed. If you think it *was* her fault, tell us what you would have done in her place."

Reesh glowered at Dinno but didn't immediately speak up, which was a surprise to no one. Dinno only waited a moment, and then he nodded.

"That's what I thought," he rumbled at a red-faced Reesh. "You needed someone to blame, and Antrie was the safest target for your mindless complaints. If you had any real innards, you would have opened your mouth to the one of us who really deserves it . . . You're all but dancing and singing at the idea of the Gandistrans leaving, Korge. What do you expect their absence will let you accomplish?"

"I'm pleased at the thought of their leaving because I dislike them so intensely, Dinno," Korge answered slowly as though explaining something complex to someone who wasn't terribly bright. "Isn't that enough of a reason?"

"No, it isn't, not with those invaders breathing down our necks," Dinno denied immediately in an even harder tone. "If you hadn't taken up . . . *slut* ways as soon as our backs were turned, the Gandistrans might not have been so impatient with us. So allow me to repeat the question you ignored a moment ago: What do you expect to accomplish?"

"He wants the same thing that fool Tal wanted, and that's to go home a hero," Cleemor said when Korge hesitated, the matter perfectly clear. "He must have convinced his Blendingmates that being stronger than the rest of us would get them somewhere, which would make them just as stupidly blind as he is. He—"

"You just *wish* you could be as stupidly blind, don't you, Gardan?" Korge interrupted with a sneer, anger in his gaze for the way everyone now spoke to him. "Even if the rest of you fools follow our example and increase your own strength, we'll still be there ahead of you and will still be stronger just as we were before. But the rest of you *won't* follow our example, will you? You just don't have the guts to do what's necessary without whining about it, so don't blame *me* for your shortcomings."

"It's your own shortcomings we're talking about, Thrybin," Antrie said flatly before Korge could get to his feet and leave. "When Cleemor said you were being stupidly blind, he stated nothing but the absolute truth. We all know how incredibly strong the Gandistrans are, but even they needed the help of another Blending almost as strong in order to make the invaders vulnerable to us. If you'd been there with us you would have known that, but your temper tantrum kept you in camp. Even if you're now *twice* as strong as you were yesterday, which I seriously doubt, how do you expect to do anything at all against the invaders all by yourself? Or does our soon-to-be hero have that all worked out?"

"Look at the fool!" Reesh suddenly exclaimed, pointing to a Korge who frowned in an effort to hide how suddenly appalled he was. "That thought never occurred to him, so he was happy to drive the Gandistrans away! I say we get *him* to go over and apologize, and maybe the Gandistrans will stay after all."

"Me, apologize to those arrogant snoops?" Korge demanded, his skin darkening further with his raging emotions. "Your cowardice is making you babble even more nonsense than usual, Reesh, so why don't you do as Dinno suggested and shut your mouth. We don't need those people to help us, or maybe I should say *I* don't need them. What the rest of you do is your own business."

And with that Korge did get to his feet and leave, stalking off toward where his Blendingmates waited. Dinno joined the rest of them in watching the man go, and then he shook his head.

"At least he knew he was lying when he said *he* didn't need the Gandistrans' help," Dinno rumbled before looking around at those who were left. "The rest of us know the same, but just knowing the truth won't help us. If we don't agree to do things their way, the Gandistrans will leave anyway."

"I say we tell them we agree, but that we'll need some time to get used to the idea," Cleemor said, mostly to fill the silence that came after Dinno's words. "I don't know about the rest of you, but I haven't changed my mind about how I feel. My marriage is too important to me to throw it away for . . ."

"Yes?" Dinno prompted when Cleemor's words simply trailed off into silence. "Your marriage is too important to you for you to throw it away just to save our country? Is that what you were going to say, Gardan?"

"Bickering among ourselves won't solve the problem," Antrie pointed out when Cleemor still couldn't find what to say. "I understand how Cleemor feels, and I agree with him. Our best course of action will be to accede to the Gandistrans' demands, but ask them to be patient while we adjust to the new circumstances. That should keep them with us until we can think of something else to do."

"But that *won't* keep them with us," Dinno immediately denied, his gaze going back and forth between Antrie and Cleemor. "It's obviously escaped your notice, but those people can tell truth from lie even better than I can. If we aren't absolutely and completely sincere in what we tell them, we might as well not bother."

"Are you trying to say that you now *support* the idea of changing our entire lives?" Cleemor demanded, looking straight at Dinno. "What happened to your not being able to bear the thought?"

"I did a lot of thinking last night, and once you put the emotionalism aside you realize that the Gandistrans are right," Dinno answered, deep sadness behind the calm of his words. "Our choice is between clinging to the traditional way of doing things and going under against those invaders, or changing our lives in order to survive. We all have our fears, Gardan, and Reesh's here is at least as terrifying as yours, but the both of you will have to come to terms with your fears or else perish. What you have to remember is that changing at least allows *some* chance of finding happiness again. Perishing doesn't."

Cleemor glanced at Reesh where he sat, understanding Dinno's reference to Reesh's fear. No one associated with Reesh unless they absolutely had to, a truth the man undoubtedly understood completely. Reesh could very well be rejected as a member of a Blending if they were all High talents, and that would leave him with no one to associate with at all . . .

"Even if we decide to change our ways, what good will it do?" Cleemor said as soon as the point came to him. "We not only have to lie with our Blendingmates, we first have to find other High talents to *be* our Blendingmates. That means lying with absolute strangers, which won't be as easy for Antrie as it is for you and me—even as hard as it would be for me in particular. Have you considered *that* at all?"

"I've considered *every* aspect of the situation, but the problem is we don't have enough information," Dinno responded with a frown. "That fool Korge rushed to lie with his present Blending, and we might well be able to do the same as a stopgap measure. Going out looking for other High talents now will take time we don't have, but we have to check the point with the Gandistrans. If we *can* manage to stay with our present Blendings, at least we'll have *that* familiarity to comfort us."

"Why isn't it possible to do something *without* lying with our Blendingmates?" Reesh asked, his voice now more wheedling than demanding. "If we pair up the way the Gandistrans did to remove that aura from the invaders, we might be able to do the same thing they did. How can we decide to throw tradition out the window before we make the least attempt to handle the matter in our own way?"

"No, Dinno, Reesh has a point," Cleemor said at once before Dinno could reject Reesh's suggestion out of hand. "We all went against the invaders individually, so we don't *know* what will happen if we team up against them. I agree that the least we can do is try, and that way we may be able to save our country and our way of life as well."

"It really isn't an unreasonable idea, Olskin," Antrie put in when Dinno's frown only deepened. "I'm sure you don't know this, but I've . . . begun to see someone. It would destroy the both of us if I had to tell him I've been lying with strangers or even with my Blending, but I'm willing to do that if there's no other option. All I ask is that we make completely sure there *are* no other options."

Dinno began his arguments all over again, but Cleemor had Reesh and Antrie solidly on his side. The three of them stood fast against every point Dinno raised, and at last the man threw up his hands in defeat.

"All right, I have nothing left to say that any of you is willing to hear," Dinno growled, glaring around at all of them. "You all have your own private reasons for wanting to keep things as they are, so you're pretending to be reasonable when what you're really being is selfishly stubborn. It isn't possible for me to force you into doing the right rather than the comfortable, but I'm telling you right now that it won't work. And when it doesn't, don't come crying to me that you did your best."

And with that he rose to his feet and stalked off the way

Korge had done, bringing Cleemor, at least, as much relief as Korge's departure had.

"He'll feel better about things when we prove that we're right," Antrie said with something of her usual smile, and then she gathered herself to stand. "Right now we'd better go and speak to the Gandistrans, to tell them about the idea we've decided to try. When we present them with a definite plan of action, they won't be able to refuse to stand with us."

"And then we won't have to worry about acting alone," Reesh said happily as Cleemor helped Antrie to her feet. "When we show the Gandistrans that we can handle things just fine the way we are, they'll also have to stop telling us to change our lives to suit *their* whims."

Cleemor felt a distant disturbance over that statement and Antrie's as well, but he needed the solution they'd come up with too badly to try picking holes in it. Instead of trying to see what it was that disturbed him, Cleemor thrust away the emotion and simply accompanied Reesh and Antrie through the camp. The Gandistrans had established themselves a short distance from the Gracelian arrangements, but it should be possible to see the first of them any moment now . . .

"Oh, no," Antrie suddenly gasped, horror in her voice. "Cleemor . . . the Gandistrans are gone!"

"They can't be gone!" Reesh denied, terror in his own voice. "They said they wanted a decision from us, so they can't have left before getting it!"

"They also said they would not wait beyond the time they were ready to leave," Cleemor said in a voice that sounded dead in his own ears. "We spent so much time arguing that they kept their word and didn't stay, and now we're on our own."

"It's all that Dinno's fault!" Reesh cried, his pallor a match to Antrie's. "He delayed us so long with his nonsense that we weren't given the chance to tell the Gandistrans that we had a plan. They would have listened to us when we said we had a plan!"

"But that wasn't the plan they wanted us to have," Cleemor murmured, still held by an odd feeling of floating.

"It's almost as if they knew what we would say and didn't care to wait around to hear it. But that's ridiculous, of course. How *could* they have known in advance?"

Antrie wept quietly and Reesh stood with one hand over his eyes, so Cleemor's question wasn't answered. Not that it *had* to be answered. The Gandistrans *couldn't* have known what they meant to say, so instead of thinking about foolishness they now had to find a way to carry on without the presence of the incredible strength they'd been counting on to support them . . .

# NINETEEN

"I can't believe those fools just argued themselves back to their original stance," Naran heard Tamrissa say from where they both rode to either side of Vallant. "I'm glad we didn't stay around to hear it, or I might not have been able to control my temper."

"That time I probably would have joined you in temper losing," Naran said with a headshake, looking at Tamrissa across Vallant. "There really wasn't much of a chance that those people would see reason, but knowing that one of their number had already started to do things right should have meant *something* to them."

"They couldn't let it mean something to them," Jovvi put in, turning in her saddle where she rode ahead of them. "Cleemor, Antrie, and that Satlan Reesh were all terrified for personal reasons at the idea of doing what was necessary, and terror doesn't let you think clearly and rationally. Their way of life is coming apart all around them, but they still can't let go of their old practices."

"And they probably never will," Naran confirmed, remembering what she'd seen glimpses of. "They're trying to keep what they have, but they'll find that their efforts have done nothing more than lose them what they were trying to keep. Especially since things are looking very hopeful for our own efforts."

"If that means we won't be wastin' our time, I'm happy to hear it," Vallant commented with satisfaction. "I don't expect *everybody* to agree with what we want to do, but as long as we have enough reasonable people to form two or three Blendin's that should help quite a lot."

*The people will be more desperate than reasonable,* Naran thought but didn't say. What they found in the village they rode toward would be far from pleasant, but the others didn't need to know that yet. They would all be upset at what they saw, what she'd *already* seen, and there was no need to bring that disturbance on sooner than absolutely necessary.

It didn't take very long for them to reach the village, the place where all those refugees had tried to take refuge. But there just wasn't enough room to accommodate all those people, not in any kind of housing. It was obviously men and probably single women who crouched around the small fires that were lit everywhere, half of the people trying to keep warm and the other half trying to cook. Someone must have done a considerable amount of hunting, but other staples had to be running perilously short . . .

"Just wait until the next group of people arrives," Tamrissa murmured as they all slowed to look around. "The people who are still alive in that other village will be heading in this direction, and there isn't even any room for the people who are already here. I think we'd better suggest that everyone able to move on should do so as soon as possible."

"Not until we find the volunteers *we* need," Vallant corrected, but he still sounded disturbed. "If enough people decide on comin' with us that will ease the situation, and then we can urge the others into movin' on."

"I think we'd better start out by helping with some healing," Lorand put in from where he rode beside Jovvi. "These people didn't have an easy time of it getting here, and they probably have worse ahead of them."

"That's two things needin' arrangin', and I think we can do them both together," Vallant answered as they all stopped, and then he looked toward Rion where he sat his horse to Jovvi's left. "Rion, if you and your people are ready for helpin' out . . ."

"We're all ready, Vallant," Rion answered with a smile. "Go ahead any time *you're* ready."

Naran had noticed that Rion was looking more thoughtful than distracted this morning, but she'd carefully kept herself from thinking about the fact. She'd also firmly kept herself from Seeing anything to do with the two of them, even though a number of possibilities had nearly shouted at her. This was *not* the time for personal problems . . .

"Please give me your attention, people," Vallant said, and with the help of Rion's Air magic groups his words rang loud a good distance across the village. "We're here for two reasons, and both of them are important. The first reason is offerin' healin' to anyone who needs it, so if you or someone close to you is in need, just let us know."

A murmur of relief and gladness grew among the refugees, doing a small bit to lift the heavy atmosphere of doom which hung over everyone. There wasn't anything like joy to be seen, but at least Naran was able to detect the relief and gladness.

"The second reason for our bein' here is that we need help against those invaders," Vallant continued, and suddenly everyone was paying very close attention. "No one's been able to touch the invaders with talent because they're bein' protected *with* talent, and only Highs workin' together have a chance to break through that protection. Are there any High talents here who are willin' to work with us?"

"You better believe there are!" a man called from where he stood by one of the fires. "I'm one of them, and I'll do anything I have to in order to destroy those who killed my family and friends. When do we start?"

By then there were other people shouting their agreement, quite a few others. Near the shouting people were those who shrank back with pale faces and shaking hands, those who seemed ashamed that they weren't also volunteering. Naran really wanted to say something comforting to those others, but Jovvi was already ahead of her on that.

"We're going to start immediately, but first I'd like to say something," Jovvi stated, and her voice also rang out across the village. "If you're not able to bring yourself to volunteer, please don't let that fact upset you. Those who fight are born to do that, and those who prefer peace are born to build again after the fighters make the world safe for you. You'll have your turn at helping, but right now those who are willing to fight need your support. Are *you* willing to give it to them?"

Those who had looked afraid were now smiling and nodding, many of them shouting out, "Yes!" and "I'm behind you!" and "I'll do whatever I can!" Everyone now looked alive again, and Vallant showed a smile as he took over again.

"I'd like those who are volunteerin' to meet me over there," he said, pointing to one side of where they sat their horses. "Those in need of healin' want to go over *that* way, to where Lorand and his people will be waitin'. If you need to be in both places, come to me first if you can to tell me what aspect you are, and then join those bein' healed. If the healin' can't wait, see to *that* first. It won't do any good havin' you fall over."

A few people laughed at that, and then everyone was moving in a different direction. Tamrissa and Rion were joining Vallant and dismounting with him, while Jovvi joined Lorand and his Earth magic link groups. The refugees were also moving in all directions, either to one of the two groups or hurrying across the village. Those hurrying away could well be going to check on people who might not have heard what was said, which took care of *that* chore.

Naran took a deep breath while thinking about what *she* could do, and then the answer became obvious. She and her link groups would serve best by circulating among the people of the village, making sure that those who needed attention by Lorand and his groups were coming forward to get it. And it might be a good idea to listen to what the people were saying among themselves, especially about Vallant's proposal . . .

Rion shared Vallant's and Tamrissa's delight with the number of High talents who came forward to volunteer their help. Those assembly people they'd left earlier were completely impossible, and staying with them any longer would have been a waste of time. Now there was the chance to see something useful done, and Rion felt eager to get on with training these new talents.

"I'd like to thank you all for comin' forward," Vallant said once it looked as though everyone who meant to join them had already arrived. "I'll start out by tellin' you that my friends and I are a Blendin', and that we have other Blendin's with us. But all the members of our Blendin's are High talents, and that's what we'd like to do with *you* folks: teach you how to Blend."

"But . . . only members of the assembly are allowed to Blend," one woman protested, her confusion shared by many others. "And the Blending *can't* contain more than one High talent, it's simply not done."

"It's not done *here*," Tamrissa corrected, her tone calm but very firm. "I don't know how that fool arrangement got started, but it's useless against the problem you all now face. We met some of the invaders along with four assembly Blendings, and those assembly people couldn't do a thing against the invaders. *We* had to take care of the matter, but this isn't our country. If you people won't fight for it, why should we?"

"No, she's right," one of the men in the crowd said as voices of protest rose from some of the others. "What's the sense in waiting around to be the major talent in a Blending, when none of us might live long enough even to compete for the position? And if the assembly Blendings are useless against the invaders, what's the sense in wanting to continue with the practice?"

"I agree," a different woman announced, also over the protests of others. "If our old way of doing things was all that superior, we would be comfortably at home now instead of running for our lives. And since this *is* my country, I'm willing to do anything I have to in order to defend it."

"But this particular anything means breaking the law as well as tradition," the first woman pointed out, her tone filled with worry. "Assuming we do drive the invaders out, what will happen to us then?"

"You'll change the law, just the way *we* did in our own country," Tamrissa said when the second woman stood silent. "Back home the people in power were able to *stay* in power by using the law against everyone, but the time came when it would have been suicide to continue to be 'law-abiding.' If your current arrangement is really meant to be kept, after the fighting you'll all go back to it. But if it's an outdated and useless way of doing things . . .'

"Then we'll develop new ways," the first woman said, surprising everyone by being the one to finish Tamrissa's sentence. "Yes, I can see that now, and we really don't have much of a choice, do we? Saving our country has to come first, and then we can worry about the consequences of *how* we saved it. So what do we do?"

There were still a few people in the group who were too shocked and outraged to go along with the proposed changes, and while two of them simply turned and walked away another two began to argue. Rion listened to the arguing for a moment while fighting to hold down impatience, and then someone next to him made a sound of scorn.

"Do you believe that ridiculous man?" the woman standing near Rion said in a murmur. "He's obviously been counting on becoming a major talent in the assembly and can't bear to give up his dream. How can he not understand that if we still have a country left after this is all over, there won't *be* Blendings with only one High talent any longer?"

"You sound very certain of that, and also very unconcerned," Rion commented as he examined the woman. She was as dirty and bedraggled as the people around her, but her condition did nothing to hide her beauty. "Since this concept should be as new to you as it is to your fellow countrymen, I wonder why you feel nothing of their disturbance."

"But the idea *isn't* new to me," the woman said with a smile that actually added to her beauty. "Some of us have been wondering for quite some time why there has to be only one High talent in the assembly Blendings. And why the composition of those Blendings has to keep changing every time one member or another is displaced by a challenger. The situation doesn't make sense for anyone but the only High talent in each assembly Blending, and that also has to be the only reason things haven't changed. The people who have the power don't want to lose it."

"Isn't that usually the way?" Rion commented, very

aware of the fact that the woman had moved a bit closer to him. "Those in power want to keep that power, even if they no longer deserve to have it."

"But from what that woman said, you and the others didn't let that stand in *your* way," the woman murmured, looking up at him with definite warmth in her dark eyes. "I really admire people who act rather than just talk, and I would enjoy getting to know you better."

Rion's first reaction to that comment was a feeling of surprised flattery, along with a definite physical interest in the very beautiful woman. But then his second reaction set in, and that was more of a surprise than the first. The woman was clearly serious in her attempt to attract him, but his mind had already rejected her scarcely veiled offer!

It took a moment for Rion to realize *why* he would reject so beautiful a woman, and then the reason became clear. As desirable as the woman was, she simply couldn't compare to his Blending sisters. And that, oddly enough, had nothing to do with physical beauty. No woman in the world could compare favorably to Tamrissa and Jovvi and—

Rion's thoughts pulled themselves up short as he suddenly felt himself filled with joy. His brothers and sisters had been perfectly right, and although he felt flattered and faintly tempted by the strange woman's interest, his decision to do nothing about that temptation was not being strained in the least. He *was* a grown, adult man, and now he could prove it to Naran as well as to himself. But there was something else he and Naran needed to talk about, something he'd been thinking about all morning . . .

"I really must ask you to excuse me, Dama," Rion said to the woman with a small bow. "Your interest is flattering, but you'll soon learn why I'm not returning it. And there's something I must do before we begin to show you all how to Blend."

He turned and walked away with that, leaving the woman with a startled expression on her face. She, apparently, wasn't used to being rejected out of hand, possibly even less used to the doing than Rion was used to performing the act. But experiencing newfound maturity was exhilarating, and the sensation put a bounce in Rion's step as he moved along. He'd seen Naran walking in this direction earlier, so she ought to be *somewhere* in the area.

It wasn't long before Rion spied Naran a short distance ahead, strolling along as she looked over the people gathered in small, excited knots of conversation. Members of her link groups were also about and doing the same strolling, which told Rion that they were probably examining the population for those who needed Lorand's attention but weren't taking advantage of the opportunity. It would be rather easy to take Naran aside for a few private words, then . . .

Rion had nearly reached Naran when he saw her hesitate and then start to move off in a totally different direction. She had been looking at the people directly ahead of her, but rather than strolling past she seemed anxious to leave their vicinity entirely. That action puzzled Rion—until he saw one man jump from his place in the group to grasp Naran's arm.

"*You're* one of those outlanders, so *you* can tell my friends the truth!" the man rasped out as he pulled Naran to a halt. "You're using this invasion as an excuse to destroy our way of life, aren't you? You're all jealous of what we've built here, and since you can't share it you want to destroy it! And come to think of it, your lot might even be behind those invaders!"

"No, that isn't true," Naran protested as she tried to free herself of the man's hand on her arm. "We're here to help you, not to destroy anything. Please let me go."

"I'll let you go when you stop lying!" the man snarled, actually daring to shake Naran by the arm he held. "You tell my friends the truth, or I'll—"

The man's words broke off as the section of air that Rion had hardened hit him directly in the face. The fool staggered backward toward his friends after having released Naran, and by then Rion stood beside his woman.

"The truth of the matter is very simple," Rion said coldly to the man and those others the man had nearly crashed into and who now held him up. "You know well enough that no one would accept you into a Blending as an equal, so your only hope to be as important as you feel you *should* be is to insist that a useless arrangement be continued. If you weren't the sort to think of yourself before you considered the safety and well-being of those around you, the matter would scarcely have become the problem it is for you. If your . . . friends are wise, they'll find someone else to associate with who really is a friend to them."

By then the people around the man had withdrawn from him to stand together at a small distance, showing they had already come to the conclusion Rion had suggested. The man himself turned angrily away from Rion and Naran, apparently about to speak to those he'd stood among, only to discover that those people had withdrawn from him. The man shook his head and tried to approach the small group, but they turned as one and deliberately walked away, leaving the man with no one to listen to his complaints. Seeing that, Rion also led Naran away to a place they could talk without being interrupted.

"I really must thank you for helping me out of that mess," Naran said before Rion could speak, her very neutral gaze on his face. "I Saw the possibility of that scene and tried to avoid it, but the man moved too quickly."

"If that fool had hurt you I would have killed him rather than simply denting him a bit," Rion returned, his words nothing but the absolute truth. "As it happens I was looking for you, though, so happily I was there to keep much harm from befalling you. But we'll ask Lorand to look at your arm just to be on the safe side."

"Lorand can't do anything for a bit of bruising, and that's all my arm is suffering from," Naran said with a faint smile and a headshake. "I'll be fine, but I'd like to know why you were looking for me."

"I came to tell you that I'm no longer uncertain about what my reaction will be with other women," Rion answered at once, wishing the revelation could be as completely a delight as he'd once expected it to be. "There's no longer even the remotest chance that I'll someday betray your love, but I've discovered that there's another consideration that could well stand between us. I would like to discuss that consideration before I try to tell you again how very deep my love for you is."

"It's hard to believe that I'm having this much trouble understanding what you're talking about," Naran said with a small headshake, her neutral expression beginning to dissolve. "You seem . . . different, somehow, Rion, and I'm not sure why that is."

"I'd like to think that the change is due to maturity," Rion answered, too well aware of the fact that his own expression must be rather rueful. "I'd like to assure you first that I'll continue to love you till my dying day, but dearest . . . I've recently come to realize that there are other women I also love. That doesn't make my love for *you* any less, but the situation could well be one you find it impossible to accept. I need to know if that's so before I bedevil you with importunities to return to my side."

"You . . . also love other women," Naran echoed, something very like fear in her eyes as she continued to stare at him. "I . . . think I should ask who those others are before I come to a decision."

"Of course," Rion agreed, wishing he had the courage to take her hand. "The other women I truly love are Jovvi and Tamrissa, both of whom are more than simply sisters to me. At first I felt that my joy in lying with them was a betrayal of *you*, and then I realized that they meant far too much to me for me to cheapen the time even in my thoughts alone. It's become clear that we'll need to continue strengthening our Blending bond on a regular basis, and I loathe the thought of hiding my true feelings from you. That's why I—"

"Oh, Rion, I was so afraid!" Naran blurted, cutting short the rest of what he'd been about to say. "I thought you meant *other women*, not Jovvi and Tamrissa! We six are all a part of each other, and if your love for them couldn't be full and true, it could never be that for me either. Will it . . . disturb you to hear that I've begun to feel the same way about Lorand and Vallant? They're marvelous men, the best in the world, and my feelings for them have been growing much stronger . . ."

"But of course Lorand and Vallant are marvelous men," Rion agreed with a laugh, finally taking Naran's hand in his own. "If they weren't, I would hardly find it possible to call them brothers. Then you agree that we can share as much of our lives as we please, as long as neither of us expects the others to be excluded? If you do, then you really are the most marvelous of women . . ."

"Oh, Rion, how I've missed you," Naran said with a sigh as he kissed her hand. "I really do love Lorand and Vallant, but *you* . . . Thank you for finding a way to bring us close again. I was beginning to think that it might never—Oh, rot!"

"Rot?" Rion echoed as he straightened, his brows high. "Is that a reaction to my kissing your hand? If so—"

"No, no, my comment had nothing to do with hand kissing," Naran said, and now she looked vexed. "I'm afraid that I Saw something that could well cause a bit of difficulty. Lorand and Vallant have been really good about changing their attitudes regarding our all lying together, but there's going to be *something* . . . I caught no more than a glimpse of the possibility, but I think there's going to be trouble with one of them."

"To borrow a phrase from Jovvi, oh, dear," Rion said, a new worry now filling his mind. "Is there anything *we* can do to lessen the trouble?"

"I really don't know," Naran said, her gaze clearly on something other than what lay about her. "That miserable flux is still doing a marvelous job keeping me from Seeing what I need to, but there are still some patterns I haven't yet tried against it. If I do manage to See some way for us to help, I'll be sure to tell you at once."

"Since I'll be right there beside you, telling me anything you like will be effortless," Rion said as he drew her into his arms. "We no longer have tents to pass the night in, but never fear, my love. I'll find *some* way to secure us privacy tonight."

"As a matter of fact, I know you will," Naran responded with a small laugh as her hands went to his arms. "I Saw that as a strong possibility earlier, and couldn't imagine how the situation would come to be. Now that I know . . . I'm just sorry that we still have so much to do before night finally falls."

Rion exchanged a brief kiss of agreement with her before releasing her with a sigh. There *was* quite a lot for them to do before nightfall, and that didn't even count whatever trouble might arise. How nice it would be if they *could* find a way to lead normal lives, whatever *that* was supposed to be . . .

# TWENTY

"Well, at least that's taken care of," Lorand said with a sigh to Jovvi as the last of the people needing attention was helped away. "A lot of these people are still suffering from exhaustion, but there's not much we can do about that. Now we can go and see how Vallant and the others are doing with the volunteers."

"You know, I've been thinking about how long training takes," Jovvi mused, her lovely brow wrinkled in a small frown. "Under normal circumstances we can show the volunteers all the patterns they need in just a few days, but right now we don't have the time to spare. If those people are willing, I just may have come up with a way to train them a good deal faster."

"Not wasting time means saving lives," Lorand said with his own brows high. "If that isn't a good enough reason for trying your idea, nothing else will do the job either. What have you thought of?"

"If we use our Blending entity to impress the knowledge we have into the minds of the volunteers, they'll have learned what they need to know without spending the time to do it the long way." Jovvi studied him as she spoke, a bit more carefully than usual. "So what do you think? Will they consider that a conscienceless invasion?"

"I don't know how *they'll* look at it, but I consider it a great idea," Lorand said, honestly meaning every word. "Assuming it does the job we want it to, impressing the knowledge on the minds of others ought to be incredibly efficient. It's too bad *we* couldn't learn the patterns like that."

"At first I thought that impressing might give the patterns to people who couldn't handle them," Jovvi said, clearly back to fretting. "Then I remembered that everyone we trained with was shown the necessary patterns, but not everyone was able to *use* what they were shown. I wonder how many new Blendings we'll be able to build. There seemed to be quite a lot of people who went to join Vallant."

"Right now I'd say there are about half that number still with him," Lorand estimated as they walked toward the place where Vallant and Tamrissa waited. "If that's the final count after they've been told everything they need to hear, we'll hopefully have four new Blendings to work with."

"But not *full* Blendings," Jovvi murmured after glancing around to be certain that no one was listening. "I've been wondering why we haven't come across anyone at all with Sight magic in this country."

"I—ah—got the answer to that question, but haven't mentioned it on purpose," Lorand said with another sigh, hating having to add to Jovvi's disturbance. "I spoke to that Reesh fool, and it was all I could do not to rant and rave at the man. In our own country, 'nulls' were sent to special villages and never talked about. Here . . . here they're 'put out of their misery.' "

"Oh, no," Jovvi breathed, tragedy in her lovely eyes. "They just put them down like animals? How can they do something that heartless?"

"To them it's being practical," Lorand told her with a headshake. "Reesh dismissed the whole thing with a wave of his hand, assuring me that they were doing a great favor for the parents of such children. Putting down the hopelessly crippled meant that no one had to suffer with the knowledge that their son or daughter would never amount to anything."

"And you spoke to Reesh about the matter because he would never see a connection between your question and anything of real importance." Jovvi now matched Lorand's sigh, and then she matched his headshake. "Well, if no one in this country ever protested that practice, then they deserve to have nothing but unfinished Blendings. You do know that these people meant to invade us, don't you?"

"Yes, I picked up that fact myself," Lorand replied. "They probably would have had no trouble against the nobles and their pet Middle Blending, but once *we* took over their chance was gone. At least the assembly Gracelians were bright enough to understand *that* point."

"And the Gracelians should continue to understand it even once they're ruled by High Blendings," Jovvi said. "These people will have us and our associate Blending to compare themselves to, so they won't be able to fool themselves into believing— Vallant, Tamrissa. Are we ready to start the training?"

Lorand and Jovvi had reached the place where their Blendingmates waited, and the two nodded in answer to Jovvi's question.

"Rion was keepin' an eye on Naran and her link group people, but he and Naran should be back in a minute or so," Vallant told them. "These people are what's left of the volunteers, and they've even formed themselves into Blendin's. There were others, but either they didn't like what real Blendin' called for, or they couldn't find anyone willin' to Blend with them."

"But we told them how to Blend before they left," Tamrissa put in, looking pleased. "If they don't use the knowledge themselves, at the very least they'll pass it on. People were free to try to join an assembly Blending in this country, but until they did they weren't allowed to know how to do it themselves. Those people who were in a Blending and were displaced were made to forget the method, so the assembly kept control *that* way. Now that part of it is out of their hands."

"Once we're through here, the old assembly members probably won't *be* assembly members any longer," Lorand pointed out. "I know I should be feeling guilty about our part in bringing them down, but this needs doing too badly for guilt to have a chance. And Jovvi has come up with an idea that could very well get these people trained a lot faster than the old way."

"But that's exactly what we need," Tamrissa exclaimed while Vallant made a sound of pleased surprise. "What have you come up with, Jovvi?"

"Something that might not work, but is certainly worth trying," Jovvi said with a smile before turning her head to the right. "And here come Rion and Naran, so I can explain what I have in mind to everyone at the same time."

The last members of their Blending came up right on cue, so to speak, and then Jovvi was able to explain her idea. Lorand listened with pleasure while Jovvi spoke, enjoying her bright mind as usual, and once she was through Rion was the first to comment.

"That's the best idea I've heard in quite some time," he said while the others showed that they agreed. "I've been feeling rather more impatient than usual lately, and I've come to believe that that's due to the fact that we have very little time before . . . *something* happens. I suggest that we get on with the experiment while we still can."

"But first we need to have those people agreein' with the idea," Vallant pointed out. "I'll tell them what we have in mind, and hopefully they'll go along with it."

That *was* the first step, so Lorand stood and listened while Vallant got the attention of the twenty people waiting to be shown how to Blend. Vallant told them what he and the others wanted to do, and then had to speak louder over murmurs and comments of disturbance.

"I can understand that you aren't sure about what we're suggestin'," Vallant said with both hands raised, palm out, toward them. "We aren't certain the trick will work either, but it's definitely worth tryin'. You can't be hurt by it, after all, and if all we were thinkin' about was gettin' control of all of you, we wouldn't have had to mention our intention. We could have just gone ahead and done it, which you'll find out after you Blend for the first time. We're runnin' out of time, folks, so please make up your minds fast."

"I say he's right," one of the men in the group said once Vallant stopped speaking. "I think we all know that a Blending can take over ordinary people whether they like it or not, and these people *are* stronger High talents than any of *us*. If their idea works, it will save us from having to learn a lot of new things the hard way."

"I've always enjoyed the idea of doing things the easy way," a woman said, clearly supporting the man's statement. "Let's do try it and see what happens, because if it doesn't work we have a lot of cramming ahead of us before we can get our own back against those filthy invaders."

That last point about getting their own back seemed to reach the rest of the group, and a moment later everyone had agreed to trying Jovvi's idea. Lorand glanced around to see members of their various link groups lounging around casually not far away, which made him feel a good deal better. Blending at a time when their bodies would be vulnerable to attack was an idea that disturbed Lorand, but with their link groups there and alert—and their Blending entity not far away—Lorand felt easier in his mind.

"We'll sit down, if you don't mind," Jovvi said to the group of hopefuls once they'd all agreed. "You'll find that after the first time or two that you Blend, sitting down while your entity operates will be much easier for you."

Lorand joined the others in following Jovvi's example, and a moment later it was the Lorand entity who floated beside his flesh forms. The Lorand entity was amused to see his associate entity floating not far away, clearly on guard against any sort of attack that might come. With that fact in view, the Lorand entity quickly examined those flesh forms waiting for his attention. Many of them were filled with doubt and fear, so the Lorand entity first calmed them and then put into their minds the knowledge that they needed.

The new flesh forms all exclaimed with pleasure when the knowledge was theirs, but the Lorand entity wasn't yet done. He also gave the new flesh forms details concerning the act of Blending, and then it was Lorand alone who sat on the ground.

"Now I'd like you all gettin' into the positions you were shown," Vallant called to the twenty people, who were still busy exclaiming in delight. "Since you all know how to do it, Blendin' should be easy for you."

Lorand felt the crackling eagerness in the air as the

twenty people did as Vallant had said. They formed themselves into four groups of five, and Lorand was pleased to see that they were all of an optimal composition. Two of the four had three men and two women, and the other two had three women and two men. Blendings of all men or all women would be optimal only for those people whose natures allowed a physical sharing among them, otherwise it would be pointless.

And then it was the Lorand entity who watched as, one after the other, the four new entities came into being. There was still a crackling awe and eagerness behind those new entities, which the Lorand entity found amusing.

—*Welcome,*—the Lorand entity said to the new ones in greeting, drawing their immediate attention. —*There still remain a number of things for your flesh forms to do, but we greet you with pleasure.*—

That was when the new ones noticed the second entity floating not far away, and had it been possible for entities to be wide-eyed, the four new ones would have been just that. The new ones were small and weak in comparison to the Lorand entity and his associate, and it was impossible for them not to be aware of that fact.

—*Your Spirit magic members must now dissolve your Blendings,*— the Lorand entity told the new ones. —*Your first efforts will be extremely draining, but that will pass in a short while. In the interim, your flesh forms must strengthen themselves as you have been shown, and then you will grow and flourish as we have.*—

The new ones did as they were bid, and then Lorand was back a second time to see the reactions of the new Blending members. All twenty of them seemed to be babbling to their new Blendingmates, and that despite their obvious weariness.

"I think that that went really well," Tamrissa said as she rose to her feet, the rest of them following. "Jovvi, you're an absolute genius. If those people are ready on time to face the invaders, it will be thanks only to you."

"She knows that and thanks you for mentioning the point aloud," Lorand said with a laugh when Jovvi just smiled and shook her head. "She's too modest to have said the same thing, of course, which is why she's glad *you* mentioned it."

"Lorand!" Jovvi exclaimed in mock outrage while everyone else laughed. "You're making me sound like an egotistical monster! Instead of teasing the life out of me, why don't you help me find enough food to bring our new Blending members back to life? Between holding to the power as long as they can and Blending for the first time, they're almost flat to the ground."

Lorand turned to see that Jovvi's description of the new Blending members was literally true. All twenty of them were now sitting on the ground, and some *were* lying flat. It wasn't hard to remember what it felt like when *they* first began to Blend, and the others apparently remembered the same.

"Oh, my, yes," Tamrissa said at once, looking the Gracelians over. "They do need to be fed now, and with better food than what they've *been* getting. And I think it's time to suggest that the rest of the escapees here in the village start to move on. That way there ought to be a brief lull until the new escapees arrive, and we might even find a place to sleep tonight."

"There won't be any difficulty in finding a place to sleep tonight," Rion said, surprising Lorand and apparently everyone else except Naran. "I've discussed the matter with my link groups, and even mentioned the same to our associates. Air magic will provide each of us with a warm, dry, comfortable, and *private* place to sleep tonight, and should take no more than a small effort. Forming each area will take the most strength, but afterward the areas can be maintained with minimal effort."

"If we hadn't had those tents the Gracelians insisted on bringing, Rion might have thought of this sooner," Naran said, holding to Rion's arm in a way she hadn't done in a number of days. "Actually, our own preparations worked against his thinking of it. When you have 'good enough,' you most often don't bother to look for better."

"You know, now that you've got me thinkin' about it, I

can see that we haven't been doin' nearly all we can to make livin' easier," Vallant commented. "I could have been providin' drinkin' water as well as bathin' water, and Lorand could have made huntin' a lot easier by bringin' the game to *us*."

"And I could have kept us warm when the weather turned a bit cool," Tamrissa added in agreement. "It's also just occurred to me to ask if it's possible to use Fire magic to keep us *cool* when it gets too warm. Maybe something combined with Air and Water magic . . ."

"We'll have to look into all of that, but first we have to take care of those new Blendingmates," Lorand said, bringing everyone back to the present. "The longer it is before they can eat, the more they'll suffer, so we'd better get a move on."

One glance told the others that Lorand wasn't exaggerating, so they separated to look for the food that they needed—and to get as many people as possible on the road away from there. Jovvi went with Lorand, which made him even happier than usual. He'd missed lying with Jovvi at night, and now it looked like he would *not* have to wait until he could do it again. He'd certainly have to remember to thank Rion as sincerely as possible . . .

Thrybin Korge left his tent after a nice nap, feeling considerably better than he had earlier in the day. Those fool associates of his had gotten him very disturbed with their maunderings, but the passage of time in logical thought had cleared up the confusion he'd felt.

The new strength his Blending now had *would* be enough to let him take charge of this effort against the invaders, and would also let him make use of the feeble strength of the others. Their five entities would work together to dispose of the trash the invaders sent against them, but it would be *his* Blending that got all the credit for their success. When they returned to Liandia victorious, his Blending would claim leadership of the assembly and the empire with no one able to deny them—

"Psst, Thrybin!" he heard, and then Restia Hasmit was beside him. "You're out here just in time for the show, so come on!"

Thrybin's Blendingmate had been whispering, but she'd also been laughing softly. For that reason he let her tugging on his arm lead him in the direction she wanted him to go, curiosity touching him lightly. Restia was obviously up to something amusing, and it should be fun to see what she considered a "show."

Thrybin was led only a short distance away, to a ring of bushes near someone else's tent. When Satlan Reesh stepped out of the tent and Zirdon Tal suddenly appeared in front of Reesh, Thrybin had a strong hint about what was going on.

"Good day, Reesh," Tal said in a friendly but formal way with a small bow. "I trust you had a decent night's sleep last night?"

"What do you want, Tal?" Reesh answered at once with impatience clear in his voice. "If you don't have any work to do, I'll be glad to help find you some."

"Does that mean you see nothing wrong in what was done to me?" Tal countered at once, his tone filled with supposed hurt. "Have you stopped to think how *you* would feel if it had been done to *you* instead? Those disgusting outlanders spoke sharply to *you* more than once, and if they did decide to ruin your life, which of your colleagues would have had the nerve to protest? None of them really likes you, you know."

"Yes, I couldn't help but notice that," Reesh answered with what seemed to Thrybin to be dry resignation. "I've been thinking about my . . . lack of popularity quite a bit, and I've come to certain unhappy conclusions."

"And one of those conclusions must be that what you need is a *real* friend," Tal said with sympathetic understanding, stepping closer to put a hand to Reesh's arm. "Yes, I already know that, so—"

"No, that is *not* one of the conclusions I've come to," Reesh interrupted sharply, shaking off Tal's hand. "What I've had to face is the fact that my lack of popularity is my own fault, just as yours was with you. Or didn't you know that not a single member of the assembly really liked you?"

"Come now, let's admit that you're exaggerating just to make your own position appear better," Tal said in such a condescending way that Reesh looked ready to hit the man. "We both know that my popularity would be rather over-whelming to someone like you—"

"You know, I never understood why so many people considered you a fool, but now I'm beginning to," Reesh interrupted, studying Tal as though he were an interesting but outlandish insect. "You weren't popular, you were feared, mostly because your opponents sometimes had terrible accidents that couldn't be traced back to you. And because of the wealth and standing of your family, which would un-doubtedly have supported you if anyone felt foolish enough to accuse you anyway. Now, though, you're without position and soon to be without family backing, so would you like to put gold on how many 'friends' you find coming to your aid?"

"Reesh, you're letting your distress make you talk fool-ishly," Tal said, a bit more sharply than he'd *been* speaking. "My position in the assembly may have changed for the moment, but my family will see to it that my place is restored whether or not I still have talent. I was treated shabbily and high-handedly without a proper accusation or any sort of proof, and because of that am due much in the way of repa-ration. If you expect anything else to be done, I'm afraid you're due for great disappointment."

"Oh, there will be lots of disappointment, but none of it will be mine," Reesh returned, now apparently enjoying the discussion. "You seem to forget, Tal, that you were stupid enough to attack a woman with your Blending in front of the rest of us. If the woman hadn't burned the talent out of all of you, you *would* have been accused on the spot—and treated to the same removal of talent. After the word about *that* gets around, do you really expect *your* family to still stand be-hind you? Aren't they the ones to whom face means so much? You've lost more face than an entire generation of them could have done on their own, and they'll disown you the instant they hear about it. In point of fact, I'm looking forward to seeing that."

"No, that isn't true!" Tal denied in a shout, all thought of cozening Reesh clearly gone from his head. "My family will know that all of you are lying, and they'll stand behind me! I *know* they'll stand behind me!"

"Lie to yourself all you like, Tal, but don't expect *me* to let the lie go unchallenged," Reesh countered, his expression now one of grim satisfaction. "Even if we did happen to be lying about what you'd done, since most people hearing about it will take it as truth, your family will have no choice but to disown you. Now get back to work and out of my sight, and don't come back to bother me again."

Tal, having no choice about obeying, stumbled away looking grey and old, and Reesh himself headed toward where lunch would be served. Thrybin exchanged a glance of amusement with Restia, and then he nodded.

"You were right to alert me to that, and I enjoyed it thoroughly," Thrybin told her softly. "I'd been thinking about pulling Reesh back as my lapdog again, and now I know I can. I'll take care of it after lunch."

"The others are all too out of sorts to oppose you the way they have in the past, so now is the best time for you to take charge," Restia told him just as softly. "Be decisive in a casual way, and they should follow along without more than a murmur or two of protest."

"I'll do that," he said, putting a hand to her face before moving away to join his current peers for lunch. She would join the rest of the Middle talents for the meal, all of them staying back out of the way while the major talents made all the decisions. Just the way it should be, of course . . .

Reesh was just getting his meal when Thrybin arrived, and the others already sat eating. Thrybin waited politely until Reesh was finished, and then he took his own meal before joining the loose circle his peers had made. No one spoke or greeted anyone else, and the air of gloom was so thick that Thrybin could have used it to stuff his bed mat. Instead of spreading his own good mood around Thrybin gave his attention to the meal, and only when he had cleaned his plate did he take a sip of tea and then look around.

"Since no one else has said it, let me be the first," he announced, gaining the attention of the others. "We have to do something about the invaders whether or not the outlanders are with us, so let's get down to planning. I say we go back to that village and wait until more invaders are sent to replace the ones we destroyed. When they arrive, we take care of them in the same way the first group was done."

"We can't destroy them in the same way," Antrie Lorimon replied, her whole bearing more than weary. "You weren't there, Thrybin, but I assure you that it took two very strong Blendings to get anywhere at all. Without those two strong Blendings, there isn't anything we can do."

"Of course there is, Antrie," Thrybin scolded mildly. "We happen to have *five* Blendings among us, so there's quite a lot we can do. If we stand together against those invaders we'll win, and that's what we came out here to do, isn't it? *You* tell her, Reesh—tell her that we're bound to be successful."

"I'm not sure we will be," Reesh answered at once in an open, honest way that surprised Thrybin. Usually the man was more than eager to support anyone who spoke to him as though he really was a desirable human being . . . "As Antrie said, you weren't there but the rest of us were. And if anyone has learned this point, I'm the one: We need to take captives to question, so if destroying the invaders was what you had in mind, you're wrong on that score as well."

"Oh, please!" Thrybin said, showing a corner of his annoyance. "Those outlanders are the ones who said we need prisoners, but if you stop to think about it you'll see how ridiculous the contention is. If we're able to destroy all the invaders, will it *matter* where they came from and what they intended? We already know that what they intend is to take over our country and kill our people, so what more do we *need* to know? Our most important task is to stop them, and I need the rest of you to join me in that work. Are you all saying you refuse?"

"No, we aren't saying that," Dinno rumbled after taking a

deep breath. "We'll all go out there together the way we're supposed to, but I seriously doubt if it will do any good. And let *me* point out that Reesh is right. If nothing else, we need to know how many men the invaders have to throw at us, and how long they'll continue that throwing if we start to destroy them. If the numbers are too great, we'll need to get more of our peers out here to help."

Lorimon, Gardan, and Reesh were nodding at that, so Thrybin had to swallow down his annoyance and pretend to smile his own agreement.

"All right, then we'll take a prisoner or two just to make you happy," Thrybin conceded. "But first we have to find the invaders before we can take any of them prisoner, so I suggest we get moving. We're much better off meeting the enemy on *our* terms and ground rather than on theirs."

That was something none of them could argue, so they all put their plates and cups aside and prepared to stand. Thrybin rose as well, and touched Reesh's arm as the man was about to walk away.

"Reesh, a word with you in private, please," Thrybin said with the smile that always reached the man. "I'd like to tell you more of what I have in mind as a plan."

"I already know what you have in mind, and if you do it you'll have to manage without *my* help," Reesh responded at once, neutrally but also, unbelievably, on the cold side. "You want to take over the empire as well as this group, but you're a fool to think you can. And don't try again to manipulate me by pretending to be my friend. You don't like me any more than the others do, but at least they have reason to feel like that. You don't, not after all the times I supported you, but it's clear that that doesn't count with you. Just stay away from me, and we'll both be better off."

And with that the man turned and walked away, leaving Thrybin to stare after him. Worse yet, the others had heard what Reesh had said, and they all seemed to approve of his outburst. Thrybin himself turned away and went to find his horse, distantly wondering if the world was about to end. Satlan Reesh, refusing to be manipulated through his need for acceptance? Thrybin never would have believed the fool capable of behaving like that, and still didn't believe it after having seen it.

Well, not to worry. Reesh would come around after Thrybin and his Blending showed the whole bunch of them how strong his new arrangement was, but that would be too late. Thrybin no longer *wanted* Reesh to support him, and when the man begged to serve him he would laugh and walk away. That would leave Reesh all alone, something that would bring the man the devastation he deserved.

It wasn't long before the other major talents and their Blendings were mounted, so Thrybin and *his* Blending led the way to the road and toward that village. There were all sorts of people clogging the road again, and getting past and around the fleeing fools was rather difficult. The extra effort necessary made the ride even longer, so Thrybin wasn't in the best of moods when they reached a stand of woods and Gardan called to him.

"Korge, we'll be leaving our horses in there, in the woods," Gardan said when Thrybin turned in his saddle. "We can see the village from the edge of those woods without having to expose ourselves to attack."

For a moment Thrybin was about to remind the fool Gardan who was in charge, but then it became clear that the others were all solidly of the same mind. The key to the beginnings of leadership was to never give a command that your followers were determined to disobey. It set a bad precedent for the future, so Thrybin simply smiled and led the way back to the others.

"If being in the woods will make you all feel safer, by all means let's stop in the woods," Thrybin told them with easy generosity. "Once you learn that those invaders can't stand against our combined might, though, I expect to see you all filled with a proper courage."

Thrybin's soon-to-be followers weren't pleased to have their courage denied even in passing, but they still followed him into the woods without comment. When Gardan indicated that it was time to leave the horses, they all dismounted, and then Thrybin gestured Dinno into leading the way. The other man gave silent agreement along with a wry bow, and then they were moving through the woods on foot.

It wasn't far to the edge of the woods, and then Thrybin got his first look at the village. It was clearly emptier than most villages he'd seen, but not completely deserted. There were at least a dozen people moving around, all of them ignoring the vast swarm of flies and carrion birds infesting the air to the far right of the last of the houses. Thrybin felt puzzled by the presence of the flies and birds, but the mystery was quickly cleared up for him.

"I see they've moved the bodies I stupidly produced out of the village," Reesh said in a soft voice. "Along with their own dead, possibly, but they probably took better care with their own. But I wonder why those people are still here. Don't they know that the invaders will be along to find out why the ones I killed haven't reported back?"

"Some people find reality almost impossible to accept," Lorimon said in a strange tone of voice. "Those people down there have probably talked themselves into believing that they're now safe, most likely because they're terrified of the idea of leaving. We all find reasons to keep from doing things that terrify us, don't we?"

"Some of us more successfully than others," Dinno commented, apparently understanding what Lorimon meant. "The most unlucky of our number come to appreciate just how foolish they're being, but still find it impossible to change their actions."

"And then there are those who decide they *should* change, but don't really know where to begin," Reesh put in as though he, too, understood what they were talking about. "I suppose it takes practice to know if you're being smart or foolish in what you do, but how do you get started with practicing the right thing?"

"You ask your friends," Dinno said, looking directly at Reesh with a smile. "When someone is serious about wanting to do better with his life, people know it and admire the someone for making the effort. See? Getting started isn't that difficult at all."

"How incredibly good it feels to have friends who are willing to help," Reesh said to Gardan and Lorimon as well as Dinno, since the other two were also smiling at him. "I wish I'd known that sooner . . ."

"There's something we all have to know," Thrybin interrupted just as Dinno was about to speak again. "If the invaders show up we need to be ready, so a little less idle conversation, please."

Thrybin had put a bit of sharpness in his tone to show his annoyance, but the four fools chuckled among themselves rather than turning shamefaced. What they found so amusing Thrybin couldn't imagine, but at least they fell silent. That was enough to satisfy Thrybin, since it showed that they *were* beginning to obey him.

But the following hours proved a good deal less satisfying. At least two of them went by while nothing at all happened, except for the others discussing something in murmurs and then going off to speak to their Blendingmates. Thrybin wondered what they were doing, but asking them would have been too demeaning. *He* was supposed to be the one in charge, and assuming that they were acting without his knowledge and approval would weaken his position. He had to assume instead that they were just wasting idle time, but suddenly Dinno spoke up.

"All right, another group of invaders is just a few minutes away," Dinno said, not just to Thrybin, as he should have, but to the others as well. "Everyone get comfortable, and then we'll see what we can do."

"I'm the one who will be giving the orders, Dinno!" Thrybin told the man sharply. He was annoyed for more reasons than the fact that they were all sitting down already, and it was time the fool understood who their leader was. "Why are you assuming that the invaders are almost here? We might still have as much of a wait as we've already endured, so—"

"You're the one doing the assuming, Korge," Dinno came back much too quickly and sharply. "You were obviously content to sit here and wait, but the rest of us decided to use our Blendings to keep an eye out. This last watch was mine, and I saw the invaders coming with my own—or at least with my entity's—eyes."

Thrybin was furious, but there wasn't much he could do about their totally unacceptable behavior right now. So what if it hadn't occurred to him to set out a watch? If one of them had mentioned the need, he would have assigned them to what they'd done on their own. How dare they act as though he weren't in charge? Didn't they know—

"Korge, they're *here*!" Lorimon had the nerve to say in a tone that suggested he was a child who needed direction. "Don't just sit there, *Blend*!"

And then Lorimon acquired the look that the others already had, the staring distraction that said they had Blended. Thrybin would have dearly loved to Blend and then destroy *her*, but that could be taken care of later, once the invaders had been seen to. Instead he nodded to Restia to begin the Blending, and then—

And then the entity containing the flesh form Korge was born, an entity much strengthened from all but the last time it had been called forth. That strength was clear when compared to the other four entities awaiting it, a fact the other entities were also aware of. Those other entities hung back, giving *it* the honor of floating out first, and it lost no time in doing so.

Those flesh forms down among the dwellings, who had been going about various mundane tasks, were no longer doing so. Instead they now ran screaming, for the first of the alien flesh forms had come into view. The strongest entity floated toward the alien flesh forms, the other entities following, and when the strongest reached the aliens it attacked.

But to no avail. The aliens seemed entirely unaware of the strongest entity's presence, its efforts against them blocked by what appeared to be an aura of some sort. Its failure gave the entity distant anger, and while it hung motionless in its frustration it became aware of the fact that the lesser entities were not equally as motionless. The four of them surrounded the aliens and attempted to increase their strength by reflecting it back and forth between themselves, and they did accomplish a surprising increase. But even so, their efforts did nothing to breach the aura surrounding the enemy.

Which brought the strongest entity distant fear. An urge came for the entity to flee and preserve itself, but instead it attempted to add its own superior strength to the effort of the others. Its presence did indeed add to the effort, but still that aura remained untouched, and now the enemy began to slay those flesh forms it found among the dwellings . . .

And then it was Thrybin back to himself, as he and his Blendingmates exchanged looks of disbelief. That protective aura around the invaders . . . How could it possibly be so strong and resistant?

"Well, now we know for certain," Dinno said, heavy despair in his tone. "Even with five of us, it wasn't possible to break through that aura of protection. We can't do anything to save those people who stayed in the village, so we'd better get going ourselves. Once the village is entirely theirs, they'll move on again."

Thrybin watched them get to their feet and start to head back to the horses, and he suddenly found himself standing as well without remembering how it had happened.

"You can't all run off and desert me!" he shouted, making them pause to look back at him. "It has to be some kind of mistake that we weren't able to reach them, it *has* to be! We can't just run away in defeat—!"

"Why not?" Gardan asked flatly, looking at Thrybin as though he were less than himself rather than more. "Don't you think we knew it when you tried to make your entity run away? The only thing that kept you with us was the fact that your Blendingmates aren't as craven as you, otherwise all that marvelous strength you're so proud of wouldn't have been added to our own. Which was supposed to be the original idea, I think, even though it made no difference."

"He doesn't want us to 'desert' him because he hasn't yet made himself the hero of this crisis," Reesh said, and he had the nerve to speak in a tone filled with disgust. "If he leaves with us now he has to admit that his marvelous plans were the daydream we told him they were, and he can't live with that idea. Just like those people in the village, he'd rather lie to himself than deal with the unacceptable."

Thrybin was furious all over again, and nearly attacked his so-called associates by himself. But then he remembered that he didn't have to do *anything* alone, not when he had the strongest Blending around to work with him. With that in mind he turned to his Blendingmates, intending to tell them what he meant to do, but they were no longer in the places he'd left them. They were joining the others in heading for the horses, and when they turned to glance back at him there was disdain in their eyes. Disdain!

Rage tried to rise in Thrybin, but suddenly all anger was replaced by fear. His Blendingmates had believed him when he'd told them how strong they would be once they bonded, strong enough to do anything they cared to. But it hadn't worked out that way, and they also knew that he was the one who had tried to make them run away while the others were still fighting against the invaders. That they'd walked away from him said something terrible, so terrible that Thrybin couldn't bring himself to think about it.

So he simply stumbled along after everyone else, promising himself that he would straighten out all the trouble once they'd put enough distance between themselves and those murderous invaders. He *would* be their leader again, the leader of everyone in the whole empire!

# TWENTY-ONE

It had been a more than interesting day, filled with work and new beginnings, and everyone seemed as glad as I was that the day was nearly over. When I say everyone, I mean my Blendingmates. The Gracelians in their new Blendings were still drunk on their recent experiences, and seemed to find sitting in one place for very long an impossible task. I found their reactions amusing and touching, remembering as I did how *I'd* reacted in the beginning. But I also found watching them tiring, so I watched instead the new groups of refugees being helped by the villagers to find places to rest.

"It's a lucky thing we got the first group of escapees on their way when we did," Jovvi commented, just about reading my mind. "If we hadn't, there would have been no room at all for *these* people."

"And thanks to us they'll even have what to eat," I agreed. "The new Blendings had no trouble Encouraging the crops that were almost ready for harvesting into ripeness and the crops only recently planted into growing faster. That way the villagers won't suffer for sharing what they have, and *they* got to share in the meat our own Blendings brought into reach."

Jovvi was about to say something else, when Naran came over to crouch beside where we were sitting. Our Blending-sister looked disturbed, and didn't wait for us to ask what was wrong.

"We need to get the men back from wherever they went,"

she told us in a soft voice. "We'll be having visitors in just a little while."

"Lorand went to check over the new arrivals, so he isn't that far away," Jovvi said, her brows high. "Vallant and Rion are with our own people, setting up watch schedules. What have you Seen?"

"The Gracelian assembly members are on their way, and a large group of invaders is only a few hours behind them," Naran answered with a sigh. "The invaders will get here in the small hours of the morning, and they won't wait for daylight to attack."

"So we have to be ready for all of them," I said with my own sigh. "Those assembly people will probably make almost as much trouble as the invaders."

"Maybe not," Jovvi said, preparing to get to her feet. "If they're coming here rather than staying in their camp, they must have discovered that they can't handle the invaders alone. That realization should make them behave politely, at least until they find out about the High Blendings we've formed. Let's find the men, and then we can greet our visitors in the proper way."

I rose to my feet as well, and then we went looking for the rest of our Blending. Rion would be disappointed that his idea about shelter for us would have to wait to be tested, and I felt a small bit of disappointment myself. It would have been nice to be alone with Vallant again, but somehow the . . . edge of my need for Vallant's complete attention had been dulled. He and I *would* be together at some time, and waiting was no real hardship.

When Lorand heard the news, he left his link group members and the Earth magic people from our second Blending to finish working with the newcomers.

"Happily, we've already got most of these people taken care of," he said with a smile that quickly vanished. "I just hope we can *keep* them in good health."

With the invaders coming there was no guarantee of that, even though we'd already stopped a different group of them. For that reason we all seemed lost in our own thoughts as we went to find Vallant and Rion, and when we located our last two, Vallant needed only a single glance at us.

"What's wrong?" he asked at once, Rion immediately joining him in coming toward us. "I knew everythin' was goin' too smoothly for it to last long."

"The Gracelian assembly members will be here soon, and a large group of invaders is only a few hours behind them," Naran said, delivering the news herself when Jovvi and I remained silent. "And from what I could See, the invaders won't wait until morning to attack."

"So we'll soon have another chance at gettin' some answers," Vallant commented, obviously feeling more optimistic than the rest of us. "What do you mean when you say a 'large' group, Naran? How large is that?"

"At least three times the size of the group we defeated at that village," Naran answered at once, her gaze turned inward the way it usually was when asked a question like that. "I'm still having trouble breaking through that flux, but I have the impression that there's even more trouble coming *beyond* that group of invaders. Exactly what it is, I can't tell yet."

"My guess would be that their leaders are movin' forward," Vallant said, now sounding depressed. "That means we'll be facin' whoever put that aura of protection around the invaders. I have to admit I'm not lookin' forward to that. Things won't go the way they did with the Astindans."

The rest of us exchanged glances, knowing exactly what Vallant meant. The Astindans had shown a sense of honor that went far beyond the usual, but these invaders had shown just the opposite. To send your forces to kill everyone they reached, to blithely destroy lives, and then move on to destroy even more lives . . . It was a vicious, heartless, *inhuman* thing to do, so there would be no coming to terms with the leaders of the invaders.

"I'd say that makes things easier for us," I put in, determined to lighten the heavy gloom that had settled on everyone. "We could have destroyed the Astindans piecemeal, but we all knew they had a right to try getting their own back.

That doesn't hold true for these invaders, so we ought to feel very little guilt when we wipe them out. Even if we have to stretch some to do it."

I'd added that last just to show I hadn't forgotten the very real possibility that the invader leaders had more strength than we did. The reminder could well have brought back the gloom, but instead everyone seemed to brighten.

"I've always been more comfortable with the idea of bestin' someone bigger than me," Vallant said with a sweet smile sent in my direction. "Takin' someone my size or smaller always felt like cheatin', and I don't much care for cheatin'. Let me tell the others what's goin' on, and then we'll go and meet those assembly people."

We waited while Vallant walked back to the others and explained what was going on, and when he rejoined us I directed our steps toward the fire where our meal had been prepared. There was still tea left, I knew, and I definitely wanted a cup.

Everyone decided they also wanted a cup of tea to brace them, and by the time we'd all helped ourselves our first wait was over. One of our people came over to say that the assembly members had just reached the outskirts of the village, so they ought to be with us very shortly. As we stood sipping our tea and waiting, I wondered which of the five major talents would be leading the group. Logic said that that Korge fool would have taken over, but I had the strangest feeling—

"There they are," Jovvi said, and it was clear she'd known of their arrival without needing to be told about it by that sentry. "And look who's riding at their head."

I did look, but I wasn't sure I believed. The man Olskin Dinno rode in front, but right beside him was Satlan Reesh. Somehow Reesh had lost that air of constantly being out of his depth, and Dinno wasn't projecting distaste at being in the man's company.

"Better yet, look who's trailing behind all alone," Lorand murmured, amusement in his voice. "I wonder what Korge could have done that it turned everyone against him."

"That everyone seems to include his own Blendingmates," Rion observed in a matching murmur. "If they aren't deliberately ignoring Korge, I've never seen the act."

A glance at Korge's Blendingmates suggested that they were bent out of shape by something, so it looked like Rion's comment was true. It's hard to imagine what someone could do to alienate his Blendingmates, especially when they've bonded, but Korge seemed to have managed it. Our sight-seeing had given the head of the column time to reach Vallant where he stood beside Naran, and Dinno looked down at the two of them with mild surprise.

"If you people are here, the rest of you can't be far away," Dinno commented. He glanced around to locate "the rest of us," and then returned his attention to Vallant. "We thought you'd decided to leave us to our own devices. What made you stop here in this village?"

"It was fairly obvious that the folks in this village needed some help," Vallant answered blandly, telling the complete truth without actually admitting a thing. "Why are all of *you* here as well? Did somethin' happen to bring you back?"

"I'm sure you already know what happened," Dinno said with a sigh, not quite meeting Vallant's gaze. "Another group of invaders appeared at that other village, and we were helpless against them even working together. And even with Korge's 'extra strength,' I might add."

"You've changed your minds, haven't you?" Antrie Lorimon said to Vallant as she moved her horse up to where Dinno had stopped. "You've found that you can't abandon us after all, so you've stopped in order to give us the help we need. I can't tell you how happy I am to—"

"No, don't start thankin' us," Vallant interrupted, wiping away the woman's smile of relief and delight. "We aren't here to help *your* group, not when you persist in refusin' to help yourselves. We'll be workin' with people who *aren't* afraid to try somethin' new when their lives are at stake."

"What are you talking about, you fool?" Korge came charging up to demand, fury clearly all through him. "*We* are the legal authorities around here, and either you help *us* or you don't help anyone! Do you understand me?"

"Better than you know," Vallant all but drawled in answer,

the gaze he sent to Korge filled with ice. "You're afraid of havin' someone steal your thunder, someone whose efforts you can't claim as your own. And as far as bein' the legal authority around here goes, you forfeited that position when you lost against the invaders. Or didn't any of you realize that?"

"How dare you tell us what *your* opinion of the matter is?" Korge came back at once while the others simply looked thunderstruck. "Who and what we are is beyond *your* efforts to change, no matter your estimate to the contrary! We are *members of the assembly,* fool, and the only way that can be changed is by—"

Korge's words broke off abruptly, as though a terrible idea had just come to him. He looked around wildly in the direction of his associates, but most of them had gone pale or closed their eyes in understanding.

"Yes, I think you're finally gettin' the idea," Vallant said to Korge in that same drawl, but his tone had sharpened just a bit. "Waitin' for those who can't cut it to step aside is a waste of time, a truth we learned really well at home. The people here wanted nothin' more than the chance to do things right, so we gave it to them. Did you really think we would abandon *them* because their leaders are fools?"

Korge had started to rage incoherently, but the others simply sat their mounts without speaking. I thought they intended to stay that way all night, but then Satlan Reesh drew a deep breath.

"It's amazing that when the worst thing you can imagine actually happens, it turns out not to be as horrible as you were picturing," the man said, surprising all of us. "I expected it to be a while before our positions were gone from us, and I thought I needed the time to get used to the idea. I'm astounded to say I'm not nearly as shocked as I expected to be, and I may even be rather relieved. The worst has happened, and I'm actually ready to pick up the pieces and go on with my life."

"You know, I think I feel the same way," Dinno said in answer, looking at Reesh with surprise. "I also expected this to be the end of the world, but it isn't, is it?"

"Of course it's the end of the world!" Korge screamed, glaring at Dinno and Reesh together. "These interfering imbeciles have broken the law and taught people how to *Blend*! That act goes counter to everything we stand for, and the outlanders must be punished—along with the dupes they forced into doing their bidding. Wake up, you fools, and work with me *now*!"

And with an imperious glance at his Blendingmates, Korge sat his horse staring at us with spite and malice. I suddenly had the impression that a Blending entity floated not far away from us, and I was about to defend us when I realized that Korge *couldn't* be part of that entity. He sat braced on his horse, but didn't have that distant, distracted look that someone takes on when they Blend. The same was true of the rest of the assembly members, so I simply held my fires ready and waited.

"Well, what are you waiting for?" Korge demanded the next moment, obviously speaking to his Blendingmates as well as to the other assembly members. "We have to Blend and do our duty, and we have to do it *now*."

"You really are a fool, but you're clearly the only fool among us," Reesh told the man with obvious distaste and a small headshake. "Even your Blendingmates know how much stronger these people are than we, so the only ones likely to be punished would be anyone stupid enough to go up against them. Why don't you take yourself off somewhere and stop bothering everyone."

The disdain in Reesh's voice hit Korge like a slap across the face, doubly so, most likely, because of who the comment came from. It was very clear that Satlan Reesh had somehow changed on the inside, and because of that now came off as a different man. Gardan looked at Reesh with faint respect and Lorimon stared at him with raised brows, but Dinno simply smiled. Korge, still apparently in shock, glanced around as though about to say something, but no words came out. He must have also noticed the expressions on his associates, and finally, truly realized that he stood all alone.

"I think we'd better ask now where it would be best for us

to camp," Dinno said once it was clear Korge's ranting would not continue. "Our people and baggage are still stretched along the road leading from our last camping place, so it might be best if we found a spot on that side of the village."

"Actually, the *other* side of the village would be best," Vallant told Dinno, his tone of voice now a good deal more careful. "Our people have done some scoutin', and we've learned that the invaders are on the move behind you, headin' this way. Since they'll be comin' up that very same road, you don't want to be between them and us when they get here."

"No, no, we certainly don't," Dinno agreed at once after exchanging a quick glance with Reesh. Reesh, Gardan, and Lorimon all looked upset now, and Korge had actually paled a bit. "We'll get our people moving as quickly as possible. Is there anything we can do to help?"

"You might want to help keep people calmed down as much as possible," Jovvi suggested when Vallant hesitated over answering the question. "The rest of us will have our hands full with the invaders."

"Yes, we can certainly do that," Lorimon agreed at once, looking relieved that there *was* something for them to do. "We'll get our followers out of the way, and then we'll start assuring people that everything will be fine."

With that settled, the Gracelians began to move away from us as they passed along all sorts of orders. Everything seemed to be under control, but I still thought I sensed the presence of an entity, so I turned to Jovvi.

"Am I imagining things, or is there an entity not far from us?" I asked her, trying to keep my voice moderately low. "I'm not unsure about the feeling, but as far as whether or not the feeling is true goes . . ."

"Now that you mention it, I think I may be aware of something myself," Jovvi answered when I just let my words trail off, her brow wrinkled in concentration. "I didn't notice the awareness until you mentioned it, but—"

"What's wrong?" Vallant asked he came up, interrupting Jovvi's slowly spoken comment. "You both look as though somethin' is botherin' you, so I'd like to know what it is."

"Tamma thinks she's detecting the presence of an entity and I may be detecting the same," Jovvi answered for both of us, also keeping her voice low. "If the two of us aren't imagining things, do you think it's possible that the enemy has sent a Blending to scout ahead? If so, we could be in serious trouble."

"Actually, there's *supposed* to be a Blendin' entity here with us," Vallant answered, his expression definitely one of surprise. "I asked our associate Blendin' to be on hand in case there was trouble from the Gracelians, thinkin' there was no way for anyone to know about the precaution. But now you two—"

"Vallant, we may be in trouble," Lorand said softly as he came up to us, taking his turn at interrupting. "I don't know how I know it, but somehow I'm certain that there's a Blending entity around here. Could it be the enemy?"

"Brothers and sisters, we may have a problem," Rion said as he and Naran also came over to join us, speaking before any of the rest of us could answer Lorand. "I became aware of an odd feeling, and I've come to believe that—"

"That there's a Blendin' entity around," Vallant said, looking at both Lorand and Rion. "As I told the ladies, the entity is the one belongin' to our associate Blendin'. I asked them to be here in case any of the Gracelians made trouble, but now I'm tryin' to figure out how all of you know it's here. Give me a minute."

We all began to speak softly about the new development while Vallant seemed to be doing an inward search. Even Naran agreed that she was aware of *something,* a something that had nothing to do with Sight magic. After a moment Vallant made a sound of satisfaction, and then his attention was ours again.

"Okay, now I've got it," Vallant said. "For a minute there I thought I was the only one who wasn't feelin' what the rest of you were, but I'm not. I must have been ignorin' the feelin' because I knew that the Blendin' entity was *supposed* to be here. Is this one of the changes we were expectin' after all that tiredness we went through?"

"It must be," Jovvi said when most of the rest of us just shrugged. "It's a definite benefit and a very useful addition to the balance of our abilities, so it's certainly worth having. I suggest that we all make ourselves aware of what the feeling means, so if the enemy *does* try to approach without warning we'll be warned anyway."

"And we need to pass the word on to our associate Blendin's," Vallant put in with a nod. "Holter's Blendin' isn't much behind our own in developin', and since we've been keepin' his Blendin' and the other lesser Blendin' with him up to date about what's been happenin', we ought to mention this as well. And it's a good thing those other two Blendin's of ours are stickin' so close. We just may have to call them to help us if the new Gracelian Blendin's don't make the difference."

"But hopefully they *will* be able to handle it," Lorand said with a sigh. "If they don't, it could get to be years before we're able to go home—if we're ever able to."

That was too depressing a thought to comment on, and everyone seemed to think the same. Vallant shook his head as he turned away to find our people, and a moment later the others were in two small, unimportant conversations. Rion spoke to Naran while Jovvi spoke to Lorand, a not-unusual pairing off—and that suddenly made me remember a thought I'd had not long ago.

When I'd found out that we would be fighting tonight instead of sleeping, I'd only been faintly disappointed that I'd miss being with Vallant. At the time the feeling seemed perfectly natural, but now I had to wonder about it. I still loved Vallant as much as I ever had, but being with him was no longer an all-consuming need. I *wanted* to be with him, looked forward to being in his arms, but all the anxiety and uncertainty I'd felt at one point was gone.

*Question number one,* I said to myself with a sigh. *Is this a good development or a bad one? Question two, how do I figure out which? And question three, a really good one: what can I possibly do about any of it no matter which one it turns out to be?*

I found nothing in the way of answers jumping out to greet me, which made it a real shame that it was the wrong time to look for someplace to hide for a while . . .

# TWENTY-TWO

Vallant went about his business briskly, as though he had nothing else on his mind, but carefree was the last thing he felt. When he'd heard that the invaders would soon be right on top of them, he'd wanted to curse out loud. He'd been so looking forward to a *private* time with Tamrissa . . .

Vallant didn't quite sigh as he stopped to talk to their people, telling them first about the new ability he and his Blendingmates seemed to have developed. Holter and his people and the fourth Blending along with all of their link groups were about an hour away, camped for the night. Vallant's associates' Blending entity was able to reach them easily, and Vallant had decided to ask them to move their camp closer to the village. Just beyond the camp of the Gracelian assembly members ought to do, especially if care was taken to keep the assembly members from knowing they were there.

With that chore taken care of, Vallant's next stop was with the members of the new Gracelian High Blendings. Those people were still floating in ecstasy over the Blending experience, but when they saw Vallant's expression their delight began to fade.

"Is something wrong?" Rangis Hoad, a member of one of the Blendings, asked almost at once. "You were amused the last time you came over to us, but now you're very disturbed."

"We've just learned that the invaders are comin'," Vallant answered, seeing a variety of expressions grow on the faces around him. "They'll be here in the small hours of the mornin', and we'll be waitin' for them. I'd like the members of your four Blendin's to get some sleep, so you'll be in better condition to join us."

"Join you how?" Alesta Vargan asked, her own expression intense. "Are we going to be standing around watching how you and your other Blending do things, or will *we* get a chance at those vermin?"

"Actually, we want *your* Blendin's to learn how to remove the aura of protection from the invaders," Vallant replied, more than half expecting the question from at least *one* of them. "We already know how to do it, so it's pointless for us to do it again. Unless we find that you haven't yet grown enough in strength to handle the job. If you haven't then we'll do it, and the rest of you will just have to practice until you do gain the strength."

"That's fair enough," Hoad decided aloud, gaining Alesta's grudging nod of agreement. "If we aren't yet able to stop the invaders, we don't want to leave them able to continue killing people. How will we handle the attack?"

"We'll clear the village area closest to the road, and go for the invaders just as they're about to enter the village," Vallant told the closely listening groups. "But one thing you all have to understand: Once the aura of protection is gone from those people, they're not to be destroyed. We need to question them to find out what we vitally need to know, and killin' the ones with the answers won't do anyone any good. And we got the impression from the first group that their bein' here killin' isn't their own idea. It's likely they're bein' controlled, and if so then we might be able to turn them back against the ones who sent them."

"Now, that's who *I'd* like to get to," Alesta said, her smile grim and not very nice. "The ones who sent those murderers to kill helpless, innocent people. Anyone responsible for that kind of thing deserves to die slowly in a great deal of pain."

"You may get your chance at that as well," Vallant said, deciding not to hold back *any* of the news. "Some of our people have gotten the impression that the leaders of the invasion are followin' some distance behind the reinforced group that will be reachin' us first. But you'd better know that it took a *lot* of strength to place those auras of protection. The leaders of the invasion could well be stronger even than *my* Blendin'."

That bit of news wasn't at all welcome to the Gracelians, and even Alesta couldn't quite find what to say. The woman's expression made it clear that she wasn't frightened, but frustrated was something else again. A small child might decide to fight against something an adult wants to do, but the child isn't likely to be very successful no matter *how* much it wants to prevail.

"Now I'm goin' to tell you somethin' even the assembly members don't know," Vallant said after making a quick decision. "We have two more associate Blendin's camped not far from here, but they won't mix in unless we really need them. I'm tellin' you this because their Blendin' entities will be there to observe what we do, and I don't want you thinkin' they're the enemy."

"You know, I'm really glad to hear that," Hoad said with a small laugh, exchanging glances with a few other people. "We talked about the fact that you seemed to have come here with only one other Blending, and that spoke of an arrogance that didn't quite fit with our observations of your actions. We decided you had secrets you weren't willing to share with us, secrets we really needed to know. Now that we do know, we feel a good deal better."

Murmurs of happy agreement came from all over, making Vallant know that there was one more thing he had to tell these people. He hadn't intended to mention the point until he absolutely had to, but if Gandistra was ever going to be honestly friendly with Gracely . . .

"If it's secrets you're lookin' for, you'll find one when your Blendin' entities see ours more clearly," Vallant said after taking a deep breath. "Your entities will probably recognize ours as bein' complete and your own as not, but there's nothin' you can do about the lack right now. There's . . . a sixth talent that doesn't . . . show up like the others, and leads people to believe that the child havin' it is . . . a null . . ."

Now there were gasps of horror and pale faces surrounding Vallant, and twenty incredulous gazes clinging to him. Then most of the gazes were gone, some because the eyes producing them had closed, some because of the presence of tears.

"Chaos take them!" Hoad whispered fiercely, sudden tears running down his beard-stubbled cheeks. "My youngest sister . . . They said she was a null, and that my parents would be heartless and cruel if they didn't let the authorities put her out of her misery. I begged my parents not to let those people take such a bright, happy, *alive* little girl, but my parents told me they couldn't afford to pay the penalties they would be assessed with if they refused. Now you're saying—"

Hoad's ragged voice broke at that point, making it possible to hear the sobbing coming from one of the women. It was clear that a number of the others had had a similar experience with a brother or sister, and now the devastation they'd felt at the time was more than doubled. In a matter of heartbeats there were four separate groups rather than one large, loose arrangement, Blendingmates sharing sorrow and trying to comfort the bereaved.

Vallant felt the suffering as easily as he'd felt the elation earlier, so he turned away from the Gracelians and quickly went looking for Jovvi. The Gracelians were going to need help with getting over the reactions of tragedy, at least for the time being. Chances were they'd never *really* get over it, which would likely turn out to be a good thing. If no other small children ever had their lives stolen from them by the country's "authorities," a dark day would turn bright indeed . . .

Thrybin Korge sat alone while the camp was being reestablished not far from him. The others had obeyed orders and put the camp where the outlanders wanted it, not where it was most convenient for *them*. They were all still members of the assembly, the ruling body of the Gracelian Empire, but the others acted as though their positions had already been taken by those abominations taught and trained by the outlanders.

Rage flared high in Thrybin again, fueled by any number of intolerable happenings. First his own Blendingmates betray him by refusing to stand behind him. Then, when he confronts them about the shameful act, they actually accuse him of lying to them!

"Didn't it ever occur to you that those Gandistra people would put together Blendings that *could* resist the invaders?" Restia Hasmit had had the nerve to demand. "You told us that 'bonding' would make us the most powerful Blending in the empire, but all the bonding in the world won't change the fact that the rest of us are just Middles. We may have more experience with Blending than those newcomers taught by the outlanders, but they have the *strength*! If you didn't realize that this could happen you certainly should have, which makes it an incredibly lucky thing that you weren't given the chance to take *anything* over. You're an idiot as well as a coward, and none of us will ever let you Blend with us again."

The others hadn't uttered a word, but their expressions said that that was only because Restia had said it all *for* them. They agreed with her completely, so Thrybin Korge, head and shoulders better than any of those other fools in the assembly, was now without a Blending.

"And those miserable outlanders have every willing High talent in this village," Thrybin muttered, his lowering stare on those people he was able to see beyond the camp. "The rest won't even consider becoming part of a Blending, not even with an actual assembly member who has experience accomplishing the act. The three I spoke with made that abundantly clear, especially that last woman . . ."

Thrybin thrust away the memory of what that woman had said to him, most of her words a confused mishmash of question and accusation. *How can you even think about forming another Blending when you already have Blendingmates?* she'd demanded, understanding nothing of the true situation. *If you'll turn your back on them, won't you do the same with anyone foolish enough to rely on you?*

That mindless woman had had no idea of what was really involved, and Thrybin hadn't been about to explain matters to her. It was his Blendingmates who had turned their backs on *him,* so didn't he have the right to look for other, more reasonable people to Blend with? Even if they *hadn't* said anything to him until he got back to camp? Their actions had made their position perfectly clear when they'd refused to stand with him, so he'd had every right—

"Well, it seems that continuing to have your talent doesn't make much difference these days," a voice drawled not far from him. "Throwing people out of the assembly has obviously become a favorite pastime of the Gandistrans, and now it's become your turn and that of those other fools. I told you all that it was a mistake to let those people come anywhere near us, and now you're all reaping what you deserve for not having listened."

"There's nothing wrong with my memory, Tal," Thrybin returned at once, more than faintly annoyed at being interrupted in his thinking. "Your pitiful stance was the great decision about whether we should offer the Gandistrans a peace treaty or demand reparations for the 'destruction' caused by their army. You never said a word about not associating with those people, you just went your usual stupid way and tried to attack one of them in secret. And now you seem to have gotten over your shock at having been told the truth by your former puppet."

"That fool Reesh spoke *nothing* of the truth!" Tal spat in answer, his face darkening to match the look in his eyes. "I hadn't realized you were sneaking around eavesdropping, Korge, but even you should know that my family will take what was done to me as a personal insult. They will *not* disown me for unsubstantiated doings that maimed me without warning and without a chance to defend myself, that I promise you. They'll bring legal action against everyone here and the assembly as a whole, and will especially make certain that none of you spreads rumors to the detriment of my family name. All the rest of you will end up working for *me,* and when that happens—"

"Oh, wake up, Tal!" Thrybin snapped, in no mood to coddle a fool. "There isn't anyone here—or back in Liandia, for that matter—who wouldn't rather starve in the streets than work for *you*. And if I remember correctly, much of your family's wealth and position has depended on the fact that they were related to two assembly members, you and your cousin. Your cousin died of the poison that freak Syant had put in our food and drink before we left the city, and now *you* no longer qualify as an assembly member. I'm sure your faulty memory has let you forget that you're responsible for both happenings, directly and completely responsible with no possible excuse to fall back on. If you think your family will overlook *that* fact—"

"It isn't true!" Tal screeched, his hands having turned to claws that rent the air in Thrybin's direction. "None of it was my fault, none of it! Those Gandistrans made me lie, to justify what they did to me without provocation! My family will believe *that,* the truth, not lies formulated out of spite and envy!"

"You really are pitiful to believe that everyone thinks as poorly as you do," Thrybin said with the nastiest smile he felt able to generate. "That Gandistran woman burned the talent out of your entire Blending as well as out of you, so you'd have to explain why you were all Blended in camp. And as far as forcing you to lie goes, you told us things none of us knew about. They were things the Gandistrans couldn't possibly have known, which is why everyone believed what you said. Unless your family is as thick in the head as you, they'll see through you at once."

This time Tal couldn't seem to find any words to throw back in rebuttal, and the desperation in his eyes was a delight to see. Tal had enjoyed the thought of coming over to torment Thrybin, but Thrybin had turned the tables on him in a totally expected way. The fool had never been able to think clearly, and that realization suddenly gave Thrybin a marvelous idea.

"What a shame that you haven't the courage to take your revenge against the people who most deserve it," Thrybin commented, as though simply continuing what he'd been saying. "It's possible that I may soon be replaced in the assembly, but that remains to be seen. You, on the other hand, *will* be replaced even if the rest of us retain what we have.

You've been maimed forever, your entire life stolen away, and you stand there talking about someone else *suing* your fellow victims."

"What else am I supposed to do?" Tal demanded, a definite snarl in his tone. "*I* can't do anything against the Gandistrans, not any longer, so all that's left to me is to convince someone to act in my place. You used to be part of my coalition, Korge. If there's any loyalty inside you at all—"

"Tal, I was part of your coalition for reasons of my own," Thrybin interrupted to say slowly and directly. "It isn't a matter now of loyalty anyway, not when the times demand that we each be loyal to ourselves. The rest of us do have something left to lose, but you don't. If anyone is to use the perfect opportunity that will soon be available to take his revenge, you have to be the one. Afterward, no one will be able to blame you for retaliating against the arrogant beasts—for all of us."

"What perfect opportunity are you talking about?" Tal asked with a frown, the eagerness in his eyes belying the casual way the question had been put. Tal the fool still thought it was possible for him to become a hero . . . "Not that I have any real intention of doing anything to those people. Any one of them could stop me without half trying."

"Not once they've Blended, they can't," Thrybin pointed out in little more than a murmur, his smile now a very satisfying one. "The invaders will be here in the small hours of the morning, they said, so they and their new High talent pets will be Blended to receive the visit. Their Blending entity will naturally be in the thick of things to show the rest of us how pitiful we are in comparison, and that will be the perfect time to strike. Do I need to tell you how vulnerable their bodies will be then?"

"No, of course not," Tal said in a matching murmur, most of his attention directed inward. "That *would* be a priceless opportunity, but I, of course, would never think of using it. It really is a pity that so lovely an opportunity will just slide by without anyone taking advantage of it. Well, I have things to do, Korge, so I'll speak to you again at another time."

Thrybin watched the fool walk away, finding it all he

could do not to laugh out loud. Of *course* Tal would never consider taking advantage of the opportunity, not when the man thought he was still in a position to play politics. Tal obviously still lived in the past when one of his thickheaded ideas had a chance to work. He was "covering his trail" before going ahead with something that there wasn't the slightest chance he wouldn't be caught at.

*Yes, things are definitely looking up,* Thrybin thought with satisfaction. Once the Gandistrans were gone it would prove easy to take advantage of the lack of knowledge and practice of the new High Blendings. That would get *them* out of the way, and with no High Blendings around to challenge the existing assembly members, things would go back to the way they'd been. Yes, tomorrow was guaranteed to be a beautiful day, as soon as he explained to his Blendingmates that he hadn't just been lying to them . . .

Jovvi had to use her link groups to soothe the disturbance of the new Gracelian Blendings. Those poor people had had a terrible shock, and those few who were more personally involved than the others were devastated. The new Blendings would have to fight later, but more importantly they were people who needed help *now* to get over tragedy. Refusing to supply what help she could was beyond Jovvi, and hopefully always would be.

"I think we'll do best leaving them alone for now," Jovvi told Vallant once she'd done all she could. "Most of them are beginning to get angry, which is a sign that they're pulling out of the shock."

"Then leavin' them alone for a while is what we'll do," Vallant agreed at once before turning and beginning to lead her back toward the others of their Blending. "And now that they can't hear us any longer, I'd like to ask a question. Were they in shock because none of them will be a full Blendin' until someone with Sight magic grows old enough to join them, or because of what was done to helpless, innocent people?"

"That's a hard question to answer," Jovvi responded with a sigh. "Many people have trouble seeing a happening as unfair or a tragedy if it doesn't affect them personally. The exception to that outlook covers those people who need a cause to champion because of their own personal reasons. The people in those Blendings seem to be decent, ordinary folk who probably felt uncomfortable with the practice of putting down those without talent. But without a solid reason to demand that the practice be stopped, they must have felt they'd be wasting their time protesting. And they *would* have been wasting their time, as you'll probably agree if you stop to think about it."

"Yes, most likely you're right," Vallant granted with his own sigh. "It's possible I shouldn't have told them what I did, but I was tryin' to head off trouble before it started."

"Telling those people the truth can't possibly be considered a mistake," Jovvi said, stopping Vallant with a hand to his arm as she looked directly at him. "I can see that something else is bothering you, but I can't tell what it is. Would you like to talk about it?"

"It's nothin' but a bit of sour grapes," Vallant replied after a very short hesitation, clearly trying to smile. "And personal sour grapes at that. I think you know how much I enjoyed my time with you and Naran, but I was really lookin' forward to spendin' an uninterrupted night with Tamrissa. Now that we've got somethin' else to do instead, I'm . . . bent out of shape just a little."

"Well, that's understandable," Jovvi said, mildly surprised. "Lorand is out of sorts for the same reason, so you do have company. But you seem to be . . . repressing some feelings at the same time, feelings you don't seem to *want* to repress. Do you understand what I mean?"

"Yes, but I *do* want to repress those feelin's," Vallant answered, his tone now a good deal more firm. "Those feelin's are irrational and have no real basis in fact, so I refuse to listen to them. And I think we're all goin' to need some help in gettin' the few hours of sleep that we're sure to need."

"Everyone will have that help as soon as they're ready to settle down," Jovvi assured him, joining in deliberately changing the subject. "Pagin Holter's Blending entity spoke to Lorand and asked if they could help, so he suggested that they help us all get some sleep. Once we lie down, we'll sleep until the invaders are almost here."

"Good," Vallant said, beginning to walk again after drawing Jovvi along with him by a touch to her arm. "I was wonderin' how I would get any rest at all, but now the problem is solved. And as soon as I make sure that everythin' is taken care of, I'll be takin' advantage of that help."

By then Vallant had returned her to where their Blendingmates were, so he touched her face gently and then strode off. Jovvi watched him heading for their associate Blending and all the link groups, sighing only on the inside. Lorand seemed to be feeling almost exactly what Vallant was, and minimizing Lorand's reactions hadn't helped to ease Vallant's. Both men were definitely fighting off feelings of jealousy, and Jovvi had no idea what she could do about the situation.

Glancing around showed that Rion, Naran, Lorand, and Tamrissa were already asleep, so Jovvi dismissed the idea of another cup of tea and went toward her sleeping pad. They would all definitely need as much sleep as they could get, and wasting sleep time with worrying that could be done later was foolish. Jovvi lay down and covered herself with a blanket, and then—

And then she was waking up with everyone else around her doing the same. It was clearly still in the middle of the night, but no one anywhere around remained asleep.

"All right, people, now's the time," Vallant called from his own sleeping pad. "The Blendin' on watch says the invaders are almost here, so it's time for us to do what *we* have to."

And for some reason Jovvi's heart began to beat a lot faster as she prepared to initiate the Blending . . .

# TWENTY-THREE

Sembrin Noll returned from the second meeting with his new tools in a filthier mood than he'd been in the night before. His entire being had turned into a growl, and he made directly for the nearest decanter of wine. When he turned away from it again with a filled cup, he found Bensia staring at him with puzzlement.

"What's wrong, Sembrin?" she asked at once, concern clear in every part of her. "I felt your return like an avalanche of stone coming down on the house. And where are the children?"

"The children have gone off about their own business," Sembrin answered after taking a good swallow of the wine, the same growl having now invaded his voice. "I took them with me to the meeting tonight as you . . . suggested, but our intentions were a waste of time. That peasant Ayl never made an appearance, just what the other two insisted would happen. Apparently Ayl came to the first meeting only to satisfy his curiosity, and had no real intention of joining our effort."

"But isn't he the one you said had more followers than the other two put together?" Bensia asked, now looking vexed. "We *need* that man, Sembrin, so letting him refuse to join us just isn't acceptable. Why didn't you have the men take you and the children to wherever the peasant lives? You could have had him seen to then, and—"

"Don't you think I tried that?" Sembrin interrupted, fight-

288

ing to keep his annoyance from turning to outrage. "That was when the men informed me that they had no idea where the peasant lives, or even where he spends his idle time. They'd contacted him the first time by leaving a message for him, but this time he didn't respond."

"Well, we'll just have to have some of the men search for him," Bensia decided, just as though *that* thought hadn't occurred to Sembrin as well. "When they find him we can make him sorry he's putting us to so much trouble, but only *after* he brings in his followers. But we do have the other two and *their* followers, so we don't have to put off getting our plans started."

"It devastates me to disagree with you, my sweet, but your newest ideas won't work either," Sembrin returned with sarcasm fueled by rage. "From what the other two peasants told me, I have to assume that finding Ayl won't be done simply by deciding to do it. Apparently the people in the new government have been after the man as long as they've been in power, and even they, who don't have to hide what they're doing, can't locate him. And finding him may even be a waste of time. The other two insist that Ayl is mad, and all his followers have been arrested by now. His claim of having more than two hundred people is most likely part of his overall delusion."

"Then it doesn't matter whether we can find him or not," Bensia pointed out, back to being coolly in control of herself. "And I really would appreciate having you watch your tone when you speak to me, Sembrin. I'm growing tired of needing to remind you that I'm not one of your peasants."

"Actually, it would help if you *were* one of my peasants," Sembrin returned, now hearing the bitterness in his voice. "If we were to consider the children as your followers, you would then have more followers than the two fools who lust after becoming members of our new nobility. Since I had the children with me, I decided to make use of them to another purpose. They took control of the two peasants who did come to the meeting, and then I asked them how many followers they'd lined up to work with us."

"Are you telling me that after having an entire day to talk

to people, they weren't able to recruit *anyone* to our cause?" Bensia demanded, the abrupt disappearance of her cool control bringing Sembrin a large measure of grim satisfaction. "I thought you told me that they were leaders in this city. What kind of leaders find it impossible to produce any followers?"

"The self-deluding kind," Sembrin answered after taking another swallow of his wine. "It seems that the peasant named Meerk actually did make the effort to speak to his 'followers,' but when they heard him say he wanted to put a noble back in power they all got up and walked away. They may be a bunch of malcontents, but apparently they aren't stupid enough to want to return to being owned. Meerk called them back and even suggested that *they* could become nobles themselves, but only one man out of the entire group actually believed him. The rest left again and didn't return."

"And the other peasant?" Bensia asked, fury lurking in her lovely eyes. "Was he able to promise as many as two others besides himself?"

"Not even that many," Sembrin told her, making no effort to soften the blow. "The one named Henris had actually spoken to only a single man, and that one had threatened violence before throwing Henris out of his shop. After that Henris was afraid to speak to any of the others, since he'd started with the man most likely to go along with him."

"I find this impossible to believe," Bensia said as she rubbed at her brow with one hand. "All that effort with nothing to show for it but two men. I certainly hope you didn't give those two the gold to spend after all. What we need are the *real* leaders of the disaffected in this city, and when we find them—"

"Now, that's something else I asked those two about," Sembrin said, again taking pleasure in interrupting. "Since *they* were obviously not the ones we needed, I ordered them to tell me who I needed to speak to instead. It seems that *they* are the most outspoken among the disaffected, and no one else is interested in ousting the new government. Or at least no one else makes their opposition a matter for public consumption."

"Those stupid peasants," Bensia growled as she began to

pace back and forth. "Give them a few crumbs that make them feel as though they're worth something, and they lose all interest in upsetting the status quo. Well, *my* ambition is made of sterner stuff, so we'll just have to go ahead without them. And I meant to ask you as soon as you came in. Have you seen cousin Rimen at any time today? This afternoon I sent the children to his apartment to wake him, but his apartment was empty."

"How utterly fitting that you ask about your cousin Rimen *now*," Sembrin answered, keeping the words from being a *snarling* drawl only through sheer effort of will. "The answer happens to be one with all the rest of what we've been discussing. I had two of our men follow your cousin last night when he left here, and it's a good thing I did. Your darling Rimen tried to murder someone with a knife right in the middle of a street, and if the men hadn't been there to stop him Rimen would have been stopped and arrested by the city guard."

"That's . . . that's probably an exaggerated distortion of what really happened," Bensia tried, clearly swallowing down shock. "Those men are certainly trying to earn more of our gold, so their claims can't be trusted. But putting Rimen in a place he can't simply walk out of was undoubtedly a good idea until I can have the children get the truth from him. And after we have the truth, the children will also see to it that he never—"

"Bensia, Rimen is dead," Sembrin told her, enjoying the need to be brutally direct. "When the men stepped in to keep Rimen from killing the peasant he'd chosen as his victim, your fool of a cousin tried to fight and kill *them*. He struggled so hard that he managed to break his neck in the process, which was truly a lucky thing. People from the city guard showed up the next instant, and only the word of the former victim cleared the men of a charge of murder."

"No, Rimen *can't* be dead," Bensia insisted, her face having turned very pale. "He's my *cousin,* my own blood, and I would never allow that to happen. This is all *your* fault, Sembrin, for not having protected him properly. You—"

"How dare you!" Sembrin interrupted her shaky rambling, his rage no longer small enough to hold back. "When I tried to warn you that Rimen was insane and needed to be watched closely, you ignored my advice and blithely went your *own* way! You knew better and so made no effort to listen, and now you dare to try blaming *me* for what happened? If I hadn't taken the proper precautions we'd have the peasants on our doorstep right now, ready to arrest us and send us to Astinda with the balance of our peers!"

Sembrin was more than ready to continue his tirade, and Bensia must have been aware of it. Instead of trying to argue or say anything more at all, she simply turned and hurried out of the room. When the door closed behind her Sembrin seethed with what she hadn't given him a chance to say, but then a bit of calm returned. And with the calm came the question of why she hadn't tried to control him the way she usually did.

"Come to think of it, I believe she did try to control me," Sembrin murmured to himself then as he gazed at the closed door. "I recall *something* trying to soothe and calm me, but my outrage was too strong for those other emotions to get through. And *that* has to mean that strong anger is a kind of shield against what she can do. I really must remember that."

Satisfaction let Sembrin sip at his wine this time, but impatience refused to let him sit down. Having what might well prove to be a shield against Bensia was all well and good, but having her and the children quietly and completely obedient under Puredan would be even better. His people had promised to *try* to get the Puredan, but they weren't as confident of success as Sembrin would have liked. Those peasants now in charge of the city had put all supplies of the drug under close guard, and casual access to the Puredan was no longer possible.

But one of them might have succeeded after all, so Sembrin took his wineglass out to the barracks with him to ask Jost Feriun, leader of his guardsmen, if any packages had been left for him. As soon as he stepped out of the house, Sembrin couldn't help but notice that there weren't any guardsmen on duty the way there usually were. The lack struck Sembrin as odd, so he had another question to ask as soon as he walked into Feriun's office.

"Why aren't there men on guard outside?" Sembrin demanded as soon as Feriun looked up. "Just because no one knows where we are doesn't mean we can afford to grow sloppy."

"I have men around the perimeter of the estate, sir," Feriun answered, taking fractionally too long to rise to his feet. And could the man's neutral expression be hiding something . . . ? "Having men standing a post right near the house is actually an unnecessary duplication of effort."

"You never complained about duplication of effort before this," Sembrin pointed out, narrowing his eyes as he studied the other man. "What's happened that you aren't telling me about?"

"There's . . . a small and temporary problem with the number of men available," Feriun admitted after a long moment of hesitation, furious discomfort now barely hidden behind his neutral expression. "As soon as I move others in from one or two of the alternate locations, the problem will be solved."

"One or *two* alternate locations?" Sembrin echoed, suddenly very attentive to what he'd been told. "There are supposed to be thirty men here, approximately the same number as that in the other places. How many men are . . . unavailable here that you need to replace them with that many alternates?"

"The number of men left here isn't our only problem," Feriun ground out at last, sitting down again without waiting for Sembrin to do the same first. "I still don't know what's happening, but late this afternoon all but seven of my men were gone from here. I went to the nearest alternate location to replace them, and found only five men left *there*. The third location had ten, and the fourth only two. I brought the seventeen back with me, then sent some of them out again to the remaining locations. Hopefully the rest are still at full strength."

"Hopefully," Sembrin echoed, staring at Feriun in distant shock. "From a total of one hundred and twenty men, we now have only twenty-four left! I want to know where the others have gone, and I want to know *now*!"

"If *I* knew, don't you think I'd tell you?" Feriun had the nerve to ask in a ridiculing grumble. "The men still here said something about a lot of private conversations going on since last night, but they don't know what the talk was all about. The others told me they had visits this morning from various of the men who were stationed *here*, and then there were also a lot of private conversations. Since two of the three men in charge of the other locations are also gone, we have to assume that the rest of the locations are known to the men in this . . . movement."

"Marvelous, absolutely marvelous," Sembrin muttered, finding himself completely incapable of coping with the thought of this newest disaster. "How long will it be before we know what size force we have left to us?"

"Not very long," Feriun answered with a clear lack of enthusiasm. "The men I sent out are due back any moment, and as soon as I have their reports I'll let you know."

"The *very* minute you have them," Sembrin emphasized, then turned to leave. He got as far as the door before another thought stopped him. "Have any packages been left for me by any of my people?" he turned back to ask. The question was a waste of breath, of course, but it *was* the reason he'd come out here to begin with. No sense in not getting all the bad news at the same time.

"Actually, two packages have been left for you," Feriun answered, shocking Sembrin again as the man reached into a deep drawer in his desk. "With everything else going on, I completely forgot about them."

Feriun produced the two small packages, and Sembrin took them almost in a daze. After everything that had happened tonight, the packages must surely contain notes of apology for failure to get the Puredan. But Sembrin would look inside just to be sure, as soon as he reached his study.

Once in his study and seated behind his desk, Sembrin sipped at his refilled wineglass for a moment before taking up the first package. He'd braced himself for disappointment, but when the wrappings fell away he found two vials of clear liquid lying on a small piece of paper with a large *G* on it. Sembrin picked up the piece of paper with the printed initial on it, and found the note on the reverse.

"Apologies, my lord, but these were the only vials I could get," the note read. "They were hidden in a private place not many knew about, and I hope they're enough. I'll be by to-morrow for the promised gold."

Sembrin smiled as he held the vials gently in one hand, knowing his agent had probably lied. The man had most likely kept at least one vial for his own use, but the offer of gold had coaxed these other two out of him. The two vials could well be enough for Sembrin's purpose, but he still put them aside to open the other package.

The second package contained three vials instead of two, but when Sembrin saw the initial *K* below them he found himself suddenly suspicious. This man had numberless con-tacts among the peasants, but almost none in the moneyed population and fewer yet among what had been the nobility. How, then, would *he* have gotten three vials of Puredan? When Sembrin's suspicions grew he decided to resolve them, and so drew out the stopper from one of the vials.

The liquid inside the vial looked flat when compared to that in the first two vials. There was no odor to be detected, of course, but a single drop of the liquid on Sembrin's tongue brought nothing of the tingling it should have. This second offering was obviously not Puredan, and was proba-bly nothing but plain water.

Sembrin sat back feeling coldly furious. If he hadn't be-come suspicious he would have given that water to Bensia and the children, and then he would have tried to put them under his control. But . . . if Bensia and the children hadn't been frozen in the typical reaction of someone under the in-fluence of Puredan, he *wouldn't* have tried to control them. How could the fool who had sent these vials expected him to do otherwise?

The question was an annoying one, but Sembrin had no time for it now. They would all be sitting down to dinner soon, and the opportunity was far too good to miss. With that in mind he checked the other two vials that had come with the first, finding them to be water as well. Then it was time to check the two vials which had come in the first package.

Sembrin hesitated a long moment, but then plunged into the test. If he were going to be disappointed he wanted it to be *now*, but the first two vials proved to be exactly as promised. Sembrin's tongue tingled twice with the drop of liquid he tried from each vial, proof that he really did hold Puredan—and freedom—in his hand. Odd how delight was able to emerge in the midst of misery and failure . . .

The two vials of Puredan were easily hidden in Sembrin's coat, and he had just disposed of the three false vials when there was a knock on his study door. Sembrin glanced around to make sure there was nothing left to show that he'd received any packages, and then he called out his permission to enter.

"Sir, all of my men have now gotten back," Feriun reported after walking inside. "I have to tell you that the news isn't good."

"Well, we hardly expected it to be, did we?" Sembrin pointed out, his good mood evaporating instantly. "Tell me how many men we have left."

"Out of our original three hundred and thirty-four, we now have less than one hundred and fifty men left," Feriun told him flatly. "My people brought them all back here, and after filling out the house complement I sent the rest to the three places we picked out as alternate sites when we got back to the city. When we need to have someplace to send our local recruits, we'll have to put them elsewhere."

"Don't worry about the local recruits," Sembrin told him, in no mood to mention there would *be* no locals they needed to house. "Right now there's only the men we brought with us to consider, and the first thing you have to do is disallow private conversations. And only certain designated officers will be allowed to visit the locations where the men are. If anyone else tries to gain entry to those houses, the anyone is to be arrested at once and held until we can talk to him. Or, rather, until we can coax him into talking to *us*."

"I've already given orders to that effect, sir," Feriun stated, looking less than pleased to have anticipated his employer's wishes. The man must really be raw over having had more than half his force stolen from under his nose . . . "Are there any other orders?"

"Not at the moment," Sembrin answered with a head-shake. "I mean to set my plans in motion as soon as practical, possibly even tomorrow, so make sure the men are ready. Once we start, there won't be any turning back."

"No, there *won't* be any turning back," Feriun agreed, a glint in his eyes that Sembrin found very familiar. "And I'll make certain personally that the men are ready."

Feriun performed a small, stiff bow and then left, closing the door behind himself. Sembrin waited only long enough to allow the man time to leave the house, and then he took himself to the dining room. Bad luck with the men seemed to have translated itself into good luck with the rest of Sembrin's plans. Not even a single servant was in sight, which meant no one saw Sembrin empty the contents of his two vials into the table's wine decanter after filling his own glass with the wine. Once the empty vials were put back into his coat, Sembrin sat at the table and took a single sip of his wine. It should be starting very soon now, as soon as Bensia and the children got to table.

The children arrived first only a pair of moments later, and by then two servants were also at the table putting out hot rolls and butter. Sembrin sat quietly with his wine, watching the children ignore him completely as they chatted idly among themselves. The only time his own children paid attention to him was when their mother gave them reason to, and then only to manipulate him. That realization brought such seething anger that he nearly missed Bensia's arrival.

But almost wasn't the same as actually being that mind-less, so Sembrin was the first to rise to his feet when his wife reached the table. His sons were a moment behind him in rising, and Bensia gave them all a faint smile of thanks as she took her place. She still seemed to be saddened by the terrible news she'd had, but it was clear the woman had re-gained complete control of herself.

Sembrin waited until one of the servants performed his

duty by pouring wine for the newcomers, and then he raised his own glass.

"After speaking to commander Feriun, I've decided to put our plans in motion tomorrow," Sembrin announced, a speech that managed to gain the attention of everyone at the table. "I offer a toast to our success, the first of many, the last of which will see the palace and the empire firmly under our complete control."

"Here, here," Travin murmured as he and the others all reached for their glasses. Bensia's smile was odd as she did the same, and they all drank as one to toast the very bright future they would surely have. After taking his own sip of wine, Sembrin looked at his wife and children. The two boys sat with their glasses not far from their lips, the girls had begun to put *their* glasses down, and Bensia still showed that odd smile. But all of them sat frozen in place, so Sembrin decided to assuage his curiosity.

"Bensia, my dear, you're showing a very odd smile," Sembrin said with extreme satisfaction. "Would you tell me why you're doing that?"

"It's because I just realized that you were going to try giving us some supposed Puredan," Bensia answered without the least hesitation. "When I learned that you'd asked one of your people to find you some, I decided to supply the 'Puredan' myself. What a marvelous joke it would be when you were told that you'd given us nothing but water."

"Ah, so *you* were responsible for those three vials," Sembrin said, finally understanding. "Did you and the children mean to *pretend* to be under the drug's influence, and then, once you learned my intentions, laugh at my presumption?"

"Yes, of course we did," Bensia agreed amiably. "We were going to laugh until *you* cried, and then put you much more completely under our control. You've been allowed far too great an amount of freedom until now, but that was necessary to have the men obey your orders without question. Now that we're nearly ready to begin, your complete freedom would have been . . . awkward."

"Awkward for you and your own plans," Sembrin said, understanding completely. "And are you pretending *now* to be under the influence of the drug, or does it really have you?"

"Oh, it certainly does have me," Bensia responded, still without showing the least disturbance. "I would say it also has the children, since I can detect nothing in the way of independent thought in their minds."

"Well, good," Sembrin said, his delight growing with his amusement. "All of you are finally under *my* control, and that's the way I'll be certain to keep it. From now on all of you will take orders only from me, obeying completely and without hesitation. As soon as you return to yourselves, you'll first remove any and all . . . strings you may have on me. After that you'll all forget the removal, and will be convinced that I'm doing precisely as you want me to. But you'll be the ones taking the orders, and you won't question those orders no matter what they are. And you will *not*, under any circumstance, make an attempt to influence me again. Do you all understand?"

Sembrin knew he'd repeated himself in his speech, but he'd wanted to make absolutely certain that his loving family was tightly chained. And that he himself was finally freed. When he received immediate agreement from all of them, he smiled again. Luck was really with him in that he had asked *five* of his people to obtain Puredan rather than just one, but Bensia hadn't known that. If she had, *he* would be the one enslaved right now . . .

"All right, then it's time we resumed our meal," Sembrin announced when all five of his marvelous slaves agreed they understood his orders. "But be sure that none of you drinks from the wine again, and at meal's end you carry away the glasses and their contents to spill out somewhere. We wouldn't want some innocent servants to accidentally swallow what was meant for their betters."

All of them had resumed normal movement again, and now they chuckled their agreement to his command. Sembrin was very much anticipating the arrival of the food now, but as Bensia rang her bell to tell the servants to begin serving the meal, an odd occurrence diverted Sembrin from his appetite. He was suddenly able to feel the calm quiet inside every member of his family, as though a screen of some kind had just been removed from between him and the world.

"Of course," Sembrin murmured with surprise that suddenly turned to anger. "I have Spirit magic just as they do, but they've been keeping me from using it for so long that I forgot all about it. Just as they wanted me to forget. Now I think some punishments are due, and in fact long overdue."

No one paid any attention to Sembrin's murmuring, but that was perfectly all right. They'd find out all about what he'd said when they were given their punishment, and he would enjoy every moment of the time—as they would not. And first on the list would be his lovely wife, the woman who had doled out her favors as a means of controlling him even more. After dinner they would retire to their apartment, and before he slept Bensia would pay the price of years and years of manipulation.

Sembrin allowed a servant to put soup in front of him, but food wasn't what his newly awakened appetite craved. First he would see to filling his belly, and then on to satisfying that other, much more interesting, appetite . . .

# TWENTY-FOUR

Driffin Codsent got back to the warehouse in a happy frame of mind. Things were going really well, and he refused to worry about what lay ahead in just a short while. If you resisted happiness when it came along, too often that made happiness start to avoid you for lack of appreciation . . .

"Driff, how did things work out?" Idresia asked as soon as Driff was in the door, coming forward to meet him. "Were my people of any help?"

"You're asking if they were of any help?" Driff returned with a laugh of true amusement. "Everyone agrees that we couldn't have done without them yesterday, and today they even added to that. You're not by any chance interested in the details, are you?"

"Only if *you're* interested in continuing among the living," Idresia countered much too sweetly, her fists on her hips. "I might come to regret destroying you for extreme cruelty at some later time, but you'd still *be* destroyed."

"Then I'd better start telling you those details right away," Driff said quickly, pretending to cringe away from her. "Will you also destroy me if I get a cup of tea while we're talking?"

"As long as the words keep coming out of you, you can get two cups of tea if you like," Idresia assured him with a small, deliberately evil smile. "In fact, I'll even pour the tea for you, but only if you start talking right now."

"Your word is my command, O Divine One," Driff said

with a bow before gathering her in under his arm. They were in the middle of the warehouse floor and the tea was in their living quarters, so he started them walking in that direction. "Yesterday that Blending I recruited followed the directions your people supplied to the house where the renegade is living, and they arrived just in time. A lone man left the house on horseback in a very secretive manner, and a few minutes later two other men appeared to follow the first."

"Was the Blending able to follow, or did they lose the three?" Idresia asked, her eyes having gone a bit wide. "Or did they want *my* people to follow?"

"I'm told that the Blending members were on horseback themselves, so they left your people continuing their watch on the house and *they* followed the three." Driff was a bit disturbed over keeping the entire story from Idresia, but if she learned too soon that it was a High Blending rather than a Middle one that was helping, she might not be able to keep the fact as quiet as it needed to be.

"The Blending members followed the three all the way back to our part of the city," Driff continued. "The lone man dismounted and tied his horse before going the rest of the way on foot, and the two who followed him did the same. When the Blending reached the place where the horses were tied, they also dismounted and then sent their entity to follow."

"It must be so exciting to be able to do that," Idresia said, definite wistfulness in her voice as they entered their living quarters. "So what did their entity see when it followed?"

"Their entity discovered that the lone man was named Rimen Howser, and his mind was as badly twisted as his body," Driff answered, faint regret still in him that he hadn't been able to help the poor fool. "He went directly to an alleyway behind a tavern, and once he was in the shadows he pulled a knife out of his clothing where it had been hidden."

"Was *he* the one who killed those people?" Idresia asked, disturbed enough to turn from the teapot before she'd even put her hand on it. "I heard about the murders, and made sure to be fully alert every time I went out."

"The Blending is certain he *was* the murderer, so that's

another feather in *your* cap," Driff said as he sat down at the table. "It was your people who let the Blending find the man, and now he's no longer a danger to the innocent."

Driff then went on to describe how the madman quickly lost patience with waiting in the dark, tried to pull someone into the alleyway from the street, and how the murderer was subsequently killed himself. Idresia listened quietly as she poured tea for the both of them and carried the cups to the table, then sat beside him.

"The two men who had followed the madman stopped him from claiming another victim," Driff said after sipping at the tea. "They didn't *mention* they'd been following him, but they also didn't kill him on purpose. The madman struggled so hard that he ended up breaking his own neck, and when members of the city guard showed up and then congratulated the two followers for being heroes, the Blending got an idea."

Idresia raised her brows, but this time didn't say anything. A faint disturbance was obviously still with her, but she also seemed to be in the process of pushing the disturbance away.

"One of the Blending members told me that they touched the two only very lightly," Driff said. "Apparently both men were shocked that they were being congratulated instead of accused, and being called heroes to boot. The men seemed to like the idea of being heroes instead of bullies, and it took only a small hint from the Blending to convince the two that they wanted to enroll in one of the training classes and then join the city guard."

"It's too bad there were only two of them," Idresia remarked. "If the renegade's whole force disappeared to come over to *our* side, it would save us all a lot of trouble."

"You don't know how right you are," Driff told her with a laugh of renewed pleasure. "The two men decided that they would be killed if just the two of them tried to walk away, so they came up with a different plan. They agreed to talk to the rest of their companions who believed the way they did, and try to convince the others to leave *with* them. They started to talk to people last night when they got back, and today a number of their recruits went to visit the guardsmen in the other locations. There were ten other locations, and we now know where they all used to be."

"*Used* to be," Idresia echoed, delight beginning to shine in her lovely eyes. "Don't tell me that those two managed to recruit *all* the renegade's men?"

"They actually got more than half, and we now have almost two hundred newly *useful* citizens in the city," Driff responded happily. "The original two had just a *little* help from the Blending in convincing the men they spoke to, but again I was told that the effort was no more than a nudge or two. Most of those men apparently *want* to be useful members of our society, but no one ever gave them the chance to do it before."

"What a waste," Idresia said, now showing heavy disgust. "Those nobles not only wasted their own lives, they forced the same on people who had almost nothing to do with them. You have no idea how happy I am that we're now changing that."

"I think I do, because I'm at least as happy," Driff assured her, then he laughed again. "What I most miss seeing is that renegade's face when he found out how many of his 'guard force' had walked away from him. His guard commander gathered up the remnants left, then sent some of them to various new locations. Your people followed to learn where those new locations are, and now we know exactly. They might as well have left the men where they were for all the good moving them did."

"If there has to be wasted effort, I'm glad it's theirs rather than ours," Idresia said with satisfaction. "That was quite a lot to have happened in just one day."

"But that's not all that happened," Driff corrected, stopping her in the midst of rising from the table. "Do you remember the meeting place the renegade used to speak to his new 'followers?' Well, he used it again today to bring the men together again, but he had a bit of bad news. Only two of the men showed up, and one of them was *not* Holdis Ayl."

"But that's not *bad* news," Idresia protested with a laugh that wrinkled her nose. "Now we don't have to worry about that madman joining his efforts to the renegade's."

"I'm told that the renegade really lost his temper when he learned that Ayl came the first time only because he was curious," Driff said, nodding his agreement. "He also had four young people with him who were all Spirit magic users, and the four linked to put the remaining two followers under their control. Then the renegade asked the two how many men they could really provide, and blew up a second time when the two admitted that between them they could only produce one other man."

"That's probably because of the new policies," Idresia said, clearly enjoying an inner picture of the renegade's fury. "The men Meerk and that other man would have recruited would be the sort who were bound and determined to get a free ride no matter *who* was in charge. Most of that sort are gone from the city, either leaving on their own or having been thrown out after being caught doing something illegal. The only ones left are those who enjoy grumbling no matter *how* satisfied they are."

"So my guess would be that the renegade won't be calling on his new followers again," Driff said after sipping at his tea. "And now that most of his guard force has disappeared, the renegade will most likely do one of only two things. Either he'll leave again to find other men to bring his force up to what it was originally, or he'll go ahead with his plans using the men he has left."

"I'll bet he chooses to go on with his plans," Idresia said after only a moment of consideration. "The man has to be made of pure arrogance to have tried this to begin with, and arrogance like that will refuse to retreat. He'll consider it unnecessary weakness, and will forge ahead with whatever he means to do."

"And he also seems to have no idea what he's up against," Driff agreed for the second time. "Almost everyone in the city now knows *something* about what a Blending is capable of, but the renegade has apparently made no effort to learn about what he means to challenge. He's still picturing things the way they *used* to be, which is the blind part of his arrogance. And speaking about people who are determined, Issini ought to be here soon with her noble friend."

"Yes, I know," Idresia said with a sigh, all amusement leaving her. "Do you have any idea what we can do about the man? From what you said, we no longer need the information he thinks he has."

"I've been thinking about the situation since yesterday, and I've finally decided which way I'll handle it," Driff answered with a sigh of his own. "The man risked his neck when he let Issini bring him here, trusting that we would not betray him. All we can do is tell him the absolute truth, and let *him* choose what will happen next. We—"

Driff broke off at the sound of a knock at the door, the knock also keeping Idresia from commenting. Her disturbed expression said she'd wanted to say something, but instead she rose and went to the door. When she opened it, Issini stood there with a very old man just behind her.

"Hi, Har," Issini said to Idresia, using the name only she used for her friend. "We're back just the way we said we'd be."

"Come on in, Ran," Idresia invited as she stepped back out of the way. "Driff is here, and he needs to be introduced to Edmin."

Driff got to his feet as the two people entered the apartment, and then Driff was able to get a better look at the "old man." Earth magic told Driff that the newcomer wasn't in the least old, and that despite the really good makeup and wig he'd been provided with.

"Edmin, welcome," Driff said, putting out his hand. "I've heard a lot about you, and I've been looking forward to meeting you."

"Oddly enough, I've been looking forward to this meeting as well," Edmin answered, taking Driff's hand after a very short hesitation. "Desperate situations aren't supposed to provide pleasant surprises, but I seem to have been getting more than my share of them lately."

"I'd say you're in for more of the same, but we'll get into that more fully in a moment," Driff replied, gesturing Edmin and Issini into taking seats at the table. "At the moment, I'd like to know what pleasant surprises you're talking about—if you don't mind sharing the information."

"I don't really *mind,* but the admission is bound to make me sound . . . unbearably pompous," Edmin said with a faint smile as he seated Issini and then sat down himself. "I had certain very definite ideas about what 'peasants' are like, but I've been learning that there are too many exceptions to that simpleminded belief for the belief to still have much relevance. Using Issini and your lovely lady there as yardsticks, I've . . . begun to believe that this is the first time in my life that I've met any 'real' people. My former peers were so busy trying to outmaneuver and best each other that they never came in touch with true reality."

"Real peers don't fence for position and advantage, they enjoy each other's company," Driff said with a nod as he also resumed his seat. "Would either of you like some tea? I can testify that it's fresh and hot."

Both of the newcomers accepted the offer, which seemed to please Idresia. Driff's beloved had been standing near the teapot, probably waiting for a chance to make the offer herself. Now that Driff had put the question and gotten the answer, Idresia would be free in a moment to sit down with them. It was mostly thanks to her that this meeting was being held, and Driff wanted her to be an integral part of it.

"All right, now we all have refreshment in front of us," Driff said once Idresia had brought over the cups of tea and then had taken another moment to fetch a plate of small cakes before resuming her seat. "Idresia told me you offered us some information yesterday, Edmin, and in return you asked to be included in taking down the renegade named Noll. Do you still want to be part of the effort?"

"Of course," Edmin answered at once, his teacup in his hands. "What would make you think I'd changed my mind?"

"Well, things have happened that make the information you have unnecessary," Driff answered slowly as he studied the man. "We're still willing to invite you to join us, but I've noticed in the past that some people become . . . uneasy if they can't feel that they've paid their way. Have you come far enough from your former life to get past that?"

"Now *that's* a good question," Edmin muttered, his gaze inward rather than on Driff. "I'll admit I experienced a moment of panic when you said you no longer needed my information, as though I, myself, had suddenly become useless. In my former life that would have been the case, but it isn't the same here, is it? Why do you no longer need to know the locations of three of the groups of guardsmen Noll brought into the city?"

"Primarily because the guardsmen are no longer *at* those locations," Driff answered, having already decided on how much to tell Edmin. "Idresia and her people were able to locate the house Noll is living in, and because of that some of our other people were able to . . . maneuver some of the guardsmen into wanting to desert Noll. That core group spread the idea a lot farther than we were expecting, and now Noll is left with less than half of the men he brought into the city with him. His guard commander moved the remaining men to new locations, ones we already know about."

"I see," Edmin said, and Driff was impressed to notice that Edmin had already adapted to the changed situation. "You definitely don't need my information, or you would have made *some* effort to extract it without promising anything. Instead you've assured me of my place among you without my having to pay for it, and that's the part I'm not sure about. If you don't need my information, why do you feel you need *me*?"

"Actually, we *don't* need you," Driff told the man as gently as possible. "But you have a legitimate need to be part of our effort, and at the moment there's no real reason to exclude you. That may change in just a little while, but we believe that every man should have the chance to do something positive with his life. If you still want to be part of our effort after you hear the rest of what I have to say, you'll be given the chance."

"Now, *that* sounds ominous," Edmin remarked, leaning back in his chair to study Driff. "What can you possibly have to say that would make so much of a difference?"

"I have good news for you," Driff said, watching the man with every bit of his talent. Earth magic let Driff know lie from truth because of bodily reactions, and those reactions would be critically important right now. "You told Idresia that you wanted to join our effort to stop the renegade Noll because Noll and his wife were responsible for your father's death. It's now my pleasure to tell you that your father *isn't* dead, only wounded, and he's currently in the process of healing quite nicely."

Edmin didn't say a word, but his sense of shock was so profound that Driff felt certain every Earth magic and Spirit magic user within a mile of the warehouse must be aware of the reaction. The man just sat and stared, but on the inside he floundered pitifully.

"What Driff *didn't* mention is that he was the one who saved your father's life," Idresia said after a moment, her tone very gentle. "He's an incredibly good healer in spite of being only a Middle talent, and that's why the officials sent for him when they found your father's wounded body. I happen to believe that no one else would have been able to save your father's life."

"Idresia's one failing is her tendency toward blind prejudice," Driff said with a small laugh, reaching over to squeeze Idresia's hand. "Your father *was* badly hurt, Edmin, but I'm sure that most other healers would have been able to do what I did. But the point is still the same. Your father *wasn't* killed by the Nolls, so now *you* have to decide whether or not you still want to help take them down."

"And if I don't, you'll simply let me walk out of here in the same way I walked in," Edmin said in a faint voice, back to staring at Driff again. "I'm willing to bet any amount of gold you name that that's true, but it's also the next thing to unimportant. Did you know who my father was when you healed him?"

"We all knew he was a noble, but we didn't know he was Embisson Ruhl until after he'd been taken to the palace to recover," Driff admitted. "Some of the servants there recognized him, and once he was strong enough he was questioned about what he was doing in the city. That's when we learned about the Nolls."

"And about me, I'll wager," Edmin said after draining his cup of tea. "I can tell how you feel about 'nobles,' undoubtedly the same way those 'officials' feel, but they still sent for you and you still healed one of your enemies. I should be finding it impossible to believe that all of you would do that, but for some reason I'm not. Where is the cell they have my father locked up in?"

"He isn't *in* a cell," Driff replied, wryly amused by the question. Edmin hadn't changed quite as much as he seemed to believe . . . "He still needs a good deal of attention if he's to recover completely, so they have him in one of the guest bedchambers in the palace. What they intend to do with him once he *has* recovered is something I don't know."

"But until then they're treating him like a human being rather than unimportant dross which has already been defeated," Edmin muttered, shaking his head. "As I said, only a little while ago I never would have believed that, but now . . . You asked me a question earlier, and now you deserve a truthful answer."

Edmin's last words had been in a normal voice, and now he stared straight at Driff with no attempt to avoid Driff's gaze. Edmin still seemed partially in shock to Driff, but the former noble had apparently recovered full control of himself.

"My answer is that I do still want to join you in stopping the Nolls, and my decision has nothing to do with the fact that they *tried* to kill my father even though they didn't succeed." Everything about Edmin said he was telling the truth, and he smiled faintly when he saw Driff's confusion over his statement. "Would you like me to explain why I've come to that conclusion?"

"Yes, please," Driff agreed. "I'm glad to hear you say it, but I don't understand *why* you're saying it."

"Truthfully, I'm saying it because I knew you *would* be glad to hear it," Edmin replied with a very small laugh. "I feel like a young child who has been given a gift so marvelous that he had no idea the gift even existed. In my old life my offered help would have been accepted and made use of, with every effort made to keep me from learning any part of the truth of the situation. Afterward, my virtual helplessness would have allowed those who had used me to discard me without a second thought. They would have had no idea how to . . . enjoy the company of a peer."

"But we do have that knack," Driff said, smiling only to himself. Edmin seemed to have learned what it was like to associate with people he could trust, and the experience had him hooked. Like the headiest of drugs, he now craved more . . . "With that in mind, why don't you and Issini join Idresia and me for dinner. We can discuss what ought to be done next to ruin the Noll effort at conquering the world."

"Issini?" Edmin said, turning to the woman who sat beside him. "Will our accepting their very kind offer ruin any plans you've already made?"

"No, Edmin, I've made no plans so there's nothing to ruin," Issini replied, the look in her eyes a glow of pleasure. "But I do appreciate your asking."

"It's a poor guest who returns rudeness for the kindness he's been given," Edmin told her, reaching over to pat her hand before turning back to Driff. "Yes, Driff, we would very much enjoy joining you for dinner—and the accompanying discussion."

"Wonderful!" Idresia exclaimed, popping out of her chair. "There's more than enough for everyone, and if I start the meal now we should be eating in just a little while. Driff, you'll have to entertain our guests without me until the food is ready."

"I'll do just that as soon as I talk to the boys on guard duty," Driff answered, also getting to his feet. "I don't want them to start worrying when our guests don't leave as quickly as they did last night. I'll be right back."

Idresia joined the others in nodding their understanding, but the look she gave Driff told him that she knew he was up to something. It was true that Driff did have an unmentioned chore to attend to, and as soon as he was out of the apartment and a short distance away from it, he stopped in the shadows.

"Are you there?" he asked the empty air, feeling the least bit foolish. "Can you hear me?"

—*This entity is present and aware of your words*—Driff heard at once inside his head.—*This entity would have you know that the flesh form you spoke with uttered the complete truth. It has chosen to join your efforts with a whole heart, a decision which will remain unchanged unless some catastrophic event occurs. This entity will monitor the flesh form from time to time, and should such a change occur you will be informed immediately.—*

"Thank you," Driff said, no longer feeling foolish. The Blending had promised to be present at the meeting with Edmin to find out how the former noble really felt, and now they'd confirmed what he'd told Driff. Driff had wanted to be able to trust Edmin completely if the circumstance called for it, and now he could.

Whistling tunelessly, Driff continued on into the warehouse proper to talk to the boys on duty. No sense in neglecting the chore and possibly making himself a liar in front of someone he expected, for some odd reason, to become really good friends with . . .

# TWENTY-FIVE

Edmin Ruhl, former noble and lord of the empire, sat in what he once would have considered a hovel and gloried in being where he was. That was rather an extreme reaction for someone who had always been cool and unimpressed with the happenings of life, but it was precisely the way he felt. New reactions for the new life he had been forced to begin, a life he now looked forward to much more eagerly than he ever had the old one.

Issini sat beside him with a quiet smile curving her lips, but the delight inside her was crystal clear to his talent. What made the delight so marvelous was that it was for *him* rather than for herself, her worry about him all but disappearing. She'd risked her safety by taking him in, had risked his anger by instructing him in those things he hadn't at first wanted to hear, and then she'd shared her friends.

And what friends! Edmin had felt drawn to and attracted by Idresia, and had come tonight with some vague plan to make the man she lived with look small and unimportant next to *him*. Edmin still felt the same attraction for Idresia, but his plans had gone by the boards the moment he'd met Driffin. The man was slight and almost nondescript, but a sense of easily controlled power fairly radiated from him.

At first Edmin had been immediately wary, having had far too much experience with men of power in his life. But then Driffin had begun to tell him things, and Edmin had had to fight not to show how shocked he felt. Most men of power used and manipulated those people around them, lying as easily as they breathed. But Driffin hadn't lied, not even once, Edmin's ability in Spirit magic confirming that fact without a single doubt. And not only hadn't Driff lied, he'd even glossed over a rather important point to keep from boasting.

*My father is still alive, and Driff is the one who saved his life,* Edmin thought for the hundredth time, once again experiencing the same delighted disbelief. If their positions had been reversed, Edmin knew perfectly well that his father would have let Driff die. But Edmin's father was the product of a twisted and weakened society, one that had *needed* to be taken down and replaced with a more viable and vital arrangement. Edmin was able to see that now, and his eagerness to join the new arrangement was far greater than his regret over losing great wealth and importance . . .

"Edmin, we're going to have to supply you with a really good false identity," Driffin's voice came, bringing Edmin out of his thoughts. He'd been so deeply engrossed, he hadn't even noticed Driffin's return. "I've been thinking, and that's something we need to get you right away."

"For what reason?" Edmin asked, surprised and curious. "As soon as we finish dealing with Noll and his sweet wife, I won't even need the disguise I'm currently wearing."

"Seeing to the renegade is just a pleasant joint venture that will soon be over," Driffin answered, resuming his seat and his cup of tea. "After that you'll still have a life to live, and you want to do that in the best way possible. The first step in achieving that best way is to join one of the classes and have your talent trained, and for that you'll need a false identity."

"To keep people from knowing that I'm also a renegade," Edmin said heavily, most of his previous enjoyment draining away to nothing. "I hadn't realized that that's the sort of life I'll have to look forward to, not in the midst of so much that's bright and new . . . Being constantly in hiding, continually fearing betrayal to the new officials . . ."

"Well, actually, that last is something you *won't* have to worry about," Driffin said hesitantly and almost diffidently, as though he'd done something shameful that he was now forced to admit. "I . . . spoke to some people I know without going into details, and got their agreement to let you join us if you really were sincere about wanting to help. Since you *are* sincere and will certainly be quite a lot of help, the new identity will just be to keep ordinary people from giving you a hard time."

Edmin sat staring at Driffin for a moment, and then he was forced to shake his head.

"I have no idea what I could possibly have done to deserve meeting you, but I will be grateful until the end of my days that I did do it." The words Edmin spoke were definitely on the foolish side, but Driffin seemed to know that they were also completely heartfelt. "The only problem is, I'll probably be searching just as long for a proper way to thank you."

"That's one search that's easily ended," Driffin said with a chuckle and a deprecating gesture of dismissal. "Just don't make me sorry I trusted you, and we'll be even."

"Adopting the street lost has become a way of life for Driff," Idresia said from where she stood preparing their meal. "He's never asked more than that from *anyone* he's taken under his wing, so you're now a member of an even more exclusive group. It's a good thing you have experience with that sort of thing."

Edmin couldn't help adding his own laughter to that of the others, laughter that felt strange coming out of *him*. He'd always wondered how most people were able to laugh so easily, and getting the answer to that question was a sudden and marvelous revelation.

"How odd to gain two fathers in a single day," Edmin couldn't help remarking to Driff, for the first time in his life feeling the urge to tease someone. "Is that how I'm to address you from now on, calling you Father as I do my other parent?"

"No, Edmin, we're not at all that formal here," Idresia put in before a grinning Driffin could comment. "When the need arises, you call him Daddy."

"Idresia!" Driffin exclaimed while the rest of them laughed again. "If he starts to call me Daddy, then he'll be entitled to call *you* Momma. Fair's fair, after all . . ."

"All right, all right, I surrender," Idresia conceded with another laugh that everyone joined in. "I'd hate to have to murder you all to keep everyone in sight from calling me Momma. Ran, could you give me a hand here? I think we'd all like to eat before midnight."

"I thought you'd never ask," Issini replied at once as she got to her feet. "I know you're a better cook than I am, Har, but only a small number of people have died from tasting the fruits of my efforts. Saving time is surely worth the risk . . ."

Edmin chuckled at the banter between the women, knowing that Issini wasn't serious. The woman was actually a very good cook, so if Idresia was better, then the meal was definitely something to look forward to.

"Edmin, I'd like to ask you a private question," Driffin said in a murmur that wasn't likely to reach the women. "If you'd prefer not to answer, please don't hesitate to say so. I promise I'll understand."

"You're suddenly feeling very serious," Edmin observed in the same kind of murmur, now studying Driffin with faint worry. "What sort of question do you have that you think I won't want to answer?"

"A personal one," Driffin replied with a sigh. "You were incredibly relieved to hear that your father is still alive, but you haven't asked about going to see him. May I ask *why* you haven't?"

"I now understand your hesitation," Edmin answered ruefully as he dropped Driffin's gaze. "I would have preferred not discussing the subject, but if anyone is entitled to an answer . . . The truth of the matter is, I'm . . . not sure I *want* to see my father. He and I were very close, but that was in another life. He would never understand why I've chosen to . . . 'turn my back on my heritage,' and it would not be possible to explain the matter to him. I have no doubt that he still plans to take over running the empire."

"And telling him you won't join in the effort isn't something *I'd* want to tell him either," Driffin admitted at once with another sigh. "Especially not if the two of you were as close as you say. But what about convincing the man that he hasn't the slightest chance of taking over? Won't *that* do any good?"

"I think . . . that that understanding would be the end of my father," Edmin said with a sigh of his own. "He was a High Lord among the nobility and a very powerful man. If he ever had to admit that he would never be the same again, the realization would probably kill him. I never had any interest in being a High Lord, only in controlling the tendency toward chaos that was life among the nobility. My father considered his title and position the only things worth having in this life, and having those things gone forever . . ."

"Would probably kill him," Driffin agreed, sympathy a heavy and comforting ocean that flowed out of the man without the least sign of condescension. "I started out envying your relationship with your father, but now there's nothing of envy left. I suppose this is the bright side of having parents who hated the very sight of you. I used to doubt that every cloud had a silver lining, but now . . ."

Edmin knew exactly what Driffin meant, and they sat together for a pair of long moments in a shared silence of emotional aching before the women suddenly reappeared at the table.

"We'll start with this soup, and by the time we finish it the rest of the meal should be ready," Idresia said as she placed a bowl in front of Driffin and one in her own place. Issini had carried over Edmin's bowl and her own, and the women were quickly seated. "By the way, Edmin, I meant to ask a question. Before you got here, Driff mentioned that the renegade has four young people with him who linked up to use Spirit magic. Do you have any idea who the young people could be?"

"Of course," Edmin said, sudden revelation stopping his spoon halfway to his mouth. "All along I've been trying to understand how Noll's wife had found it possible to put my father under her influence with *me* around. I was present once when she exercised her talent briefly, so I knew that her strength was weak compared to mine. If she had the help of others, then the answer becomes perfectly clear. And those others are her and Noll's children. One of my people saw and recognized the children, but I had no idea that they were being used to help Noll."

"Then his efforts are a real family affair," Driffin said after swallowing the spoonful of soup he'd taken. "Do you remember what Noll's wife was doing when she used her talent the time you were around?"

"I certainly do remember," Edmin answered after tasting his own soup, finding it as good as he'd hoped it would be. "The woman clearly wanted something from Noll, so she used her talent on him as she spoke to him privately. The fool had no idea he was being manipulated, and he granted her request at once. Afterward she was downright smug, but not out where anyone could see it."

"You know, that could mean something," Issini commented as Driffin nodded his understanding. "Her being secretly smug, I mean. If she influenced her husband so casually, that could mean she was used to doing it. And if she *was* used to doing that influencing, she could be the one in charge rather than her husband."

"Without his having the least idea of the truth!" Idresia pounced in agreement just as Edmin was about to gently ridicule the idea. "All those men they brought into the city with them would never have taken orders from a woman, but with her husband supposedly in charge they probably never hesitated to do as ordered. So just how much of a puppet *is* he, Edmin?"

"Actually, I'm not sure now," Edmin answered, surprised to find that he'd changed his mind. "Noll claimed that his brother Ephaim had trusted him completely because *he* had none of Ephaim's ambition, and now that I think about it that claim might be true. All the ambition in the family might really be Bensia's, and if it is then I really *don't* know how much of a puppet Noll might be. The man seemed totally wrapped up in his wife, and so might simply be doing as she wished because of his feelings for her."

"That comment tells *me* how much of a puppet he is," Issini put in, her expression one of excitement. "Don't you remember, Edmin? I told you that Bensia Noll had a courtesan friend of mine hurt because one of her clients was Noll. Men who are completely wrapped up in their wives don't visit courtesans, so the woman must have . . . adjusted her husband's feelings about her to keep him pliable. If his mind and body filled with desire every time he looked at her, wouldn't he be more eager to do everything she asked him to?"

"No question about it," Driffin said after exchanging a glance with Edmin. "A man who's really wild about a woman will do anything to please her, and will also *want* to do that pleasing. People like that can't seem to understand that mutual pleasing is better than the one-sided variety— even if they *are* getting something of their own out of it."

"So that means the renegade is really Bensia, and her husband is just being used," Idresia summed up as she looked around. "I hope neither of you men think that that means our efforts against the Nolls will be *less* of an effort because a woman is in charge?"

"Do I *look* as if I've turned addlebrained?" Driffin asked with a sound of ridicule, saving Edmin from saying that what Idresia had said was exactly the way *he* saw the matter. "I know from personal experience that women make the worst adversaries because women will do absolutely anything to win. Most men, even the most ruthless, will draw a line *somewhere* beyond which they just won't go. Most women think lines are good for nothing but hanging wet clothes on."

"So what's your point?" Issini asked very mildly, which made Idresia join the laughter Issini produced right after the comment. Driffin simply shook his head in a helpless way, which was exactly how Edmin felt. A helpless babe in the woods who knew almost nothing about the world about him, despite all the knowledge he'd *thought* he had. But he was a very lucky babe in the woods, as he now had guides all about him to help him find his way. And he *would* find his way, that he was determined to do. He would take the path to true happiness, and his step would never falter—until the day came when he had to face his father again . . . and maybe even ask about his brother Ophin . . .

\* \* \*

Honrita Grohl strolled into the shop projecting an air of complete innocence. The shop sold food, and Honrita found it pleasant that the shelves were well filled instead of almost empty. Food shipments were reaching the city again on a regular basis, but Honrita wasn't there to do any buying. She had a much more important objective, the final leg of what had proved to be something of a difficult search.

The man she was waiting for arrived no more than a few steps behind her, a nervous little man who made the same stops every day. The new arrival went straight to the woman who stood behind the counter of the shop, and didn't even have to speak. When the woman saw him coming she took a small envelope out from under the counter and handed it to the man when he reached her. The man took the envelope, put it in his old, worn tunic, then turned and left again.

Honrita drifted out of the shop after the small man, right now only interested in whether he would make his next stop or go directly to deliver the note he'd picked up. His next scheduled stop was rather close to this last one, and that was why she'd chosen to leave her note here. The man's next actions would be easily seen . . .

And they were. The small man went directly to his next stop, making no effort to take off in another direction. That left Honrita free to go somewhere herself, namely the place she'd lost the man two of the times she'd tried to follow him. But those times she'd been behind the man instead of in front of him, so to speak, and she hadn't been certain about where he was going. Now she *was* certain, and was also determined not to lose her guide again.

The area she got to first was very nearly deserted. It had been allowed to become very run-down during the reign of the nobles, and had therefore housed beggars and thieves and others who lived on the shady side of the law. The new government officials had rid the city of everyone who was unwilling to work an honest job, but hadn't yet gotten around to rebuilding the neighborhood. It would certainly be taken care of in its turn, but there were other, more populous, places that had to be rebuilt before this one would be done.

A doorway stood open and inviting, its door hanging from its one remaining hinge. Honrita made sure that no one was in the rickety building, and then she accepted the doorway's invitation. It was the perfect place to wait for the small man, just ahead of the spot where she'd lost him twice. She hadn't been able to hurry and still remain unnoticed, so when she'd reached this street the small man had been nowhere in sight.

"It would have been nice if I could have taken control of that little messenger boy, but for some reason it didn't work," Honrita mumbled to herself as she stepped into the dimness that would hide her presence. "His Spirit magic isn't quite as strong as mine, so I don't understand why I couldn't control him. That second week of class probably could have taught me how to get around the problem, but they didn't let me *take* the second week of class. I'll have to show those people just how much I appreciate being cheated."

It would have been nice to let her justified anger start to roil again, but Honrita knew she couldn't allow that luxury. If she did, the small man would know instantly that someone stood in hiding, just as she would have known. Her only chance was to calm herself so completely that she was serenity itself, and that she did know how to do. Then the small man would have no idea she was there and would continue on to the place—and the man—Honrita was determined to locate.

Honrita was already wrapped in silent balance when the small man appeared. She visualized gently rolling clouds to keep herself from thinking and feeling, and was therefore able to watch the small man closely. He hurried to a place to the right of where Honrita stood but on the opposite side of the street, looking around himself constantly. When he felt confident that he was alone, he went to a blank wall and pulled on a torch bracket. Part of the blank wall popped open inwardly to make a door, and the man was inside instantly to close the door behind himself. That left nothing but a blank wall again, and Honrita allowed herself a faint smile. No wonder she'd lost the man twice . . .

There was no way to know how long the small man would be in coming out again, so Honrita began to compose herself for something of a wait. Just as she was settling down the secret door opened again, and the small man reappeared. He reached to the bracket that had come forward with the opening of the door and pushed it back straight again. The straightening of the bracket caused the door to disappear into the wall again, and then the small man hurried away.

Honrita waited until the small man was completely gone, and then she left her hiding place. The small man's mind and talent had been ragged with fear and uncertainty, the relief of his departure only a small glow behind the rest. Honrita thought she knew why the man felt like that, an understanding that hastened her footsteps toward the silently waiting blank wall.

It was necessary for Honrita to stand on her toes to reach the torch bracket, something the man she'd followed hadn't had to do. The man wasn't small physically, only in his own self-image, so that was the way Honrita saw him. Even his talent was decently large, but his inner attitudes kept him from being anything more than a messenger. Honrita had been that way herself before the training class woke the proper self-image, so she had very little patience for the man's lacks.

It took a bit more strength than expected to pull the bracket forward, but once Honrita accomplished it the hidden door opened smoothly, quickly, and silently. Three steps brought Honrita far enough inside to close the door behind herself, which was rather easily done. The door had been hung with superb balance, so pushing it shut was no problem at all. It was—

Honrita broke off the useless, foolish thoughts about the door as she turned away from it, no longer willing to keep from thinking about what she was soon to find. She'd been dreaming of this moment, and hesitating with nervousness now was completely unacceptable. Her dreams were about to come true, but only if she behaved in the proper way.

With the door to the outside closed, the fairly long and narrow hallway she stood in was dim with the light of only a single lamp. Directly ahead of her she was able to make out what seemed to be another door, and there was definitely someone alive behind that door. For that reason she quickly made her way over to her objective, pulled on the latch-string, and stepped into a fairly large room.

"How clever of you to find your way in here," a man's voice said with amusement, the man himself standing only a few feet away. "It pains me to tell you that this intrusion won't accomplish what you expect it to."

"But of course it will," Honrita disagreed at once with a smile to match the one the man showed. He was tall and thin, just as he was supposed to be, and the burning stare of his gaze was almost painfully familiar. "I've come here to ask to be allowed to join you."

"Dama, you've managed to surprise me," Holdis Ayl replied as he continued to stare at her. "What makes you think that I *will* allow you to join me? One more follower added to the numbers already dedicated to my cause will make no difference whatsoever."

"Adding *this* follower will make a great deal of difference," Honrita countered, looking around to see the sparse furnishings she'd expected to find. The chairs were all straight-backed and unpadded, the eating table small, the bed barely larger than a cot . . . "The man who was just here has Spirit magic, but he's afraid to use it properly. I'm stronger than he is, and I'm *not* afraid to use my talent. You've been in hiding for much too long a time, and I'm determined to see that change. You deserve to be in *charge*, and I want to help make it happen."

"You made that statement without using your talent in an effort to convince me," Ayl commented, still staring at her unblinkingly with that faint smile curving his lips. "If I knew your reasons for coming here like this, I might be better able to judge how much truthfulness you speak with."

"My reasons are quite simple," Honrita murmured as she drifted a bit closer to the man. "My father was just like you, a man meant for greatness that everyone feared, but he was never able to accomplish that greatness. I wasn't old enough or strong enough to help *him*, but now that I'm both I'd like to make up for my previous lacks, so to speak. If I help *you* gain what's rightfully yours, it will be like giving *him* help when he needed it."

"I do mean to rule, but it won't ever be directly," Ayl said, now studying her in a different way. "I know what I need to accomplish to gain my due, and you would merely be a tool to facilitate that accomplishment. You will never have the power in your own hands, a fact you must be able to understand and accept."

"I do understand, and I do accept," Honrita assured him in the same murmur, now close enough to look up into those very familiar eyes. "All I ask is the chance to serve you—in every way possible."

"I believe I *will* allow it, at least for the time being," Ayl agreed after a long moment of silence. "Would you care for some tea while I explain what I'll require of you first?"

"Yes, yes, I would love some tea," Honrita answered, all but breathless over her acceptance. "I knew you would be able to make use of my talent at once, so I'm ready and eager to begin."

"Excellent," Ayl said as he moved past her to walk toward a tea urn. "What I require first is another four people with your strength, but in the other four aspects. You must put those people under your influence one by one, and once you've accomplished that the five of you must Blend."

"So that you'll have a Blending of your own to use," Honrita exclaimed as she watched Ayl pour her tea. "How delightfully delicious an idea. And what will you use our Blending *for*?"

"Why, to gain control over the members of a High Blending already in an official position, of course," Ayl answered as he turned back to her with the teacup. "Why struggle to oust those in power when you can make them your puppets instead? Members of High Blendings will be cautious around other High talents, but Middle talents will be all but ignored. That's always been a blind spot just waiting to be taken advantage of."

"And we're about to use that blind spot to gain you the place that was meant to be yours," Honrita said as she accepted the cup of tea. "Yes, the first step in the process is to find other strong Middle talents, and I'll get right to it as soon as I finish this tea. Do you have anyone in particular in mind, or will just any strong Middle talents do?"

"I've already located the people I want, so I'll give you their names and where they can be found," Ayl replied as he gestured her to a chair before taking one of his own. "I meant to use that fool you followed here to get the rest, but his cowardice for anything but fetching messages delayed my plans. And I appreciate the warning you gave in the message *you* sent. Telling me you would soon be here saved your life, as I would have destroyed an unexpected caller. Destroying you would have been such an incredible waste."

Honrita smiled at the compliment before taking a sip of her tea, so excited she could barely contain the emotion. With *her* help Ayl's plans *would* become a reality, and then they would be in control of a High Blending able to defend the position they would be required to take over. Ayl pictured himself as the only power behind that puppet Blending, and that was perfectly all right. By the time their puppets were in place, Ayl himself would be *her* puppet.

Ayl began to tell her about the other talents he had already picked out for her to control, and she listened carefully with most of her attention. She herself had no way of knowing who had the proper amount of strength, but knowing things like that was Ayl's strong suit. Honrita would do exactly as he said, giving him just what he needed when he needed it— in the way of pawns. Honrita had heard many people talking about the elusive Holdis Ayl before she'd been sent to that prison house, and just before she'd escaped she'd realized that she *had* to find the man.

The temptation was there for Honrita to sigh, but that reaction was part of her old self. These days Honrita acted instead of sighing, and her plans were well on the way to becoming reality. She'd tested Ayl by letting him know that he could have her body if he wanted it, and rather than accept her offer he'd asked if she wanted tea. That made the man *exactly* like her father, and the situation would have been funny if it hadn't been so filled with bitterness.

Honrita had been deeply in love with her father, and had wanted nothing more than for him to return her love. Instead, the vile man had ordered her around and used her in every way but the way she yearned for, ignoring her completely as though she were invisible. And then, before Honrita had found a way to gain the love she needed so desperately, the miserable man had suddenly died.

But Ayl would *not* do the same, at least not until Honrita had everything she wanted from him. He'd already accepted her to do his chores, and in a little while he would give her the love her father never had. Her father had *known* he was born for greatness and had made every effort to achieve it, but the accomplishment had slipped through his fingers. Helping Ayl *would* be like helping her father, and she would see that he did achieve his greatness.

And then she would take it right out of Ayl's hands, paying her father back for all the hurt he'd given her. *She* would have the greatness, the worthless female offspring her father had scorned so well and so often, proving her father had been wrong in everything he'd said and done. It would be marvelous, and she, too, would never flaunt her power for others to see. That way she would be able to keep the power . . .

# TWENTY-SIX

Kail Engreath returned to the very large house he shared with fifteen other people, his mood so good that he should have been whistling. After only five days his training was over, and so was that of most of the people who would be in his group of experimenters. That meant they could all get together in the house's meeting room tomorrow, and start to talk about what they would do. There had to be any number of things possible to do with talent that weren't already being done, and his group would earn Astindan citizenship as soon as they began to find those things.

"Kail, I'm delighted to see that you're back early too," Kail heard, and he turned just inside the door to see Renton Frosh. "Does this mean that you've also finished your training?"

"It certainly does, Ren," Kail answered with a grin as he closed the door. "Did you get that tea in the sitting room, or did you have to go to the kitchen for it? I can definitely use a cup of it myself."

"It's in the sitting room, which means they expected some of us to get back early," Ren replied with his own grin. "Isn't it nice when people have confidence in you?"

"It's something I've certainly been getting used to," Kail said as he and Ren headed for the sitting room open to the use of all the house's residents. "If someone suddenly started to doubt me again, I might not even remember how to act."

Ren chuckled to show he appreciated the joke, but he didn't comment. Kail knew that that was probably because Ren was fully aware of the fact that it would take years before the two of them got over what their fathers had done to them. Assuming they *ever* got over having been told for so long that they were useless and failures. They both knew perfectly well that they *weren't* useless failures, but deep down there was still that tiny whisper of doubt . . .

But thoughts like that were for another day, one that wasn't as pleasant as this one. Kail walked into the sitting room and headed straight for the tea service, nodding to the other residents of the house who had gotten back before him. There were only three of them, and they—as well as he and Ren—wore the new clothes the Astindans had provided. The clothing wasn't fancy, nothing like what they'd worn in Gandistra, but they were pleasantly colored and decently made from material that would not wear out too quickly.

"Don't be so disappointed that Asri isn't back yet," Ren murmured from Kail's left as Kail poured himself a cup of tea. "Somi—Tansomia—isn't back yet either, and I happen to know that she's doing *very* well in her class. Have you managed to speak to Asri about joining our group?"

"Not yet," Kail answered with a sigh as he turned away from the tea service with his cup. "I've made up my mind to do it a dozen times, but somehow she and I end up talking about everything *but* the group. Now that the group will be having its first meeting tomorrow, the subject should come up all on its own."

"And about time," Ren said, obviously in a teasing mood. "We're all so good we ought to start to get results almost immediately, and it would be a shame for Asri to lose out on the credit."

"I'll definitely speak to her before we sit down to dinner," Kail promised, the words for himself as well as for Ren. It had been lovely seeing Asri every evening, but it would be even lovelier to see her during the day as well.

Kail and Ren and some others chatted until almost dinnertime, and then they joined the others in setting the table and carrying out the various dishes. There were four Astindans employed in the residence who did the cooking and general cleaning, but Kail and the others had been told that that didn't mean the residents could just sit around. Each resident was responsible for keeping his or her own bedchamber neat and tidy, each had to pick up after him or herself, and all had to help at mealtimes. After their time working in the fields no one had protested, and in fact they each seemed to enjoy helping out.

But the thing bothering Kail was that Tansomia had gotten back only a few minutes after him, but Asri hadn't shown up until the usual time. Granted she was no *later* than usual in getting back, but that shouldn't have been. If she'd finished her training the way the rest of them had . . .

It would have been nice if Kail could have spoken to Asri as soon as she walked in, but that wasn't possible. Asri had to feed her baby son and then put him to bed before she could get her own meal, and interfering with the effort would just have delayed Asri even more. Kail waited for Asri to join them at table, but by the time she did he'd decided to wait a bit longer to ask the most pressing questions. No sense in asking about something that might be embarrassing for her where everyone could also hear all about it . . .

Meals at the residence were tasty and filling but never lavish. Kail was as hungry as ever, and everyone else seemed to feel the same. The food disappeared with its usual rapidity, and afterward everyone carried plates and bowls and cutlery and cups into the kitchen so that they might be washed by the staff. Only then was Kail free to take Asri aside, so that they might speak privately.

"The rest of us got home early today, and I was really worried when *you* didn't," he began, once again delighting in the smile that she reserved for him alone. "You did finish your training today, didn't you?"

"I . . . haven't been training," Asri replied after a definite hesitation, her lovely smile fading. "I . . . have a position that I really enjoy, one that lets me keep Dereth with me. Most jobs for women don't allow them to take their babies along, so I consider myself very fortunate."

"It would be easier yet for the both of you if you worked

here in the house," Kail pointed out at once, pouncing on the opportunity. "The group I'm a part of will be meeting for the first time tomorrow here in the sitting room, and there's no reason to believe that we'll be moved elsewhere for quite some time. If you start right now I'm sure you could get through the training really quickly, and then we could—"

"No, Kail," Asri interrupted immediately, giving him no time to mention how much more time they'd be able to spend together. "I've already asked to have my job made permanent, so I'm afraid it's too late to change my mind. But I appreciate your interest, really I do . . . I . . . had something of a hard day today, so I think I'll go straight to bed. I'll see you again tomorrow at breakfast."

The smile she gave him then was nothing like the usual one, and then she was gone toward the stairs. Kail watched until she disappeared upward, and then he turned to Ren and Tansomia, who had come over to join him.

"What did you say to her, old fellow?" Ren asked with gentle concern. "I could feel her agitation and distress all the way over on the other side of the room."

"All I did was ask her to join the group," Kail answered, feeling more bewildered and upset than he ever had before. "I don't understand why she reacted that way, Ren. She hasn't *been* in one of the training classes, and doesn't even want to hear about starting one."

"Maybe she has so little talent that she's ashamed," Tansomia suggested, sympathy clear in her tone. "We're all rather strong for Middle practitioners, don't forget, so a really weak Low would feel completely out of place with us. What aspect is she?"

"I really have no idea," Kail answered, realizing that Tansomia might be right. "The subject never came up, so I never asked. But now I can understand why she reacted like that. An overgrown fool tried to talk her into something that she's unsuited to do, and almost refused to take no for an answer. She should have hit me over the head with something hard to get my attention, and then explained the facts of life to me. Maybe then my foot would not be so firmly wedged in my mouth."

"I suggest that you wait until tomorrow morning to apologize, and then merely mention the apology in passing," Ren said with a hand on Kail's arm to keep him from going after Asri immediately. "If you follow her now you'll have to say why you've changed your mind, and that will be just as embarrassing for her. Tomorrow you can just say you didn't mean to demand that she leave something *she* enjoys doing for something *you* enjoy. After that you promise never to do the same again, and then you change the subject."

"Yes, I can see you're right so I'll wait," Kail said with a sigh after thinking about the suggestion for a moment. "She's so strong and vital a woman, it never occurred to me . . . Yes, waiting is definitely a good idea, but now I'm not fit company for anyone. I'm going to turn in early, and I'll see you two at breakfast."

Ren and Tansomia both obviously understood, so they just wished him a good sleep and let him walk away from them. Kail climbed the stairs slowly, most of his inner being yearning to go to Asri so that he might comfort her, but that was a bad idea. Comforting someone without mentioning what you're comforting them *for* isn't easily done, and telling Asri that her weakness of talent didn't matter to him would just be giving her more pain. No, better to take Ren's advice and leave the whole thing for the morning.

Kail expected to be up tossing and turning all night, but he'd worked too hard finishing up his training. Sleep had no trouble finding him not long after he lay down, and he was already awake when the glass chimes in his bedchamber were rattled to let him know it was time to get up. One of the servants had Air magic, and the woman would walk past each room rattling chimes to wake the residents. She was also obviously a morning person, and so had no need of help herself to wake up on time.

In spite of the need to speak with Asri this morning, Kail couldn't keep from feeling excited. This was the first morning his group would be meeting, and he looked forward to the time as he had little else. He still wished that Asri could be a part of it and him, but if she couldn't be with him then he would just have to share the time with her when he saw her. That way she *would* be a part of it all, just not as a participant.

Asri was already downstairs when Kail reached the dining room, so he joined her in setting the table and then in carrying out the food from the kitchen. Asri looked a bit down to Kail despite her efforts to seem as pleasant and happy as usual, so Kail didn't hesitate. When they were settled in their places and reaching for the food, he took the first step toward easing her mind.

"I really do have to apologize for trying to bully you last night," he said in a murmur that hopefully only she would hear. "If you enjoy the job you do, I had no right to insist that you do something else. If you forgive me, I'd like you to stroll with me tonight after dinner. If you're not too tired, of course."

All those "ifs" in his little speech made Kail want to wince, but apparently they didn't bother Asri. She gave him the smile he'd loved from the first time he'd seen it, true warmth and happiness behind it.

"I should have known better than to think you would try to run my life the way my husband always did," Asri answered in a matching murmur. "Thank you for proving me wrong, and I'd love to stroll with you tonight after dinner."

*So that was it*, Kail thought as he did his part in passing around the platters after helping himself to some of their contents. Asri had reacted so strongly because she thought Kail was acting the way her husband always had, and that had never occurred to him. Maybe it meant she wasn't a Low after all, and once she heard what his group was doing she would decide to join them after all. If not it would still make no difference to the way Kail felt about her, but now he had even more of a reason to see that the group came up with good ideas as quickly as possible.

Breakfast disappeared behind idle but pleasant chatter, after which Asri went to get Dereth. Kail waited until the two came down so that he could wish them a good day, and once Asri and her son were gone it was *time*. Ren and Tansomia had waited for Kail, so the three of them walked into the meeting room together.

"About time the three of you showed up," Belvis Drean said with a wide smile, most likely to let them know he was just joking. "The rest of us have been here since we helped to clear the breakfast table."

"We would have been here as well, but we had someone to speak to," Ren said at once with his own smile, speaking to everyone in the room. "I hope you'll forgive us, as we're just as eager to begin as the rest of you. Has anyone thought of anything for us to begin *with*?"

No one spoke up to say *they'd* thought of anything as the latecomers—and Drean—made their way to chairs around the large table, but Kail had a different question.

"There are only the eight of us here, and we're all from the residence," he remarked as he sat down. "I was told that an equal number of native Astindans would be joining our group, so I wonder where they are."

"Possibly they couldn't find anyone willing to work with us," Drean suggested, faint disturbance behind his words. "I can't say I really blame the Astindans, but we're all trying so very hard . . ."

Ren exchanged a glance with Kail, most likely even more aware of Drean's disturbance than Kail was. Drean had been a different man since the time they'd helped to bury that family on the road to where they were now, and the new Drean was actually pleasant and likeable. It was as though Drean had never before been allowed to show his pleasant side, and so now took great enjoyment in showing nothing else.

"That may not be the truth of the situation," Kail said after a moment of thought. "It's possible that it took longer to *find* Astindans for this group, so they haven't yet finished their training classes. If no one shows up in two or three days we can ask someone about it, but right now *I* have a question. Someone here has Air magic, I hope?"

"Yes, I do," an older woman responded with a smile, a woman Drean had sat down next to. Her name was Vantin Flain, and she was actually a bit smaller than Drean. "What question do you have?"

"Well, in a manner of speaking the question is personal, but it's occurred to me that there might be a broader application for the solution as well." Kail felt vaguely uncomfortable asking for something personal that might *not* have other applications, but with no one ready to discuss anything else . . . "As most of you probably already know, I've been . . . spending most of my free time with Asri Tempeth."

"Anyone not living locked in a wardrobe knows *that,*" Vantin replied with a wider smile. "Are you asking us to comment on your relationship with Asri?"

"No, I'm not," Kail replied very firmly at once, matching the woman's smile. "What I wanted to say was that Asri and I enjoy strolling together after dinner, but we've never been able to go very far or stay out very long. Asri worries that her son, Dereth, will wake up crying without her knowing about it, so she never stays away from their bedchamber long. Is there some way to . . . do something with air that would . . . let Asri listen in on her bedchamber from a distance? I don't know if I'm explaining my question clearly, but—"

"No, no, you're being very clear," Vantin interrupted to assure him, her amusement obviously gone. "And you're right, the solution to that problem *would* have other applications, some of which I can see right now. For instance, if it's possible to hear things from a distance, it might also be possible to speak from that same distance. Speaking to someone without one of the two having to go to where the other is . . . What a treat *that* would be!"

"More than just a treat," Drean enthused as everyone else began to comment with excitement. "It would save everyone so much time and effort . . . But, Vantin, you haven't yet said if any part of that is possible. Can you *do* something like that just by manipulating air?"

"A week ago I would have said no," Vantin answered, her renewed smile now showing delight. "After going through the training class, I'm now convinced that all parts of the idea *should* be possible. I simply can't do it alone, so we're going to have to ask for help. Oh, I can't *wait* to get started!"

Kail felt the same delighted enthusiasm, and apparently so did everyone else in the room. They'd produced their first good idea, and all because Asri had a baby she worried about. Kail knew he'd have to thank Asri for helping out the group even *without* being a part of it.

"I have a question for Spirit magic that I've been thinking about," Dobranin Corb said suddenly from the other side of the table. Corb was tall and thin and very much on the quiet side, as though he were most often wrapped up in private thoughts. "I have Water magic like Kail there, so I have no idea if what I want is possible. And I think I ought to mention first that there are too many times when I have to . . . fight off feelings of believing that everything I try to do is . . . futile."

"We all have moments like that, so please don't feel that you're alone in the experience," Ren told the man at once, his tone gentle with understanding. "If you ever need help with regaining your proper balance, you have only to ask."

"Yes, I know, but there's a limit to how often a man feels comfortable asking something like that," Corb pointed out with a smile that contained almost no amusement. "Just because you're a decent man who's willing to help, that doesn't mean you want to spend your life doing nothing else. Which is why I'd like to know if it's possible to . . . put 'balance' in a corner of a room, somehow. That way anyone who needs the help can just step into the corner and get it without bothering anyone else."

"You know, it would probably take the help of someone with Air magic, but I think it just might be possible," Ren said, his voice filled with awe and revelation. "And if everyone had a corner like that in one of their rooms, people would no longer have to start the day in a foul or miserable mood. Or bothered by nervousness or anger or any of the other disruptive emotions."

"Well, it looks like a personal question has done it again," Tansomia said with a delighted laugh. "Two questions, two bright new ideas. Does anyone else have a personal problem, I hope?"

That question produced laughter in everyone including Corb, but Kail knew it wasn't at all a joke. It became clear that the others knew the same when Vantin held up her hand.

"As a matter of fact, I had a passing thought just yesterday," Vantin said to everyone. "During dinner I managed to get a stain on my skirt, and I had to bother Belvis to use his Earth magic to remove the stain. It occurred to me to wonder if there could be some way to treat material *before* it's made into clothing that would keep it from getting stained to begin with. Do you know if that's possible, Belvis?"

"Why, it just might be," Drean said after a moment, his expression filled with surprise. "There are substances like resin that resist everything at a certain point, so why couldn't material be coated with something like that? Not resin, of course, or our clothes would be too heavy to wear comfortably, but one of the others . . ."

"I . . . hate to interrupt, but I have a suggestion about that," a tiny voice said, sounding as though the woman producing the voice had had to force herself to speak. The woman was Effella Tantor, a very shy little thing who rarely joined a discussion unless deliberately invited. Kail and the others had made a point of inviting her to comment on a regular basis, and now the effort had apparently paid off.

"Yes, please give us your suggestion, Effella," Drean told the woman in a kindly way. "Your Earth magic is every bit as strong as mine, and you've never wasted our time yet with nonsense."

"I . . . I appreciate that, sir," Effella answered with a blush covering her young and pretty face. "My . . . father liked to make things from wood, a hobby that relaxed him after a long day working in the government. Once he made a cabinet, and he didn't use ordinary varnish as a finish. He used a very thin extract of resin, so thin that once it dried it was almost impossible to tell that it was there. The wood looked as if there was nothing on it, but even dust found it impossible to cling. If that substance could be used on cloth . . ."

"Then we would have the perfect protection against staining, and maybe even dirt in general," Drean finished when she didn't, his nod clearly distracted. "That would make it unnecessary even to wash the clothing, which couldn't be done in any event. The only question I have would be about odors, and also how the extract would behave in the presence of dyes. I think we'll just have to try it and see."

When Effella realized that Drean's "we" included *her,* the shy young woman beamed even while she blushed. The man beside Effella, Jadro Marth, patted her arm gently with murmured words that were probably congratulations. Marth was as interested in Effella as Kail was in Asri, and the young Fire magic user always made sure to give Effella as much encouragement as she needed.

"All right, now *I* have a question for our Water magic users," Ren said suddenly, looking between Kail and Dobranin Corb. "If the two of you laugh at me I'll probably turn violent, but there's something I've always wanted to ask about."

"And I've always wanted to see *you* turn violent," Kail couldn't help commenting with vast amusement. "For that reason I just may laugh even if I don't think your question is funny."

"You're a true friend, Kail, and I knew I could count on you," Ren came back with wry amusement that was on the dry side. "So I'll admit that I *won't* get violent, but I'm still going to ask my question. The first time I saw a water wheel that powered a mill's grindstone, I was fairly young. For that reason I wondered why carriage wheels couldn't be made with water inside, so horses would be unnecessary to make the carriage go. Now, of course, I know that it was *falling* water that turned the wheel, but I still wonder if there isn't some way for Water magic to make the water fall *inside* a carriage wheel . . ."

Ren had been glancing around as he'd asked his question, possibly looking for the laughter he'd mentioned and might even have expected. For himself, Kail felt stunned, and if the expression on Dobranin Corb's face meant what Kail thought it did, Corb was just as stunned.

"You know, *boiling* water roils by itself," Tansomia commented into what had become a very deep silence. "I wonder how boiling water would do inside that wheel, and how much water would be necessary to make that carriage go."

"However much it is, the wheel would have to be sealed with resin or something against a loss of the water or even of the steam," Drean put in, his brows still high. "But keeping all four wheels turning separately might not be necessary. If all the water was used to move something that in turn moved the wheels, there would be only a single device that needed Water and Fire magic applied."

"But the water container *couldn't* be sealed," Vantin said, distractedly putting her hand on Drean's. "The steam would cause so much pressure against whatever held it that the whatever could well rupture explosively, with violently moving air doing the dirty work. Haven't any of you ever seen a teapot filled with water heating on a stove? Not everyone uses Fire magic, after all, so some of you *must* have seen it."

"A teapot has something that lets the steam escape with a high-pitched whistle," Effella offered with less shyness. "Would that something also do the job for our device that moves the wheels?"

"Maybe it would also do the job of calming the device instead of having to use Spirit magic," Ren put in, now obviously as deeply into the matter as everyone else. "The water in the device would have to be replaced, of course, but that's what people with Water magic do. So how do we get started with building this device?"

Everyone agreed that they *ought* to get started with building the device, but they also had the other ideas to work on. Just before Kail dove into helping to decide what they ought to start with first, he paused to pinch himself again. Yes, he still seemed to be awake, no matter how unreal the marvelous situation felt. This was what life was *meant* to be like, and he blessed the day the Astindan enemies had first made him a slave . . .

# TWENTY-SEVEN

Kail and the others in the group were so excited that they all decided to go together and ask for the extra help they needed. It wasn't far to the building they'd been interviewed in so they walked over, still discussing the ideas they'd come up with. Deslin Fodro was in his office, and at first the Astindan was startled to see the whole group descending on him. Once they explained the purpose of their visit, however, Fodro grew almost as excited as they were.

"This is a good deal more than we were expecting," Fodro said, gazing from one to the other of the group. "Those ideas are actually useful, and I'd personally like to see the one concerning distance-speaking put in use at once. Then I could just *speak* to the person I want to consult, rather than having to go to her office. Come with me, and we'll see about getting you the help you need."

"Some of us have what might be considered a delicate question," Kail said as Fodro rose from behind his desk and began to lead the way to the hall. "You told me that we would have Astindans working with us, but so far none of your people have joined us. Is that because we're still considered . . . outsiders?"

Kail had originally meant to use the word "enemies" rather than "outsiders," but at the last moment had changed his mind. Fodro paused near the door to the hall, and his faint smile seemed to show that he was aware of Kail's original intention.

"No, the delay in getting you others to work with the group is because of a shortage in man- and womanpower," Fodro answered in a way that convinced Kail he spoke the complete truth. "There weren't that many extra workers in this town to begin with, and putting the field-worker encampment so close used up what few people were available. Now we have to bring others in, just as I was brought in, and getting people moved isn't easy. First you have to convince them to leave their homes, and that's hard enough even if the people involved don't have a family. If they do have others in their lives . . ."

Fodro shrugged rather than completing his sentence in words, and then he continued on his way. Kail and the others followed, and Kail, at least, needed nothing in the way of more clarification. But the explanation did cause Kail a bit of worry. If unoccupied people were that scarce in the town, where would the Astindans find the help the group needed?

Fodro led the way to another part of the building, stopped in front of a closed door to knock, then gestured the group after him when he was invited to enter. This time there was a woman seated behind the room's desk, and she looked surprised to see so many people coming in.

"Kestri, there's a happy problem," Fodro said to the woman, giving her one of his faint smiles. "Our group of researchers met for the first time this morning, and they've already come up with so many new ideas that they need people to help put those ideas into practice. Or to find out that the ideas *can't* be put into practice. But after hearing the ideas, I'm hoping they'll find success rather than failure. By the way, people, this is Kestri Somore."

The woman nodded distractedly to the group, acknowledging the introduction, and her expression was downright comical.

"They've thought of things *already*?" the woman asked, putting her expression into words. "My goodness, that really is impressive. Can you give me an example of what the ideas are like?"

"Well, the one *I* like best is a way to speak to someone from a distance," Fodro replied with a smile that had actually widened a bit. "It would involve doing something to the air, I'm told, and if the procedure works it would save us from having to run over to each other's offices when we had something to say."

"That could well make us fat and lazy, but I'm willing to risk the danger," Kestri answered, her brows now high with obvious interest. "So what would be needed for *that* idea would be Air magic users, probably the stronger the better. I think there may be two or three Highs we can kidnap for you, people who are here resting from their shift at the work camp. Let me arrange the kidnapping first, and then you can all tell me about your other ideas."

Kestri Somore rose from her desk and hurried through the crowd in front of it, her smile making Kail believe that the woman should have been chuckling instead at the very least. Most of the members of the group *were* chuckling at the idea of kidnapping High talents, but they also looked suitably impressed. Their suggestions were being taken very seriously, almost as satisfying a reaction as coming up with the ideas in the first place.

Fodro chatted with the group while they waited for Kestri to get back, but the woman returned a good deal sooner than Kail had expected.

"That went a lot more easily than I expected it to," Kestri said as she made her way back to her desk. "I've been assured that the Air magic High talents will lose no time in kidnapping themselves and delivering the victims to your residence, so you'll want to be there when they arrive. But first I'd like to hear about the rest of your ideas."

Fodro started to mention the rest of what he'd heard, but the man got bogged down when it came to Ren's idea of using water to turn wheels. Ren and Kail and the others added clarifying comments, and finally ended up doing *all* the explaining. Fodro stood and listened along with Kestri, and when the explanations threatened to become discussions on how to accomplish the results they wanted, Kestri held up a hand.

"Please, my friends, please have some pity," Kestri said with mock distress. "If Deslin and I were the kind of people who were capable of doing this kind of thinking and planning, we would already be part of your group. But we're *not* as creative as you obviously are, so all you're doing is making us feel confused and bewildered. I can see, though, that you'll need more than just Air magic High talents to help you. If you'll all go back to doing what you're obviously so marvelous at, I'll arrange for more people to assist you. And then Deslin and I can return to our plodding paper shuffling."

"At least until you work out a way for us to talk without leaving our offices," Fodro put in with what was, for him, a wide grin. "When that happens, I intend to ignore my paperwork in order to play—ah, practice with, I mean—practice with the new arrangement. Please get it worked out as soon as possible."

The plaintive plea in Fodro's voice made the entire group chuckle, and then they offered sincere thanks before taking their leave. Ren's clear satisfaction told Kail that the Astindans hadn't simply been saying what the group wanted to hear. Both Astindans had meant what they'd said, and that made the whole situation even better.

Kail and the others lost very little time in getting back to the residence, and that turned out to be a lucky thing. No more than minutes after they got back, one of the house workers came into the meeting room to tell them that they had visitors. There were three callers, the Air magic High talents Kestri had promised to send, and the two women and one man demanded a more detailed explanation of what was wanted as soon as they walked in the room. They'd been given only a part of the story, but even that part had captured their imagination.

Vantin Flain, their own Air magic user, took over for the group, and the discussion quickly passed beyond the point of understanding for everyone else. Sorting air currents, setting vibrations, and creating tiny and limited echo-chamber effects may have meant something to Air magic users, but those with other talents were left lost in confusion.

So Kail and the others abandoned the Air magic people to the arcane part of their talent, and began a discussion about other possible ideas. Kail wondered aloud why bath house water was kept heated by talent, but was never agitated briskly in a way that would invigorate a person's body.

"Probably because people aren't laundry," Dobranin Corb put in morosely, but then his head came up a bit. "You know, come to think of it *I* might enjoy something like that even more than you. Soaking in warm water usually made me feel a bit better, and so did massages. If it were possible to combine the two . . ."

That comment sparked another discussion, of course, but Kail found that he had to "throw cold water" on his own idea.

"Agitating bath water is practical if you have servants with a wide variety of talents to do the job," he said, quieting everyone else's comments. "For those people who live more simply, which most Astindans seem to do, there would be no way for them to get the agitation unless they had Water or Air magic."

"Or unless they could use whatever talent they did have to make the water agitate itself," Ren mused, apparently surprised by whatever thought he'd had. "That device we were talking about to make the wheels move on a carriage without the use of horses . . . Would it be possible to adapt the device to other ends?"

"Wouldn't the . . . device have to be . . . useable by anyone with *any* talent?" Effella Tantor asked in her usual painfully shy way. "I have . . . Earth magic, you know, and I don't see how . . . *I* would use something like that."

"Now *that,* I think, is the best comment made by anyone yet," Ren stated, the excitement in his gaze clear. "Everyone has been taken by our suggestion concerning the possibility of distance-speaking primarily because it won't be necessary to *have* Air magic to use whatever the Air magic people arrange. It might be a good idea if we use that concept as a framework for the future, that the best ideas will be the ones that can be used by anyone."

"We should have realized that sooner," Kail said, looking around at the others. "Ren and Effella are absolutely right, and the only way our ideas will be good for everyone is if everyone can use them. If we come up with something that only people with a specific talent can use, we'll have to put the idea on a secondary list for later consideration."

"To be considered once we've put out some things that everyone can use," Jadro Marth, the Fire magic user, said with a nod of agreement. "That kind of thing will be useful, but less useful than the first kind."

"I wonder . . . if there's a way to use Earth magic . . . without someone with Earth magic being there," Effella ventured, her gaze partially distracted. "Like if someone has a headache or can't sleep . . . and doesn't want to bother a healer with something so unimportant . . ."

And with that comment they were off again, linking the idea to Dobranin's earlier one about a corner with Spirit magic that would soothe the troubled. Quite a lot of time went by like that, and then they were interrupted by Vantin and the High talent Air magic users.

"We think we've got something worked out," Vantin told the group, her eyes glowing with pleasure. "Would anyone like to help us test what we've done?"

It came as no surprise to anyone that everyone in the group volunteered immediately, and that included Effella and Dobranin. For that reason the group was divided in half, and Vantin joined the three people in the second division. The other four were led away by the High talents, and Vantin gestured the others after her to a far corner of the meeting room.

"Please notice the pink ribbon that was put on the wall over here in this corner," Vantin said, speaking to Effella and Jadro as well as to Kail. "When your turn comes, I'd like you to place yourself in the corner in a way that lets you just reach up and touch the ribbon. Do all of you understand that?"

"The idea isn't particularly hard to understand," Kail pointed out mildly with a smile. "But how will we know when our turn comes? And where were the others taken?"

"You'll find that out in a moment," Vantin answered, her

own smile much wider. "That assumes the arrangement works for someone other than Air magic users, of course. We tried it ourselves, but that doesn't—"

"Kail, Kail, are you there?" Kail suddenly heard in Ren's voice. The voice was rather soft, but it was so clear that Kail looked around for where Ren might be hiding.

"Go ahead, Kail, step up to the ribbon," Jadro urged with amused excitement. "And don't forget to ask him where he is."

Kail, feeling a bit foolish, did step up to the ribbon hanging on the wall. He could have reached up to touch that ribbon, but instead pretended to be cool and uninvolved.

"Is that you, Ren?" Kail asked, resisting the urge to speak loudly. "If it is, where are you?"

"I'm in the dining room, old son, and this is unbelievable," Ren's voice returned, sounding even closer and clearer. "But it just occurred to me . . . What if you want to speak to more than one other place and person? And what if you *don't* want to speak to anyone but the person in the same room with you? Does this arrangement mean having to give up one's privacy?"

"I heard that, and I can answer his questions," Vantin said, now looking smugly delighted. "And I can even answer one he didn't ask but should have. We're all close enough to hear someone speaking from another place, but even a foot farther away would change that. The High practitioners and I decided that we would put up differently colored ribbons for different locations, so it would be possible to speak to more than one person—and know which person you were calling out to. If you want privacy for a face-to-face conversation, you'll just move out of range of the ribbons. The one thing we can't decide on is whether the various locations should be arranged together or put in separate parts of the room. After all, you might want to speak to someone without everyone else knowing about the conversation."

"That decision might well be left to the people who are involved," Kail heard, this time in Belvis Drean's voice. "What *I'd* like to know is, will you very fine people be willing to arrange for certain connections for *us* before you go back to the interviews building? After the rest of us try out *this* connection, of course."

Jadro moved forward as Vantin laughed, adding his own plea to Drean's. Kail moved out of the way so Effella could also get closer to the ribbon and be in line to take her turn, but he listened carefully to whatever the answer to Drean's question would be.

"Vantin has already asked us that," a strange male voice came through from the other end of the connection. "Since the arrangement doesn't take very long to do once you know what you're about, we'll be glad to oblige you folk. After all, if not for you we wouldn't *have* this lovely idea to put into practice."

The marvelous answer made more than one pair of the group happy, and once everyone had had a chance to try the new arrangement the four Air magic people went off to start making good on their word. The rest of the group came back from the dining room, and then those who wanted the connection installed were called out in pairs to tell the Highs where they wanted their "ribbons" to be.

When it became Kail's turn, he cheated just a little. He had one end of the connection placed near the side of his bed that he never slept on, and the other end above the place in Asri's bedchamber where her baby's bed stood. Asri might never decide to use that side of Kail's bed, but if she did then she'd have no worries about the well-being of her son.

Just before the last of the connections was made, the group was told about additional visitors. This time there were two Highs in Spirit magic, which meant that all three of the Highs in Air magic did *not* return to the administrative building. One of the three stayed to work with the Spirit magic Highs on the next idea, which would put a "balancing" corner into certain rooms. Drean gently took Effella's arm and coaxed her along with him, and then told the Highs about Effella's idea concerning a "healing" corner.

After a bit of discussion, it was decided that putting everything into the corner at once might be easiest, but there weren't any High talents in Earth magic present yet. The lack was frustrating, so everyone involved decided not to wait. If the group's two Earth magic talents linked up, they might be able to do almost as well as a High talent. It was worth trying, and if it didn't work they would *then* sit down and wait for the Highs.

This time the rest of the group decided to go along and watch what was done, so the time really flew. The Air magic High somehow . . . *prepared* the air in a corner of the meeting room, the Spirit magic Highs added to the preparation, and then the linked talents of Drean and Effella took their turn. None of those watching understood anything of what was done, but when the effort was over Drean turned to Dobranin Corb.

"All right, Corb, you're the logical one to be first to test this newest arrangement," Drean said with a warm smile. "If it works on the rest of us the doing won't mean much, but if it works on *you* then we've accomplished something."

"Since I'm the one who wanted this, I *will* test it first," Corb said as he stepped forward with his usual sour expression. "I'm not expecting it to be really effective, but I might as well—"

Corb's words broke off as he stepped into the prepared corner, and for a moment there was no sound in the room except for everyone's breathing. Then Corb turned around very slowly, and the smile on his face was so wide that it took another moment before Kail noticed that the man's eyes were closed.

"This is the most marvelous experience I've ever had," Corb said, the words an actual murmur. "Every worry and disturbance in my mind has been calmed, and even a headache I didn't know I had has been soothed. If I were to lie down now I would fall asleep at once, but I won't sleep because I don't really want to. I think I've been made into a new man."

"What *I'd* like to know is how long the effect lasts," one of the Spirit magic Highs put in. "Would you step out of the corner now, Dom Corb?"

"Certainly," Corb answered in the most pleasant tone of voice Kail had ever heard from him. Kail and Ren and the others exchanged glances, all of them obviously worried that the man would revert to his original feelings and attitudes as soon as he was out of the corner, but it didn't happen.

"Yes, that was exactly what I'd hoped it would be," Corb said after opening his eyes and taking three steps away from the corner. "I know somehow that my original feelings *will* return at some time, but that's nothing to worry about. When I do start to feel sour again, I'll just come back to this corner."

No one was able to hold back on their congratulations after that, and the words were spoken to the talents who had developed the corner first and then, not surprisingly, to Corb. It was Corb who had turned a personal problem into a solution for more people than himself, and Corb joined in everyone's delight with no trace of his sourness left.

After that everyone had to try the corner, Effella being the one who was urged in first. The small, shy woman emerged glowing, and when it became Kail's turn he understood completely why everyone was responding so well and so completely. The corner assured Kail that he was a perfectly decent and useful human being, and that everything he attempted would turn out well. The tiredness he'd been feeling was also soothed away, and if Kail had lain down to sleep he knew he would have been able to do so without any difficulty. But there was also a small but definite insistence that he leave the corner, otherwise he might have forgotten to walk out again . . .

"Good," that same Spirit magic High said when Kail stepped out of the corner. "Apparently everyone is responding properly to the buried command not to stay in the corner indefinitely, including the gentleman with Spirit magic. Now the only things we don't yet know is how long the effects last, and how long before the corner needs to be . . . refreshed."

"Now, that's a good point," Ren said with raised brows, apparently understanding the comment more fully than Kail did. "The implanted . . . 'auras' probably *will* weaken over time, but how long a time they'll remain effective is something we don't yet know. We also don't know if the use of a large number of people will weaken the auras more quickly than use by only one or two folk. It seems our experiments are not yet done."

"We can get the rest of the people in this residence to try the corner," Kail suggested, now understanding the problem. "At the same time, we might want to have a second corner 'prepared' elsewhere for the use of only one or two people. That arrangement would give us more answers than having only the one corner to use."

Everyone considered that an excellent suggestion, so another corner in the meeting room was "prepared." This time Kail sat down in a chair instead of joining the others in watching the process. He felt absolutely marvelous, and couldn't wait until Asri got home. Things were going so well that this was probably the best time to ask her to be his wife. Not to mention the fact that Kail knew well enough that he might lose his nerve once the "treatment" in the corner wore off.

"So my best bet is to act as quickly as possible," Kail murmured to himself happily. Life was really becoming worth the living, and would be even better once he and Asri were really together . . .

# TWENTY-EIGHT

Kail felt tempted to wait for Asri at the front door to tell her how his day had gone, but then he realized that she would be tired and first had to feed and settle her child before she herself could sit down to eat. For that reason he waited for her at the table as usual, but when she took the chair beside his, he gave her a smile that was warmer than usual.

"Today was really incredible for me, and I'll tell you all about it later," Kail said, putting his hand on hers. "I just hope your own day was as good."

"My day," she echoed, oddly asking nothing about his first comment. "My day was . . . only to be expected, I suppose. Do you mind if we do talk later? I'm really very tired right now, and would rather just eat my food without any conversation."

"Of course I don't mind if we talk later rather than now," Kail agreed at once, belatedly noticing how drawn Asri looked. "You just enjoy your meal and don't worry about anything else."

The smile Asri gave him was on the wan side, and that worried Kail. She was always so alive and cheerful and full of hope for the future . . . Right now she looked as though she expected the roof to fall in on them at any minute and didn't expect to be able to avoid the fate. Kail very much wanted to ask her what was wrong, but he'd agreed to save all conversation until after dinner.

So Kail spent the time while he ate his meal watching Asri

out of the corner of his eye. She took just as much food as she usually did, but she ate mechanically as though eating were a somewhat distasteful duty that she performed only because it was necessary. Everyone else at the table excitedly discussed what the group had accomplished today, but Asri never noticed. She had sunk down into her own thoughts, a place she seemed to be held despite the apparent unpleasantness of the location.

By the time the meal was over, Kail had completely changed his plans. He'd meant to take Asri on that walk they'd agreed to the night before, even though he hadn't remembered to ask for a "ribbon" place to be established outside that linked to Asri's room. Instead Kail wordlessly guided Asri to the meeting room, where members of the group were demonstrating how easy it was to speak to others still in the dining room. Asri continued to be too distracted to notice what was going on around her, and so she stepped into the "soothing" corner without a protest. Kail let her stand there for a moment, and then he touched her arm.

"Are you feeling any better now?" he asked in a soft and gentle voice. "If you need to stay in the corner a bit longer, that's perfectly all right."

"No, I *want* to come out now," she answered with a bit of confusion as she stepped out to rejoin him. "What *was* that, and where did it come from? And while I'm asking, what are those people doing over there near that ribbon?"

"That's what I was trying to tell you about earlier," Kail replied with something of a smile. "Our group was more than a little successful today, and now we have things in this house that everyone can use. What you just tried was what we decided to call a 'comfort corner,' but it doesn't seem to have worked as well with you as it did with the rest of us."

Kail had added that last observation because of the clear signs of disturbance that had returned to Asri's expression. The comfort she'd gotten had turned out to be only momentary, and when she shook her head to dismiss Kail's unspoken question about what was bothering her, Kail suddenly decided to broach a topic he hadn't meant to cover until much later.

"Asri, things are going much better for me a lot faster than I ever expected them to," he said, taking her hand as he groped for the best words possible. "For that reason I've reached the point that I've wanted to reach ever since the day we first met. If you'll have me, I'd like to be your husband and Dereth's father."

Kail expected his proposal to give Asri *some* kind of pleasure, even if she just smiled and said she wasn't ready to marry again. Instead Asri stared at him for a moment with tragedy in her gaze, and then she hurried out of the meeting room without looking back.

"Well, *that* answer's clear enough," Kail muttered to himself as he watched her go. Asri obviously felt horrified at the thought of marrying him, and had been so upset that she hadn't even been able to voice a refusal. Kail was so disappointed and downright miserable that he couldn't stand being in the same room with anyone else. The fact that the others were enjoying themselves was completely unbearable, so he quickly headed for the stairs and the solitude of his own bedchamber. He felt as though he were carved out of pain; knowing that the woman he loved detested him was enough to bring him thoughts of ending it all.

Closing the door to his bedchamber severed Kail's connection to the rest of the world, but it did nothing to calm the turmoil of his thoughts. Asri couldn't possibly love him, otherwise she would never have acted the way she had. And *he'd* been foolish enough to think that she might want to share his bed when she agreed to share his life. What a joke *that* had turned out to be.

Kail wanted to laugh bitterly at dreams that were now dead, but laughter of any sort was beyond him. Instead, he walked slowly to the side of the bed that would have been Asri's, and sank down on the bed to put his hand to the quilt. To have had her there, to have had her love, would have been his life's greatest gift. Now, though . . .

For a long moment Kail sat unmoving and almost unliving, but then he became aware of an odd sound. At first he couldn't identify it, but then he realized that it was muffled crying. Where crying could be coming from he couldn't imagine, but just as he remembered the connection he'd had established with Asri's bedchamber, he also heard her voice.

"Oh, Dereth, I wish you were old enough for me to really talk to you," Asri said in a whisper, the soft words coming out ragged in between sobs. "Kail asked me to marry him, the very thing I've been dreaming about ever since I met him, but all I could do was run away to cry. After what they told me today, you and I will have to leave. But Kail is happy here and finally as successful as he deserves to be, so how can I ask him to go with us? I *can't* ask him, and now we'll never see him again."

The sobbing finally overwhelmed Asri's words, but all Kail could do was sit very still from the aftereffects of shock. Asri *did* love him as much as he loved her, but for some reason she felt she couldn't say so. And she meant to leave, all alone except for Dereth . . .

For a very long moment Kail was filled with nothing but conflict, all of it centering on the very thought of leaving. Kail's entire life had been spent searching for acceptance and success on his own terms, and he'd finally found both precious things in Astinda. They'd given him the chance to prove his capability, and soon would offer him full acceptance. How could he possibly walk away from that?

An odd numbness had taken hold of Kail, and for a short time his mind was held in cold motionlessness. Then it slowly came through to him that he hadn't been *asked* to leave what he'd earned, in fact the exact opposite had been done. Asri loved him so much that she was prepared to leave him with what she knew he needed so desperately, but it suddenly came to Kail that she was wrong.

*That was what I* used *to need,* Kail thought, knowing it was the truth. *I had to prove myself* to *myself, but now that I've done it I don't have anything left to prove. Except, possibly, that Asri's love isn't being wasted on a self-centered fool . . .*

Relief flooded Kail as he got to his feet and headed for the door to the hall. Now that he'd shown himself that he could be part of a successful effort, he knew he could find that success again anywhere. What he would *not* be able to find was a woman who loved him as much as he loved her, a woman who might even love him *more* than he loved her. It was now up to him to show that his own love was just as great, otherwise he didn't deserve to have her.

Kail almost knocked on Asri's door, but remembering that Dereth slept inside kept him from doing it. And Asri might even ignore a knock, especially if she guessed that it was Kail at the door. With that in mind Kail simply turned the knob and walked in as quietly as possible, and Asri was still too deeply absorbed in crying to notice.

"I'm going with you, Asri," Kail said softly once the door was closed again, the only thing he could *think* of to say. "Wherever it is you feel you have to go, I'm going with you."

Asri's head had jerked up in shock at the first of Kail's words, and it took a moment for her to understand what he'd said. After the moment her face paled, and she hurried over to hold him as he held her.

"Kail, you can't do that," she objected, her voice still ragged from the crying she'd done. "You don't understand what's involved, and you can't leave what your talent and ability have earned you."

"Asri, what I've earned is the knowledge that my talent and ability will work anywhere," Kail disagreed gently as he delighted in the feel of her in his arms. "What I can't and won't give up is the woman I love, even if I don't know what's troubling her. Do you think you can tell me about it now?"

"I was about to refuse, but refusing isn't very bright," Asri said with a sigh, looking away from him even as she stepped out of his arms. "You deserve to know the whole story, and then you'll have the chance to change your mind. If you do, I certainly won't blame you . . . Come and sit down."

Asri led the way to the two small chairs standing on the opposite side of the room from where Dereth lay sleeping. Kail felt disturbed over what Asri had said, but it didn't seem to be the time to argue with her. Once he heard what she had to tell him, he would then know what to argue against.

"I . . . don't really know where to start, so I suppose I might as well work backward," Asri said, her words now coming out with a great deal of reluctance as she continued to avoid Kail's gaze. "My job here has been in a child-care residence, a place where people leave their young children during the workday when there's no one else to look after the children. There are so many jobs to be done and so few people to do them that women are *encouraged* to leave their homes if they have even the smallest amount of ability . . ."

"Yes, I know about the shortage of workers," Kail put in, just to be encouraging and supportive. His brief statement seemed to do the job, as Asri took a breath and continued.

"I really loved working with the children, especially since it was possible to keep Dereth near me at all times," Asri said. "The other people in the residence were really nice— but today a small group of strangers came through the house. We all thought that they were there to see if we were doing a good job, but when I was taken aside by one of the women I found out differently.

"The woman told me that they were there to do an unofficial assessment of what talents the children have. The official assessment would come when the children reached five years of age, but a preliminary examination would tell the Astindan leaders what sort of diversity and strength would eventually be available. That was why the woman wanted to speak to me privately, to give me the bad news before I heard it from an official source when Dereth got to be five."

Asri's voice had been getting lower and lower, until Kail could barely hear her. He felt a chill when she mentioned bad news, and couldn't bring himself to interrupt with a question. He had a feeling he knew what she would say and couldn't bear to rush the time when he would *have* to hear the truth.

"The woman told me that Dereth . . . showed no signs of talent whatsoever," Asri went on in the same whisper, confirming Kail's worst fears. "I'd had the feeling that I ought to stay home from work today, and I wish I'd listened to that feeling. The woman also told me that I would have to . . . give up Dereth at the age of five so that he could be trained for some menial job where he would come in the least amount of contact with normal people, so I might want to think about giving him up now, when it would be easier on both of us."

"Easier!" Kail echoed with a sound of scorn, no longer able to stay silent. "How easy would it be for *her* to give up her own child? But maybe for her it *would* be easy, so I withdraw the question. I hope you told her what to do with her advice."

"I . . . couldn't quite do that," Asri said, still avoiding Kail's gaze even after she knew how he felt. "You see, she was angry with me and had a right to be angry. As she put it, I should have known that my own complete lack of talent could well be inherited by any children I had, and so I should have remained childless. It didn't matter that my former peer group dismissed my lacks as unimportant in light of my social position. *I* should have known better, and now I had no right to complain."

Asri's comment was made in so even a voice that Kail should have missed what she said, but his immediate inner turmoil proved that he *hadn't* missed it. Asri wasn't a Low talent, she was a null. That had to be why she'd reacted so strongly when Kail had tried to talk her into joining his group. She didn't have the *ability* to join his group, but the shock of that realization came and went surprisingly fast. With or without talent, Asri was still the same woman he'd fallen in love with.

"So instead of complaining, you've decided to take Dereth and leave," Kail said when it became clear that Asri had nothing further to add. "Since I agree completely, where do you think we ought to go?"

"Somehow I knew you were going to say that, but don't you understand that you mustn't?" Asri all but begged as she finally looked up at him again. "If you leave with me you'll be throwing away everything you've always wanted, and eventually you could come to hate me for making it necessary that you do that. I'd rather leave you behind than see you come to hate me."

"Since I'll never come to hate you, I don't see the problem," Kail returned with all the lighthearted relief he actually did feel. "Being part of a successful group and having Astindan citizenship means nothing to me if I can't share those things with *you,* so leaving them behind is no real hardship. Now that we have *that* settled, tell me where you'd like to go."

"I . . . really have no idea," Asri answered, her gaze now filled with all the love Kail himself felt for *her.* "Where do *you* think we ought to go?"

"At the moment I have no idea either, but I fully expect that to change," Kail assured her. "Since we don't have to leave this very instant, I'm going to take a day or so to think about the matter. But I don't expect to take very long with my thinking, so please be ready to leave at any time. And make sure you don't let *anyone* know what we mean to do. We may not be working in the fields any longer, but we still haven't earned the citizenship we were promised."

"Which means that technically we're still slaves," Asri agreed with a nod, understanding the point at once. "I'll have to pretend that I'm still depressed when I go to my job, which shouldn't be too hard. I was really looking forward to making a new life here, but now . . ."

Kail nodded to show that he understood, but instead of saying anything else he stood and drew Asri up from her chair by one hand. Once Kail had his arms around her Asri was the one who initiated the kiss, and they shared each other's essences for a wonderfully timeless time. Kail had wanted to lie with Asri, but something told him it was the wrong time for that. They had the rest of their lives to share their bodies, and once they were on their way to the new lives waiting for them, Kail knew Asri would feel a good deal better about the matter.

So Kail simply enjoyed the kiss, and once it was over he went back to his own bedchamber to sit down and think. When the group's experiments had proven to be a success today, someone had mentioned in passing that there would be gold for all members of the group that had produced so much for Astinda. Kail had been too wildly happy to think about something so mundane at the time, but now he did think about it—and about how much he could do with gold.

"It would be nice to have a wagon, but I think we'll do better with two saddle horses and two packhorses," Kail murmured to himself. "We'll be able to move faster on horses than we would in a wagon, just in case they decide to chase after us. We'll pretend to be heading deeper into Astinda, but in reality we'll be going back to Gan Garee."

Back to Gan Garee. The last thing Kail wanted was to return to the place he and Asri had been so unhappy, but that was the whole point. It was also the last place the Astindans would think to look for them, and if he and Asri pretended to be ordinary people rather than members of the former nobility . . .

"It will work," Kail said aloud, making the promise to himself as well as to Asri. "No matter what I have to do, I'll *see* that it works . . ."

Deslen Voyt walked into the room where the class would be held, more excited than he'd ever have admitted aloud. He and Brange had come to the building together, but they'd had to separate once they arrived. Deslen was a Low talent in Water magic, while Brange had a Low talent in Earth magic. Two different talents, two different classes . . .

Deslen only glanced around before taking a seat, pretending he knew no one else in the room. The fact was he knew three of the other people already there, but they were pretending to be strangers to each other just as he was. They all really wanted a chance to join what these city people had going for themselves, and showing up in the class as a group would have made Deslen and the others stand out and look suspicious. At one time standing out from the crowd had been fun, but now . . .

A man Deslen didn't know appeared in the doorway to the room, pausing before walking in. For a moment Deslen wondered if the man was their instructor, but then he noticed the man's nervousness. The man obviously worked to hide how he felt, but Deslen had no trouble recognizing the reaction for what it was. He himself felt excited to finally be in the class, but behind the excitement was the same kind of nervousness. What if his talent proved to be *too* small to be trained? What if he didn't measure up even after the training?

Those questions were enough to destroy the self-assurance of anyone, but the stranger in the doorway forced himself to enter the room in spite of the near certainty that he shared those terrible feelings. The man, who was almost Deslen's size, came over and took a seat not far from Deslen, then sat just as quietly. No one in the room spoke to anyone else, and the silence was almost painful.

Deslen knew that if they all had to sit there like that for very long, chances were good that at least half the people in the room would leave again. Excitement was waning and nervousness was rising, and then suddenly another newcomer was entering the room. This time it was a woman, though, and rather than choose a chair among those already present, she went to the desk in front of the room.

"If at any time during this class I scream and faint, please just ignore me until I come to again," the woman said as she looked around. She wore a faint smile, but it was obviously a forced reaction. "I've been telling myself that there's no need to be shy in front of so many very brave people, but I . . . can't help feeling a bit overwhelmed. Everyone has been saying how impressed they are that you're all here, so I've come to feel . . . more than impressed."

"What are you talking about, woman?" a voice rumbled from the other side of the room. It was one of the men Deslen knew, just about taking the words out of Deslen's mouth. "You sound like you think we're all High talents, but if that's so, then I'm the only Low in the room."

"No, no, of course I don't think you're High talents," the woman protested with a small laugh as a mutter of comments trickled through the room. "I've met High talents, and although I wish *I* had their strength, I wasn't particularly impressed. It's the fact that every single one of you *is* a Low talent is what's making everyone notice."

"We still don't understand what you're talking about," Deslen said over the next circulating mutter, an understatement if there ever was one. "No Low talent has ever impressed *anybody,* and that's something I know better than I like."

"Obviously I haven't been making myself clear, so let me explain," the woman replied with a warm and friendly smile for Deslen, then she spoke to everyone again. "I'm sure you all know that this is hardly one of the first training classes. The first classes had almost all Middle talents, with just a smattering of very self-confident—or very brash—Lows. People who were very sure of their talent showed up first, and then came the ones with a bit less assurance. Now . . ."

The woman looked around again, and now her gaze came from shining eyes.

"Now we have the people who know they have very little talent, but still have the courage to try to do the most with it. It doesn't take much to step forward if you *know* you have the strength to handle what you're shown, but to step forward even when you're uncertain . . . I think all of you people are just marvelous, and I mean to try very hard to justify the honor of teaching you. If you have any questions, please don't hesitate to ask them. Chances are there are others with the same questions, so you won't be wasting anyone's time."

The woman directed her smile toward everyone in the room, and it simply wasn't possible to doubt her sincerity. Deslen had been conned more than once over the years, so he'd developed a recognition of sorts to protect him from being fooled again. He usually knew when someone was lying in his or her teeth, and realizing that the woman spoke what she considered the truth was incredibly warming.

A glance around showed that the other people in the room seemed to feel the same, and that let Deslen relax completely. With someone so much on his side, he knew he would *not* fail to do the best he was capable of. When people go so far as to believe in you, it just isn't possible to let them down.

The woman began to say things about touching the power as long and as often as possible, and Deslen listened closely with an inner smile. He'd always wondered what it would be like to have someone believe in him, and now that he knew he refused to even consider losing the experience again. He would do his absolute best in the class and then he would become a city guardsman, and someday he might even recapture the incredible feeling of being a hero again . . .

# TWENTY-NINE

"All right, people, now's the time," Vallant called from his sleeping pad. "The Blendin' on watch says the invaders are almost here, so it's time for us to do what *we* have to."

"Just how close *are* they?" I asked, having the feeling that Jovvi was only a breath away from initiating our Blending. "It would help to have some tea first to counter the jangle of waking up this abruptly."

"That's a good idea, so let me ask," Vallant said, and then his gaze seemed to go inward for a moment. After the moment he nodded, and then he was back with us. "The invaders are still about half an hour away, so we do have some tea drinkin' time. Assumin' there's tea available for us to drink."

"There is," Jovvi said as she joined the rest of us in standing up. "I made sure of that before I lay down, knowing I, at least, would need some. And once we have the tea, we really ought to speak to the new Blendings one more time. They're certain to be strung wire tight right about now."

We all agreed that that was a good idea, so we got our tea and then carried the cups over to where the members of the new Gracelian Blendings waited. Most of them looked as nervous as we'd expected them to, but one set of Blending members looked more amused.

"If you've found somethin' funny in all this, you really should share it," Vallant gently told the ones who were smiling. "I think we could all use somethin' to laugh at right about now."

362

"I think the matter is more one of justified comeuppance than being funny," Alesta Vargan, one of the members of the Blending, said with a wry smile. "Just before I lay down to sleep, I was approached by a very important person. The charm flowed out of him as he made sure to mention first just how very important he was, and then he made a once-in-a-lifetime offer. He told me that if I found a way to include him in my Blending instead of whoever we had now in his aspect, our entire Blending would end up ruling the empire. And it would be perfectly legitimate, because he was already a member of the assembly."

"Korge," three or four of us said at the same time—and with the same inflection—which brought smiles to the faces of everyone listening. "And what did you say to that very . . . interestin' offer?" Vallant added.

"I told the man he must be feebleminded to think even for a moment that any of us would seriously consider listening to him," Alesta answered with a wide and happy smile. "If he was a member of the assembly, then he was one of the fools who had made sure that everyone continued to do everything wrong. I then suggested that he find a job somewhere digging ditches, because that would be the only position open to him if we all survived this invasion."

Everyone standing around was chuckling by now, and a few people called out things like, "Atta girl, Alesta, you told him right!" My own Blendingmates found the situation just as amusing, but my suspicious nature had begun flexing too hard for me to feel the same.

"That man is going to make trouble for us if we don't do something about him," I said once the noise had died down. "He's perfectly capable of helping the invaders to win against us if he thinks there's even the smallest chance that doing so will advance his own cause. If we leave him behind our backs when we turn to face our enemies, we'll definitely regret it."

"There's no arguin' with *that* truth," Vallant agreed after taking a deep breath, all amusement gone. "So what are we goin' to do about it? We can't justify jumpin' on him before we have a concrete reason, since there's always the chance that he won't do anythin' at all."

"He's definitely a coward, so that's very true," Jovvi said, her expression filled with frustration. "He might *want* to do something against us, but might not be able to force himself to action. But just in case he does, I think I have a way we can protect ourselves. If we establish a ring around ourselves with Air and Spirit magic, anyone trying to pass that ring will have his mind changed to the exact opposite of what his original intentions were. We'll have to tell all of our own people so they don't stumble into the ring by accident, and that will leave just enemies to have their intentions changed."

"And that might even make Korge useful for a change instead of being the total loss he is now," I said at once, liking the idea. "Simply stopping the man would be easier, but this is the better idea."

Everyone seemed to agree with that estimate, so we arranged to show the Gracelians what to do once we'd all Blended. It would be foolish to assume that we would be Korge's only targets, especially after what Alesta had said to him. And then it was time for us to Blend, to make sure that the invaders didn't get *too* close.

My Blendingmates and I went back to our original positions and put our cups of tea aside, and after Vallant spoke a brief warning to our people we then got comfortable on our sleeping pads. The pads made easier sitting than the bare ground, and then it was no longer me but the Tamrissa entity who looked around herself.

I had no trouble remembering the ring I was to establish, therefore I performed the necessary manipulations quickly. But not too quickly for the new entities to follow what was done, for they hovered near, watching me closely. Once I saw that they, too, would have no difficulty in protecting their flesh forms, I then turned my attention to those who approached with total destruction in mind.

Those flesh forms termed invaders were nearly to the point where my own flesh forms meant for them to be stopped, therefore I looked about myself. My three associate Blendings hovered in the vicinity, just as they were supposed to do, and on the far side of the group of dwellings I became aware of four lesser, unfinished entities which merely hovered to watch what was being done. It was proper that the lesser, unfinished entities stay back out of the way, therefore I dismissed thought of them and turned my attention to the new entities.

The four had finished with establishing their protective ring, therefore did I quickly give them knowledge of what was necessary in order to remove the aura of protection from those who approached. The matter would be more easily seen to were I and my associate entities to have acted instead, but it was necessary that these new entities be taught. For that reason the knowledge was given over, and then I hovered to one side with my associates and merely watched.

The new entities wisely chose caution over pride, and therefore all four of them arranged their positions in the proper way. Two entities hovered to either side of the enemy, and then they began to radiate power back and forth between themselves. Their strength grew more slowly than the strength of older and more complete entities would have, but the level did eventually reach a high enough point that they were just able to cancel the aura of protection of about half of the flesh forms approaching.

Had I not been watching the new entities carefully, I might well have merely waited for them to do the same to the other half of the enemy flesh forms. I *had* been watching carefully, though, and then there was an occurrence which, for a brief moment, struck me as odd.

*They aren't able to handle the balance of the invader flesh forms*, I heard inside myself, another part of my own entity-being speaking, that part known as Rion. *They've spent their strength on their first efforts, and now won't be able to continue.*

*Yes, I became aware of the same fact myself*, I replied in the proper way, which had come to me an instant earlier. *With that in mind, the doing now becomes our task again.*

As there was no disagreement as to my—our—course of action, I signaled to the strongest of my associate entities and took up my position to one side of the invader flesh forms. My associate entity took a position on the opposite side, and we quickly radiated enough power between us to remove the protection from the balance of the flesh forms.

Once the aura of protection was gone, however, the radiated power wasn't simply allowed to disappear. Instead I used it to put *all* of the invader flesh forms under my control, which immediately stopped their forward movement. The entire column of them simply stood and waited, therefore it was time to return to my own separate flesh forms . . . Separate . . .

"In the name of the Highest Aspect, how *did* that happen?" Rion immediately demanded as soon as Jovvi dissolved the Blending. "Tamrissa, was I dreaming, or did we actually speak to one another while we were Blended?"

"Well, if *you* were dreaming, then I dreamt the same thing," I answered, filled with at least as much confusion as he apparently was. "Are we moving backward instead of forward? We haven't been able to speak to one another since the first time or two that we Blended, and then it was because we were only surface Blended. What can it possibly mean *now*?"

"Am I understanding this right?" Lorand asked, looking back and forth between Rion and me. "You two were able to speak to each other while we were Blended? Then why wasn't *I* aware of the conversation? And now that I think about it, was I the only one who wasn't aware of it?"

"No, you weren't the only one," Jovvi assured him, her face showing concern. "I wasn't aware of the conversation either, and from their expressions I take it that Naran and Vallant were also excluded. So let me repeat Tamma's question: is this a step forward or a step back?"

"How can we know until we see where we go from here?" Vallant asked, obviously trying to be reasonable and calm. "Since whatever it was didn't harm us, discussin' the point can wait until we see what our prisoners have to say."

"Yes, before someone *else* decides to wipe them all out in the name of caution," I agreed at once. "I hope you set one or two of the other Blendings to protect the prisoners until we talk to them. I remember seeing the assembly Blendings gathered and watching from the far side of the village."

"You bet I set two of the Blendin's to protect the prisoners," Vallant agreed with a firm nod. "There are too many fools in this world to take any chances, so let's get to it."

No one spoke up to disagree, so we all began to make our way toward where the invaders would be waiting. It was still completely dark, of course, so I kindled my own version of a torch and set it to move just ahead of us.

"Thank you for the help, Tamma," Jovvi murmured as she came up to me. "Now that I can see the ground clearly, I don't have to worry about tripping over something I *don't* see . . . Will you look at those people? I seriously doubt if there's a free thought in the head of any of them, and not just from what *we* did. I have the impression that it's been a very long time since they were allowed to think for themselves."

"But at least they're in better condition than *our* people were in," Lorand added as he appeared on Jovvi's other side. "These people obviously haven't been feasting, but they haven't been starving either."

"Which only proves that the ones in charge of them are smarter than our former nobles, who might well have starved their army members even without being forced into it," I said, glancing over toward Lorand. "It doesn't mean that these leaders are better than the nobles, not when this bunch is set to kill any human being it comes across. I don't like the ones who sent these murderers out, and I intend to find *some* way to reach them even if they *are* stronger than us."

"You can count on the fact that I'm with you for that," Lorand assured me, an odd hardness in his expression. "I'd say we're probably *all* with you, so let's find out what we can from these people."

We'd reached the front of the column by then, and were no longer staring at its members from a distance. Most of the people in the column had very light coloring—skin, hair, *and* eyes—making even Vallant look dark despite the fading of the deep tan he'd started with. Vallant had been looking around at the rings of metal on leather that the men—and they *were* all men—wore, and then he stepped closer to one of them.

"You have four strokes of black paint on your metal hat

instead of the one or two strokes of these others," Vallant said to the man. "Does that mean you're in charge of them?"

"Yes, it does, sir," the man replied with an odd . . . lilt to his words. "How may I serve you?"

"You can tell me who's makin' you do all this killin'," Vallant answered at once, his voice hard with authority. "Where do you come from, and why were you brought here?"

"The Leaders have instructed us to prepare for their coming by removing all lower life-forms that might appear in their path," the man said, his voice showing nothing at all of inflection. "We come from West Tallvin, of course, which is home to many of us. We were brought here to spread the benefits of civilization to the barbarians on this shore."

"Oh, great, another group with its own definition of civilization," I muttered. "Just what we needed."

"Another thing we need is to know exactly what their definition consists of," Jovvi said, aware that Vallant had heard the both of us. "I'm going to use my link groups to see if I can't break through this man's original conditioning. If I don't, we'll never learn anything but what his leaders want us to know."

Vallant nodded his agreement both with her idea and her conclusion, and then he stepped back a bit. The rest of us simply stood and watched, but a number of minutes passed with nothing happening. Jovvi's face began to look strained, and then she wilted before shaking her head.

"It's just no use," she said in a much fainter voice than she'd *been* using. "Even with my link groups, I just can't break through the commands set in this man's mind. Vallant, will you ask our associates to see what *they* can do?"

Vallant showed nothing but a neutral expression as he nodded before turning away to speak to our other Blendings, but I knew he felt as disturbed as I did. Lorand used one arm around Jovvi to support her until she regained her strength, but he also exchanged quick glances with Rion, Naran, and me. We just weren't used to not being able to do what was necessary, and this new experience wasn't terribly pleasant.

"I think, perhaps, that we need to look at this time as a

learning experience," Rion said slowly after a moment. "Until now we've found nothing and no one able to stand against us. That kind of situation is not a healthy one, no matter that our motives are pure and unselfish. The nobility found people unable to oppose them, and look at what *they* became."

"All right, you have a good point," I grudged after another moment, looking at Rion bleakly. "But that doesn't mean I have to *like* this situation, so I'm not going to. What I'm going to do instead is look for a way around our lacks, and worry about learning a necessary lesson another time."

"I cast my vote with Tamrissa," Lorand said, his smile definitely wry. "We do need something to keep us from going the way of the former nobility, but a method that means the end of a lot of lives isn't my idea of the best way. We'll take care of these so-called leaders first, and then we'll worry about not getting too arrogant."

Rion matched Lorand's wry smile as he agreed along with the rest of us, and then we had no more time for conversation.

"The other Blendin's are goin' to try to free this man, but they want us to be braced and ready," Vallant said as he rejoined our group. "They've got the impression that he'll . . . run amok in some way once he's freed, and if we have to chase him down, then someone is likely to get hurt."

"Yes, I can understand why they feel like that," Jovvi said, suddenly able to stand straight and without help. "I get the same feeling, and by the way, thank you both for sharing strength with me. It's more than just handy that we can now do that."

"Handy" was certainly too mild a word for what the other entities had done to help Jovvi, especially since she was one of those who would control the invader once the associate Blendings released him. I could have controlled him myself, of course, but making the man run through a ring of fire was not likely to do him much good . . .

We had just enough time to get ready before things began to happen. One minute the man Vallant had spoken to just stood quietly in place, and the next he began to scream as he tried to run. Vallant and Rion held the man's arms as Jovvi and Lorand touched him in their own way, and then the man was still obviously frightened but no longer trying to get away from us.

"It's all right, we aren't goin' to harm you," Vallant said, the same thing he'd been repeating ever since the man was released. "Just calm down and tell us your name."

"I—I'm Borvri Tonsun," the man choked out with the same lilt to his words, apparently on the verge of terror. "It wasn't my fault or choice, so please don't hurt me! I hated what they made me do, but I couldn't stop doing it!"

"Yes, we know that," Jovvi said in a soothing voice, also giving the man a smile. "We know that every man here is under control, so we don't blame any of *you* for what's been happening. Can you tell us about the people who *are* responsible?"

"If I do they'll kill me horribly," Borvri Tonsun said in a whisper, his fear increasing instead of easing. "You have no idea what they're like, and you won't be able to stand against them any more than my own people could."

"Then you'll be working in *their* best interests by telling us about them," I pointed out as soon as the idea came to me. "If you make us believe that we don't have a chance against them, we'll surrender without giving them the trouble of forcing us to it."

"You know, that makes sense," Borvri said with a frown of consideration, his fear finally easing. "Yes, it makes a lot of sense, so they might not hurt me after all. What would you like me to tell you?"

"Why don't you start with where those people come from," Jovvi suggested after exchanging glances with me. The glance told me that she was the one who had made the man believe what I'd said, showing how well we all worked together.

"No one really knows where the Leaders come from, but it certainly isn't from West Tallvin," Borvri said, his brow still creased in thought. "Most of our Blendings were Middle and Low strength, but enough of them were Highs that no one should have been able to conquer us. Our very strongest High Blendings went out to meet the forces of the Leaders, but even though there weren't a *lot* of forces our

Blendings couldn't stop them. Those forces just killed everyone in their path, and when our people began to run away in terror the killing stopped. But that was because our people were being put under control instead of being killed, and the dead might have been the lucky ones."

A lot of bitterness had entered the man's voice, and he didn't seem to realize that he'd told us more than Jovvi's question had asked. Borvri seemed to *want* to talk about what had happened to him and his people, and I could understand that without the least trouble. Some part of him was clearly hoping that we'd be able to defeat those leader people after all, but my own determination had slipped just a bit. If Borvri's people had had lots of Blendings of all sorts, their Highs must have had a lot more experience than we did . . .

"How long ago did those people invade your country?" Vallant asked the man, the quietness of his tone telling me he felt just as bothered as I did.

"It's been almost ten years," Borvri said with a heaviness that was painful. The man had removed his metal hat, and the pale hair under it lay in sweat-soaked limpness. "A lot of our people tried to hide or run, but the forces at our borders kept them from running. When they decided to hide instead, they were found as easily as those who had gone into hiding to begin with. Searching Blending entities aren't easy to hide from."

*We* knew well enough how true that was, so my Blending-mates and I just looked at one another. There were still a lot of questions to be asked, but it would be a while before the most important one was answered. The High talents from Borvri's country had failed to defeat the ones who had invaded them; was there any reason to believe that *we* would do any better? Even with the help of three other experienced Blendings and four new ones?

We'd promised to help save the Gracelians; would we be able to save anyone, including ourselves? And what would we do if we discovered that the invaders had put forces elsewhere as well as in eastern Gracely? How close might that elsewhere be, or how far away? Possibly as far away as our own homeland . . . ?

* * *

Zirdon Tal was already awake when the Gandistran intruders were brought back to consciousness by the Blendings they obviously had guarding them. He stood in the shadows watching and waiting, and had even had a brief bit of amusement earlier. That fool Korge had tried to talk himself into being a part of one of the new High Blendings, but he'd failed just as Zirdon had known he would. Not only hadn't the woman Korge had chosen fallen to his charms, she'd told the fool off without the least hesitation. Korge had stalked away into the night with the blackest expression Zirdon had ever seen, and the incident couldn't have happened to a more deserving person.

But soon there would be another incident, and the recipients of Zirdon's attention would be even more deserving than Korge. Once those interfering outsiders of Gandistrans were dead, Zirdon Tal would be hailed as a hero for not letting even the maiming he'd had stop him from doing what was right. If something wasn't done Gracely would soon become an extension of Gandistra, but Zirdon was about to keep that terrible fate from happening.

It wasn't long before the Gandistrans settled down to Blend, so Zirdon forced himself to wait another short while before leaving the shadows. He wanted everyone's attention firmly fixed on the invaders they meant to stop, and then *he* would be free to stop those who had already invaded his country. As he moved slowly and quietly, Zirdon pulled out the knife he'd made sure to bring with him. Being talentless didn't also mean being helpless, a truth he was about to prove beyond all doubt.

Joy rose in Zirdon when he made it to within five feet of the Gandistrans without anyone trying to stop him. Everyone else was paying attention to other things, so Zirdon raised the knife in his fist and took one more step forward—and then stopped as the world spun wildly about him. The urge to scream was gone before it could be acted upon, but the whirling didn't stop. There was something Zirdon had to understand, something he had to think about . . .

It seemed a very long while before Zirdon's mind was

clear, but it took only a moment to realize that it hadn't been very long at all. He'd been confused about any number of things, but now that the confusion had cleared away he knew exactly what had to be done.

To begin with, the Gandistrans weren't the enemies Zirdon had thought they were. The Gandistrans had only the best interests of Gracely in mind, so those who opposed the Gandistrans had to be the real enemies. Zirdon knew exactly who those people were, the ones who refused to listen to the wise council of Gracely's good friends. Lorimon, Gardan, Dinno, Reesh—and Korge, of course. They were the ones who had to be stopped, before they undid all the good work the Gandistrans were attempting.

A smile of satisfaction curved Zirdon's lips as he turned around and took his knife in the direction of those who had to be stopped . . .

# THIRTY

Wilant Gorl sat at his desk reading a report with more satisfaction than he'd expected to feel. These days some things were actually starting to go right in Gan Garee, which was a great relief after being surrounded by nothing but trouble for so long. When the real Seated Blended got back to the city, they ought to enjoy the progress made almost as much as he did.

Suddenly there was a brisk knock on the door to his office, and then the door opened to show Oplis Henden and Eslinna Mansor, two members of his Blending, striding in. Oplis had Air magic and Eslinna Earth magic, but both of them looked as though they'd only just discovered that they had really strong talent.

"Wil, you're a genius!" Oplis exclaimed as soon as he saw Wilant, the man's smile threatening to break his face in two. "Eslinna and I have actually found it!"

"When you wondered out loud about where the information on Blending could be, I thought you were wasting our time," Eslinna added in obvious agreement. "It hadn't occurred to me that the information had to be *written down*, not even when Jovvi and the others told us that the nobles who trained everyone for the competitions were scheduled to be killed as soon as the competitions were over. The higher nobles made sure never to learn anything that would cost them their lives, so the information had to come from some source that was considered safe. If they killed everyone but their pet Blendings who knew how to Blend, then there *had* to be something in writing."

"And we found it," Oplis said with that same wide grin. "For a little while I had private doubts, because it was just possible that the ones who trained everyone in how to Blend were given the information by the outgoing Seated Blending. Then I realized that there *had* to be another source of information, otherwise there was nothing to stop the Seated Blending from refusing to pass on the knowledge. If no one but them knew how to Blend, they'd be able to stay in power for their entire lives."

"And the nobles who really ran things would never have allowed that," Eslinna said in continuing agreement. "So we started to look around, and guess where we found the books?"

"Probably in the last place you looked," Wilant answered blandly, just as excited as his Blendingmates but needing to do a bit of teasing. He'd *never* expected anyone to find what he'd known *had* to be there . . . "You understand how that works, don't you? When you search for something and find it, the place you find it is the last place you search. That means—"

"Okay, okay, we get it," Oplis interrupted with an amused shake of his head. "That means you always find something in the last place you look. In this case that was the vault of the oldest bank the nobles had established. Would you like to join us in examining those books? There are six of them, one for each aspect excluding Sight magic, and one for Blending itself. The last book, the one on Blending, is the largest."

"It looks like they really *didn't* know about Sight magic," Wilant said as he rose from his chair and walked to the other side of his desk. "Which doesn't make much sense, if the books are as complete as they actually should be."

"Vin said he had the impression that there was a volume missing, even though there was no real evidence to prove the feeling," Eslinna told him as they all headed for the door. "According to Vin, the balance was wrong or something, and only someone with really strong Spirit magic would be expected to notice."

"Which none of the nobles actually had," Wilant said with a nod, leading the way out into the hall. "The nobles also probably made very sure that they didn't read any of the books, or even look at them closely. The information would have put their lives in danger for what they believed was no benefit at all, so they stayed away from the books. Too bad they were as wrong about *that* as they were about most things. Where did you leave the books?"

"In the main meeting room, with the rest of our Blending-mates to guard them," Oplis said, easily keeping up with the pace Wilant set. Eslinna had just a bit more trouble keeping up, but not so much that they left her behind. "They said they'd wait to open the books until we fetched you, but they may have been lying."

"That's a fine thing to say about your own Blending-mates," Eslinna scolded Oplis with a laugh of real amusement. "It's exactly what *I* happened to be thinking, but I made certain not to *say* it."

Wilant ignored the banter that the two kept up until they reached the main meeting room. That *was* the best place for the books, so that all of them could be read at the same time. If there were comments or questions, no one would have to run to someone else's quarters to make those comments.

The other three members of their Blending simply sat at the table where the books had been placed, each book in front of another place. The books obviously hadn't been opened yet, but as soon as Wilant, Oplis, and Eslinna walked in, their three Blendingmates immediately opened the volume in front of them with big smiles. They'd kept their word about waiting, but now the wait was over.

Oplis and Eslinna ran to their own chairs, and Wilant lost no time in taking his own place. The volume left for him was the one on Fire magic, of course, and it was big and dusty and large enough to be called a tome. Wilant opened it carefully and began to read, giving the book all his attention just as his Blendingmates were doing. Their new Sight magic member had taken the volume on Blending, but later Wilant meant to see personally what it said. Right now he had his own volume to read, and very quickly he sank right down into it . . .

"But why can't you just *tell* me what's wrong?" Driff asked for the tenth time as he hurried in the servant's wake. "And why did the temporary Seated Blending send a guardsman to get me? Usually they send one of their own."

"Please, sir, there's nothing I can tell you until you see the problem for yourself," the servant said over his shoulder, the man's voice actually trembling. "We would never have bothered you, but we know everyone considers you the best healer in the city. Please, it's just a short distance ahead."

Driff gave up asking questions, but not with very good grace. If he hadn't been so worried he probably would have dug his heels in until he was given some answers, but the servant—and the guardsman sent to fetch him—was just about beside himself. Driff knew it shouldn't be much longer, and it wasn't. The servant turned into the large meeting room in the public corridor, and when the man stepped aside, Driff almost stopped short.

"In the name of chaos, how long have they been like that?" Driff demanded as he forced himself to walk closer to the large table the room held. All six of the temporary Seated Blending members were unmoving in their chairs, and Driff had been able to tell at once that they were almost unliving as well.

"One of us came in here to remind them that it was time to eat lunch," the servant answered, sounding as though he were about to cry. "More often than not they forgot about meals, so we usually— Can't you do something for them or the others?"

"Others?" Driff echoed, turning to look at the man. "Do you mean to say there are other people taken in the same way?"

"It's . . . every High talent in the palace," the man whispered, as though not saying the words aloud might keep them from being true. "Please, sir, please say there's something you can do for them."

Driff turned back to the people who had become his friends with shock clanging in his head. *Every High talent in the palace was like this? But what about the High talents who* weren't *in the palace?* That would have been the logical question to ask next, but Driff found himself helpless to speak the words. The people seated so close to him were all but statues, their life essences so faint that the essences seemed miles and miles out of reach. He'd never seen anything like this before, and worse than that hadn't the first idea of how to treat it.

"I need to talk to other people about this," Driff said at last, turning away from the unmoving bodies with a relief that shamed him. "Meanwhile, who's in charge of the city?"

The servant simply stared at Driff, and it took a moment before Driff was able to admit that he knew what the servant's stare contained. The man looked at Driff with dread hope and stark pleading, two emotions that answered Driff's last question completely. At the moment there was *no* one in charge, but the servant was praying that Driff would agree to change that.

*Me?* Driff thought with even stronger shock, finding it impossible to accept the idea. *I'm the outlaw dedicated to getting around the authorities. I can't up and* become *the authority!*

Not to mention that he hadn't the first idea of where he would start. He'd have to do something to bring back the people who were legitimately in charge, but how was he supposed to do that? Every High talent in the palace—and possibly even in the city—was the same? What in the world *could* he do? What, in the name of the Highest Aspect, could he do . . . ?

# THE BLENDING WORLD

*Sharon Green*

All science fiction and fantasy starts with someone thinking "What if . . . ," and the world of The Blending is no exception. Most worlds that allow magic contain the chosen few who are the only ones capable of performing magic. But what if everyone can do magic to a greater or lesser degree? What kind of society would be there be?

That line of thought produced the world of The Blending. In a world where people have "personal protection," so to speak, the development and use of weapons would be at a minimum. Hunters would be Earth magic or Air magic users, and possibly even Water magic users.

With Water magic you might conceivably kill game by drawing out all water in its body, and then immediately replacing the water. Air magic could kill game by smothering it or concussing it, and Earth magic could simply stop a heart. Crops and domestic animals would be encouraged by Earth magic users, possibly with the help of Spirit magic users. Metals would be worked and tempered with the help of Fire Magic users . . ."

But people with special abilities aren't easily ruled, even by others of their kind, and having a lesser talent doesn't necessarily mean having a lesser desire to control those around you. Historically speaking, the more desperate a ruling body is to completely control its citizens, the more that ruling body curtails personal freedom. That truth set up the political situation in Gandistra, along with the claim of historians that most ruling elites start to decay along with their form of government after three to four hundred years.

So we have a society that's just about run its course. The time has come for reform and change, but not just anyone can become a leader of rebels. And what about those abilities that people have been denied the use of? Is there anything about them that remains unknown?

When you start to investigate the unknown, it isn't possible to *know* where the investigation will take you. "Well, just keep on with it, no matter *what* you run into," but it isn't as easy to follow. The loving support of others does help, but in the end, for the most part, you have to face what comes by yourself. Most people find it very hard to be in that position, but they need to remember one thing: the next step may be frightening, but the step after that could be the most wonderful you've ever taken in your life.

I'm the kind of dreamer who believes that there's always something wonderful around the next bend, waiting for us to discover it. When people, either in The Blending world or in our own, let themselves be kept from going around the next bend, they're depriving themselves and everyone else of unknown wonders. The road leading to that next bend is far from nicely paved, but once you get around the corner you find that the bumpy trip was worth it.

People complain that every discovery can be turned to the dark side, but that's been true since the discovery of the wheel. Just because your wheel can be used on a tank, that doesn't mean the wheel should be destroyed as a weapon of war. Raise your children gently but firmly with a lot of love, and they won't *want* to use your wheel on a tank.

And one of those children just might find the way to let *us* Blend in a way very much like the one our heroes and heroines use . . ."